THE DAMNED

TARN RICHARDSON

Duckworth Overlook

First published in the UK and the US in 2015 by
Duckworth Overlook

LONDON
30 Calvin Street, London E1 6NW
T: 020 7490 7300
E: info@duckworth-publishers.co.uk
www.ducknet.co.uk
For bulk and special sales please contact sales@duckworth-publishers.co.uk,
or write to us at the above address.

NEW YORK
141 Wooster Street
New York, NY 10012
www.overlookpress.com
For bulk and special sales please contact sales@overlookny.com,
or write us at the above address.

A catalogue record for this book is available
from the British Library
Cataloguing-in-Publication Data is available
from the Library of Congress

ISBNs:
UK: 978-0-7156-4954-1
Typeset by ketchup

Printed and bound in Great Britain

DEDICATION

For Linnie,
my beginning, middle and end

and Sam and Will,
everything in-between

In memory of Harry Garbutt
1889–1915

PART ONE

"I know that after I leave, savage wolves will come in among you and will not spare the flock."

Acts, 20, Verse 29

ONE

23:32. MONDAY, OCTOBER 12TH, 1914.
THE FRONT LINE. ARRAS. FRANCE.

As the first mortar hit the British trench, Lieutenant Henry Frost drew a line through the unit's diary entry predicting a quiet night. He'd written the forecast more in hope than expectation, as if writing the words within the journal would somehow sway the actions of the Germans and ensure a quiet night. A private prayer for peace for just one night, for some rest from the infernal shrieks of falling shells, the bursts of distant gunfire, the intolerable cries of the wounded and the dying.

Already it felt as if the war had stalled, trapped under its own ferocity of hate. After the Germans rolled, seemingly unstoppable, through France, they had eventually found themselves snagged by the most fragile of lines east of Arras, checked by the British and French armies and stymied by their own over-stretched supply lines. Now the Germans had taken to unleashing an almost relentless nightly barrage of artillery upon the front and support lines. 'The Evening Hate' the Tommies called it. You could almost always set your watch by it. Eleven twenty eight. Every night. On the dot.

In expectation, when the minutes ticked over the half hour mark, Henry had checked his wrist watch and updated the diary entry. So when the first shell burst, he cursed himself for his impetuousness, his reckless optimism forever now recorded in the diary under the firm black line through his naive prediction. Whilst only weeks old, this was a dreadful war. Already there was no time for optimism in this conflict.

Above his corrugated iron bunker, a rancid welt of grey black earth burst amongst his soldiers, spraying metal, mud and blood into the night.

Someone yelled to take cover as a second shell screamed overhead. Moments before it fell, mortars hissed and clunked from emplacements along the German front line two hundred yards away, fierce red tongues licking the night sky.

The thunderous clap snatched the breath from all within its blast, as the second shell exploded in a ball of fire and gristle. Within the officers' bunker below, lanterns swung and dirt fell from the ceiling onto Henry's paperwork. He tilted his eyes upwards towards the incessant screams of the injured in the trench above, the hopeless cries for a doctor, the splattering patter of debris blasted high from the last shell.

Seconds later, three more shells fell on the trenches, all in quick succession, blasting bodies from their holes, obliterating corpses away from where they'd laid just moments before. Killing soldiers twice.

A fourth mortar landed, battering the entrance to the dugout and sending a pall of smoke and dust down into the yawning mouth of the front line bunker. Henry crouched over the unit's diary, as if the hard-backed tome was the most precious thing in the world.

"A doctor!" a voice wept through the barrage above, choking on soot and dust. "A doctor! For God's sake, get me a doctor!" came the desperate plea, before a fifth mortar landed.

The Germans had found their range.

"Get your bloody heads down!" Henry cried down the front line, appearing from the bunker and leaping through the clods of showering earth to reach his men. He stuck his head between his legs and prayed like the rest of them.

Another shell landed ten feet away, depositing scrambling soldiers into No Man's Land, leaving behind a sodden bloodied clump of mincemeat, splintered bone and boots where they had once stood.

And then, as quickly as it came, the barrage stopped.

Silence flooded into the trench, like the creeping cordite clouds blown on the midnight breeze. As the roar of the shells fell away, once more the screams of the injured, the moans of the bewildered, the pleading for mother, from those moments from death, renewed their dreadful chorus.

Cautiously, Henry looked up out of the hole he had found to shelter in, and peered both ways down the trench. He suspected a trick. In his memory, no onslaught had ever been so short. Out of the smoke and dust, figures stumbled over bodies and blasted earth. He was aware of weeping, the whinnying of horses, a vague ringing in his ears. Everything sounded very far away. He looked down at his hands. They were shaking, trembling like a newborn infant's. He drew them into balls and crushed the shuddering out of them. After a month on the front line, nothing made Henry shake like artillery barrages. He'd amputated a man's leg, half hanging by its sinews of flesh, with his knife, shot a German through the eye and stuck a bayonet into the ribs of a young German soldier no older than the boys who used to play football in the green opposite his house back home, watching him writhe and whimper for twenty minutes before dying, gagging on his tears and blood. He'd even ordered the shooting of a sentry for deserting his post without a second thought for the soldier or his family's honour. But artillery barrages? They tore through every fibre of his body. It was the uncertainty of where the next shell would land, the indiscriminate roaming of their destruction which so terrified him.

When no further shells fell, he coughed the dust out of his lungs and found his feet uneasily, levering himself up and into the pitch of the trench. Without question the barrage had ended. Strange for it to have stopped quite so suddenly – for it to have been so short. A creeping cold fear drew over him.

"Get to the bloody walls!" he roared, trundling into a run. "Check your sentries!"

The enemy! They would be coming, storming across No Man's Land, the thump of their boots, the glint of their bayonets in the moonlight.

"Check your posts! Check for approaching enemy!" Henry cried again, charging to an observation point and knocking the quivering sentry aside. He heard someone call, "There's nothing there, sir!" as he peered wildly across No Man's Land, wishing for a periscope to aid him. Smoke drifted across his view, smoke and moon-cast shadows. He stared wildly across the scarred ground between them and the German front line.

Nothing.

Nothing was coming.

But there was something. The noise from the German trench, gunfire, savage shrieks of alarm.

Henry strained to look closer at the enemy line. He could see its front parapet in the moonlight, recognise the tangle of barbed wire and the sacking of sandbags in front of it.

He narrowed his eyes and stared.

After the initial barrage the air was thick with smoke and sulphur. Battered and bloodied soldiers sat puffing on cigarettes in silent rows or moaned beneath crimson stained bandages. Dropping from his post, Henry patted shoulders and shook hands with his men as he trudged past, planting his boots into the prints made by the Sergeant he was following.

"Barrage a bit bloody short tonight?" suggested Henry, peering down the length of the trench and regretting his words immediately upon seeing the butchered lying still within it or the injured struggling their way out of it, leaning heavy on the shoulders of mates.

"Yes, sir," replied Sergeant Holmes, peering into his periscope, "and that's the very thing, sir."

"How'd you mean?"

The barrel-chested Sergeant stared down the lens, reacquainting himself with the scene captured within it, before standing to one side and offering the chance for the young Lieutenant to look.

"I mean, sir, have a gander down that."

"What the devil ...?" Henry exclaimed in the instant his eyes fixed to the horizon. "Is that us ... attacking?" he asked. If it was, it was no form of trench raid the Lieutenant was familiar with. "Do we have any activity targeting the enemy's forward trench this evening, Sergeant?" Henry asked intently, his eyes still locked to the periscope's sights.

"No, not to my knowledge, sir. This whole line is on a defensive footing."

"Not according to that," Henry retorted, turning to Holmes and raising an eyebrow. He looked back into the lens and allowed his eyes to focus once again. At the very range of the periscope's view, frantic figures were leaping and charging along the enemy trench line, fearsome silhouettes against the silvery light, sporadic gunfire lighting the darkness.

"We've got units in Fritz's trench," Henry mumbled with dumbfounded amazement. "No wonder the barrage came to an abrupt halt!" Henry blinked the dust out of his eyes and peered hard. "What on earth's going on?" he muttered. "Who the hell is that?"

"Whoever they are, they're winning!" cheered Holmes, allowing himself the beginning of a fiendish grin. "Shall I ... rally the men, sir?" he asked expectantly.

"Over the top, Bill?" Henry stuttered. "But the men ... aren't they ... are they up for a fight?"

"Oh yes, Lieutenant!" roared Holmes, his face now beaming. "My boys are always up for a fight, sir! Just need the order and we'll go over the top in a flash."

Henry hesitated and cursed himself for his indecision, a trait for which his schoolmasters had long admonished him. Exhaustion, from days without sleep, tugged at every facet of his body, weariness almost overwhelming him. But there was a fire now beginning to catch within him, ignited by the scenes revealed through the periscope and fanned by the enthusiasm of his Sergeant.

"Too good an opportunity to turn down, sir!" Holmes suggested urgently. "And a near full moon to light our way!" he added, indicating the night sky. "Whoever's doing our job has put Jerry on the ropes. I don't mean to put words into your mouth, sir, but it would be my view that we get over to their trench and give Fritz the knockout blow!"

"Very good then," cheered Henry, casting any more doubt aside. He allowed himself a nervous smile. "Well done, Sergeant. Let's get ourselves organised and head on over!"

Holmes saluted the officer and turned on his heel. Storming back up the trench, he called for the men to fix bayonets. "We're going over the top, lads!"

Exhausted and bruised groans returned the order.

"Come on! Step to it!" the Sergeant cried, marching past the slowly assembling pockets of soldiers. "Let's go and teach Jerry a lesson about throwing shells at us, shall we?!" he cried, accompanying the command with repeated peeps on his whistle. "Come on, you bastards! Over the top then! Over the top!"

TWO

1889. Kraków. Poland.

"The boy is broken."

Sister Angelina of the Catholic hillside monastery almost seemed to spit the words at the Father, as if the child were a rancid piece of meat. She stared at the hunched shape on the bed and wrinkled her nose. "Broken," she repeated, remarking on how the child's lifeless eyes peered vacantly at the rain splashed window of the room.

But Father Adansoni refused to accept her assessment. He shook his head and drew the folds in his face taut with the palm of his hand. Adansoni had nourished the boy back to a semblance of physical health with all the guile and skill he possessed. And whilst he accepted that the wounds within would take longer to heal, for everything that he was worth, the Father was determined to draw the child out of the living corpse which sat before him.

Since their arrival a few days ago at the small monastery south of Kraków, the young boy called Poldek Tacit had done nothing but sit on the edge of the bed, staring to the rolling fields and mountains beyond, partaking in a little soup silently, wordlessly, whenever it was brought to his side, standing and walking lifelessly around the grounds without murmur or resistance whenever it was commanded that he do so for some restorative air.

On a night, he could be heard to whimper and cry, both as he dreamt and when his nightmares threw him awake, drenched and panting, knotted tight within his sheets.

"Send him to the sanatorium in the city, Javier," the Sister pressed. "They will make his life more comfortable."

"No, Angelina!" the Father replied sternly, his fists clenching into balls against his cassock, his eyes on the boy, desperately trying to fathom the thoughts in the child's inaccessible mind. "I'm taking him back with me to the Vatican."

"You cannot mean that, Father! You don't drink from the cup which is cracked!"

"As long as it holds water, then why throw it away?" Adansoni countered, drawing his arms about his chest. He didn't look at her. Instead he continued to study the boy, looking for anything which proved his hope was not in vain. There was something which captivated him about the child. He felt an ownership over him, a responsibility, a belonging, the likes of which he'd never known before, with either object or person.

After a long while he said, "Sister Angelina, you have always offered wise council. May I ask you something?"

"Of course, Javier."

"Do you believe in prophecies?"

"Depends of which prophecies you speak? There are plenty which are given voice but few that deserve any credence. Why do you ask?"

"When I found him …" and then Father Adansoni's voice trailed off, as if the memory of that scene in the mountains was still raw, too grievous for even the man to recollect. "When I found him, he was the only one alive. His mother and father, both slain, the murderous Slavs who had attacked their home, dead too."

"What are you trying to say?"

He turned his eyes slowly onto her. "I think some divine power saved him," he said, before looking back at Tacit. "Either that or this child killed those men himself, trying to save his family."

The Sister could barely contain her snort. "A twelve year old child? Kill … how many did you say you found?"

"Four of them."

"Kill four grown men?" She scoffed and flapped a hand in mockery. "A passing soldier maybe? A mercenary, perhaps, came to their assistance? But the boy?!" She forced a cold, short laugh.

"Surely had it been a soldier or a mercenary, they would have aided the child further? They would have stayed with the boy, or would have taken him away to safety?" He looked back at the lifeless shape sitting on the bed. "But there was no one, no one but this child amongst the dead."

"Then if you ask me, it sounds like you have brought something tainted into the church. Have you not asked the boy what happened?"

"He has not spoken of the event. Indeed, he has barely spoken all the weeks he has been with me."

"Well, when he does," Sister Angelina said quickly, "he will reveal the truth. There are good samaritans yet in the world, many good things which still happen to people, many miracles. He was saved by good chance and the miracle of a passing stranger. Mark my words." She touched his arm kindly, as she turned from the room. "You'll see."

"Yes," Father Adansoni replied, looking to the window out of which Tacit was staring, "you are probably right. But from where the miracle first came, I do not know," and he allowed his eyes to turn in the direction of Italy and a sky heavy with greying clouds.

THREE

23:37. Monday, October 12th, 1914.
The front line. Arras. France.

The British soldiers charged over the scarred and barren stretch of No Man's Land, the whites of their eyes gleaming out of their filthy battered faces. They ran forward over the detritus of the month-old battlefield, curses on their breath, hearts in mouths, their rifles raised, the moonlit-gleam of bayonets at the ready, towards the silent trench ahead.

Whether day or night, No Man's Land was a dreadful place to cross, the stench of rotting soldiers, churned amongst the earth and blasted trees, their bodies left to the torment of the elements and the hordes of rats and crows. But in the dark, the hateful blindness was almost overwhelming. Shadows swept and spun before one's eyes, every rustle was the swish of an enemy's trouser leg, every crack the setting of an enemy's bolt. Every step closer towards the German line brought a growing sense of fear and trepidation, all waiting for the eruption of light from a German flare, the hard clack of the machine gun, the sharp bark of the rifle. But the closer they drew, and the longer not a single shot was heard, the more they realised that someone ahead of them had been busy with the enemy.

Sergeant Holmes set his pistol forward in one hand and raised his mace high in the other in readiness for what might greet him as the first to enter into the trench below. He peered over the lip of the parapet, and the mace slowly dropped to his side.

"What is it?" Henry hissed, stepping up. He looked down into the trench and lowered his own pistol. "Jesus Christ," he muttered, under his breath.

All along the front, a low rumble of surprise and revulsion from the approaching British soldiers gathered against the lip of the trench. Across every inch of the enemy trench, wherever one looked, the remnants of body parts and blood covered the ground, as if it had been used as an abattoir in hell.

Nothing could have survived that butchery. Nothing stirred. All that remained was a grisly carpet of blood, ruptured organs, torn uniforms and broken weapons, splintered bone and ripped skin, cruelly slashed and discarded like disposed filth from a butcher's yard. Every now and then, amongst the muddied crimson waste, soldiers spotted a discernible body part, the top of a skull, a collection of fingers, the fleshy round of a thigh bone.

Soldiers turned and vomited back into the decay of No Man's Land. They had seen shell strikes and their bloody aftermath, had witnessed first-hand the evisceration caused by the sniper's bullet, the carnal gore of the bayonet's twist. But this scene had a horror beyond anything they had witnessed before, a mass and brutal killing the entire length of the trench.

"Is there anybody left, do you think?" Holmes asked Henry, his dry mouth slackening, his wide eyes trying to comprehend what they were telling him.

"Can you hear anyone?" replied Henry brusquely, feeling a hardening in his stomach.

Holmes shook his head. "What you going to put in the unit diary, sir?"

"What we've seen," the young Lieutenant said, turning away and covering his mouth. "A massacre."

FOUR

1889. The Tatra Mountains. Poland.

It surprised the young boy to see how quickly the man died.

He'd only ever used his sharpened stick to stab at fish from the pool at the bottom of the valley. He'd always watched in wonder as skewered fish flapped and threw themselves about the river bank in their long drawn out dances of death. They would always fight for survival with every drop of their might until their life finally bled out of them. But this man, this Slovak gypsy, who'd pulled a knife and had laughed wickedly, had gone down and hadn't moved from the moment he'd been struck. The stick stood protruding upwards from deep inside the man's right eye, a fine rivulet of blood oozing from the socket.

The child crouched a little way away from the body, his fierce unblinking eyes on the corpse as if suspecting a trick. As if he expected the man to spring back to life and reach out at him, to choke the life out of him. The rat-faced man lay there, his back flat on the ground, his scowling, unmoving face turned upwards and to the side by the weight of the stick.

The boy could feel the blood beat in his ears. He was aware of the thumping in his chest and the ache in his clenched fist. His father had often told him of the Slovaks, bone-jawed and filthy, looting and stealing from the decent folk of the valleys and mountainsides of the southern Polish mountains, but he'd never seen one in the flesh. To him they'd been just stories, like those of ghosts and werewolves. Used by adults to keep him polite and quiet on a night. Now he felt guilt that he'd not believed his father, that he'd doubted monsters ever existed.

A strangled cry from away up the mountainside tore his eyes from the body. The cry came again from the ramshackle wooden house, teetering three hundred yards away on the rocky ridge above, this shriek even more desperate and shrill.

His mother.

An anger and a passion, the likes of which he'd never known in his twelve short years, coursed through him. He wrenched the stick from the man's punctured eye and shot away up the mountainside, not even looking to see how he planted his shoes between the stones of the steep climb. His eyes remained fixed on the house and the wicked noises coming from within. There were men in the house. He could hear them now clearly –

cruel laughter and shouts. He thought back to the dead gypsy at the river bank and imagined his house full of their type, pushing and taunting his mother, demanding food and money from her. There was only one aim in his mind. To act as his father would act, as any good shepherd would, to protect his own.

He leapt from the rocks of the river bank onto the dirt track, a short way from the front of the house. He landed and his left foot went from under him, skidding on the gravel. He went down, gashing his knee amongst the stones, skinning the knuckles of his hand holding the stick. The shutters of the house were closed against the morning sun but inside he could hear the angry growl of coarse voices and hard laughter, joined now and then by the pleading voice of his mother.

He whimpered and staggered to his feet; years of working atop the treacherous high ridge of the Tatras had taught him to ignore pain. He stumbled on towards the door, reaching out to the handle the very moment it was pulled open from inside. Instantly he knew it wasn't his father framed in the doorway. The thin figure could only be one of them; his father always having to stoop his vast bulk beneath the lintel of the door. Without thinking, he closed his eyes and thrust his stick forwards with all the force he could summon from within. It snagged against something soft and then, moments later, continued its drive upwards, more slowly now, as if some force was pushing against the sharpened point. It reminded him of how he sometimes had to force his knife through chunks of mutton on his plate.

The stick slid five inches beyond the hang of the man's shirt. He grunted and sank to his knees, his hands clutching weakly at the shaft. The handle of a knife glinted in his belt and instantly the child gathered it into his hand, leaping over the tumbling figure and through the open doorway.

A heavily bearded man stood to the right of him, the sneer on his hairy face foundering in surprise as the child leapt inside. Something lay curled in one corner of the room and he saw his mother, her clothing torn to shreds, on her hands and knees. A man, stripped beneath the waist, was forcing himself towards her.

At once his mother turned her head and cried out, pleading for the boy to be left alone. The hairy man spat something dark and reached forward to strike at him. Instinctively, the boy ducked and, finding himself between the man's legs, drove the blade of the dagger upwards to the hilt with all his might. The man shrieked and staggered backwards against the wall, clutching at his butchered parts, blood pouring between his legs, out over the blade and his hands, onto the floor in a wild torrent.

The boy looked back at the man behind his mother. He'd now pushed himself away from her and had turned, his yellow-white thighs flecked with froth and blood, a monstrous looking member bobbing evilly between his legs. It confused and repulsed the child, how it wavered and hung like a weapon tilted towards him. The man shouted something in a language the boy didn't understand and charged, kicking out with a mud-caked foot. The child was too quick for him and had turned and reached the far wall cupboard by the time the Slovak had regained his balance. As the boy passed the body curled in the corner, he recognised it instantly as his father, his face submerged in a pool of his own blood, wickedly slain with a knife in the back. A weight of grief and sickness crashed into him, almost dragging the child onto the floor.

The man shouted again. The boy tore open the cupboard drawing the revolver he knew his father always kept. The man's eyes flashed and he ran forward, his tone more urgent, his hands raised.

The revolver blew itself out of child's hands in the same instant that the man's head blew backwards, sending him tumbling to the floor, the wooden floorboards showered in a vanilla and crimson spray of flesh and bone.

Finally silence flooded into the house and enveloped the room, the only sound now being the ringing of the boy's ears from the gun. He wondered if he'd been deafened, until he heard his own voice call out.

"Mama!" he cried, racing to his mother, throwing himself into her side with a wide embrace.

He thought it strange how she didn't wrap her arms around him, at least until he drenched his hands on the deep gash in her neck.

He never saw them arrive. He never heard their footsteps on the front porch of the house, their horrified cries when they first laid their eyes on the carnage in the room, capped their hands to their mouths in an attempt to hide their revulsion and mask the stench from the bodies. Trapped on the faint edge of unconsciousness between hunger and grief, the first time the boy was aware of the Fathers was when one of them knelt forward and gathered him from the half-naked woman, believing the child to be a victim amongst the dead.

They'd come to the valley as missionaries, to spread the word and message of their Catholic faith, to shepherd the desolate and the unguided towards the light. They'd never expected to find such horror as this.

The boy remembered how the Father had muttered about miracles the instant that he'd stirred and had his cheek cupped by the Father's hand.

"What is your name, my child?" the Father asked, his eyes full of concern and sorrow.

"Tacit," said the boy to the Priest, feeling very small under the heavy eyebrows of the missionary. He sniffed and brushed the hair weakly from his dead mother's face. "Poldek Tacit."

FIVE

23:37. MONDAY, OCTOBER 12TH, 1914. ARRAS. FRANCE.

Father Andreas always found pleasure from extinguishing the candles at the end of evening mass. Like the drawing of a veil across a stage at the end of an evening's performance, the snuffing out of each flame with the small metal cup gave one the chance to reflect on the day's achievements, whilst drawing one day to a close and heralding in the promise of another.

But not tonight.

Tonight there was no peace to be found for the Father in this slow and measured act. The deliberate smothering of each flickering flame brought no respite to his own flickering thoughts. How could the snuffing out of candlelight in any way halt this raging torment within the mind of a man who had, in one single act, snuffed out his worthiness to his faith?

For seven weeks Father Andreas had tended his flock at St. Vaast's Cathedral of Arras, an ambitious post for one so young. He remembered, as if it was yesterday, when he was first approached to take up the role. He wasn't sure if it was his impetuous enthusiasm Cardinal Poré had recognised, or his seemingly endless commitment to doing good which had secured him the post, but at twenty four he was the youngest Father ever to be awarded the position at the Cathedral.

Almost immediately, he became a figurehead amongst the local population of Arras, adored by the existing, and ever swelling, congregations. He was young, handsome, brave, devout, possessing a natural way with people, words and deeds. The older members of the congregation loved his godliness and his piety. "A local saint achieving his rightful place," they would say, being born, as he was, in the city. The younger attendees at the church were inspired by his style and ardour. People joked that the Cathedral would need to be rebuilt to house the new influx of worshippers coming to witness and find sanctuary there thanks to this wondrous new appointment within the Catholic Church.

His ambition could sometimes overwhelm him, not his personal aspiration for he was meek and humble before his faith, but his ambition for his Church and its capacity for correcting the wrongs of its past and solving the problems of today. That ambition never left him, like a voice forever taunting in his ear, and it was the very thing that led him to make choices that he knew ran counter to the will of the Church.

Momentarily distracted from his thoughts, Father Andreas became aware of the silence in the Cathedral. He stood and listened, turning his head slowly from side to side to check that he had not simply been struck deaf. Out there, in the east, at the front where the German, French and British forces had fought each other into the earth, there was, for the first time in weeks, a silence almost too beautiful to bear. The guns had stopped. It was usually at night that they were at their most terrible, pummelling the darkness and those beneath their trajectories with their dreadful payloads. Arras had been already been cruelly pounded, an inexorable killing within the city and its people, which had seen hundreds killed, many more injured. It was not unknown for Father Andreas to blow dust from the holy passages of the Cathedral bible as he celebrated Mass. Homes had been set on fire or had been blasted to rubble and shabby silhouettes of their former selves. Many residents had forsaken the city, abandoned their homes and moved west to wherever they could find some liberation from the churning machinations of war.

Father Andreas closed his eyes for a moment, bathing in the moment of stillness. Then he knew he had to press on.

With the left hand of the ambulatory now cast into darkness, he crossed to the opposite side and raised the conical lid of the snuffer to the sixteen candles on the right, their flames dancing gently in the still cool of the Cathedral air, oozing white wax onto their dais. A trail of smoke snaked lazily from the first extinguished candle, up into the rafters of the building. Andreas looked to watch it rise. The ceiling of the Cathedral of St. Vaast never failed to inspire him. His head spun as he craned his neck to see, the blood pooling in the base of his skull from the crick in his neck. He wavered a little gingerly on his feet and closed his eyes, enjoying the lightheadedness that his stance gave him, a feeling almost like a wave of righteousness washing over him from the Lord above.

"I trust I have not failed you too greatly, Lord?" he murmured quietly to himself, as if in prayer, as if in reflection. "I mean only to do right."

He lowered his head and felt his senses settle themselves squarely back onto his two feet, his mind clearing. "Thank you, oh Lord, for the gifts you have given," he added, almost as a liturgy.

He opened his eyes and looked at the candles, now raising the lid to extinguish them quickly. It was time to return the whole of the Cathedral to blackness, to permit it rest for the night, to let Father Andreas himself rest. For he was gravely tired.

Was it guilt that made him feel that way? Was it the dishonesty he felt so keenly, knowing he had failed himself in everything he had ever been taught to do? He'd tried to tell the Cardinal, to reveal his doubts and his concerns as to what he had done, the part he had played in the plan. But as he'd stood before him, fighting back at the grief which was trying to consume him, the words had failed him. How could he speak so openly of his blasphemy to one who had showed him such faith and belief?

Each candle died with a hiss, as he flattened the lid into the wax. Sometimes he liked to choke the life out of the candle by holding the lid a fraction above it, watching the flame slowly splutter and die, as it was starved of oxygen. But not tonight. Their slow, tormented dying reminded him too much of how his own soul felt. Tonight Father Andreas thrust the lid down and snuffed the flames out firmly into the wax, wicks and all.

Suddenly, those candles still alight flickered in unison. He felt the draft from an open door. Andreas turned and peered through the gloom of the Cathedral. The side door to the Cathedral's transept stood ajar, wide enough for a figure to have slipped through, narrow enough for the wind to have blown it open. Father Andreas strained his eyes to try and spot a figure standing near the doorway, someone stepping up the aisle towards him, perhaps someone returning to the Cathedral having left something behind at Mass?

He called out, quietly. "Hello?"

He lowered the snuffer and peered hard through the gloom. A peculiar sense of fear gripped him. His voice sounded small as it left his throat, but it echoed around and up into the vaulted ceiling of the Cathedral, as if God himself was taking the timid voice and empowering it with his grace.

No one returned the greeting, but Father Andreas knew he was not alone. Someone had entered the building. He could feel a presence. It wasn't due to any special talent or divine intuition. He could now hear the sound of heavy breathing, a scratching on the hard tiled floor, perhaps from hobnailed boots. He wondered, for a moment, if a soldier had entered, looking for respite, maybe injured at the front? After all, the front was only a few miles from here. It *might* be possible.

"Hello?" he called again, a little stronger this time. "Is any one there?"

He tilted his head to one side and listened intently. The grating of a chair being pushed roughly to one side drew his eyes into the darkness in the middle of the nave. He peered, but all he could see were shadows.

"I know there's someone there," he called, trying to sound both assured and welcoming, but aware that his voice wavered with the final words. He could feel his heart beat hard within his chest, a trembling in his hands.

He placed the snuffer on the candle tray and stepped cautiously to the front of the ambulatory, as a servant might do when called before a tyrannical king. He peered out over the Cathedral blackness, his eyes flicking backwards and forwards, urgently trying to see someone, something. He tried to speak again, but the shadows cast from the few remaining candles appeared to rise up amongst the pews and overwhelm him. There was someone who chose not to be seen with him in the Cathedral, of that he had no doubt. He drew back, defeated with fear, his hand to his chest, his eyes wide. He stole past the candles to the antechamber. He was already tugging off his top garments by the time he'd reached it. He heaved the robe over his head and hurried to the cupboard to hang it on the peg.

It was then the shadow came at him.

It was the beast's eyes which snagged him first, like a hook in a fish's mouth, the smouldering rage of its glare grasping and holding his gaze. He tried to scream, but his tongue was lame, even after he felt sharp teeth tearing into the soft flesh of his left arm.

There was no pain, no fear, just surprise when he looked to his side and saw the tattered remains of his butchered limb gushing blood onto the crouched feral figure in front of him. Vast and repugnant, its fetid coat knotted, its wicked eyes staring upwards into the Priest's with hatred and malevolent rage. It readied itself to spring.

Father Andreas fell backwards as the thing leapt, a filthy thick taloned claw catching him hard on the side of the face. It sliced effortlessly through his skull, gashing open the Father's eye socket, splattering the far wall of the chamber with torn shards of bone and flesh from his face.

He stumbled, trying to raise his one remaining arm in defence or supplication. Blood gushed out of his face, pumping down his cheek and into his mouth. Finally he found his voice, as if the rich liquid had invigorated his tongue. All he could do was scream. He managed to get to his feet and shuffled around in a circle, disorientated, trying to rebalance himself against his missing limb, staggering like a drunkard towards the door.

For a moment, the beast sat back on its haunches and watched, its head turned to one side like a cat teasing a dying mouse. It lingered, almost hidden in the shadow of the antechamber, as if in that moment finding pity in the floundering, weeping figure of the Father. It watched him stagger through the opening and out onto the ambulatory, before rising up and bounding after him with giant, effortless leaps.

There was a swagger to the way the thing moved, a terrible elegance and might, as if every step brought the beast pleasure, a pride in the magnificence of its prowess.

Andreas threw himself down the steps of the apse, tumbling into the pews at the front of the assembly. His head spun. He could feel the life blood pumping out of him, the front of his cassock drenched, his face sticky and tasting of iron. He held up his right hand, slick with gore, and turned it over in attempt to kiss his signet ring.

A dreadful weight thudded into the back of him, his chest thumped hard, as if he had been shot. He felt his legs crumple and he tried to let himself fall, to collapse into the thick embracing darkness of death creeping in from the periphery of his vision. But he found his legs wouldn't buckle, as if, in his final moments, they had found new vigour, new life. He allowed a last joyous thought to wander through his slowly dying mind, that the Lord had granted him new strength at the end.

He turned his one good eye downwards and despairingly saw how the beast's taloned claw had punched straight through his body, the wicked thing dripping with his lifeblood from the gaping hole in his ribs.

He realised he was unable to move, unable to breathe. His mind faded. He felt his body rise and be thrown backwards as the clawed hand pulled away, thudding him hard into the bottom step of the apse. He slumped over onto his back, staring up at the Cathedral's ceiling. How he loved that ceiling, he thought, as death swept in and his vision faded to blackness.

SIX

1889. THE VATICAN. VATICAN CITY.

"We all have to face our own demons," Father Adansoni insisted, before the prying eyes and questions of the Holy See. "This boy here is no different." he said, indicating the cowed figure of Tacit next to him.

It was the first time Adansoni had been called to the Inquisitional Chamber. It was the first time he'd brought a child, found during one of his missions, with him back to the Vatican. He felt dwarfed by the size of the chamber and the council that circled before him. But he also found that the command in his voice had not failed him. "Demons he may have," he called, "but he has taken such giant steps since I found him. His progress has been remarkable!"

He took a step forward and thrust his hands before him, clenched, as if in chains. "When I found him he was malnourished. He could not speak. Now, he is stronger and has refound his tongue. He speaks Polish, his native tongue, but already he has a grasp of many languages. Italian. French. German. This he does but a month since I began to work with him. His capacity for learning is incredible. Physically he is like no twelve year old I have known. He is strong, like an ox."

Adansoni let his hands drop to his side. "I feel he is also my responsibility," he continued, his voice now plaintive, "and I must do the best for him. I found him. I rescued him from that place. I have brought him into the Church."

"No, you have not brought him into the Church," croaked an ancient white haired Cardinal from beneath a skull cap of scarlet, seemingly too big for his shrunken head. "You have brought him into the Vatican. You had no right to do so."

"But there is something about the boy," Adansoni replied firmly, "something I cannot define."

"If you expect him to stay, Father Adansoni," spat another from the council gathering, "which undoubtedly you do, for why else would you have brought him here, you must explain your actions to us."

"We do not take in waifs and strays on the whim of travelling missionaries," the decrepit white haired Cardinal continued, only his mouth moving so the rest of him appeared to be made of stone.

"There is a strength within him, a strength about him, an almost tangible feeling of power. I have never felt anything like it before from one I have met. One can almost feel it emanate from within him."

"You use bold words," a voice from the right of the watching council called. "What exactly are you trying to suggest?"

Adansoni paused and gathered his breath. His heart beat hard in his chest. He steeled his resolve and turned to face the Cardinal. "I'm not trying to suggest anything," he lied. "I merely feel he would be an excellent addition to the ranks of young acolytes in the Catholic Church, here, in the Vatican."

"If you bring young ones to the Vatican, it is usually a sign that you think them of the calibre to join the Inquisition. Is that what you are suggesting?"

"No!" answered the Father firmly, feeling a heat rise within him. "Absolutely not. Not all who come before the Holy See are bound to that path. I see this boy achieving much within the office of the Vatican. I do not see him joining the ranks of Inquisitors."

"It is most unusual," a voice to the left of the white haired Cardinal called, "to take in acolytes from unrecognised sources. We have standards. We only pick from the very finest families and recognised seeds."

"Then perhaps we should change?" Adansoni retorted, to which there was a sharp intake of breath from the congregation. The Father felt foolish at his hot-headedness and quickly moved to soothe the pricked emotions. "Forgive me, Cardinals. I say only that I feel … no, I *know* he will be a good addition to our Catholic family and faith. Do not ask me how I know, but I do."

"And what do you say, boy?" the white haired Cardinal asked, putting his eyes onto Tacit. "What have you got to say for yourself?"

Tacit raised his head and stared vacantly around the room. His impression was that the place smelt wrong. There was no warm odour or earthy richness in the bewildering dark of the chamber, no comforting fragrance of the mountainsides that he knew so well, no stench of freshly-cut goat leathers hardening in the autumn sun, no heady nourishing bouquet of succulent soups and freshly baked bread. Cold stone and metal, along with the hint of wood smoke and pork flesh now long gone, were all Tacit could detect, as he stood bowed in fear close to Father Adansoni in the centre of the room.

And then in a voice and a language Tacit never realised he possessed, words formed on his tongue. "*In Deo speramus*," he spoke, lifting his head to face his questioners – *"In God we trust."*

SEVEN

23:40. Monday, October 12th, 1914.
The front line. Arras. France.

"It's like staring into fucking hell's abyss," Henry heard one of his soldiers mutter darkly, between puffs on his cigarette.

Henry looked across at Sergeant Holmes. "We need to go into the trench, Sergeant," he said resolutely, recovering enough of his wits to consider their predicament. They couldn't stay where they were any longer, exposed on the parapet of the German trench. He looked back to the ditch full of of slaughter. "We need to search it."

He'd never gone over the top before, never raided an enemy's trench. For the last month Henry's unit had been told to dig in and hold their position. All he knew was defence. The responsibility of taking the offensive to the enemy terrified him. He swallowed at his dry throat and thought of his schoolmasters, what they would say if they could see him now. "Round up a few groups of men, Sergeant, those willing to go forward. I don't expect them all to go."

"Will do sir," Sergeant Holmes replied, storming along the trench lip and barking orders to the waiting soldiers.

Henry looked about the blackened broken landscape and wished to God for a little more humanity to be found somewhere in the world to put an end to this dreadful conflict. Further up the line, heavy guns pounded and the horizon burned yellow. He looked down at the earth and noticed his right boot stood on a piece of paper. It was a picture of a family drawn by a child, a drawing of a father, mother and two children alongside a dog and a cat, disfigured and partially erased by mud, blood and water. But underneath were written the words, clearly visible in careful and precise German writing, 'Möge Gott Sie sicher zu halten' – *May God keep you safe.*

Those unfortunate men selected to go beyond the German front line found only decimation in the support trenches. Most had refused to climb into the infernal squalor, sitting firmly within No Man's Land, unwilling to go back, unable to go on, even under the caustic bark of their Sergeant's threats. Those who had the courage to enter quickly paled and scampered back before they had ventured too far into the complex of twisting high- sided trenches. There was a wickedness which had befallen this place, far greater and more inexplicable than the usual horrors of the war, that even the most sanguine of men felt. Their fear was made all the more terrible by the need to shuffle forward by touch, moon and torchlight alone. A pall hung over the place, blacker than anything created by man's own invention.

The patrols came back not long after they had headed out, their hands and uniforms crimson from the blood sodden earth, their senses shaken from the scenes within, and no signs of life to report.

"The thing that is puzzling me, sir," confessed Sergeant Holmes, stepping forward to light Lieutenant Frost's cigarette, "the thing I cannot understand is, well, where are all the bloody bodies?"

"Good question," Henry replied, drawing deep on his cigarette. He noticed blood on its paper and quickly withdrew it from his mouth. "I was thinking exactly the same thing." He corrected the cap on his head, pulling it tight with its peak. "And if our lads did this to Fritz, where the hell have they gone to?"

Standing in the German front trench, they could feel the moisture of freshly spilt blood seep through the leather of their boots. Henry moved his weight uneasily from foot to foot in a vain attempt to stop the oozing into his socks.

The plod of heavy feet in the sodden mud drew the Lieutenant and Sergeant's attention away down the trench. Henry used the interruption to discard his bloodied cigarette. A squad of Tommies were driving a dishevelled group of German soldiers like cattle ahead of them. The prisoners looked half insane, moaning and crying, clawing at their faces, tearing at their uniforms. They yelped and yelled unfathomable words, as if their minds had been broken, their tongues somehow too fat for their mouths.

"We found these poor buggers," said a British soldier, peering at them pitifully, "just down the way, in a dugout. They'd blocked up the entrance with stones and mud, sir."

Another soldier from the squad squeezed himself forward in the narrow trench, eager to be heard, to have his role in their discovery recognised. "There was bits of uniform and all sorts over the opening. I had to put my foot right through it. To make a hole. To peer through. Took some doing. The buggers didn't want to be found."

"We found 'em though," the first Tommy continued, "but they're all we found of old Fritz," he added, swallowing and curling the edges of his mouth up disdainfully. "Looks like the rest of them they've scarpered, sir, good and proper. That's if they even got away. We've been quite a way in, sir, and there's nothing but, well, blood and bits all the way." He went to wipe his eye, but caught sight of his bloodied hand in the flicker of torch light and decided against it.

Henry turned to the muttering, jabbering group of six prisoners, behaving as if maddened by a cruel sickness. He called out to them in German, but they continued their inane babble, seemingly oblivious to anything except their own private torment. Henry spoke again, more strongly this time, commanding one of them, a Corporal, to speak. He took hold of him by the shoulders, turning him sharply.

"Soldier!" he said, trying to shake him into some semblance of consciousness. "Tell me, what has taken place here?"

The soldier waggled his head, his face scrunching up with pain and bitterness. He began to weep, falling forward into Henry's body and clutching hold of him in a deep embrace.

"Wölfe," he wept bitterly into Henry's shoulder. "Wölfe!"

Henry held the soldier to him, the Corporal shuddering and weeping like a wounded child. He could feel the shape of his uniform against his, the weight of his body pressed into him, the smell of earth and blood in his hair. The enemy held on, tightly buried into Henry's chest. Henry drew his hand to the back of the soldier's head and pulled him tight to him.

For several moments they stood like that, enemies embraced, until, finally, Henry turned his eyes to Holmes. The Sergeant gave a knowing nod and turned to address the British patrol.

He cleared his throat, almost apologetically at first. "Right then, let's get these poor buggers out of here." He stepped forward to usher them along the trench.

"Take them back behind our forward line, Bill," said Henry, extracting himself from the Corporal to watch the shambling mob stumble past. "I doubt any of our men would fancy bunking down in this trench for the night, do you?"

"Not bloody likely, Lieutenant," muttered the Sergeant, finding a pathway out of the bloodied killing ditch into No Man's Land. "Mind you, sir, they is all soft. They could all do with a bit of hardening up, if you ask me."

"How about you, chaps?" asked Henry to the three nearby soldiers. "Fancy a night in this trench?"

"With all due respect sir," the nearest soldier replied, "not on your bleedin' Nelly!"

Henry chuckled grimly. "Go on then, get back to our hole."

Eagerly they bolted for the lip of the trench.

"Want us to send the word, sir, up the line?" asked one of them, peering back into the trench and the popular officer, "to pull back I mean, sir?"

"Pass it on to any you see, Dawson. I'll walk along now and order any I find back. I think the Hun has buggered off. There doesn't seem to be anyone about. Oh, and Dawson," Henry called, "well done with those prisoners."

"Not a problem, sir," replied the young soldier, standing to awkward attention, his chest puffed with pride. He made as if to leave but something held him at the lip of the trench. "Sir, excuse me, sir, for asking but what do you think he meant when he said 'Wolf'?"

"Dawson, I have no idea." Henry muttered, looking up into the dirty pitch of the sky. "Seems to me are many strange and terrible things in this war. Whatever demons those poor bastards witnessed, I sincerely hope we never have to face them ourselves."

EIGHT

19:43. Monday, October 12th, 1914. Paris. France.

Cardinal Bishop Monteria stood silently in the gloom of Notre Dame's central aisle, bowed by the weight of his advanced years and the month's labours. A darkness was falling across Paris and the Cardinal's mind.

Resting heavily on a cane long carried for ailments in his hips, he watched with eyes possessing an eagerness and anticipation at odds with his elderly frame. From every corner of the far nave, the church's army of Priests, pastors and church hands scurried about their duties, ordering, erecting and arranging the pulpit and transepts for a large forthcoming congregation, as if their very lives depended on it. On Saturday, October 17th, within just five days, many of the world's leaders, dignitaries, aristocracies and religious officials would descend upon the Cathedral for an unparalleled and combined prayer for peace. A single act to stop the war, an attempt to bring the carnage to an end before the slaughter grew even worse.

A Mass for Peace.

The architect of the event passed the cane over into his right hand and shifted his weight onto his stronger right leg. He knew that he'd never dream of accepting credit for having brought the event so close to realisation with so much ambition and belief. To him he was just one piece in a giant puzzle, a puzzle which, when unlocked, he hoped would reveal a new way forward for mankind. He was just glad that he was here to see it. To witness its results.

In the grey dusk, which had cast much of the Cathedral into darkness, he looked smaller and more insignificant than usual. It was how he liked to appear. Just like Francis of Assisi, the Saint he most admired, Monteria always believed that the meek's path towards achieving their goals was easier than the path for those who telegraphed their deeds at every opportunity. After all, didn't the Lord himself say that the 'meek shall inherit the earth?'

The venerable Cardinal rubbed his palms together, as if removing the last crumbs of a meal, and exhaled loudly, looking up into the heights of the Cathedral and then back down towards the nave. Inexplicably he was suddenly caught in an embrace of fear and trepidation at the enormity of what he was planning to do. He was relieved when a voice called out and rescued him from his anxiety.

"Tired, Cardinal Bishop Monteria?" a young black-cassocked Bishop asked, stepping out of the shadows of the north transept, where the candles had yet to be lit. A scarlet coloured *fascia* around his middle gave the stout figure a dash of style and verve, inconsistent with his portly appearance. The voluptuousness of his voice mixed beautifully with his French tongue. "You have every right to be. You must be very proud to see preparations moving at such apace, so near completion."

Cardinal Bishop Monteria straightened the front of his own cassock and looked across at the Bishop with heavy, drooping eyes. He smiled and proffered a hand. "Bishop Guillaume," he said in greeting to young Bishop he knew well from Notre Dame. He looked back to the rear of the Cathedral and the bustling figures. "No, not tired," he said, tapping the foot of his cane on the tiles. "More worn, like a cord which has been tied too many times. But, there is no need to worry. Everything will work out fine."

"It sounds like you're planning something," Bishop Guillaume Varsy replied, raising an eyebrow and a smile.

"I am," said Monteria, looking about the glorious building. "Peace."

A sharp yelp from somewhere in the blackness of an adjourning chamber broke the reverent silence for a fleeting moment. Monteria pretended not to hear it, but when Varsy asked what it was, the Cardinal was quick with an answer.

"A local man. Was caught speaking in tongues."

Varsy pulled a face and shrugged, drawing himself alongside his colleague to look down the length of the Cathedral with him. "Is that so bad?" he asked. "Many of my congregation have claimed to have spoken in tongues at some point."

"He was speaking in tongues *backwards*," elaborated Monteria directly.

"Ahh." Varsy puckered up his face and gave a knowing nod.

"They said he spoke words of the devil, something he chose *not* to deny." The Bishop looked again, briefly in the direction of the chamber from where a second yelp came, and then back to the arrangements in front of them. "They're excommunicating him at the moment," Monteria revealed.

"Oh, he's a ranking Catholic, is he?" Varsy asked, appearing captivated at the news.

"Cardinal Deacon." Monteria anticipated the next question and spoke before he was asked. "Cardinal Deacon Travert."

Varsy gasped. "Cardinal Deacon Travert?!" He stuttered the name out of his mouth in amazement. He'd known the Cardinal Deacon since they were children. Monteria knew Varsy would be shaken at the news.

"He is resisting," he continued, "but that's only to be expected. He's come to this Cathedral for over twenty years."

"Longer than most," Varsy added, moistening his bulbous lips with his wine-coloured tongue.

"They'd tried exorcism," Monteria revealed, aware that his colleague's head was now fixed firmly in the direction from where the pained cries of the excommunication were coming, "but they quickly realised that Travert wasn't possessed. He'd just … fallen from his faith." Without warning, the elderly Cardinal leaned his body forward to trot down the main aisle towards the nave, his stiff torso rocking from side to side, as he waddled above his short, quick strides. "Some do fall, of course," Monteria mused, almost to himself, the tip of his cane clacking on the hard stone slate. "It's a narrow path we walk."

The younger Bishop had now joined him at his side, surprised by the speed at which the old Cardinal could move when he so chose. "And to think of what we used to do to them," Varsy muttered darkly, a last final look towards the chamber behind him where his friend was being held. He leaned a little closer to Monteria's ear and lowered his voice, like someone passing on a secret. "Full excommunication, I mean."

Monteria had known what he'd meant without the need for elaboration. The comment had surprised the old man and he flickered his eyes briefly over the Bishop before casting them back onto the Cathedral in front of him, slowly being brought into life with the lighting of candles.

"We toll a bell before we excommunicate them now," Monteria replied, his tone more considered than his excitable colleague's. "That's quite enough."

Monteria liked Bishop Varsy. He believed he showed promise and occasional wisdom, but he still had much to learn, particularly, at times, in how to behave, what and what *not* to say. He would blame it on the young man's age, but he knew he would never have mentioned such dark things when he was Varsy's age.

"I heard we used to cut their gall bladders from out of them with silver knives, or so I was told," the young man continued, like a child revealing macabre secrets. "And only on full moon nights, as well."

Cardinal Bishop Monteria felt a heat coming to his cheeks. He was neither in the mood, nor did he deem it the place to discuss such things. Indeed, such matters were no longer appropriate for discussion, full stop, nor had they been for many decades now.

"We live in a more civilised time now," he retorted, a firmness suggesting the subject was closed.

"Really? If times are so civilised, why do we need to hold a Mass for Peace?"

It was a fair question and Monteria was unable to give it a suitably considered response. So he chose to say nothing and instead the old Cardinal quietly ruminated on the vulgarity of youth.

As they walked, the Cardinal admired the frescoes on the Cathedral's walls. The scene which caught his attention depicted the opening of a door to hell, all the devil's minions pouring forth in an army of death and retribution. Monteria swallowed and pulled his eyes away.

"Have you ever carried out a full excommunication?" Bishop Varsy asked suddenly, still unaware of Monteria's reticence to discuss the topic.

Monteria tutted sharply and sucked on his tongue. "You know there hasn't been such a thing for over forty years!" He hissed the words, both to keep others in the Cathedral from hearing what was being discussed and as a final veiled effort to show his disapproval of the subject. "We are paying a high enough price for the choices we made in the past as it is."

"I heard that their limbs popped when they were the cast out in the old days, as a sign of how the transformations would affect them once they were bound up within them. That their screams followed them into the moonlit hours. I was told that they cast out blood from their orifices for three days and nights, after which they could taste only blood and desire only blood to satiate their hunger."

"They say a lot of the old days. They are only stories."

"Have you ever seen a werewolf?"

It was the frankness of the question, asked without the slightest deliberation or discretion, that appalled the Cardinal. He stopped and drew Varsy by his sleeve to face him. "Why are you asking such questions?" he demanded, his knuckles white clenched to the Bishop's robe, his eyes flashing over the young Bishop's face, looking for anything which might reveal more.

"I am just interested," he replied.

"Well curtail your interest in such things!" Monteria warned. He studied the fine lines and folds on the young man's face, his eyes slowly cooling. "They were from another time. When things were different. Things have changed. Let us focus on what we have now and the tasks of our age which we must tackle."

He was aware he was still grasping the young Bishop's sleeve and let go of it, almost apologetically. He drew a shaking hand across his forehead and then waved it over the Cathedral behind where Varsy was standing. "This is where the de Lecluse family will be sitting, yes?" he asked, control gradually returning to his voice and his movements.

"Yes," replied Varsy nervously, never having seen the Cardinal so animated. He felt shameful that he'd angered the old man as he had. It had never been his intention. "I hear Henri de Lecluse has been recalled to the army?" he said, in an attempt to draw the conversation back to more shared and conservative interests. "He must be forty five? At the very least?"

"France's army is desperate for good men," Monteria replied, bleakly. "This whole area is designed for the French aristocracy, yes?" he asked, continuing his review of the seating plans.

"Yes. And the block to the right," Varsy said, waving with his hand.

"We should move them to the front," the Cardinal announced suddenly. "They should have the best view. Hear every word that is spoken. See every action. It will do the cause good to have so many powerful families so close to where the service will be taking place. Do we have many from outside of France attending?"

"We have representatives from almost all western countries. We even have members of the Social Democratic Party of Germany attending."

Varsy dared to allow a smile to tease his face and was relieved when

Monteria's face lightened too. A warmth, like the afterglow left by a passing torch, grew within him, swelling his heart with pride and munificence, as if the spirit of God had burgeoned inside it. It was a sensation Varsy often felt, whenever he saw the comfort he brought to people during his sermons, God's grace upon him. If ever asked of the proof of God's existence, he would tell people to simply 'feel it in their heart'. Emboldened, he continued with the other news he had gathered.

"'Le Figaro', 'Le Matin', 'Le Siècle', 'La Justice', they and many other newspapers are covering the event, some even writing in advance of the day itself to provide a prelude and backdrop to the Mass, its intentions and hopes."

Monteria nodded, a wry look on his face.

"We also have papers from other countries," Bishop Varsy added quickly, keen to show that news of the Mass for Peace was not to restricted to France alone. "'The Times' from Britain are attending. 'Coburger Zeitung' from Bavaria. The corridors of the Hotel de Crillon fairly rattle with the babble of a thousand accents and voices from the different countries of the world."

Varsy noticed that the old Cardinal's lips glistened in the dim light of the Notre Dame. Monteria's protruding adam's apple worked its way up and down his ashen skinned throat.

"And politicians?" he asked, furtively. "You mention representatives are attending. Do you have any names? Important persons?"

The young Bishop's eyes flashed in the candlelight from above. "Britain is sending Foreign Secretary Edward Grey, 1st Viscount of Fallodon."

The Cardinal seemed to shudder briefly, his breath snipped, as if snagged by a trap. "So Britain shares our view that this war must be stopped and stopped forthwith?"

"One would hope all nations share such a view? Count István Tisza, Prime Minister of Hungary, is also attending. Long he has been an advocate of peace to resolve Europe's issues. Léon Descos, French Ambassador to Belgrade, he has returned home to show his allegiance to the pursuit of peace, and I have just heard that the German Ambassador to Vienna, Heinrich von Tschirschky, is also in attendance."

"A global audience," smiled Monteria. He closed his eyes for a moment in an attempt to comprehend what he had achieved, Bishop Varsy's earlier indiscretion long forgotten in light of this latest news. "Let us hope our message is afterwards taken away by those who attend to their own peoples around the globe. Shall we sit?" He indicated the line of chairs beside where they were standing.

"Yes, it's sometimes good to sit and watch others work," Varsy replied lightly, and the two of them chuckled.

"You do realise that we've been here before don't you, Guillaume?"

"What, with a Mass for Peace?"

"The Catholic Church, in a direct parley for peace. Francis of Assisi. With his attempt to broker peace between the Crusaders and the Arabs. With the Sultan al-Kamil."

"Yes!" the young man replied passionately, pleased to recount a topic he knew well and with much fondness. "I remember the teachings. Francis offered the Sultan a trial by fire to prove his and his faith's worthiness. Putting his life in the hands of his Lord in order to achieve peace." They nodded and then Varsy looked across at Monteria nervously. "If I remember rightly, he did not succeed though?"

"It depends how you define 'succeed', Guillaume? To broker peace no, he did not succeed, but perhaps that was never his, or God's, intention?"

Varsy shook his head in doubt, making his double chin wobble. "I don't understand. Why would God not want peace?"

The old Cardinal raised his hand gently from the top of his cane and lifted an index finger from it. "I never said that. When he reappeared from the flames of his trial unharmed, his clothes unblemished, Francis was immediately heralded as the true embodiment of God, by both Christians and the Sultan's subjects. Francis was given free reign to wander unmolested amongst the Sultan's lands, speaking directly to his people of the Lord's wonder. He never stopped the wars but his humility and his grace won him many admirers and followers on his return to Italy." Monteria looked across at Varsy. "Yes, the wars continued, but such was the adoration on his return, on the humble nature of his achievements, and his failure, that the Church made Francis of Assisi a Saint. And it was as a Saint that Assisi's legacy achieved so much, for when people follow his path of humility and respect for all things, far more is achieved, has been achieved, than the ending of the Crusades could ever have done." He looked back to the nave. "So you see, it's not always the path that we think is destined for us by God that God in fact wants to us to take." "Perhaps they'll canonise you, Cardinal Bishop Monteria?" Bishop Varsy asked, with a wry smile, " – once you achieve peace in Europe?" But the aged Cardinal said nothing, instead closing his eyes and hanging his head in silent prayer.

NINE

1889. The Vatican. Vatican City.

The dormitory into which Tacit had stepped looked anything but welcoming. After the opulence of the Vatican, lavished with gold and rich fabrics, the dormitory looked more like a prison rather than a home.

Grey. Monotonous. Correct.

Down its length were beds, grey covers masking white starched sheets beneath and small bedside tables alongside upon which were set bibles, black bound and silver edged. Each bed was spaced the same distance apart from its neighbour across the grey stone floor, grey walls behind, grey ceiling above, the only decoration being a large black stone cross, hanging on the far wall facing the door through which Tacit had been pushed. Two small windows in the roof of the room gave everything a thin and grainy appearance.

Stretched out on beds, or gathered in groups, some standing, others crouched on the floor playing jacks, were the twelve boys, laughing and chatting idly. At once they fell silent and looked up, gathering themselves slowly in front of Tacit, peering and murmuring between themselves. Tacit checked quickly over his shoulder and realised that Adansoni had not accompanied him inside the dormitory. He looked back and felt the cold burden of dread fall heavily upon him. He felt pressure in his bladder, a tightness in his throat. He trembled and fought against the urge to run.

He hesitated beneath the enquiring glares and made to speak when suddenly, one of the tallest of the boys stepped forward, his face brightening in welcome. "Hello!" the boy said cautiously, reaching out and attempting to take Tacit's case from him. Tacit resisted, his fingers locked tight to the handle.

Another of the boys spoke. "You're Poldek?" he asked gently. "I'm Georgi."

Now there were only smiles and inquisitive glances pressed in his direction. Tacit swallowed and felt the weight inside of him shift, just a little. His fingers uncurled from the case and he watched the boy take it and place it on a bed nearby, his immediate thought that it was some sort of trick.

"How's your Italian?" a toothy boy enquired in the same language, pushing forward and proffering a hand. Tacit hesitated in taking it but the boy forced his hand into his. "You're Polish? That's right, isn't it?"

"It's alright," another called and Tacit speared him with a suspicious glare. "They've told us. Well, told us a little of what happened."

"A few of us here were abandoned too," another revealed. "You're not alone."

The edges of Tacit's mouth trembled and he nodded. "Yes, I am Polish," he said eventually, careful not to reveal too much of himself to these strangers. Not yet.

"I'm Ivan," the tall boy announced, putting an arm outlandishly across his shoulders and making Tacit flinch. Ivan ignored him, or didn't notice. "You're most welcome!" He pushed him forward gently through the crowd of boys to his bed. Tacit could feel hands on his shoulders and back, slapping and thumping, as he supposed children must do when they greet others of their kind.

Another child called Antonio pushed forward and proffered a hand. Tacit surprised himself by reaching forward slowly and taking it. "We've been told what happened," he said, looking hard at Tacit, his friends and then back at the new boy. "We're sorry, all of us. But you're safe now. The Church will look after you. We've all made a promise to look after you. We're your family now."

TEN

09:07. Tuesday, October 13th, 1914.
The Vatican. Vatican City.

"In God I trust," Cardinal Bishop Adansoni muttered to himself, "but I don't trust your time keeping, Javier."

The elderly Cardinal's shoes rapped hard on the pristine marbled floor of the Papal Palace, sharp clipped echoes bouncing about the arched dome high above. It had been many years since he had hurried anywhere. A sedentary life, once his missionary work had been drawn to a close, dedicated to prayer and careful reflection in the Vatican's gardens, colleges and smaller churches, suited the seventy four year old Cardinal far more than the hurry and bustle around the labyrinth of corridors and halls of St. Peter's Basilica the younger Cardinals and Priests so enjoyed.

Breathing hard, he recalled the day the old Pope, Leo XIII, was close to death and Father Adansoni had been requested by name to hurry to his side before he passed on. There'd been no similar request for his presence at successor Pope Pius X's passing. In truth, after what had been said and done in the final few months of Pius X's reign, Adansoni had been relieved not to have been summoned that time.

"I am late," Adansoni accepted, raising his hands in admission to the Bishop waiting for him in the pillared vestry. "Cardinal Berberino," he muttered, catching his breath, "you know how he likes to talk."

Warm sun streamed into the domed walkway, enriching the blood red of the tiles on the floor with its glow. Impassive, the Bishop turned the moment Adansoni stepped into the bright shards of light.

"Shall we walk?" he called over his shoulder, "or do you require time to recover?"

It was said as much as an insult as a question, its tone suggesting the Cardinal Bishop would be wise not to waste a moment longer in hastening to the council meeting. Bishop Attilio Basquez's chief role within the Holy See was to ensure that meetings were arranged to suit the needs of the day, ran on time, and that any late stragglers were brought to the chamber without further delay; that, and other occasional more indelicate tasks put aside for members who momentarily stepped out of line.

"No, let us walk," Adansoni replied breathlessly, joining the younger man at his shoulder and relieved to find the pace leisurely. "I am sure the Holy See are all assembled?"

"They are," the ambitious Bishop replied, his dark eyes looking out over St. Peter's Square. "They all arrived on time."

"And I would have too, if I hadn't been delayed," countered the Cardinal sternly.

There was something about the short-statured Argentinian Bishop which reminded Adansoni of a snake. He moved with an ungodly silence and his eyes seemed to flicker rather than move with a natural easy manner. From the cloistered walkway running alongside the Apostolic Palace, Basquez directed the Cardinal Bishop, with a guiding hand on his elbow, away from the palisade towards the stairs down into the bowels of the Basilica.

"I know where I am going!" Adansoni retorted, and then instantly regretted the sudden pique of anger. Basquez bowed his head dutifully, but Adansoni was sure he spotted the hint of a smile on the young man's lips.

He had attended Holy See meetings thousands of times but still the charge of adrenaline and anxiety snatched at his heart and teased his gut whenever he entered the Inquisitional Chamber. Beneath the flickering gas lights, strung on chains tens of feet above, the circular chamber rose up and around in perfect symmetry, seemingly pressing down on any who ventured inside it. He shuddered to think how an accused must feel when brought before the council of the Holy See, all seated at the arching wooden table circling the central dais in the very middle of the room upon which the defendant would sit.

Places were set for twelve senior Cardinals, each one allotted a place on the council every other week, one seat for each month of the year and a thirteenth chair set at the head for the Supreme Pontiff himself. He rarely attended any but the most pressing of cases, his lavish gold seat even more imposing for its emptiness.

A gentle murmuring welcomed Adansoni to the chamber and he raised his hand by way of acceptance and apology.

"Cardinal Korek was just updating us with news from Russia," announced an orange robed Cardinal, skull cap tight to his balding head, "whilst waiting for you to arrive."

"The war," the pointed-faced Korek elaborated helpfully.

Adansoni nodded, correcting his robes as he made himself comfortable in his chair. Naturally, the war was of great concern to the Church, the eastern front being of particular interest.

"As you will no doubt know, the Russian Second Army was utterly destroyed at the Battle of Tannenberg, the First Army all but obliterated," the orange gowned Cardinal Bishop Casado revealed for the elderly Cardinal Bishop's benefit. "The Germans have pushed the Russians all the way back to their borders and beyond. We have just heard that the Germans have reached the Vistula and are laying siege to the town of Ivangorod."

"But for the main, there is stalemate on the borders," Korek added.

"A situation similar to the western front then?" Adansoni suggested, bowing his head with a shake. "This confounded war!"

"Indeed," muttered Cardinal Casado, clearing his throat, as if he was about to commence with a long sermon. He flicked at a spot on the left sleeve of his cassock. "Anyway, now that you're here, Javier, we'll deal with the main business of the day."

"There's been a murder," he announced without additional ceremony. "A few hours ago. Inside the Church."

"I am sorry to hear that," replied Adansoni, aware that all eyes were on him. Whilst murders within the Catholic Church were not uncommon, considering the nature of the Church's work and the enemies against which they were set, there was something about the way the council looked at him that he found unsettling. He swallowed and pulled at the collar of his gown. "Where?"

"Arras. In the Cathedral."

Adansoni turned his head to one side and leant forward. "I'm sorry, you will need to remind me of the Cardinal there. My memory's not what it was."

"It's not the Cardinal who's been murdered," Casado replied, his small ferret-like eyes on the perspiring Cardinal Bishop. "It's the Father. Father Andreas."

"And what makes you sure it's murder?"

"If you saw the body, you wouldn't need to ask."

"Beaten?"

"Torn apart," Casado revealed, a sneer wrenching at his lip.

"Do we have a suspect?"

"It's awkward. The Cardinal there, Cardinal Gérard-Maurice Poré, is making worrying suggestions concerning our problems of the past. We've warned him against saying such things in public. To name such abominations."

"The offspring of our work keep wanting to return home, do they not?" Adansoni replied, fighting the urge to look around the individual faces of the council members. He nodded. "I understand the delicacy of the situation. You've sent an Inquisitor to investigate no doubt?"

"We have one in the city already."

Adansoni was impressed. He knew there was barely a town or city in the world which didn't have the eye of the Catholic Church upon it, or the feet of its agents on its streets and boulevards. No country could compete with the strength of the Catholic faith, no army had the resources or the power to overwhelm and destroy a nation quite like the Catholic Church. But an Inquisitor sent to the scene within a few hours of a crime? His admiration and unease at the Church's might swelled in equal measure. He was about to ask why it was so important that they waited for him to tell their news, but then a dread crept once more over him. He feigned an uncertain smile, cocking his head expectantly.

"It's Tacit," said Casado.

"Oh," Adansoni replied hollowly, feeling his soul sink inwards. "Heavens."

"Indeed. We thought you'd want to be told."

"What's he doing there? I thought he was in Turin? Sorting out the coven of witches?"

"He was. He'd finished with that."

"Eradicated them?"

"Eradicated them?" scoffed a Cardinal to Adansoni's left, even more heavily set than the old Cardinal was. "When our agents eventually went in, there was nothing more than a small collection of finger bones and a plate-sized remnant of their cauldron."

"After that he had crossed over the border," Casado continued, checking his notes in front of him.

"France?" asked Adansoni, desperately trying to pick up the tangled threads of Tacit's numerous missions.

"Slovenia," corrected Casado. "Slavs mobilised in the war trying to force out the Catholic Habsburg Dynasty from the west of country. Tacit processed the heretics and hung thirty two of them from the main gate at Bovec as a warning to others." The Cardinal looked down at his papers. "Now he's in Arras. An *assessment*."

"Whose assessment?"

"His."

Adansoni swallowed, understanding what the severity of an assessment meant. He tried to mask the noise that his dry throat made but he was painfully aware it was audible to everyone in that forsaken chamber.

"Why choose Arras for the assessment?" he asked.

"A suitable subject became available upon which to test Tacit's faith," Casado answered smoothly.

"I don't understand why he needs to be assessed?"

"Really?" the senior Cardinal retorted, raising an eyebrow in mock surprise.

"Even if we choose to ignore his past indiscretions and forays away from the path of truth, he recently beat a man unconscious," another of the Cardinals explained, "at the witches' coven."

"He's beaten a lot of men unconscious," Adansoni replied, defensively.

"He was drunk," the Cardinal spat.

"Sadly he often is. But, so what? After what he's achieved? Again, I don't see why –"

"The man he beat was a Bishop."

"Ahh, I see."

"They say the Bishop will never walk again," growled a hooded Cardinal, away to Adansoni's right. "If he ever regains his ability to speak, it'll be a miracle."

"He's bad, Javier," continued the orange robed Casado, his unmoving eyes boring into Adansoni. "Worse than ever."

"I don't see what this has to do with me?"

"He's your boy."

Adansoni could feel the back of his neck prickle with sweat. Now he felt he was the one being assessed. "I'd hardly call him a boy. And he's certainly not mine. I didn't make him what he is."

"You found him. You brought him into the Church. You know him best."

"That was twenty five years ago! A lifetime for an Inquisitor. I don't think anyone knows Tacit. Not anymore. Certainly not me. Go and ask those who trained him within the Catholic Church. They made him what he is!"

"They simply took what you brought to them."

Adansoni hissed at the accusations being constructed around him. But also he felt strangely protective of the child he found all those years ago in that mountainside hut, clinging to his dead mother, the child he'd brought up as his own son, at least for the first few years until the Church took him and honed him for the path he was eventually to take.

"If there is something on the loose in Arras, we need an experienced Inquisitor investigating." The Cardinal grabbed at his eye sockets and caressed the exhaustion out of them. "It'll also provide us with an excellent opportunity to appraise Tacit in further detail."

"So one assessment isn't enough for you then?!" Adansoni cried, no longer able to control his temper. "Tell me, what assessment had Tacit been set originally in Arras?"

"Exorcism."

Instantly Adansoni cooled and shrugged. Exorcisms were a forte of Tacit's.

"A particularly difficult one," Casada added, noting Adansoni's impassive response. "Three Fathers died trying with this particular possession."

"What's the date of the assessment?"

"It's already been completed."

"And?"

Now it was Casada's turn to shrug impassively. "He exorcised the demon."

Adansoni felt the breath he'd held inside of him slowly release. "So he passed?"

"Questions are still being asked. Hence the reason we feel we need to evaluate him further."

"Questions such as what?"

"He drank a lot of alcohol during the exorcism."

Adansoni shrugged again and looked around the table. "Who amongst us has not taken a little wine during a sermon? To oil the vocal cords?"

"He emptied his full vial of holy water over the poor victim. The guidelines clearly state never more than five castings, not the whole bottle."

"You also make it sound like you felt pity for the demon?" He shook his head and leaned his weight forward onto his elbows. "Tacit's not designed for delicate work, such as a murder investigation. Send him out into the field, assess him from a distance."

Casada rocked his head from side to side on his shoulders, as if weighing up his options. "It would give us the opportunity to watch him closely. We have an assessor in Arras at the moment."

"How convenient. Who is it?"

"Sister Isabella."

Adansoni chuckled disdainfully and shook his head, looking down into his lap. "So, you think he's failing in other ways, do you? I've heard of this Isabella. A new recruit to the Holy See, isn't she? Specifically trained to assess those confused with the weight of celibacy?"

"Amongst other things. She has many assets."

"Yes. I know of which assets you speak. She's young and inexperienced. You really think she can handle Tacit?"

"She's perfect for him."

"And she's in the city," another Cardinal added.

"Father Strettavario's in Arras as well," Casado went on, "overseeing the original assessment. What do you say, Javier? Do we have your agreement to continue the assessment? We'd rather do this with your blessing."

Adansoni looked about the council members, pursing and unpursing his lips like a fish gasping for breath out of water. He sighed and sat back in his chair, raising a limp hand in resignation. "Very well, I agree to the assessment but I still think it's unnecessary and foolhardy. I can't believe he's fallen. Not Tacit. He's one of the best. If not *the* best we have. Lord help us if the likes of him stray from the path."

"I am sure you're right, Adansoni," assured the orange cassocked Cardinal, passing around the order for the continuation of Tacit's assessment to be signed, "but we know that all Inquisitors eventually do fail. After all, when you spend your entire life staring into the abyss, eventually you must fall in."

PART TWO

"I looked, and there before me was a pale horse! Its rider was named Death, and Hades was following close behind him. They were given power over a fourth of the earth to kill by sword, famine and plague, and by the wild beasts of the earth."

Revelation, 6, Verse 8

ELEVEN

11:13. Tuesday, October 13th, 1914. Arras. France.

"Are you Tacit?" the woman asked him.

She hadn't needed to ask if it was him. She recognised him from the painting hanging in the Vatican, in one of the private chambers, of course. The Vatican didn't like to publicise its Inquisitors.

She asked the question nevertheless, hoping against hope that the rough looking figure would say he was not him. The painting of Tacit hanging unseen in Vatican City had captured a determined, dashing man in his twenties, jet black hair, strong features and fierce blue eyes, full of passion and faith. This figure, whilst obviously him, displayed none of the vitality or spirit layered so deep within his painting. For want of another word, he looked damaged, like the city in which he drank.

It was a dingy and morbid place, the bar – much like the figure of the Inquisitor – set several side streets back from the main streets of the city, desperately in need of a woman's touch. Or demolition. She prayed that the German bombs would see to it sooner rather than later. It was ironic that a mediaeval tannery and adjoining stables next door to the decrepit, seedy establishment had been decimated in a recent barrage. Of course, every head had turned to watch her as she entered, dressed as she was in scarlet, her wild red hair surging around and down over her breasts, a cape of velvety crimson drawn tight around her shoulders and tied in a bow above the plunge of her cleavage. The bar and its clientele were not averse to having women in their midst. Whilst prostitutes and escorts were well received and welcomed at the bar, a woman like this, alluringly dressed, an air of confidence and majesty bound up in the way she moved, was of a type not usually seen in such a place. All eyes watched her as she stepped towards the corner of the room, tongues flickering greedily over fat lips, dark eyes watching her every move in the gloom of the bar. They spied the large dishevelled looking Priest whom she approached with jealous envy, and exchanged filthy jokes about how even the Priests were now taking to whores in these dark, war torn days.

Tacit shovelled a last morsel of food into his mouth from oily remains on his plate and sucked his fingers greedily.

"I asked are you –"

"Who wants to know?" he growled, his eyes fixed on the half full bottle of spirit and glass alongside. He reached his greasy fingers forward and gathered up the tumbler, necking the amber liquid in a single quick gulp.

The woman paused and looked at the Inquisitor hard. She'd met a few of them in her time, Inquisitors. The experienced ones; they all looked haggard, spoiled, bruised, a symptom of their line of work. But Tacit, he looked more ruined than any she had seen before. He looked old as an oak tree and as rough as its bark. His deeds were legendary in the Catholic Church and she refused to let his appearance undermine her impression of him.

"I asked, 'Who wants to know?'," his broad jaw set firm.

"Sister Isabella," she replied.

Tacit thrust the glass firmly down beside the bottle and refilled it. "You don't look much like a Sister to me," the Inquisitor muttered, despite his eyes having never left the table.

"You don't look much like the man I was told about."

Tacit paused, considering the gall of the woman's words. Now he raised his eyes up to her. She noticed they settled on her cleavage a moment longer than she would have expected. If Tacit was merely a man she wouldn't have expected anything less. But Inquisitors were supposed to be above the petty frailties of men.

The chair next to where Isabella stood was kicked roughly from beneath the table by one of Tacit's heavy black boots. She drew it still further away from the table edge and seated herself, watching Tacit intently.

His eyes were back on his drink, the tumbler back in his hand. He necked the glass in two gulps and pulled a face of revulsion.

"If it tastes that bad, why drink it?" the Sister asked, her eyes hardening on him.

Tacit put the glass down, more measured this time, and sat back. He crossed his arms and peered at her disdainfully. "What do you want, Sister?" He hissed the word 'Sister' as if it offended him.

"You're needed."

"So soon after my last assignment?" he growled desolately. He saw a sense of contempt harden the Sister's features at the Inquisitor's apparent relucance to work and grimaced. "Don't judge what you don't know," he spat. "I was serving the Lord whilst you were still sneaking kisses from the choristers behind Cathedral chapter houses." He coughed roughly to clear his throat. "So, tell me, what does the Church want now? Another exorcism? Breaking of some protestant heads? Hopefully something to get me out of this God-forsaken city. It was bad enough before the war came to its borders."

"It's Father Andreas."

"Priest of Arras Cathedral?" Tacit knew of them all – every Father, Brother, Cardinal and Saint in the whole of the Catholic world. He made it his job to do so.

"*Ex*-priest of Arras cathedral," Isabella replied, her eyes not leaving Tacit's face, waiting for any reaction from him. "Father Andreas was killed last night."

If Tacit was shocked at the news, he gave no hint of it in his face or his manner. He reached across for the bottle and refilled his glass. He looked across at Isabella, the bottle still in his hand. "Do you want a glass?" he asked gruffly, more in an attempt to deviate her steely glare than a willingness to share his drink. Inquisitor Tacit had no problem drinking alone.

The Sister's silence gave him his answer. He set the bottle down and drank most of the glass in a single pull. He put it down and sat back in his chair, crossing his arms once again. The chair beneath him creaked as he shifted his weight backwards. He weighed up what he had been told.

"If it's murder, call the police," he said, eventually.

Sister Isabella glared at him, her cold unmoving eyes fixed firmly on his. He stared back, their gazes locked in a silent but fierce battle.

After a few moments, Sister Isabella spoke. "You're drunk. I can see it in your pupils."

Tacit sneered and shook his head, reaching to fill his glass again. "If you think I'm drunk now, you haven't seen anything."

The Sister's hand took hold of the neck of the bottle the moment Tacit's hand was on its body.

"*Hombre Lobo*, Tacit," Isabella hissed, leaning forward towards him across the table. Spoken with her rich Spanish accent, the words took on an even more apocryphal form.

Tacit ran his eyes over the mysterious red haired woman, judging and evaluating. If she was a Sister, she was like no Sister he'd ever met before. She looked more like a prostitute than a patron of divinity. He should know, he'd *dealt* with enough of both in his time. She wore no emblem of Christ, at least none that he could see. She overtly sexualised herself with how she dressed. She wore makeup. Early twenties. Daring young women, looking to take over the world. All looking like she did, though, they might. There was a scent of incense, perhaps even perfume, about her. He could detect it clearly through the pervading odour of stale alcohol and tobacco which hung heavy in the bar like the stench of death. But there was something else, something besides her using the rarely uttered word for one of the Catholic Church's most damned of enemies. There was an almost tangible sense of godliness emanating out of her, almost as much as her comeliness. She was a beautiful woman, in every sense of the word.

"How many cases have you worked?" Tacit asked, his unmoving eyes firm on her face.

"A few," she replied, tossing her hair out of her face.

Tacit spat dismissively, shaking his head.

"Enough," Isabella answered back firmly, her eyes on his. "It's not my first murder case, if that's what you mean? And you're not my first Inquisitor. I have been sent here to guide you in the course of your investigation."

Tacit's face creased with the suspicion of a joyless smile. He let go of the bottle the Sister was still holding firm in her grasp and sat back. "And if the dear Father is now deceased then on whose authority are you here?"

"The Vatican."

"Not good enough."

"Why do you need a name?"

"I always have a name with every case."

"You know as well as I that you'll never have a name." Inquisitor assignments were almost always given anonymously by the Holy See, so that if an investigation led back to one within the Church itself, there could be no opportunity for retribution against the original instigator of the case.

Tacit nodded. The fact she knew the routine for issuing them convinced him she was who she claimed to be, whoever that was.

"Why do they suspect Hombre Lobo?" he asked, pursing his lips.

"Come and see the body."

"They have a body?" Tacit asked, surprised.

Isabella picked up the bottle by the neck and poured a long stream of liquid into the glass in front of her. As she set the bottle down, Tacit reached forward to grasp the glass but Isabella was too quick for him. She gathered it up and put it to her lips. Tacit watched for any sign of revulsion or grimace to the hard liquor as she swallowed.

None came.

"It's in a crypt," she said, setting the glass down. "In Arras Cathedral."

TWELVE

1890. The Vatican. Vatican City.

Years of dedicated service made the Cardinal Bishop feel older than he was, but when he watched the young boys playing in the Vatican grounds, he felt the years lift from his shoulders. He rested his hands on his cane and leant his weight against the wall of rock beside which Father Adansoni was standing watching. The acolytes were playing across the way from them in the full sun of the Rome spring.

"He looks very happy," the Cardinal Bishop said, nodding towards the figure of Tacit darting about the group of boys. "You must be very pleased, Javier?"

The Father worked an eyelash out of his eye and drew his fingers through his slowly greying hair. He nodded and smiled benevolently.

"The laughter of children is one of the Lord's greatest gifts," the Cardinal continued, stamping the cane into the ground, as if to affirm his words, "and the laughter from a child once thought of as lost the most priceless gift of all."

They perched against the stone and watched the children playing for a little time in silence until the Cardinal Bishop asked, "I hear they say he is a natural leader?"

Adansoni nodded. "People naturally gravitate to him, as if there is a power within him that you cannot see but which draws you. It is nothing that he knowingly does. It is just there, as if he is a magnet for souls, drawing you towards him. It is a gift. I have never known anything like it before with any of the acolytes."

"And of what went before, there's no issue, no mention?"

"He will not talk about it, Cardinal Bishop," Adansoni cautioned.

"And the other boys, they don't enquire or press for the truth?"

"If they do, he mentions nothing of it. He says he cannot remember the episode. Whether that is true or not, I don't know. Nor I am intending to press the question. It is not my place, nor is it right to pick at that wound any longer. He is recovered. He is happy. He blossoms. That is all that concerns me. I am pleased."

"You should be. He will make a good Father, like his mentor." the Cardinal Bishop added, reaching over and squeezing Adansoni's wrist, as he pushed himself up from the wall.

"Father? Ha!" Adansoni chuckled, standing up himself and stretching his back after too long leant against the cold stone. "I am thinking more a Cardinal!"

Both men laughed and the Cardinal asked if Adansoni was returning indoors. He said that he was.

"The world needs warm good people like Tacit," the Cardinal continued, drawing his hood up over his head to fend off the morning chill, "to help spread the message of restraint, to be more considerate of others, to help people recognise that their behaviour influences outwards."

Father Adansoni looked across the grounds for a final time before turning indoors into the Apostolic Library. "He is a guide many could learn from," he said. "A mirror into which we should all look."

THIRTEEN

06:30. Tuesday, October 13th, 1914. Arras. France.

Sandrine Prideux rose naked from the bed, making no effort to avoid waking her sleeping companion. In a single graceful sweep of her body, she vaulted from beneath the sheets and stepped with elegant strides to the shuttered bedroom window. The room hung heavy with the smell of cigarettes, alcohol and human sweat. It was only six thirty in the morning but already the day was turning hot. She threw the shutters wide, feeling the warmth of the sun upon her body, letting the light flood into the room. The figure in the bed groaned and rolled over, its head under a pillow.

Sandrine lit a cigarette and sat facing the low window ledge, her feet on the sill, her knees wide enough apart to allow the fresh air between her legs. Beneath her the French city of Arras was waking up. The street below buzzed with the sound of traffic, the crank of a cart, the swish of a horse's reins, the occasional honk of a wealthy merchant's car horn. Soldiers marched in neat lines, heavy packs on backs, rifles tucked tight into shoulders. British Tommies, weary heads staring down at the toe caps of their mud caked boots, puffed on roll ups and pulled uncomfortably at their heavy khaki uniforms in the early morning heat.

Across the dilapidated skyline of the city, clipped and disfigured by German shells, Sandrine could see traders begin to gather in the square. In the house opposite she saw the occupant watching her with a look of surprise and delight from his window. She waggled her knees and waved at him. Immediately, he turned away flustered, embarrassed, and pretended to busy himself in other business, snatching another brief look moments later before shutting the shutters altogether, as if the temptation was too great and it had to be hidden behind closed doors.

"Can you not shut the window and come back to bed?" came a feeble voice from behind her. "It's too early."

"But it's a beautiful day!" she laughed.

"It's not even seven!" the voice retorted.

"And it's a beautiful day!" Sandrine reiterated brightly, peering briefly over her shoulder and then back to the street. And she felt it, the beauty of the day, not just in the weather, but within the essence of it too. A new dawn. A new beginning.

Every day she met people piling their belonging onto carts and heading west, away from the oncoming German forces. They would tell Sandrine to come with them, that a beautiful woman like her should not be left behind to the mercy of the enemy, to the ruinous destruction of war. But all her life she felt she had been running, running to the beck and call of others. She had decided she had run as far as she was going to and she would make her stand amongst the ruins of the front line. And whilst she did so, she would savour life in whatever time she had left.

She peered from the broken city skyline to the heavens, rich and blue, and then back to the street again when the bright dawn hurt her eyes. Sandrine sat back in her chair, feeling the heat from the cigarette on her fingers and the heat from the rising sun on her breasts. She closed her eyes and lounged like a lizard on a hot rock.

"Are you smoking?" the man croaked from the bed incredulously. His British officer clothes were still arranged neatly in a row along the end of the bed. Even the heat of passion and the recklessness of alcohol could not unseat the conformity of this British officer's order.

When Sandrine had met him last night, drinking wine and laughing too loud with his raucous officer chums, she considered how handsome he must have been in his youth. He still retained a glimmer of his former features but a penchant for alcohol, rich foods and nicotine had blunted his charm.

They'd all watched her greedily, the officers, as she'd joined them at their table, devouring her body with their eyes, joining easily with her rich laughter and luxuriant manner, each taking turns to fill her glass, placing hands upon her knee and imploring her with their deep and beseeching gazes. One, a sandy haired and balding officer, his thin lips concealed by a generously coiffured moustache, salted with speckles of ginger and white like a tabby cat, had even had the audacity to touch her breast and run his hand up the inside of her thigh. She'd allowed him the briefest of touches against the soft fabric of her panties, before her hand had dropped to his and a raised eyebrow insisted he withdraw it, however reluctant he felt. He'd whimpered like a scolded child and tried the same trick a short time later, only to be rebuffed sharply and pushed drunkenly from his chair. Afterwards he'd taken to staring menacingly at her from the distance of a next door table, no longer partaking in idle flirtatious advances.

Any other night she would have spurned the slow and subtle advances of the dark haired officer who now languished in his bed behind her, rejecting his suitability as a lover and choosing one of the younger officers to satisfy her deep and carnal yearning. But there was something about the way he watched her with his slate grey eyes and a quiet confidence, which both intrigued and excited her. Whilst around her officers fell over themselves to fill her glass and chirp excitedly at her jokes, he joined the revelry at a distance in an assured and measured fashion, an enticing mix of experience and command. Her passion was charged with his smouldering reserve, her own pursuit of recklessness, the noise and banter within the bar, the temerarious urge of alcohol. Four miles east from them, the Germans had begun a short and savage barrage of the British front line, pounding them with eighteen inch mortar rounds. But here, within the dark hot confines of one of Arras's most secret of drinking venues, passions of a different sort ran wild.

As a lone bell tower tolled one o'clock, she'd slipped an arm through his and told him to take her back to his lodging and make love to her.

They'd tumbled drunkenly onto the bed, his wet mouth on her neck, Sandrine's hands in his hair, around his neck and back, feeling more impassioned with every passing second. He surprised her when he pulled himself from her longing embrace and undressed quickly beside the bed, telling her to do the same, as if the act of undressing each other in their lovemaking was somehow too awkward or slow for him to consider. She giggled as he laid out his uniform in neat lines along the end of the bed, climbing onto her knees and reaching out to him when he was naked but for his undergarments. Their mouths locked in a tight embrace, their tongues tasting alcohol and cigarettes, his hand slipping between her thighs.

He made love like the British army made war, manoeuvring himself tactically within the bed and then applying himself with a sense of ruthlessness once in position.

They talked for a little time afterwards, of inconsequential things mixed with occasional brief laughter. But soon his eyes rolled in his head and he fell asleep without warning, his pursed lips slightly ajar, snoring softly in his easy drunken sleep. Sandrine had left him and sat at the window smoking, listening to the sounds coming up from the city, the sudden bark of rare laughter, the sharp rap of footsteps, the far distant falling of shells. But for the main, Arras had been silent.

Sandrine took a long and loud draw on her cigarette and, tilting her head back, exhaled into the air above her. Her darkly curled hair fell almost to the seat of the chair on which she sat.

"How can you smoke at this time of day?" The body moved between the sheets. "How can you feel like smoking after … after last night? Don't you … don't you feel just fucking awful or is it just me?"

"Just you," she said as she took another drag, enjoying the early morning bite of tobacco in her throat, and leant forward, drawing the smoke deep into her lungs. She marvelled at a vast unit of soldiers marching past, heading east. Something was happening, a manoeuvre perhaps out there, at the front? And then the realisation settled on her like a fine dust falling from above. There had been no barrage on Arras last night, the first quiet night in the city since she had arrived in it.

She spotted a face she recognised in the crowd of market sellers heading for the main square and called out to him, feeling empowered and irresistible by her nakedness.

"Alessandro! Alessandro! Good morning to you!" she cried, her breasts swaying before her.

The man turned and looked towards the voice. He laughed when he saw her. "You're a shameful woman, Sandrine Prideux!" he cried.

She'd met the young butcher on the day she had arrived in the city, her spirited manner appealing to his sense of adventure and dreams. He admired her for arriving in the city alone. She admired him for his fiery ambitious talk of his political dreams. They drank long into the night together, discussing the war, the politics behind it. He'd been kind enough to offer her a bed for as long as she needed whilst she acquainted herself with the city. He assured her he would remain the true gentleman and sleep on the couch, but she'd drawn him into his bed and made love to him in return for his generosity. Over the following days he introduced her to his friends, his contacts, even his brother, a Father at the city's Cathedral. After that she had gone, slipped away into the depths of the city, like the crackle of thunder after a storm. Every now and then he caught a glimpse of her around the place, snatched a few hurried sentences with her before one or the other had to be away.

He felt no bitterness towards her. Sandrine, it seemed to Alessandro, was like a green horse, unbroken, refusing to follow the customs of the herd, living by her methods, her choices. He knew he could never tame her and claim her as his own. She was unbreakable and perhaps that thing which so captivated others would be lost if ever anyone succeeded in shackling her to a life of anything approaching conformity.

"What do you think you're doing up there, eh?" he called, "looking so beautiful so early in the morning, eh?"

"Watching the British invasion."

"Why are you not down here kissing me, eh?" A group of men gathered around Alessandro and were looking up longingly.

"Kissing all of us!" shouted one of the other men.

"Where are all the soldiers going?" she asked, suddenly feeling exposed and wrapping an arm across herself. There were limits to even Sandrine's daring. "What has happened?"

Several of the soldiers looked up as she called and cheered at the sight of her, a naked woman leaning brazenly from the window.

"The British," Alessandro yelled up, putting his arm to his forehead to block out the low morning sun. "There is talk that they have broken through at Fampoux."

"Fampoux!" exclaimed Sandrine, raising a hand to her mouth in delight. She felt her heart twitch with the prick of hope.

"You can go home with a pair of Tommies on your arm!" Alessandro laughed. He blew her a kiss from the palm of his hand and, waving, headed off towards the market.

"Why don't you come back to bed and climb into my arms, hey?" invited the voice from the bed.

Sandrine pulled a face and extinguished her cigarette. She swivelled on the chair and peered back at the dishevelled looking individual. He looked terrible. His eyes were bloodshot, his hair, slick with oil and sweat, caked tight to the side of his head. She considered one more spell of passionate lovemaking with him, but his appearance this morning was anything but appealing. She raised a suggestive eyebrow and got up, skipping past the bed to gather clothes she had discarded last night in a far more haphazard fashion than the officer.

"Didn't you hear?" Sandrine asked cheerfully, "the Germans have been driven out of Fampoux?"

"I doubt that very much." the Lieutenant Colonel replied, struggling to sit up in the bed. He winced at the pain in his head and clenched his eyes tightly shut for a few moments. "Now, why don't you come here and make love to me like you did last night, you naughty delicious little thing?"

Sandrine curled her lip and dropped her clothes into a chair, slipping a leg delicately into her panties. "I'm surprised you think like that, Nicholas," she said, with a slight wave of her hand. "I would have thought a man of the British army would feel more enthusiastic about its achievements." Sandrine slipped her second leg in and drew her undergarments up her long mocha-coloured legs. "What makes you so sure there's been no breakthrough?"

"Well, because it's my battalion stationed just outside of Arras." He laid the sheet across his belly and swept back his hair. "And they're on a defensive footing. They should only move forward when I give the order and seeing as I've been otherwise engaged," he raised an eyebrow and smirked with a little shake of his head, "I think we can safely assume they are still several hundred yards from the German lines and Fampoux, or what's left of it, still resides firmly in the grubby paws of the Boche." He tilted his head to one side. "Come on, give me a kiss, won't you?" he begged.

Sandrine tutted and rolled her eyes, clasping her brassiere about herself.

"What's that look for?" he asked, laughing gently.

"If you have men at the front, you shouldn't leave them. You shouldn't even be here!"

"If you think that, then you shouldn't have seduced me," the officer chuckled playfully.

She smiled, a little sadly the officer thought, and then she stepped into her yellow dress.

"Are you really leaving already?" He asked the question with a touching despondency, as Sandrine drew the dress up over her body. "So soon? I was hoping maybe –"

"Why would I want to stay here?" she replied without hesitation.

He laughed at the abrupt honesty of the reply and shrugged. "To be loved?" he suggested, as if it was as good a suggestion as any. "Why, do you have a better offer?" She stepped across the room to the bed and bent down to kiss him gently goodbye. His hand closed around the back of her leg and worked its way up the inside of her dress. She tutted and smacked at the wandering arm playfully.

"Goodbye Nicholas," she said, kissing him one more time and turning on her heel towards the door of his room.

"You Catholic girls!" he called lightly after her, smiling sadly and nestling down into the covers of the bed.

Immediately Sandrine stopped and turned in the doorway. A shadow had fallen across her face, her mouth now open, her neck bent forward. "What did you say?" she hissed, anger flushing away any pleasure which had been held within her features. "What do you mean by that?" she demanded, as if this assumption had caused the utmost offence.

"Sorry!" the officer called back uncertainly, the smile slowly eroding as he saw the anger in Sandrine's face. "Have I said something – ?"

"That!" Sandrine spat. "Saying I was Catholic."

"Sandrine, I'm sorry," he stuttered, sitting up in bed with more effort than should have been necessary. "I just thought … well, aren't you?"

"No!" she retorted, as if the accusation was poisonous. "How dare you!? Why do you say such a thing?"

"It was just that yesterday … leaving the Cathedral. I saw you."

"I don't know what you mean?"

"I saw you," he muttered, testing the atmosphere with a smile. He saw the testiness in Sandrine's face quickly and dropped it from his own. "I was in the square. I'm sure it was you. I watched you come out, out of the Cathedral."

"Well it wasn't," she snapped, her mouth tightening into a sneer.

"Sandrine. I'm sorry. If I've said anything …"

She took a step forwards and thrust a finger towards him. "Never say such a thing again!" she spat, jabbing at him and his raised hands.

"Sandrine. I'm sorry. It's just, I'm Catholic myself and I thought … "

"You thought what?" she cried, feeling sickened by the revelation and almost overwhelmed by the urge to bathe and clean herself. "You thought what?"

"Just … perhaps we might see each other again? Visit Mass together?"

"Let me tell you this, Nicholas," she said, taking another step towards the officer so that she towered over him in the bed. "I'll never see you again. Do you understand? Never! Stay away from me! You, your Church and your God can all stay away!"

"Now listen here," the officer retorted, a tension now beginning to rise in his own voice. "There's no need for that!" He swung his legs over the edge of the bed and gave the impression he was about to stand.

"Nothing will save you in this war!" she hissed at him, casting an arm at him before turning to leave.

"You should watch your filthy tongue!" he warned, striding over to where she watched him with her fierce eyes. "We're here to save you French." He stabbed at her chest with an index finger. "You should be more respectful."

"Save us?!" Sandrine laughed cruelly, tossing her hair from her face. "Save us from what?"

"The Germans, of course, you silly woman."

She scowled and rolled her eyes dismissively. "Germans? Pah!" she spat, raising an arm in a way that the officer thought she was about to strike him. "There is more to fear than the Germans. There is no more hope for you. Go to your Catholic Fathers. Get down on your knees and pray. But I tell you this, no God will save you from the hell that is to come!"

FOURTEEN

06:45. Tuesday, October 13th, 1914. Paris. France.

Cardinal Monteria stood in the very centre of his room, his head held aloft, his arms angled away from his body, as if receiving a divine blessing. About him Silas, his personal servant, hurried, dressing the Cardinal in the vestments for Holy Mass, an exact and ordered procedure, long studied by the young man who dreamed one day of being dressed in such a manner by his own servant.

Usually early morning Mass would be held at Notre Dame, a short walk from the Cardinal's residence, but whilst preparations were being put in place for the Mass for Peace within Paris' main cathedral, one of the smaller churches close to Notre Dame would have to suffice for today's service. Monteria closed his eyes and contemplated that it might be standing room only for most of the congregation in the smaller building. A church filled to the rafters. There was no more gratifying sight for a Cardinal.

Silas buttoned the last tie of the Cardinal's starched white alb and turned to the cupboard to gather the cincture to tie around his master's waist, the hint of a tune on his lips.

"Something cheers you, Silas?" asked Monteria, following the young man with his eyes, a smile coming to his own face.

"One is always happy ahead of Mass, sir," Silas replied, approaching with the long cord of white in his hands, which he proceeded to fix round Monteria's middle. "A chance to reflect on the sacrifice of Christ at Calvary."

"Ah, yes! Sacrifice!" announced the old man, nodding his head knowingly. He turned back to the window and looked over the morning streets of Paris. "To sacrifice something in order to show others the true path. It is the greatest act of all."

FIFTEEN

1891. The Vatican. Vatican City.

They were running, a whole pack of boys and young men, drawn from the different years and classes of the Vatican, stripped to their shorts and vests, hair clamped tight to sweat drenched foreheads, racing from the Lourdes Gardens, through the New Gardens and on to the monument of Saint Peter. Ahead of them waited a huddle of Fathers and Priests, recording their achievements within their books, noting those showing prowess of strength and stamina.

At the head of the pack ran Tacit, a lead of ten yards, now twelve, now fifteen, his head down, his arms pumping, his legs like pistons working against the gravel of the path. Unlike the other boys, his face wasn't snarled in a knot of determination and hurt, but beamed with joy, cracking with laughter as he tore up to the monument for the second and final lap, his energy seemingly boundless, his speed unmatched.

"That's Poldek Tacit," muttered a Father to another as the boy flew past. "He's quick!"

"The fastest of any of the ages." another added.

"They must have plans for him?"

"They are saying he's a prime candidate for joining the Inquisition."

"I'm not surprised. Look at him go. He's strong. He has spirit."

"His master, Father Adansoni, seems less enamoured with the idea."

"Well, Adansoni has never been an advocate of the Inquisition. Felt it should have been closed in its entirety sixty years ago. Not allowed to … how does he say? Fester?"

A studious looking Father with thick rimmed glasses tutted and shook his head. "But he never was a soldier was he, Adansoni?"

"He spent the first twenty five years of his Catholic service as a missionary!" a Father with a hood drawn up over his head added, cheering on the following pack now passing them.

"Strange then that he has stayed so close to the Vatican since Tacit was brought here."

"They say he thinks of him as his son."

"A foolish thing to think. Once a child is brought into the Church, the Lord is his father."

"Seems to me the boy has too much spirit to be tied to anyone. Goodness me, look at him go!" the bespectacled Father cried, as Tacit sped across the lawns. "He's, what, a hundred yards ahead of the others now?"

"Of course. I hear they're saying things about him," a Priest with a daring shock of brown hair revealed.

"Who, Adansoni?"

"Tacit."

"Go on," the Father replied, clapping the remaining stragglers past them and the monument.

The brown haired Priest lowered his voice and lent closer to his colleagues. "They say there's something about him. Whispers amongst the record holders and the keepers of the ancient writings. Whispers that he is the *one*."

"They say a lot of things," the hooded Father replied, blowing through his lips. "One of what, exactly? A good athlete?"

"A popular child?" suggested a Priest.

"He certainly has a cheerfulness many of the Cardinals could learn from, that much is true!" another of the group blurted, and some of the others laughed.

"Pope Leo XIII claims to have seen visions," the brown haired Priest continued.

The Father's face next to him dropped his head and his eyes widened in his skull. "Go on," he said, intrigued.

"Visions that a young boy will come from the east. The preordained one. That he'll be found abandoned on high and will be rescued from the clutches of death. That he'll display incredible and deft skills of hand and eye. That he'll master languages. That warmth will follow him and emanate from him. That death will follow in his wake."

With that, another in the group said, "I have heard similar things spoken in the Holy See. That the one will come, and that the fate of all nations will be decided by him and him alone."

"Well, if that's true, unless he becomes Pope himself, it sounds like the Inquisition is the only path for him."

"Adansoni won't be pleased."

"Maybe not," muttered the brown haired Priest, dragging a hand across his head, "but Tacit'll never change anything as a Father inside the Vatican."

"Unless he runs for Vatican City at the Olympic Games in three years' time," the Father with the hood suggested and they cheered as one as the runner sped over the line.

SIXTEEN

06:52. TUESDAY, OCTOBER 13TH, 1914. ARRAS. FRANCE.

A sluggish stream of French soldiers, horses, wagons, guns, ammunition carts and pack mules was passing the door of the Lieutenant Colonel's billet as Sandrine tore out from it. She fell back against the heat of the sun scorched wall of the house and watched the soldiers pass. They looked dashing and irresistible, dressed like exotic flies in their blue uniform overcoats with flashes of red pantaloons and caps. They trudged past, muttering amongst each other in their ranks, faces set grim for the journey towards the east. Occasionally one would look over and wink at Sandrine, who, despite her anger at that ignorant English officer, returned their attentions with a blown kiss or a little wave of her fingers. Their Sergeant called them to order and urged them down the street. Sandrine watched them turn out of sight and a little shadow suddenly fell across her, as if her heart was a sun which had slipped behind a cloud.

She looked back up at the window of her ex-lover's house and then hurried quickly across the road, as if scurrying from prying eyes. The street into which she rushed was dark and cool, masked by tall buildings and wide roofs which blocked out any of the warmth. She felt her skin prickle with goosebumps as she lightly danced along it, heading for the shimmering glare of the main market square beyond. She plunged into the light and heat and came to a halt a little way in, standing with her head turned skywards, her arms tight by her sides, letting the sun wash over her like clear water. For how long she stood there she didn't know, but she was aware of people shuffling hurriedly past, mumbling quietly to themselves as they were forced to step around her. Eventually she lowered her eyes and opened them on Alessandro and his stall.

She didn't go to Alessandro immediately. She watched him from where she stood, serving the staccato stream of nervous hurried customers shopping for their weekly meat, always showing disapproval of what Alessandro was able to offer by their heavy shrugs faced with his war-rationed offerings – returned with a good-humoured shrug from him. The war had taken its toll in many ways. The armies needed feeding, with both men and produce. Some families gave with their wares; others donated to the cause in more devastating ways.

"Alessandro!" she called, skipping forward.

"Sandrine!" Alessandro cheered, wiping his bloodied hands on his towel as he saw her approach. He gave them a final rub on the front of his apron and leaned forward to greet her with kisses. "How is it that you look even more beautiful with your clothes on than with them off?"

"Alessandro, I always feel more beautiful when I see you," she teased, and kissed him again, this time on the forehead.

Alessandro's name suggested a heritage more exotic than the truth. He had been born in Arras twenty six years ago to Henri and Margot Dequois. Henri was so certain that he was directly descended from Roman emperors that he gave his first son a Roman sounding name. You could tell in an instant by Alessandro's pallid complexion that his roots were firmly buried in the benign rolling hills of north east France rather than the rich heat and romance of southern Italy.

Alessandro's fame as a butcher had originated courtesy of his father, from whom he inherited the business when arthritis forced Henri to sit out his days on the veranda of his modest townhouse. Alessandro's prowess in butchery, and his eye for recognising the best farmers, quickly took the business from being simply admired to being city renowned. All the best cooks used Alessandro's produce, all those wishing to impress dining guests chose from his choice wares. At least they did, before the war came. Now, he sold what he could to whoever was left in the city.

"Why are you not with your lover?" he asked, his eyes glinting.

Sandrine blew loudly through her lips.

"He was a fool!" she replied. "And a terrible lover!" she lied.

Alessandro roared and slapped his thigh.

Sandrine laughed too. "I hope the British are better fighters than they are lovers."

"Ah, so he was British?! Well, I am not surprised to hear he could not make love. What do the British know of making love? They are too busy burning their beef and building their railways." Sandrine laughed and Alessandro laughed with her. He watched the way her breasts moved beneath her dress and longed desperately to reach out and pull her to him, the sensation almost overwhelming. He thought of her in the arms of her lover last night in an attempt to subdue his passion. Their laughter slowly fell away. "So what are you doing now?"

"Now? I was going to find out if there was any truth in the news of Fampoux. What have you heard? Tell me what you know!"

"Only rumour," replied Alessandro. "Some say it was taken last night after a terrible battle. Others," he turned his head to one side and scratched behind his ear, "they say the Germans still hold it."

"There is a lot of movement," Sandrine said hopefully, looking around the square, "of soldiers going east."

The butcher nodded. "There is. Now, do you want some of my finest produce?" he asked, as if the talk of battles unsettled him. "I'm afraid I don't have much. This war, it is taking its unfair share. They take it, Sandrine, the authorities they take it and they boil it and put it into tins! My finest cuts! For the soldiers! To think of it. My award winning liver, boiled and pushed into little metal pots."

"I was wondering if I could stay with you tonight."

The question came quickly and unexpectedly. It struck Alessandro like a stunning blow. He stood stock still, his face frozen like a mask.

"You can always say no," Sandrine said, but her hands were clasped expectantly tight to her chest.

"No," Alessandro said. Sandrine at once blanched and Alessandro heard a noise come out of her. "No," he said again, stutteringly, his face brightening with each word he was able to get out. "I mean, no, please, yes, that would be ..." His spirit flashed with elation and desire. "I would love you to stay but ..." He laughed thinly and shrugged, racked with uncertainty. "But ... why?" He was standing with his hands held awkwardly by his side, his fingers twitching like the tails of irritated cats. He crossed his arms. They slipped together but instantly slipped apart and he found himself an uncomfortable and inelegant pose against the counter of meat, where he rested his clumsy body. Of course, he knew he was being used, as he'd been used before, but as he gazed at her loveliness, faced with her heart and beauty, he knew without a moment's doubt that he didn't care.

Sandrine giggled and rose, her clasped hands raised to her face, framing her delicate features.

"Why? Well, I say why not?"

She smiled and Alessandro felt he could fall long and deep into her wide and beseeching eyes.

"Why not indeed!" he chuckled breathlessly, and then he shrugged and the pair of them both laughed. He could feel a force between them, an enchantment pulling their bodies together. He allowed himself to be drawn towards her, but stopped short of draping his arms around her, despite so longing to do so. "So, you know where …"

"Alessandro, I know where you live, my darling," answered Sandrine, leaning forward the remainder of the short distance between them and kissing him briefly on the lips. "I will see you at …"

"Five?"

"Five is perfect," she said, catching sight of a contingent of Catholic Priests stepping purposefully across the square towards them. She reached forward and kissed Alessandro again. "Till later," she called, and then vanished into the hubbub of the market.

SEVENTEEN

1892. The Vatican. Vatican City.

The figure that entered the hall that morning during prayers looked like no Cardinal or Bishop the boys had ever seen before. He was clad in black, matt finished and with tanned leather about his wrists, elbows and knees. There was darkness in his features and a weight in the way he carried himself. He wore boots rather than shoes and they cracked hard on the tiled floor as he walked, as if studded on their soles. The light seemed to dim as he passed by a window or candle, as if his very presence sucked the joy from the room.

The boys muttered quietly amongst themselves, snatching glances over shoulders and above text books, transfixed by the tall and daunting figure of the man.

He walked the aisles of desks, his head turning from side to side like a pendulum, from the backs of boys hunched over their desk on the left of the aisle to the right and then back again, his pace unchecked, his glare unwavering. When he had walked the full length of every aisle, he returned back to the door of the chamber and fell into quiet conversation with the Father standing there so that none of the acolytes, despite their best endeavours, could hear.

"So, that is Tacit?" the man murmured under his breath to Father Adansoni alongside, indicating the boy in the middle of the classroom. He spoke in Latin, his language sounding exotic and mysterious. Tacit caught the man's cold eyes on him and shivered, pretending to look away and focus on his studies.

"It is," Adansoni replied. "But he is *not* to go with you."

"So you have said. But I have heard great things about him from many quarters. We need good new blood. Our battles are endless, our enemies merciless. We lose men every day in our eternal struggle with the Darkness. From what I have heard, he would be perfect for our ranks."

"But *you* would not be perfect for him."

"I don't understand," the black clad man hissed.

Adansoni lowered his gaze onto the boy and watched him with the love of a father. "He has experienced too many terrible things in his early years. He is not suitable. He never will be. Pick from the others for your army."

"But he's the quickest and the strongest, from the reports I have read."

"You are correct. He is the strongest. But it is what lies inside, which is so fragile. Despite the years, despite his achievements I do not think he should go. There is nothing which convinces me he is ready, or that he will ever be ready for the role you wish of him."

The black clad man turned from the room to stride into the dark of the corridor beyond. "Tell me," he growled loudly, so that his words could be heard by all studying in the chamber behind him, "what use is ability when all the use you put it to is to read prayers and extinguish candles?"

EIGHTEEN

07:03. Tuesday, October 13th, 1914.
The front line. Arras. France.

It was the sound of a car motor which drew Henry out of his bunker. The heavy crank of an engine seemed foreign when, during those rare moments of respite from the enemies' attentions, the heavy stomp of boots, the whinny of horses or barked orders from Sergeants were the usual sounds to disrupt the quiet.

Henry trudged down from the trench complex and peered onto what was left of the Rue D'Arras, the main road out of the city, which had been eaten up into the churn of a great network of trenches. Everything, for as far as the eye could see, to the north and south, had been consumed by support trenches, dugouts, officer posts, ammunition stores, latrines, feeding stations and hospitals. The front line – all that stood between Germany and the French coastline.

A four seater motorcar shuddered to a halt in the middle of the quickly disappearing road. It rattled itself to silence and out of it climbed a sandy haired officer, his belt drawn tight, exposing his middle aged spread, his pallid hungover complexion all the more sickly looking under the glaring sun. He stepped briskly and theatrically away from the vehicle, like an arriving dignitary, donning his cap to hide his liver spotted scalp from the light.

On seeing him, Henry swore quietly under his breath and marched out of the mishmash of tunnels to meet him.

"Major Pewter!" he called, trying to sound pleased to see his commanding officer.

"Lieutenant!" Pewter snapped back. "What the devil is going on here?" he demanded, whipping a glove from his hand and giving the impression he was about to strike the junior officer with it.

"What's what, sir?" asked Henry, a dread clutching at his throat.

"What's this I hear about you disobeying orders?"

"Disobeying orders, sir?"

"You heard me. Moving forward, when you were told to defend our position?"

"Well, I ..."

"Never mind about that. Why the blazes aren't you further up the field?"

"Up the field, sir?"

"I heard you were at Fampoux?" Pewter scowled, pulling off his second glove. "Why are you piddling around here?"

The direction and ferocity of the questioning muddled Henry's thinking. He flinched and rubbed his forehead. "We're waiting for patrols, sir," he replied hesitantly, and then stood to attention to give a more assured performance.

"Patrols?" retorted Pewter, spitting the words contemptuously. "I heard on good authority that you'd taken the German front line. Why aren't you in the blasted thing?" Henry wavered and the Major strode past him, diving into the confusion of the trenches. Immediately, Henry hurried after him.

"Complications, sir!" he called.

The Major stopped and put his cold eye onto Henry. He was tired and he was hungover. He'd been humiliated back in Arras by *that* woman. No one ever turned down *his* advances. From what he'd been told after his early morning enquiries, she'd gone home with the Lieutenant Colonel. The dislike he already felt towards his debonair senior officer had been further deepened by envy of this latest sexual conquest. He had a good mind to write home to the Lieutenant Colonel's wife and spill the beans, no matter how bad the form. The man was a fool. They all were fools, especially the senior officers under whom he had to serve. They tested his patience at the best of times, the senior officers. He was certainly not in the mood to be disappointed by one of the junior ones.

"I don't give a damn about complications, Lieutenant. Either you've taken the trench or you've not taken the trench. This is war, Lieutenant. It's black or white. Live or die. Win or lose. There is no third option." He turned and marched onwards into the labyrinth of the trench complex. "Pray to God, Frost, that the trench is not lost."

"There was no counter-attack by the Germans," Henry added quickly, as a means to reassure the Major, hurrying after him, like a servant keen to accommodate a master. "It's been quiet, all night. There's been nothing. Nothing at all. No noise. No movement. Nothing. There's nothing for as far as we've been able to glimpse."

"What do you mean, 'nothing', Lieutenant?" Pewter hissed, marching with purpose and speed. He recalled to himself the words of his previous commanding officer in South Africa: "March with purpose. Fuck with purpose. And when you kill, kill with purpose."

"Exactly that, sir. Nothing. There's nothing there. It seems the enemy have been obliterated."

The Major's ears pricked up at the word 'obliterated'. He liked obliteration, especially when it involved the enemy. There'd been far too little obliteration, at least as far as the enemy was concerned, for his liking. A breakthrough in his area might yield results, not least in possible promotion for him. But Pewter knew he had to be realistic. Face facts. This was war. The enemy didn't just vanish.

"Obliterated is a bold word, Lieutenant. Clarify."

Henry, as briskly as he could, explained what they found, or more to the point hadn't found, in the trench.

"And you say there was no barrage? The scene you describe would explain the devastation you found."

"There was no barrage, sir," Henry insisted, "not from us." He shivered to think of what might have taken place in those dark tall trenches. He thought it wise not to mention what the German Corporal had muttered, as he'd fallen into Henry's arms.

Pewter chortled and swept back what was left of his thinning hair with his hand. His pulse raced. He liked what he was hearing, mystery or not, as to the enemy's disappearance. His main concern now was getting into the trench. That was the key objective, the only objective. Why on earth Frost hadn't got his men into the trench and entrenched them there, the Major didn't know. But, so too, he recognised that Frost's decision to pull back might have played well into his own hands. Whilst British units to the north and French to the south were battling tooth and nail to take tiny portions of ground from the Germans, Pewter might now be the officer giving the final order to secure an entire trench and village. All that and without even firing a round! It was known military policy to raid a trench and then pull back. Frost's decision to have done exactly that might have proved delightfully fortuitous for the Major.

"We need to get into that trench, Lieutenant," Pewter announced, "and then hold it!" he warned, indicating with a finger.

"Yes, sir."

"You say you have patrols coming back?"

"Imminently, sir, yes. They were sent out at first –"

"Good. Hopefully their news will be promising. If it proves to be, we'll move the entire contingent of troops forward, perhaps even into Fampoux itself. Intelligence maps show the Hun trench network feeds directly from the village. If they've left the trenches, they might have left the village."

"Yes, sir. That's our impression, sir."

The Major slapped a glove into his hand and gave a short cheer.

"By jove, Lieutenant," he chuckled, "I think I might be making some progress in this war at last!"

They swept around a bend in the trench, dug wider to provide temporary accommodation for the injured brought back from the front line. It was here, in this chamber of chalk and mud, that they would be assessed and granted a break from the killing or be sent back for immediate service. Along one wall, the six Germans taken from their trench the previous night sat on a long bench, silent and numbed, covered under blankets, vacant stares onto the grey brown of the earth or the steam trails rising from their mugs of soup.

Immediately Pewter froze and glared, the veins in his temple pulsing. "By all that is holy in the world, who are these people?" he hissed, catching sight of their soft pillbox hats and German uniforms beneath the blankets.

"These soldiers … these prisoners," Henry corrected, swallowing and pursing his lips, "they're the only survivors that we've so far been able to find from the trench. Thought they might –"

"Yes, but what are you doing with them? That's what I want to know?"

"We thought they might be able to provide useful information," Henry lied.

"And why, in heaven's name, are you feeding them?" the Major demanded, kicking a mug of soup from one of the soldier's fingers and wrenching the blanket away from him. The soldier yelped and hung on to it, as if it was his only possession in the world. Pewter lunged forward and struck him hard in the face with the back of his hand, bloodying the prisoner's nose. The prisoner cowered pathetically, guarding his face, his head down, a childlike whimpering coming out of him, whilst the others sprang to their feet, howling and gathering themselves into a tight group. They drew their arms firmly around them, as if protecting themselves from another blow.

"There's no contingency for taking prisoners, Frost."

"But sir," Henry replied, looking at the Major and then back to the pathetic huddle of figures, "we couldn't leave them where we found them?"

"No, precisely," Pewter agreed, taking out his revolver and levelling it at them.

Without pause, Pewter pulled the trigger. The first round shattered the silence, sending the revolver vaulting back into the Major's hand. The German with the bloodied nose collapsed backwards, his head snapping to the side, showering blood over the wall and on the prisoners behind him. His face had been blown clean open, become a flaccid wrap of skin like a sagging door to his skull.

Pewter fired again. Another prisoner, one making an infernal racket of moans and wails, dropped to the floor, half of his head blown clean off. Henry knew he was pleading for the Major to stop, but he couldn't make himself heard above the thunderous clap of the Major's pistol.

Pewter fired a third round, blowing a blackened crimson hole clean through the eye socket of the Corporal Henry had comforted. Without pause he fired again and again, until only a single German remained, stumbling over his fallen colleagues, screaming and pleading with bewilderment and pain, his hands held up in prayer and for mercy. Pewter levelled the smoking revolver at the soldier's forehead and pulled the trigger.

The gun clicked.

"Bloody thing!" he cursed. He pulled the trigger again. The cylinder clicked over empty.

"Sergeant," said Pewter, spotting Holmes shielding himself tight to the far side of the trench. He turned his eye back onto the German and drove the side of the empty revolver into his face. He went down with a grunt in a shower of blood and broken teeth. "Kill him." He stomped away, holstering his revolver and muttering vaguely to himself. "Lieutenant Frost!" he called sharply over his shoulder. "A word, in my headquarters, if you please."

There was little which surprised Henry after a month on the front line, but the speed by which normality returned to the trench after the flash of violence almost choked him. The cries and clamour of the pistol shots were almost immediately replaced with the distant muffle of chatter and the labour of the digging crews, the mutter of soldiers as they passed, the bright cheer of a laugh somewhere in the trench depths.

Henry stared at the bloodied jumble of bodies and the German sprawled on the trench floor, clutching at his broken teeth and weeping. He was aware of Sergeant Holmes organising the disposal of the bodies around him, leading away the distraught figure of the last remaining soldier. But he didn't realise he was alone until a passing Tommy interrupted his private thoughts and asked if he was okay. He nodded and closed his eyes, allowing the reverberations of the violence to pass out of him.

Exhaustion and anger hit him like an army transport train. He fought hard against the urge to weep, drawing a shaking hand up under his nose to fight back against his emotions. He remembered his rank and his officer training, and straightened himself, brushing himself down briskly and tugging at his uniform. But he never remembered being taught how to act during such times at officer training. He swallowed hard on his anger through gritted teeth, before taking firm strides away.

Major Pewter had reached his bunker by the time Henry sought him out. He turned from his desk when Henry entered the dugout, adorned with an elegance and style befitting his class back in Blighty. In his left hand he held a solid cut glass tumbler of amber liquid, in his right a square glass decanter.

"Ah, Lieutenant!" he called, chirpily. "I wondered where you'd got to. Whisky?" he asked, pouring a handsome measure into a tumbler on the desk.

"Thank you, sir, no," Henry replied, flatly.

"Nonsense." replied Pewter, setting down the decanter and picking up the freshly filled glass, which he thrust into Henry's hand. He turned and looked for his favourite chair, placing himself slowly into it. "It must be said, Lieutenant, I have the most frightful of headaches this morning. Come on! Drink up, for God's sake, Frost," he demanded, noticing that Henry stood unmoving in the middle of the dugout. "You look like you've lost the bloody war!" He sat back and crossed his legs, sweeping the wisps of hair across his scalp whilst he sipped at his whisky. He grimaced and immediately wondered if he'd made an error in judgement, choosing to drink so early in the morning after last night. "Come on, take a bloody seat, Frost," Pewter insisted, indicating a chair opposite him, his tone growing as cold as Henry's demeanour. "Sit, before you fall down. You look half done in."

"I am," replied Henry. "Sir," he added, to bring ratification to his exhaustion and grievance.

"Well, take a bloody seat then, you fool!" Pewter cried, waving at the empty chair. "Can't have you collapsing, can we?" Henry begrudgingly stepped forwards and sank into it. To sit in the presence of the Major ran contrary to everything Henry believed in but he could also feel his legs rejoice at the weight being taken from them.

The Major drank deeply from his glass, his eyes firmly set on the officer opposite.

"It's been a terrific few hours," he announced. His eyes were bright but there was coolness within them, like a sharp winter's frost. "We need to capitalise on these successes. Push on. You know, back there," he said, waving absently. "That nonsense, with the Hun."

"The prisoners." Henry replied.

"The enemy," Pewter corrected. "I didn't like what I saw there, Frost. Really shouldn't have happened, Lieutenant. We can't afford to take prisoners in this war. Jerry wouldn't do the same to us, we shouldn't with them. We have enough of a challenge ahead of us as it is without taking half of the bloody German army into our care. Understand?"

Henry looked into the corner of the bunker.

"You've got a good heart, Lieutenant, but you're not here for your kindness. Consider hardening yourself up. You're not at Eton now, Frost."

"Winchester, Major," Henry corrected. How, his college seemed a world away to him now.

"Crikey, no wonder you're soft," Pewter retorted. He allowed himself a smile but, as soon as the warmth appeared, his features hardened again: "Don't let it happen again," he warned. "Understood?"

Henry nodded, directing his eyes briefly towards the Major and then casting them aside.

"Good. Now," said Pewter, draining his glass and stepping over to the sideboard to refill it. He felt mildly revived by the alcohol. A noise at the entrance to the dugout drew both of them to it.

"Excuse me, Lieutenant Frost, Major Pewter," said a soldier, ducking into the narrow mouth of the bunker.

"Stevens!" Henry called, climbing out of his chair.

"There's no one in the trenches. Looks like they've retreated back beyond Fampoux, sir."

"Excellent!" called Pewter, setting down his glass and striding into the centre of the room. "Seems like you've been let off the hook, Lieutenant!" he said, accusatorially. He looked at the soldier at the entrance to the dugout. "Go on, push off now," he ordered, shooing him with a hand. The Major switched his eyes, enflamed with excitement, back towards Henry. "Let's get over to Fampoux and secure it without delay! It's a big gain. We should expect a retaliation from the bastards."

"Yes sir," replied Henry gloomily. His men were exhausted, battered and frayed. Even deserted as the village seemed, he felt Fampoux was a stretch too far, knowing the Germans would make them work hard to keep it.

"Hopefully we won't live to regret your decision not to have pushed on last night. I don't quite know what is going on out there at Fampoux, but it sounds like what was discovered in that trench was nothing short of a miracle. And you can put that in the unit's diary. The miracle of Fampoux!" he barked and chortled into his whisky.

NINETEEN

1893. The Vatican. Vatican City.

Tacit supposed he'd never see his friends again. It was the way the man in black had called their names, the way they risen from their desks, as if called before a firing squad, and filed from the room without ceremony or cheer, out from the hall, past the black clad man who watched each passing acolyte with cold unwavering eyes.

The finality of proceedings struck Tacit. As if days were coming to an end.

His friends had grown and they had been recognised. They were now men, at least in the eyes of those who had selected them. Their journey, whatever it was that lay ahead of them, was about to begin. No longer would they look behind to the remainder left in the classroom, with their jotters of bible phraseology, left to tidy the hymn books, nor extinguish the candles at the end of Mass, nor hang the cloaks after choir practice. Their focus now was on the future.

"Where are they going?" he asked Father Adansoni later, as they walked together around the Vatican grounds. He felt grievous and barren.

"Have you ever heard of the Inquisition?" Father Adansoni asked absently, his feet crunching through the last of the morning's frost on the grass.

"Of course. Why do you ask? And why are you speaking to me in French?"

"To make sure you're doing your studies!"

"Well I am." He slipped seamlessly into German. "Just to prove to you I am."

"I'm impressed." Adanonsi replied, now talking in Latin. "I don't know why I need to say I'm impressed. I've long been impressed by you and told you so many times. Your head must already be swollen."

Tacit laughed but then thought of his friends now gone away and the joy was snuffed out of him.

"Why do you ask about the Inquisition?" he asked, burying the sadness deep within him.

"What do you know about it?"

"That is was a bad time."

"And?"

"That the Church had to act, to try to bring honour and faith back to the world. That the world had grown dark. That, through the actions of the Church, light was returned to the dark places of the world when it had gone out and it was feared that it would never return."

"And?"

"That witchcraft and sorcery was usurping the honesty of religious faith, that heretics and non-believers were poisoning the world with their lies. That our wise leaders felt they had to act, had to adopt more determined techniques to correct the misguided, punish the wicked, restore the faith."

"And?"

"Father!" Tacit cried, a little annoyed he was being both tested and teased by his master. He looked at Adansoni and whilst he saw that his eyes were on him, they were kindly. He continued, the words coming easily to him; years of study and recital proving their worth. "That in 1834, the Inquisition was finally brought to a close and a more considered and conservative approach was adopted by the Church to spread its message and teaching."

Adansoni nodded and smiled. "I'm impressed. Now, what would you say if I told you the Inquisition had never ended?"

"I would laugh."

"Really? And why would that be?"

"Well, of course it ended!" laughed Tacit, and then he saw the Father's face and the laughter was swallowed up. "How could it continue?" he asked. "I mean, look at our times today. We're not savages any more. Nor is the world full of them. The Inquisition's work was completed. We no longer need to behave as we did. And anyway, we couldn't behave as we once did, surely?"

"If only that was true."

Adansoni stopped and looked up into the sky, his eyes closed, feeling the warmth of the sun on his face. After a little time he spoke again. "What if I told you the Inquisition was still very much alive. But was now hidden from public, its actions covert, underground, unspoken, unrecorded; that its work continues, continues with more energy and determination than ever before? But no trace of it you will find amongst ordinary people, no knowledge of its servants' existence is apparent or is reported. That they work in secret. Complete secret. That those friends of yours who have left – they are going away to train to work for the Inquisition."

"I'd say you had been at the sacramental wine!" Tacit chuckled. But then he stopped and thought of the black clad man and a shadow passed over him. He studied the gravel of the path onto which they had now walked. "I know there are bad people in the world. I am not naive. But is it really the place of the Church to behave in such a way? Surely we should be better than that?"

Adansoni smiled and looked across the Vatican grounds.

"Your honesty and faith does you credit, Poldek," the Father said.

Tacit nodded, supposing he should be pleased at the response. But privately he felt wounded with sorrow and envy towards those friends who had been chosen and had now gone away. Their path sounded far more tantalising than the one offered to Tacit leading to the rigours of prayer alone.

"You would have liked to have joined your friends, wouldn't you? You know where they've gone, don't you, Tacit?" Adansoni watched Tacit turn away. "I'm sorry. I don't think you're ready. After everything, I don't know if you'll ever be ready. I'm sorry."

Tacit turned his eyes towards the Father. They were heavy with tears but he smiled and fought against his emotion. "You've done so much for me, Father. You have nothing to apologise for."

TWENTY

11:41. Tuesday, October 13th, 1914. Arras. France.

The hard crunch of hobnailed boots on the tiled floor of Arras Cathedral drew the pale faced Cardinal out of the antechamber. "Cardinal Gérard-Maurice Poré?" Isabella called, as she and the imposing figure of the Inquisitor appeared out of the Cathedral gloom.

"Sister Isabella," Cardinal Poré answered, stepping forward to peer at the figure she had brought with her. It had not been long since she had left him, alerted to the killing of the Father courtesy of the Catholic Church by means known only to them. She said she was intending to return with someone, but her reappearance so soon surprised Poré. "Good to see you again, I think," he added, his cold eyes on Tacit. "So, I see you have found an Inquisitor to investigate this … attack?" Both Isabella and Tacit noticed how he picked the word 'attack' with care.

"This is Inquisitor Tacit."

Even without the introduction from Isabella, Poré would have recognised the tell-tale signs of the Catholic Church's most infamous of servants at once, the immense hulking figure of the Inquisitor, clad all in black save for the starched white of his dog collar, striding down the central aisle of the nave, his dark eyes staring coldly ahead from beneath his black capello romano hat. Poré was old and experienced enough to recognise what Tacit was, being well seasoned in all aspects of his faith's arrangements. The sharp sting of past memory, when Inquisitors had intruded into his own childhood, could still catch him unawares all these many years later and leave him heaving for breath and clawing for answers.

Some wounds never truly heal.

Throughout his time as a Priest and then a Cardinal, Poré had delivered his services to all manner of people, devout Catholics, lapsed and heathen, angels and demons. But of all the people he had met, none were as distant or grim as Inquisitors and silently he hated their very existence.

There was never anything specific in their appearance which singled them out to be the people they were. Some Inquisitors were broad and strong like warriors, built for taking the battle to their enemies. Others were sly and slight like magicians, as quick with their hands as they were with their minds. It was always the haunted look which gave them away, as if they had gazed into hell and hell had left its reflection upon them. Nowadays, many Cardinals viewed Inquisitors as a vile and uncouth relic of a past age. Most Inquisitors were quick to remind Cardinals that it was they who first recommended their creation not far from a thousand years ago.

But Cardinal Poré also knew of Tacit by name and reputation. He tried to hide the swallowing in his throat and watched him with the cold of his eyes.

Just as Cardinal Poré knew Tacit, Tacit knew Poré, not because of Poré's reputation, but because Tacit liked to make sure he was well acquainted with all senior members of the Church. When crimes were committed against it, experience told him that the crime usually originated within it. Knowing the suspect-list by heart was always a distinct advantage. He knew Poré's rhetoric was as severe as his haircut, cropped short to his skull, as if he was undertaking some sort of penance. Tacit also liked a lot of what he'd been told about the Cardinal, that he was a straight talker, a devout Catholic, a scourge of minority religions and blasphemers. But he'd been made aware of inconvenient aspects too, that Poré's parents had been removed for Inquisitional processing when he was younger, that he was a radical as well as a forward thinker, that he wanted to evolve and change the Church to better suit and serve the times. That sort of talk was dangerous, in Tacit's mind. After all, Poré had recruited Father Andreas into his role at the Cathedral and that was a dangerous mistake, because Father Andreas was now dead.

A disapproving grimace spread across Poré's face. "I didn't think murder enquiries were your domain, Inquisitor? I trust you'll find the decency to treat this murder with the dignity it deserves."

Tacit ignored him and walked straight past to stare down at the pool of dried blood still staining the bottom step of the ambulatory. There were splashes, spots and trails across most parts of the ambulatory and over the first two rows of pews. Poré caught the odour of Tacit as he passed, a combination of stale alcohol and poor living, and scowled. He watched him through slitted eyes.

"This is where we found him," the Cardinal spoke gravely, stepping alongside, dwarfed by Tacit's size.

"He was found right here, then?" Isabella asked. Poré nodded, his eyes fixed to the dark crimson stain on the tiles.

Tacit grunted disconcertingly and turned his back on the spot. He stepped up onto the ambulatory, his heavy boots clacking hard on the white and black marble.

He dug his hands into his deep jacket pockets. A hand closed around the half-finished bottle of spirit from earlier. A sudden thirst gripped him. He cursed under his breath and then remembered where he was. He raised his eyes to the large cross hanging suspended on taut wires in the air above him, by way of an apology. He could feel the hard edge of the silver six-shooter in his holster hidden beneath his coat. Killing was, of course, against the Catholic faith but, two hundred and fifty nine Hail Marys later, he was still counting the corpses and the penances. He reasoned that he mostly only ever killed the bad guys. And Tacit met a lot of bad guys in his line of work, amongst other things.

He turned back to the front of the ambulatory, directly beneath the hanging cross, tracing an invisible line between the front of the pews and where the body had been discovered. The splatter marks showed how the body had been picked up and thrown, and where it had landed. Ten feet. That would take some strength.

"What have the parishioners of the Cathedral been told?" Isabella asked Poré. "They'll want to know why the Cathedral's closed, where Father Andreas is."

"The Holy See have suggested the usual procedure of silence and denial. Temporary closure of the Cathedral to refurbish after recent bomb damage."

"And Father Andreas?"

"Heart Attack." The Sister winched. "I know," nodded the Cardinal. "Unlikely. He was young, but there was obviously a deep-lying medical condition within him which none of us knew about. Clearly." The lies came easily to this Poré but Isabella knew that few reached the heights of Cardinal without being able to lie and lie with sincerity.

Tacit turned his head from one side to the other, as if acquainting himself with the shape of the Cathedral.

"Well?" Isabella asked, stepping towards him.

Tacit turned and stepped with heavy, considered feet towards the vestry room, his head down, following the trails of dried blood left by the fleeing Priest. He stopped, all of a sudden, and crouched down onto his haunches, examining the appearance of a mark through one of the splatters of blood, at closer hand.

"It's not human," the Cardinal called, following Tacit from a distance and watching him hunch over the trail. "That which made the mark. Animal. Or something," he added in a tone which suggested mystery, looking over at the Sister and nodding gently.

The Inquisitor lifted his eyes to the wall at the back of the Cathedral and sneered. Cardinals. They always had an opinion, always had a theory. When he was younger he'd been told by the Priests that he showed so much promise in his studies that he could become a Cardinal. He'd laughed at the suggestion. It was the last time he could ever remember laughing.

He flicked his eyes left and right, mapping out the route the Father had stumbled from the antechamber just ahead. He guessed Andreas had been unbalanced, stumbling mainly to the left. Tacit predicted that the Priest had lost his left arm.

"And the body? It's in the crypt?" Isabella asked.

"Yes, in the crypt," the Cardinal replied, his eyes falling to the dark archway to the right of where they stood. "I'm sure that will reveal everything."

The cool of the crypt wrapped itself about them as they descended the first few steps into the darkness below.

"I'm surprised that the Vatican still remembers us here in Arras," the Cardinal said, feeling his way into the gloom with the help of the stairwell wall. There was a lantern hanging on a metal hoop at the bottom step some fifteen steps below. He retrieved it and fumbled in his pocket for matches with which to light it. "Sometimes one can feel so very far away, especially during these times, what with the war."

"Arras is very much within the thoughts of Pope Benedict," Isabella assured him, reaching across and offering to light the lantern for him.

"That is good to hear," Poré replied, accepting the Sister's offer. She struck the match and held the small flame to the wick till it caught, whilst Poré said, "I didn't know if the war had drawn the Pope's eye to other places besides France? Already the conflict is so broad and wide."

Sister Isabella handed the lantern back to him. "Not in the least,

Cardinal. Benedict feels greatly for the peoples of France. The Mass for Peace in Paris in a week's time is of particular poignancy to his worshipfulness," she added, with a gentle smile.

The Cardinal took back the lantern with a nod of appreciation. "It's the least the Church can do," he said gently. "I am proud to have had a small part in its realisation. Having secured the services of Cardinal Bishop Monteria to help lead the planning of the event, surely we have a greater opportunity to achieve our goals."

The flicker of amber torchlight caught in Tacit's face, revealing a doubting sneer upon it.

"You don't share the view that the Mass for Peace is a good thing, Inquisitor? That the power of prayer can achieve great things?"

"A massed prayer or massed armies facing each other?" replied Tacit. "I know which my money would be on."

"We have attracted the attention of Britain's foreign secretary!" Poré retorted sharply.

Tacit yawned and thrust a fist across his nose. He thought it strange that a bitter, radical Cardinal like Poré should share a vision with an arrogant old man like Monteria and for them to then work together to try and achieve it. Tacit made a mental note to visit Monteria after his assignment in Arras to ensure the Cardinal was not getting above his station.

"The Mass will take on extra significance with a Cardinal so senior within the Church," remarked Isabella, breaking the rising tension between the Cardinal and Inquisitor, but also genuinely impressed that Poré had recruited one so highly respected within the Church as Cardinal Bishop Monteria to help plan the service.

"If the power of diplomacy fails to halt this dreadful and bloody war, perhaps the power of prayer will have more luck?"

"We certainly hope so," said Isabella.

Poré caught the lack of interest shown by Tacit, staring into the depths of the crypt, and took the hint. "Shall we?" he suggested, before squeezing past the pair of them and into the gloom of the passageway.

The tunnel leading into the crypt was tall and broad, with walls smooth as marble and china white. Such was the wall's finish that it possessed a sheen like glass.

"These are incredible tunnels, Cardinal," said Isabella, impressed at their size and finish, brushing her hand along them as they walked.

"It's the chalk rock," replied Poré, waving the lantern light to indicate the white stone. "Very easy to mine and work. Arras is built on it. The whole region is. There are tunnels under Arras which go on for miles and miles, some dating back to medieval times. Used for the storing of goods during the rich times and people during the less favourable."

Isabella swept her red hair behind an ear. "Are they still used?"

Poré shook his head. "The ones beyond the city's limits, no, but the ones directly under it most definitely. People have been using them during barrages on the city. As you can see," he said, knocking the stone with the flat of his hand, "they're solid. As good as any shelter."

"So, was there anything which suggested Father Andreas might have had any enemies?" Isabella called after the Cardinal, who was walking the tunnels ahead of them at a fair pace, his gown rippling between every urgent stride. "Anyone who might have had a grudge against him or the Church?"

"No, nothing," Poré replied, as he hung the lantern on a nail on the wall and unlocked the rusted iron gate to the main crypt. "Father Andreas always seemed so … complete."

The gate creaked open on heavy hinges and the Cardinal led on, holding up the lantern so that as much light as possible penetrated the path ahead. The further they walked the colder the air became, till their breath turned to mist in front of them.

"He was a good man, Father Andreas," Cardinal Poré continued, peering back as if to assure them of his words. He turned left into the blackness of a side passageway. "I cannot believe anyone would wish him dead." He stopped at an open doorway and turned to face them both. "But then again, there are some who are unable to control their actions." He said the words with the raise of an eyebrow and tone in his voice, clearly meaning to leave some impression on the visitors from the Vatican.

With that, Poré looked towards an ornately carved archway, its rim a mesh of interconnecting stone strands. He turned, as if he was about to say something, but deemed whatever it was he was going to announce, unnecessary. He stepped to one side and gestured for them to enter the room beyond.

On a slab in the centre of the room was laid the body of Father Andreas, the sweet aroma of death hanging around him in the cool air. The Cardinal followed Tacit and Isabella in and hung the lantern from a hook in the ceiling so that the room and body were as fully illuminated as possible.

Tacit looked down at the body. He was suddenly aware of the growing dull ache of a headache etching itself to the left side of his brain. He needed a drink. He pinched the side of his head and eye and rubbed hard. The dead Priest's skin had taken on a vague pearl sheen and the skin around the face had tightened as one would expect in a body so freshly deceased. He peered over it, breathing in the cool air, trying to detect anything within the smell of cadaver which might provide evidence the Church would have undoubtedly missed.

Tacit peered fiercely but not for long. *Significant blow to the head, destroying left eye socket and removing eyeball in the process. Wound caused by clawed hand or talon. Significant strength required to tear skin and* – he peered in towards the Priest's yellowing head – *partial skull bone.*

He looked down to the Father's chest. The gaping wound in it was made all the more dramatic by the tearing of the cassock robe through which the clawed had ripped. *Well, that's the killing blow,* Tacit thought to himself. He looked over at the left arm and was delighted to see it was missing.

"Anyone else witness the attack?" Isabella asked, noticing Tacit's vague pleasure at something. It was the first time she'd seen him show anything approaching satisfaction since she'd met him. "Did anyone see his attacker?"

"No. Father Andreas was alone."

"What about any other Priests?"

Poré lowered his head and shook it. "No. No. It was the end of Mass. Everyone had left."

"Including the choristers?" Tacit asked, looking up through his hooded eyes.

"Choristers? How'd you know about them?"

Tacit shrugged. "Saw their cloaks hanging up in the antechamber. Besides, it's a church service. You have choristers."

"Yes, you're right," the Cardinal replied hesitantly. Tacit's eyes drilled into him. "The choristers, they left after Mass. The head chorister, he left a short time before the attack. Thankfully just in time, so to speak."

"You have spoken to the boy, then?" Sister Isabella asked, gentler in her questioning than the Inquisitor.

"Uh, yes, the boy says he saw nothing. Which is good. Would have been awful for him to have witnessed ... to witness a werewolf attack."

Tacit's eyes narrowed on the Cardinal. "It's not a werewolf attack," he growled, looking back down at the body.

Tacit was surprised to find the Cardinal chuckle thinly. "Not a werewolf attack?" he retorted, closing his eyes and shaking his head, as if Tacit had muttered an obscenity in front of him. "So, how else would you explain this?" he asked, raising his hands to indicate the wounds on the body. "No normal human could have –"

"Not a werewolf," Tacit repeated forcefully, his nostrils flaring.

The Cardinal lowered his gaze onto the black clad Inquisitor. "Inquisitor Tacit. There's no need for us to be quite so coy. Let us not play games. I know of the cursed ones and unlike some of my colleagues I am not afraid to utter their name. Hombre Lobo! Werewolf!" He almost shouted the words, so that his voice echoed through the labyrinth of tunnels. The Cardinal's eyes blazed with a fire.

Isabella leaned across the body towards him, her voice almost a whisper.

"Cardinal Poré, you have been warned about uttering such things openly by the Holy See."

"And I am not afraid to utter them here, within my Cathedral!" he called back, as if delivering the final lines of a sermon. "I know the history of the Church, what has gone before, what has been and what has been created by it. So let us put aside our little game of denial. Let us not talk falsely or in riddles. I know of this . You do not need to shield me from such things. We both know what it is."

"Not werewolf," Tacit spat back, in a voice as hard as iron.

The Cardinal scratched at his forehead, rubbing the flat of his hand backwards into his short cropped hair and folding his arms. "So, Inquisitor, how else would you explain –"

"Murder."

Poré scrubbed a hand over his face and sighed, his hands dropping to his sides. "Very well, call it murder if you will! But that is exactly why I say it is a werewolf attack. Look at the wounds!"

But Tacit shook his head, his face darkening like the shadows of the crypt. "This is murder. Intentional. Werewolves don't act with intention. Werewolves attack to feed. Consumed by hunger and rage. They don't set out to murder. They set out to fulfil their bestial desires, to satiate the insatiable." He looked down at the poor figure on the slab. "And they don't leave much behind when they do. Certainly not this much." He looked up under his eyebrows, passing his eyes from Isabella to Poré and then back again. "Someone took on the form of a werewolf intentionally to kill the Father, but they're not a true wolf, not Hombre Lobo."

Tacit stood back from the body and bowed his head, as if in a final act of respect for the fallen Father. Then he turned and vanished into the dark of the outside passageway. "Murder," he called back assuredly, as he traced the path back to the steps.

Poré and Isabella caught each other's glances, whilst Tacit's footsteps were lost into the depths of crypt tunnels.

"And send for the chorister," they heard him call. "I want to talk to him."

TWENTY ONE

07:46. Tuesday, October 13th, 1914.
The front line. Arras. France.

In the growing light of day, the British soldiers scurried forward through the trenches, blackened by drying blood and littered with remains dashed and discarded in the haste to escape. In places, the blood and mud formed sticky cloying patches of crimson, which clung tightly to soldiers and trapped misplaced boots, as if trying to drag the individual down into the cursed depths below.

Ahead of them the low sprawling village of Fampoux lay, powder blasted into grey and black, the trees all burnt and smashed away so that only shattered stumps remained. The tallest building in the village, the church, had been broken clean in two, one half blown over the surrounding houses, the standing half tilting to one side so severely it looked like only the slightest of breezes would bring the whole lot tumbling down.

The soldiers could make out lines of quaint little houses standing in long rows along the outskirts of the village, no wider than half a mile. Cafés and shops encircled small squares, all now smashed or damaged by shells or dissected by a web of trenches.

Litter and filth were everywhere, over the fields and across the road down which the soldiers marched. Bits of machinery and broken tools could be seen wherever one looked but strangely, the vast cannons and artillery units, concealed behind ridges or driven into the depths of shrubbery, appeared undamaged, abandoned in the Germans' haste to leave. Flapping papers floated and tumbled across the landscape on the breeze now slowly picking up.

There was also a sharp smell of coal smoke which embraced the soldiers as they drew into the fabric of the village, a clinging acidic stench that clung to nostrils and the backs of mouths. The only sound was that of the soldiers' boots crunching and kicking in the rubble as they passed through it. Even the guns had fallen silent. A noisy crow took up its squawking from the roof of a crumpled terrace, the walls emerging from the ground like the bones of a dinosaur regurgitated from the earth.

Major Pewter drew his horse to one side and watched his men march past. Occasionally a soldier would call out to him with good wishes and he would acknowledge them with a stiff hand.

Every now and then a dog would bark, the noise punctuating the severity of the silence. Nothing else stirred, save for the occasional creak of a broken shutter or the knock of a door swinging free on its hinges.

Pewter could barely contain his joy. A mile or two to the north the British, French and Germans were locked in a bloody impasse, mired down in trenches and the dirt of the Arras Salient, whilst here he was walking into German territory without even firing a round. They would write about him in despatches, of that he had no doubt. He often imagined himself a Colonel, in the dark of night when the shells had finally fallen silent. It was all very well commanding a company of men but he aspired to more. Goodness knows he was capable of handling more than one hundred odd men.

An oval faced child pushed forward from a shamble of buildings on the main thoroughfare. He had ears that stuck out too much and dark eyes which seemed too close together. But it were his teeth which caught the attention, a broad set of immaculate looking teeth, beaming from between his cracked and dirty lips. He appeared head to toe covered in dirt and dust and he carried with him a torn dusty union jack flag which he shook energetically as he stepped forward towards the approaching troops. He let one corner of it drop and raised a small clenched fist of victory.

"Vive la France!" he called. "Vive la Grande-Bretagne!" showing his delicious white teeth.

The appearance of the single welcoming child gave the village a now haunted feel. The desolation and silence within it was profound.

"What have you found there then, Lieutenant?" Pewter called down from his saddle.

"Something the Germans have left for us, I suppose?" replied Henry, studying the board. "A message."

"Oh, and what would that be? Terribly sorry for causing all this trouble, Tommy?" Pewter laughed a high pitched haughty laugh.

"Beware the moon, Tommy," Henry read off the board, looking around him and then back at the sign. "Wonder what they mean by that?"

"Probably some sort of empty threat," the Major replied, sitting up in his saddle and looking east. "Giving us a clue as to his next attack. Probably planning night time barrages." He admired the troops marching past him. "Chance'll be a fine thing. They'll have a hard time levering us out of Fampoux, the fools. Nevertheless, no harm in being prepared. We should set up a defensive perimeter around the town, just in case Jerry decides to take a pot shot at us."

"I'll pass the order down, sir," Henry replied, looking back at the sign. There was something about the way it had been written, the scrawled letters scratched into the wood in haste. "Beware the moon, Tommy," he said again, his hand to his chin.

"Yes, beware," spoke the boy, who had sidled himself alongside. He placed a hand on Henry's side. "Beware the moon," he said, his eyes very serious.

Pewter stood up in his stirrups and peered down on his soldiers. "Goodness me, Frost!" he exclaimed. "Do you know what?"

"No sir."

"I didn't think this war was going to be quite this fun," he chirped, before turning his horse and searching out a building in the village still standing that was suitable for one of his rank.

TWENTY TWO

14:03. TUESDAY, OCTOBER 13TH, 1914.
THE VATICAN. VATICAN CITY.

Cardinal Bishop Casado jumped the moment Bishop Attilio Basquez's shadow fell across him whilst he sat in the atrium of Old Saint Peter's Basilica, his head having been bowed in deep thought.

"Bishop Basquez," he called in greeting, looking up and meeting the cold of the man's eyes with a smile. "You made me jump!"

"Troubled with your thoughts?" the sly Bishop asked.

"Troubled," replied Casado, nodding contemplatively, "but not with my thoughts. These are troubling times. For us all, even here within the safe walls of the Vatican." He peered around the shadows and dimly lit crevasses of the pillared atrium. "Old Saint Peter's Basilica. I often come here to think. It grants one a reflective ambiance to suit one's mood."

The dark haired Bishop briefly followed Casado's eyes to look about himself but he quickly put his attention back onto the Cardinal Bishop.

"Tacit has begun his assessment," He spoke the words like an obscenity.

"He has."

"I heard that Adansoni questioned the decision to assess the Inquisitor."

The venerable Cardinal turned his attention to Basquez, surprised at the Bishop's line of conversation. "Cardinal Adansoni looks on Tacit like a son, although he denies it. He is bound to resist an assessment which might result in the imprisonment, even the death, of the Inquisitor."

"Perhaps he has something to hide?" Basquez asked, his voice like the hiss of a serpent. The question surprised Cardinal Bishop Casado, watching the dark haired man closely as he stepped away, leaning back and breathing deeply on the midday Vatican air. "I raise the question only as a matter of principle." He looked back, an eyebrow raised. "If the student has been accused of falling, perhaps the master has as well?"

"What are you suggesting?" Casado replied incredulously. "Surely not that Cardinal Adansoni himself be assessed?"

"Absolutely not," Basquez assured him, a cold smile coming to his face. "But there is always the Sodalitium Pianum?" his eyes narrow.

Cardinal Bishop Casado knew of the Sodalitium Pianum well, a small group of agents, set up in recent years by Pope Pius X before his death and headed up by the unflinching Monsignor Benigni, working independently of the Inquisition to investigate rumours of early signs of heresy and combat the growth of Modernism within the Vatican's own walls. Whilst less feared than the Inquisition, their name still brought consternation to the hearts of many.

"I know that Monsignor Benigni has been busy rooting out possible weakness and the beginnings of nonconformity within the Vatican," Basquez continued, his tone now lighter, "passing any details on to the Inquisition. Perhaps he could be asked to scrutinise Adansoni's affairs? Just gently, of course."

Casado threw his eyes to the far end of the atrium, as if greatly troubled with the suggestion. His mind churned in rhythm with the flicker of his eyes darting blindly between the pillars of the square before him.

The Bishop raised a hand and inspected his nails, flicking his thumb absently against his fingers. "During these troubling times, as you call them, we should be doubly vigilant. Doubt leads to arrogance, arrogance to insubordination, insubordination to nonconformity, nonconformity leads to taking one's actions into one's own hands. Such as I hear they are doing in Paris with this Mass for Peace." Basquez spat the words from his tongue, as if they were filth.

"You do not like what Cardinal Bishop Monteria is trying to achieve then, Bishop Basquez?"

"No," he replied coldly. "It has not been sanctioned by the Holy See. Such behaviour suggests the Catholic Church is divided, something our enemies will be keen to use against us."

"Very well," Casado said, as if convinced by Basquez's final argument, turning with a resigned look on his face. "Ask Monsignor Benigni to investigate Cardinal Adansoni. But gently," he added, raising a finger to press home his insistence.

Basquez bowed curtly in agreement.

"Such treacherous times," lamented the Cardinal, closing his eyes and letting his head sag. But Basquez was quick with his retort.

"The times would be less treacherous if we had a Pope upon whom we could rely to share our vision and guide us with an unflinching hand. Like Pope Pius, God rest his soul. He was a true leader, not like Benedict!" The younger man's voice had risen to a crescendo, his eyes suddenly fierce.

But Casado shook his head, looking up into the far end of the atrium. "No," he replied softly, as he played the ruffles from his cassock, "Pius was unflinching in his vision, as you rightly say, but that meant he could not be led, could not be influenced. His vision, firm though it was, was his and his alone. Though many agreed with it, there were many who did not, and others who wanted him to go further with his plans. You talk of division? He caused division and disharmony in many quarters with his austere ambitions. And how can the Holy See guide its Pope if its Pope refuses to listen? No, Pius was a true leader but not a good Pope. Whereas Benedict ..."

"Is weak, talking of peace with our slavic neighbours," spat Basquez quickly.

"... is someone we can influence, command, set to do our bidding. In these treacherous times, we need someone without arrogance or conceit, whom we can control and who will carry our message out to the masses with benevolence and clarity."

Casado's voice had fallen to a whisper, as if the words he spoke were of great perfidy.

"I still prefer the brand of fire and brimstone," retorted Basquez, the corner of his thin mouth rising in contempt.

"You would not think that were the same brand to be set against your tongue by the Inquisition for treason, Bishop Basquez!"

The Bishop's cold eyes narrowed and he seemed to shrink back, as if fearing arrest. But Casado's tone remained calm and measured.

"No," he said, running his palm slowly across his face, "the Holy See has chosen its Pope wisely this time. It now falls to us within the Holy See to adopt a wise and enlightened policy to place upon his lips."

TWENTY THREE

AUGUST 24TH, 1914. PARIS. FRANCE.

In the dark of the southern transept, beneath the purple coloured moonlight cast from the south rose window of Notre Dame, two figures met, one bent with age, the other tall and gaunt beneath his robes.

"Cardinal Bishop Monteria?" the tall gaunt man asked in a hushed whisper, stepping closer to catch sight of the man's face.

"Cardinal Poré," Monteria replied, with a courteous bow of his head. "Well met, at last. I have heard much about you."

"And I of you," Poré replied, "of your quiet resolution to the path you have chosen to follow, of your dedication to Francis of Assisi."

A light seemed to catch within Monteria's face at the mention of his favoured saint. "And how your conviction drives you," he countered, watching for any sign of the anger Poré was reputed to carry.

"Such things do not need to concern you, or our alliance," he replied calmly, his unmoving eyes holding Monteria's. He bowed his head, as if in subservience to the older man "We come together for one thing."

"Indeed, our shared purpose. I thought I was alone in feeling such things."

"Not alone. Many share our beliefs. Just lack the conviction to act. They are weak. Like our new Pope."

"Such talk is treason."

"Then let me be found guilty."

Monteria chuckled gently. "No. Not yet," he said, the trace of a determined smile on his lips. "Let me share my plan with you for this Mass for Peace and let us see then if we be found guilty before God."

Poré craned his neck upwards to peer at the line of sixteen tall stained glass windows beneath the large magnificence of the south rose window. "Perhaps we should see if we are guilty before them first?" he asked, indicating the painted figures held within each of the windows.

"Ah! The heavenly court of the sixteen prophets," Monteria replied and he turned his eyes heavenwards towards the windows and spoke in a louder, clear voice, quoting Bertrand, the Bishop of Chartres from the thirteenth century, "We are all dwarves standing on the shoulders of giants. We see more than they do, not because our vision is clearer there or because we are taller, but because we are lifted up due to their giant scale."

"Well said," replied Poré, his dark eyes glistening. "So, let us hear this plan and let us pray to God that we be not found guilty until it has been put into action."

TWENTY FOUR

1893. The Vatican. Vatican City

Tacit was running, running through the winding streets and courtyards of Vatican City, rushing before an almighty storm, Father Adansoni's hand on his shoulder, driving him forward, out of the rain. He was running and he was laughing as he ran, bathing in the joy of belonging, of feeling safe under his master's counsel despite the downpour, laughing, and the Father laughing too, at their folly, at getting caught in the storm.

They were drenched and it cheered Tacit's heart to see how the Father didn't care that his robes and cassock were drenched either. And in that moment, Tacit wondered perhaps if that was why he was put on earth, to bring joy and good cheer to all whom he met. He thought it a good life then, to bring hilarity and joy wherever he went.

That was seconds before the old man fell. Or was he pushed? Tacit didn't know, or couldn't recall. All he remembered was turning and seeing faces, men with torches, drenched heavy coats, resentful sneers, enemies of the

Church, bearing down on them from the shadows. From where they had come, he didn't know, but he recognised their look from somewhere far off, long ago.

He remembered a club being lifted and brought down on the old man as he lay scrambling on the cobbles of the path, the wicked chuckle of voices, voices the like of which he remembered from … from …

He drew back from his memories as he felt the sharp jar in his elbow of his fist connecting with bone. He heard the crack of a jaw and a cruel voice swearing. A club, like a truncheon, a bobbing member, was being waved in front of him. Red rage tore out of him, followed by a sickening guttural choking, the sudden sound of liquid gushing onto the floor, a stickiness between his fingers.

He was aware of his hands moving before he had time to even consider where they should go, as if guided by another greater power. Wherever they went there followed a weeping and a pleading from voices quite unlike his, the splintering of limbs, the falling of bodies, then a tight intake of breath and then a slow release as death came.

And lights. Everywhere about him were lights, hanging in the air around him, embracing him, nourishing him with their rays.

And then, as quickly as the brawl had begun, it was over. Tacit picked the Father up off the floor and ushered him away from the lifeless bodies strewn about the courtyard.

Adansoni threw his eyes onto the boy and stared, a look speared somewhere between fear, disbelief and wonder at what his young pupil had done.

"You are, Poldek," Adansoni muttered, his eyes wide on the young man. "You are," he repeated.

"I am what, Father?"

But Adansoni could, or would, say no more.

TWENTY FIVE

12:53. Tuesday, October 13th, 1914. Arras. France.

The proprietor of the hotel had insisted on showing Sister Isabella personally to Tacit's room. He said the little act of goodness for a servant of the Lord would serve him well when he came to meet his maker, although this didn't stop him staring longingly at her cleavage as she enquired as to the whereabouts of Tacit's lodgings as they climbed the dark and winding stairwell, as decrepit and filthy as the bar downstairs. Every few steps, he stopped and looked back to examine the gently bouncing breasts, checking they were still safely secured beneath her tightly drawn top. She made no attempt to cover herself from his prying eyes but glared at him unremittingly outside the door to Tacit's room when he tried to make small talk, until he slipped away awkwardly like a scolded dog caught stealing food.

She turned to look at the cracked and blackened door. She wasn't surprised Tacit had chosen to stay here. Its decor matched Tacit's charm. She knocked and the Inquisitor growled, "Open," from the other side.

She turned the handle of the door and stepped into the dirty, pokey little room. There was a smell of stale sweat in the air. A single filthy unmade bed ran alongside one wall, its one measly sheet ruffled and marked. To the right of it was a casement window, bent and broken lattice across the glass. A sideboard stood on the wall opposite the bed, a jug and bowl set alongside a number of bottles, all showing different heights of brown coloured spirit inside, glasses set beside them.

A circular table, far too big for the room, stood in the centre of it. There was no chair. The only place to sit was the bed. Tacit stood by the window peering out into the early afternoon light.

She pulled a face and curled her fingers into her palms, as if to avoid dirtying them on any of the surfaces. She looked again at the bed and the stained sheet. She chose to stand.

"Just got up?" she asked with a smirk, looking again at the bed, and then folded her arms, resting back against the wall.

Tacit ignored her. He pulled a large leather bound case out from beneath the bed and thumped it down onto the table. He unbuckled the strap holding it shut and thrust it open, taking a moment to examine its contents.

He didn't look up. He stared hard into the case, as if reacquainting himself with an old face.

Isabella stifled a yawn. "Cardinal Poré's on his way," she said. "He's bringing the chorister with him. Says the chorister's lost his tongue."

Tacit looked up.

"Not literally," the Sister assured him. She lent forward and untied her cape, looking around the room for a hook upon which to hang it. Despite the state of the room, it was at least warm. Too warm.

"Is there somewhere I can hang this?" she asked.

Tacit's eyes rose to the curvaceous form of the Sister, emphasised by the clinging cotton of her gown. They rested on her breasts, her shoulders, the curve of her back, the round turn of her buttocks. He wrenched his eyes away and whispered something under his breath, forcing his attention back to the case and its contents.

Isabella caught a sense of the Inquisitor's embarrassment and felt the draw of a smile on her face. She pursed her lips and held up the cape. "No hooks, no?" she asked, breathing in deeply so that her chest was even more pronounced.

Tacit, his eyes still locked on his belongings, pointed to the end of the bed. Isabella stepped over and laid the cape down upon it, whilst Tacit began to unpack the contents of the trunk: two silver crucifixes, one grey revolver, two vial racks, each with a row of vials tied securely within, three round bellied bottles containing unknown potions, three silver tipped crossbow bolts and a hand crossbow, a collection of wooden stakes, a mallet, one silver mirror, a bag containing a fine powdery dust, a heavy weighted tome, a short length of fine rope, a net bag containing herbs, bulbs and other flowery assortments. He huffed gruffly when the case was empty and its belongings covered the table.

"You really should learn to travel lighter," Isabella suggested, stepping to the sideboard. "Must take you an age to get through customs. Do you have anything to drink other than ..." She let her words trail off, as she looked along the bottles of liquor. "What's with the booze?" she asked suddenly.

"What's with the questions?" Tacit shot back, picking up the crossbow and feeling its weight.

Isabella leant back against the sideboard. She stared around the walls of the grubby room, taking in its shabby gloom.

"You've not put the symbol of our Lord up."

"Meaning?"

"Where's the crucifix? Standard protocol for travelling Priests. To hang up a crucifix so –"

"I'm not a Priest," Tacit scowled, slamming shut the lid of the case and placing the crossbow upon it.

Isabella looked at the weapon and then the Inquisitor, crossing her arms beneath her breasts. "So why do you drink?"

She watched as Tacit raised his head, staring straight ahead to the empty wall with his cold, dark eyes. "So why do you dress like a prostitute?" he shot back.

"I dress how I like. It doesn't affect my work."

"You're a Sister. You should dress accordingly."

"Meaning?"

"All those eyes on you."

"Like yours?" Isabella retorted, raising an eyebrow and the edge of her mouth.

The air around Tacit darkened. "You should remember your vows of celibacy," he warned.

"I never took them."

With how he was standing, she couldn't see Tacit's face. He was relieved.

A knock on the door drew them both away from the rising tension.

"It's open," they called together. The door was pushed open, Cardinal Poré standing in its doorway, a small and terrified looking boy in front of him. The Cardinal's hand was on his shoulder and he gave the boy a gentle nudge to encourage him inside.

"Cardinal Poré," Isabella called, stepping around the table to welcome them. "I didn't expect you to have accompanied the boy. You could have sent him alone."

"As feared, the boy is terrified. His tongue is lame," the Cardinal replied. "I thought it wiser to accompany him, especially as there are ill tidings abroad."

Isabella crouched down so she was level with the boy's eyes.

"Hello," she said, smiling warmly. "I'm Sister Isabella. What's your name?"

The chorister looked at her with wide terrified eyes and turned his head to the Cardinal.

"I am afraid you'll find the child will not speak," Cardinal Poré announced, closing the door behind him gently. He drew his hands into the cuffs of his sleeves. "He has been … shocked into silence by events," the Cardinal continued, looking over to the hunched figure of the Inquisitor staring hard and suspiciously at the child. He then looked about the room with disdain. "Are the surroundings adequate, Inquisitor Tacit? I could reserve you a room at the Cathedral residences which would perhaps suit you better?" he suggested, looking dismissively around the shoddily cleaned and decorated room. Tacit ignored him.

"Did he ever speak?" he growled, his cold unmoving eyes on the boy.

"Who, the boy? Yes, of course," replied Poré, placing an arm across the child's shoulder. "He has a beautiful voice, both in speech and song. But these terrible events, they have choked it from him, the poor boy."

Tacit grunted, making the child turn to look. Isabella cupped the child's face in her hands and drew his gaze back to hers. He had a beautiful face, pale skin like china.

"Has the voice got lost somewhere inside you, little man?" she asked, kindly, her French fluent, as if she was a local of Arras.

The boy nodded cautiously in reply, before looking up at the Cardinal for guidance.

"Well, what we need to do is find that little voice again because we need to ask it some questions about yesterday. Would that be okay, to try and do that?" Isabella pressed gently.

The child began to nod his head but, as he did so, he stopped and began to shake it instead.

"It's Julio, isn't it?" she asked.

A nod grew out of the shake.

"That's a lovely name," the Sister said to the boy. "Okay, why don't you sit yourself down here on the end of the bed, Julio, and we'll try and find that little voice inside of you? Okay?"

She led the boy to the bed and sat him down on her gown, crouching before him. Isabella trusted that the boy's backside was cleaner than Tacit's bed. Tacit looked down at them contemptuously and made no attempt to a hide a yawn.

"So, my name is Sister Isabella," she began in a warm and deliciously inviting voice. "I am here to help find out what happened and to try and make everything all okay? Okay, Julio?"

The boy nodded, looked up at the Cardinal and then looked back at the Sister, nodding again.

"So, you've had a horrible fright and you don't want to talk about it and I completely understand that." She rested her hands on the thin thighs of the boy in front of her. "It was awful what happened to poor Father Andreas and that is why we need you to tell us what you know, what you saw, anything that might help us find who did this to the Father."

The boy looked up at the Cardinal and then back down into his lap. Isabella smiled and rubbed the side of his head.

"Did you like the Father?" she asked.

The boy nodded slowly and sniffed.

"Was he kind to you?"

The boy nodded and sniffed again, twisting his hands together in his lap.

"Oh, poor lamb," Isabella continued. "Then help us find who did this thing to your friend."

The boy twitched with his mouth and looked up from Isabella to the Cardinal and back again. He pursed his lips, as if willing himself to speak, but then shook his head and dropped his eyes back to his lap.

"Speak boy!" shouted Tacit, resting an elbow on the top of his case. Isabella shot him a glare. The child stared up at him wide eyed. "Stop wasting our time! Tell us what you know!"

"Please, Tacit!" the Cardinal cried, his hands together in prayer. "Be gentle with your questioning. This child has witnessed much and his torment is terrible. He's scared witless!" As if the words had awoken a sudden protectiveness within the Cardinal, he strode forward, his hands held aloft. "Enough!" he announced, reaching out to gather the child from the bed.

Instantly, Inquisitor Tacit picked up the steel revolver from the table and pointed it directly at the child.

"Speak," he growled, staring down the long barrel of the gun into the wide terror of the child's eyes.

The chorister cried out and froze. The Cardinal fell against the wall muttering, his hand to his mouth.

"Tacit, have you lost control of your senses?" he cried.

Tacit gritted his teeth and cocked the pistol.

"Speak!"

Isabella hung her head in a hand and shook it gently. She slipped to one side, her back against a wall, her face deep in her fingers, hiding a look combining disbelief and shame. The child began to sob uncontrollably and looked fearfully from the barrel of the gun to the Cardinal. He began to raise his hands to the Cardinal as a means of rescue.

"Please, for all that is holy in the world," Cardinal Poré begged, stepping forward to guide the Inquisitor's aim to one side.

Tacit stepped beyond him and pushed the barrel tight into the forehead of the child. "Speak," he said. "Last chance."

"For goodness sake!" the Cardinal cried, but at the same time the chorister blurted out, "The woman!" through tears and sobs.

"The woman, what?" Tacit asked, the gun still tight to the child's forehead.

"She'd come to see Father Andreas, yesterday, earlier on, that morning, before lunchtime." He ran the words into each other, as if he couldn't get them out quick enough. "She came to see him. She carried a parcel. She gave it to him. Father Andreas seemed upset, but he took the parcel."

"Parcel? What was it like?"

"Wrapped in paper. Size of a, I don't know, a baby or a large fish."

"What did he do with it?"

"Put it in the antechamber of the Cathedral."

"In its paper wrapping?"

The boy nodded despairingly, moans and tears clutching in his throat.

"What's her name? The woman?"

"I don't know," the boy whimpered.

"Seen her before?"

"No."

"Did you hear what they said to each other?"

The chorister tried to shake his head but found the revolver made any movement difficult. "No, I was sent away to collect the hymn books for the Mass that evening, while they talked."

"How long did she stay?"

"A few minutes."

"Did she say anything to you as she left?"

"No. She just left."

"Had you seen her before?"

"No."

"What did she look like?"

"Dark hair. Tall. Slim."

"Do you recognise the description?" Tacit threw the question at the Cardinal.

"Good heavens, no!" Poré roared back, his face crimson with fury.

"Did Father Andreas say anything else, after she had left?" Tacit asked Julio again.

The boy hesitated, misunderstanding what Tacit was asking.

He scowled and raised his voice even louder. "Did he say anything more about the woman to you, after she had gone?" the Inquisitor hissed, pushing the barrel hard into the skull of the child.

"No. No, he didn't."

Tacit's finger tightened around the trigger of the gun. The chorister cried out, pleading to be spared. Cardinal Poré screamed, reaching forward for the revolver.

The gun clicked.

Tacit turned and wandered nonchalantly back to the case, Isabella staring open mouthed at him.

"It's okay," he grunted, as he put the revolver back onto the table. "The gun was never loaded."

TWENTY SIX

1893. The Vatican. Vatican City.

The man Tacit was introduced to had kindly features, but there was a distance and darkness within his eyes. He pressed his hand firmly into Tacit's, so that the bones in the young man's palm crunched.

"Inquisitor Tocco," he introduced himself, and rose up to his full height over the young man. "So, you're the one they've been talking about, are you?" he asked, his hand still tight around Tacit's clammy fingers. "The new Inquisitor?"

"Well, I don't know," Tacit hesitated, finally managing to extract his hand and giving his fingers a surreptitious test behind his back. "I've just been told to come and see you."

"How old are you, boy? Sixteen?"

"Fifteen. But I'm nearly sixteen."

"Makes all the difference, that one year," Tocco joked, feigning a smile, and Tacit realised he was being mocked. "Can you handle yourself?"

"I ... I wouldn't know."

"You've seen blood before?"

Somewhere buried deep in his mind, a woman's voice screamed.

"Again, I wouldn't know."

"Course you wouldn't," the Inquisitor hissed, and his eyes burnt hard into him. For several moments he stared into the depths of Tacit's eyes, as if trying to retrieve memories from the young man's mind. Then, without warning, he snapped himself straight and looked the young man up and down.

"Well, you look strong enough. Are you up for a new challenge?"

"I suppose so," Tacit replied, watching the man leave the hall.

"About time," the Inquisitor said. "Come with me."

"Where are we going?"

"Into Rome."

"Rome?"

"You want to be an Inquisitor?"

"They've told me I should be one."

"Then let's see if *they* are correct."

They walked unmolested through the streets of the Italian capital, raising no suspicion, drawing no glances. But why should they, a dark clad Priest and his young acolyte pacing through Rome on an errand?

After a little while walking, the Inquisitor said, "They tell me you have a past. My advice to you, boy, is don't ignore it. Use it. You'll need it."

"Need it? I don't know what you mean."

The Inquisitor stood back. He looked away up the street. Tacit saw scars on his cheek, through the bristle on his jawbone. They ran down his neck into the collar of his cassock. "Toughest job in the Church," he said, putting his attention back onto the boy. "Guard yourself against the demons. And not just the ones around you."

He tapped his skull and stared hard at the boy, before reaching into his pocket and drawing out a small glass bottle encased in tendrils of metal across its surface. He unscrewed the lid and put the lip of the bottle to his mouth.

He champed against the bitterness of the tincture. "Use what you can to get through," Tocco said, raising the bottle to the boy. "You'll find a way. Most do."

"What about those who don't? Those who don't find a way?"

The Inquisitor stowed the flask into the folds of his jacket and removed a revolver from a deep pocket. "Then they're doomed," he replied darkly, before turning the handle of the door next to where they stood and stepping cautiously inside.

TWENTY SEVEN

1893. Rome and the Vatican. Vatican City.

That first moment when the apparition fell shrieking upon Tacit, he knew he'd been irretrievably changed, the fervour and panic as the thing came out of the shadows at him forever now branded on his brain. Instantly the air froze, turning Tacit's blood to ice. He fell away, shielding his eyes, enveloped in a cloud of dust as he tried to roll away from it.

He could feel the cold tendrils of the thing's tattered arms raking his back, the sound like a scream in his head. He felt lost in the darkness, swirling mists of unconsciousness engulfing him. He tried to cry out, but no sound came. He whimpered and then, when he thought he was lost for good, he heard a voice, growing louder and louder, calling out: Inquisitor Tocco, barking at the apparition to 'Get back! Get back!'

Tacit rolled over and looked straight up into the face of the wraith. It turned its wrathful eyes from him onto the Inquisitor, as Tocco leapt into its swirling gaseous form, whipping out his crucifix and at the same time pulling a strange looking gun from his holster.

At once the ghost knew it was beaten and reared away, attempting to find some hole into which it could hide. Tocco lowered the pistol and fired.

"How d'you feel?" the Inquisitor asked Tacit straggling behind him, as they strode through the bowels of the Vatican. He shouted the question into the air above his head, heaving open a heavy oak door and stepping through it. Tocco caught sight of Tacit peering about the dour surroundings. "They don't decorate down here," he said, turning right at the next split in the corridor. "Weapons mark the walls too easily. So, how d'you feel?"

"Fine," Tacit lied. He swallowed and realised he was shaking.

"Ghosts are one of the easiest things you'll face," the Inquisitor continued, unhelpfully. "They can't hurt you, not unless you let them in. You just have to remember what they are. Memories, on the wind." He touched the point of his index finger to his skull. "Sadly, there's plenty else out there that can hurt you."

"What was that thing you fired at it?" Tacit asked, recalling the Inquisitor's revolver. "I didn't think ghosts could be hurt by bullets?"

"They can't. It was a special revolver. Fired silver charms. Good for dissipating ghosts. Not so good against Hombre Lobo, witches, demons or heretics."

"Hombre Lobo?"

"Werewolves," the Inquisitor replied, smiling.

"Where would you get a gun like that?" Tacit asked, wide eyed.

"Come," replied Tocco. "I'll show you."

They stepped through an archway into a vast hall. Along one wall was a wide opening against which Inquisitors stood, leaning forward across a counter towards figures scampering back and forth on the other side. Tables and chairs, backpacks on table tops, black clad Inquisitors seated or standing in groups, covered every available space in the chamber.

"What is this place?" Tacit asked, mesmerised. He'd never seen so many assembled in one hall, not even in St. Peter's Basilica.

"Stores," the Inquisitor replied, guiding Tacit towards an available space in the opening. "We can't fight with our hands and crucifixes alone."

Tocco nodded at the figure behind the opening and wordlessly a high sided tray, piled with various items and oddments, was placed on the counter in front of him. The Inquisitor pulled it towards him and rummaged carelessly through its contents. "Here, take this," he said, producing a silver revolver from the pile of contents and handing it absently to Tacit. "My gift to you."

Tacit gasped. "But … I can't take this. It's a gun!" He shuddered at the weight of the weapon in his hands, turning it over to peer at its intricate mechanisms and the shimmer given off from its metallic parts. "It's too beautiful. I can't accept it."

"You don't have a choice. I'm not giving it to you out of the kindness of my heart. You'll need it. Every Inquisitor needs to be armed."

TWENTY EIGHT

16:26. Tuesday, October 13th, 1914. Arras. France.

It had taken Cardinal Poré several hours to calm the chorister and an hour more to calm himself after what had taken place in the Inquisitor's lodgings. He had never seen anything like it. He knew Inquisitors were cruel and harsh, but Tacit's behaviour was beyond anything he would ever have expected, even from their bitter kind.

Once the shaking had worked its way out of his body and he'd tried, and failed, to understand how and why Tacit had done what he had, there were still errands to run and people to see. Only now, late into the afternoon, had Cardinal Poré found a moment to rest. The war had taken its toll, not just on those at the front line but also on those in the nearby towns and cities, caught by the seemingly wanton barrages cast their way. There were so many in his congregation who needed help, a prayer for safety, or simply a kindly word from someone who perhaps could make some sense of the madness which had been thrust upon them. Not that Poré chose to make sense of what had befallen their nation. Instead, as his eyes turned increasingly to the east towards the sounds of war and the plumes of smoke rising from blasted outposts and abandoned homesteads, he found that the grim resolve was growing ever stronger inside him.

Poré was willing to give all succour who wished it, but right now he needed just a moment's rest in the quiet of his residence close to the Cathedral of Arras, a moment of peace and reflection, before continuing with his endeavours amongst the population of his city.

He took a little water and sat with his sad eyes upon the city before him, his mind turning from Tacit and the chorister to the many drawn faces he had looked into that day, reliving the touch of their trembling hands as he'd taken hold of them.

But nothing, not even their horror etched into their faces, could remove the image of Tacit or the outrage of his behaviour from his mind. A hatred began to catch within him, fuelled by a memory from long ago. He recalled the cruel regime under which he himself had once served, for just a short time when a boy; a terrible time of harsh voices, physical and mental abuse, the stench of leather, blood and soot, coloured only with black and flame and horror. He closed his eyes in an attempt to silence the sneering ghosts of his past, but doing so only worsened his torment, the shriek of wicked things in the dark places of the world rattling within his mind, remembering how he sobbed at his eventual expulsion from the Inquisition, the inhuman taunts from his inquisitorial teachers as he was sent from the school, the shame which forever followed him in those years after.

And then, some time later, when the Inquisitors appeared at his home calling for his mother and father to go with them, their plaintive cries of resistance, his tear-drenched pleading for them to be saved, the sharp sting as a subduing truncheon fell across the back of his head. The darkness which flooded in after he'd been hit, pulling him down into an endless blackness; he had never recovered or returned from it.

So many voices he could never silence. So many questions. Had his failings to make it as an Inquisitor led to their arrest? Had his actions, or inaction, tied his parents to those ghoulish instruments of torture? Had they been made to confess? If so, what did they confess to and what had been done to draw the confessions out? Had their torturers used fire, blades or blunt instruments?

How had they died?

Poré never discovered the charges which had been placed against his parents. He had never been given the chance to see them again, once they had been taken that day.

Their loss drove him to the very edge of madness and beyond, an overwhelming sense of responsibility and shame which, in turn and with time twisted and writhed into anger and hatred, and to the sworn promise to his dead parents that one day he would take his revenge upon the Inquisition and the faith which had created it.

Wrath bristling within him, he snatched up his scarlet zucchetto skull cap from the desk beside him and stormed from the room.

TWENTY NINE

21:51. Tuesday, October 13th, 1914. Arras. France.

Father Aguillard looked over his shoulder and tried to put the key to his door in the lock. It wouldn't go, as if the key was too big for it, as if he'd drawn the wrong one from his pocket. He drew a sleeve over his eyes, stinging with sweat, and peered with renewed focus at the small dark slot, knowing it had to be the right one for he only carried the one key. As a travelling Father of the Church, what need had he of chests or doors? He'd been given the key by the Church on his arrival. He knew it must fit. He tried to breathe a little slower and be more measured and deliberate in his actions. He thought about, once he was packed, returning the key to the Church courtesy of the mail service. Certainly not by hand. He had no intention of staying in Arras a moment longer. Not now, not any more, not now the city wasn't safe.

He cursed, a foul word he'd learnt whilst travelling in Northern Spain, for which he immediately made an apology under his breath. As if by way of thanking him for acknowledging the sincerity of his regret at the offence, the end of the key vanished into the hole and the lock gave a welcoming click, the key turning smoothly in the mechanism. The rotund Priest breathed a little deeper and slower. With a final glance over his shoulder to make sure he hadn't been followed, he pushed the door open and stepped inside.

He shut the door to the small, but perfectly acceptable, accommodation provided to all travelling Priests and Fathers at the Cathedral fast behind him, and locked it with a single turn of the key. He tested the door and leaned against it. Finally he felt a little capitulation in the fear and panic inside him. He was now safe, for the moment at least. He could pack and leave within the hour, maybe thirty minutes if he was quick. He could commandeer a horse from the Cathedral stables and ride like the wind from the city. Or perhaps he could slink from the city silently on foot, using the darkness which now embraced Arras, not stopping until he was miles from the accursed place. Once he was in the wilds of France, no one would ever find him, not unless he wanted to be found.

The options excited and emboldened him. For the first time since he heard the news of Father Andreas' death, he felt confidence returning. And he always prided himself on his confidence. After all, wasn't he the Father who walked where others feared to tread? Was he not the Father who'd entered the beasts' lair, had conversed with the enemy and had won the trust and loyalty of those shunned and feared by others of his faith?

But Father Andreas' death had scared him, Father Andreas who had shown so much willing and so much spirit. Aguillard had known at once, as soon as he'd heard the news that Andreas was dead, that the game was up, that things were changing, that they were closing the loop. He never believed for an instant the story about the heart attack. Aguillard was many things but he wasn't stupid and he wasn't naive.

But he was impetuous, he always had been, and he'd lost his temper. He'd shouted at his fellow conspirators and he'd said that the plot had gone too far and then he'd threatened to reveal it. He regretted the words now. Of course he knew he would never reveal the plans. He'd invested too much, he'd worked too hard considering, preparing, making sure everything was followed according to the plan, making sure everyone knew what their tasks were and that they followed them to the letter. That no one talked. That no one let slip what was being undertaken. But he wasn't sure that anyone believed his word was safe anymore. And so here he was running because, in a moment of maddening rage, he'd played a hand he'd feared Father Andreas had played the day before.

Father Aguillard reached the end of the narrow corridor and paused.

Strange. He could feel a breeze coming from an open window, the chill of the night time air in the apartment. And yet he was sure he'd shut the windows before leaving earlier in the evening? And that smell, a quite dreadful smell, like rotting drains coming up from behind the door. He crinkled his noise and went to push it open, rubbing his eyes with his thumb and forefinger.

A voice greeted his entrance and he swallowed, a chill creeping over him not brought on by the cool of the open window alone.

"Why don't you sit down, Father Aguillard?" the voice asked gently. "You look like you've had a terrible shock."

"I have."

"I'm sorry to hear that."

"Father Andreas, why did he have to die?"

"Why do you need to know?"

"You're going to kill me too, aren't you?" Aguillard asked the figure, sat before the open window.

"Goodness me, Father Aguillard, you do ask a lot of questions!"

"I should have asked more," he growled, finding some of his old spirit others so admired.

"Quite." The figure moved, shifting something from under its legs. "So, have you spoken to anyone about what we have done?"

Aguillard throat tightened and went dry.

"No," he said, the spirit immediately seeping out of him. He shook his head like a scolded child. "No, I haven't said a word."

"That's good." The figure lent down and dragged the thing it was lifting up over its head.

Aguillard leapt up from the chair, knocking it sideways, and cried out in a voice he never knew he possessed, instantly bursting into tears. He walked backwards, eyes fixed on the figure before him. It was then that he fell. "Please!" he cried, as the shadow stalked over him. He smelt its breath, hot and putrid. He screamed, but only until his face was ripped clean off in a single crisp bite.

THIRTY

22:34. Tuesday, October 13th, 1914.
The front line. Arras. France.

The night was as black as coal when the British patrol went forward from Fampoux and stole silently, breathlessly, into the land beyond. Above the six men, crouched close to the churned and pitted ground, the oval moon flitted in and out behind thick clouds, its weak silvery light unable to penetrate the gloom of the land below.

There was never any question of the squad not accepting the task of making a forward patrol out of Fampoux. Despite having only spent a few hours in the place, many already subscribed to the fact that there was something unsettling about the village. They couldn't agree on how or why the Germans had retreated from it almost willingly, not fighting hard for every square inch of the invaluable location. There was the cloying stench of death which hung heavy within it, as if the slaughter of the war and the trenches before it had sunk into the very earth. And there was the silence, as if an almost aberrant veil had been drawn over the village suffocating the life within it.

The men had talked, as all soldiers do as they work and to fend off boredom, about what new weapon had been created to have secured such an easy victory and at such a cost to the enemy. They shivered and trusted that whatever it was never fell into German hands. The reek of the recent slaughter and the prevailing sense of doom about that place unsettled every soldier. When the request was made for a patrol to leave the village and examine the way ahead, volunteers were quick to be found.

"Can't see a bloody thing, sir!" hissed one of the soldiers, as he felt his way forward blindly in the dark.

"Keep your bloody voice down!" the Lance Corporal snapped back under his breath. "Neither can I but I'm not harking on about it."

"How far are we going, sir?" another called, putting his hand on something soft in the dark and retracting it quickly.

"Bloody hell!" the Lance Corporal cursed, pushing back his cap. "Do you want to go back to that village?"

"No, sir!"

"Then keep your bloody trap shut!"

"Just asking, that's all."

"We'll go out for an hour or so."

"An hour?!" someone cried.

"Have a good look about. See how far the Hun have pulled back. Come on, this is bloody ridiculous," he said, standing up and peering east, "crawling around in the dirt. We're through the barbed wire. Let's go forward on foot. It's so dark. No one'll see us." He turned back to peer at his men through the blackness. "If a flare goes up, remember to drop."

"If a flare goes up and they follow it with a machine gun, we might not need to worry about remembering to drop."

"Alright, keep it bloody shut."

They walked on, shuffling figures in the darkness, tripping over unseen objects on the ground or stumbling sideways into holes and craters. There was a smell of mud and iron in the air. Behind them they could see an occasional light twinkle and then go out.

Every now and then, further along the front, the far skyline flared orange and red and the low thump of a barrage followed a little time later. A portion of the distant horizon in the south caught a dull yellow and burnt for a longer period, maybe a building burning from the onslaught.

"Poor buggers," one of the soldiers mumbled, glumly.

"Shut up, Jones," another hissed back.

The youngest of the soldiers listened to the sounds of the night, the rustle of uniform and leather belts, the soft jangle of strapping from the soldiers around him. Far behind him, he was sure he could hear the sound of conversation coming from the lights of Fampoux. It made him feel relieved. He turned his ear to the darkness ahead to see if he could hear anything.

A wolf howled somewhere in the night.

Ahead of them, the Lance Corporal raised a hand and dropped to his knees. The line of soldiers followed his lead, one after the other.

"Didn't know there were bloody wolves in France!" someone said.

"What is it, sir?" the second in the line asked.

"Thought I heard something," the Lance Corporal whispered.

They stayed there, crouched tight to the ground, for what seemed an eternity to the youngest soldier. When his legs started to ache, he sank onto his knees and turned over to sit on his backside, rifle across his lap. He looked up at the sky and thought about his sweetheart Mary back in England. He was surprised how little he had missed her. But then, he'd not had much time to sit and think about home since he'd been out here. Digging trenches, doing drill, marching for days and days, cleaning rifles, keeping sentry, staying awake nights on end, trying not to fall asleep during sentry duty, seemed to get in the way of thinking fondly of home. He was glad of it, too. He felt so far from anywhere here. He knew if he thought too much about home, he'd get sick.

At the head of the line, the Lance Corporal heard a noise again and asked, "Did you hear that?" to the nearest of the soldiers behind him.

"Hear what, sir?"

"That noise. Something moving about, up ahead."

"No sir," the soldier replied, discernibly quieter.

The Lance Corporal bent his head to the side and listened harder.

"I'm going forward," he said. "Stay here. I won't be long."

"But sir!" the second soldier in the line said, clutching blindly at the Lance Corporal's heel. "What if ..."

"I won't be long. Just having a look up ahead."

"But if you don't come back?" the Private asked awkwardly.

"If I don't come back, you take the men back to the trench."

"Very good sir."

The Lance Corporal rose and shambled his way forward. Within a couple of steps he was lost in the black of night.

"What's going on?" someone asked.

"It's Lance," the Private whispered back. "Thinks he heard something. He's going to have a look."

"Bloody great. Just what we need. Jerry in the dark."

The Lance Corporal stepped on, keeping bent and low, little steps in the dirt in the darkness. He stopped and sank to his knees, listening intently, and then rose and went forward again, his rifle gripped tight in his hands. He stopped once more, sinking down on his haunches. He looked back to the way he had come, entombed in sheer black. He swallowed and for the first time worried about finding his men again. But it was quiet and he knew could find them by calling out to them if need be. After all, there seemed to be nothing else in this God-forsaken place.

He turned back towards where he thought the enemy to be and screamed as the beast launched itself at him from the dark, ripping the windpipe and sound from out of him.

The Private pricked up his ears and peered into the gloom. As he listened, he was sure he could hear something, like the dull crunching of stones, the snap of sticks.

Something was there.

"Go back!" he hissed, standing and pushing out at the soldier behind him. "Quick! Go back! Fucking go back!" he called, his voice rising with his fear.

The soldier behind him stumbled blindly onto his knees and then up, reaching out and pushing at the soldier behind him. "We're going back," he called. "Come on! Orders from the front! We're going back!"

The bumbling, ragged line turned and began to trot back down the route they had come.

Something came out of the east and fell upon the Private at the rear of the line, vast bloodied jaws clamping hard into the crook between his neck and shoulder. The soldier cried out as the jaws tore a great chunk from his body, taloned hands grappling around his middle, holding him firm. A second bite took his head from his body, gushing warm gore over his assailant.

The remaining soldiers could hear the feral sounds, the clamouring of excited animal feeding, like a pack of hounds around a captured fox, but they didn't turn round. Now they were sprinting, charging headlong into the dark, tripping and falling into the dirt and detritus of No Man's Land, picking themselves up and running again, only to fall moments later. They were crying too, calling out for the attention of the trench ahead, for those there to help, to send up flares to guide their way forward.

But no flares were sent and in seconds the soldiers' cries were silenced.

The creatures fell upon them greedily.

THIRTY ONE

August 20th, 1914. The Vatican. Vatican City.

Cardinal Bishop Casado stood in silence at the end of the Pontiff's quarters, his unblinking eyes burning into the closed doors of the Pope's private chamber. For five days, ever since the Feast of the Assumption of Mary when Pope Pius X had been taken ill and carried away to his chamber for the Vatican's physicians to do what they could, there had been no word from the Pope or from those closest to him, a quiet stream of doctors and selected persons entering and leaving without word or emotion.

But now Casado knew the end was close. The faces of those leaving had grown increasingly bleak over the last few hours and it had been twenty minutes since the last of the visitors had reappeared.

He swallowed and allowed his eyes to fall to the floor of the corridor, a moment's rest to ease the pain growing behind them. With that, the handle to the door turned and slowly opened, a black robed senior Cardinal Casado knew well, stepping silently from inside, his eyes cast to the floor, his features drawn and white. At once Casado knew to fear the worse.

As if sensing Casado's presence, the Cardinal turned and walked quickly towards him.

"Is he ...?"

"He is," the Cardinal replied. There were tears in the man's eyes, his nostrils flared in attempt to fight back against this emotion. "Pope Pius X passed away ... peacefully." Casado went to speak but the Cardinal, perhaps sensing the words would be meaningless, continued.

"He asked that I give you this," he said, pressing a sealed letter into Casado's hand. Casado looked down at the small crushed white envelope in his palm.

Again, Casado went to speak, but the Cardinal had already turned away from him. "Oh, and Cardinal Bishop Casado," he added, pausing to turn back and talk over his right shoulder. "German forces have just marched into Brussels. War has come to Europe."

THIRTY TWO

1895. The Dolomites. Northern Italy.

It had been a hard climb and Tacit noticed how Inquisitor Tocco was out of breath by the time they reached the summit and the yawning black of a cave. Tacit followed his teacher's way and threw down his pack alongside Tocco's, his eyes drawn to the dark shadows of the cave mouth.

"Do you know what lies inside?" the Inquisitor asked mischievously, setting himself down on a rock and checking the position of the sun away to their left.

Tacit swallowed and shook his head. He knew whatever it was would put up a fight. It seemed to Tacit that whatever they visited in their line of work, wherever they seemed to go, there was always something to fight, something to destroy, to extinguish, to remove from the world.

There was always blood.

"The children of our faith," chuckled the Inquisitor, drawing out his small bottle and taking a short sharp sip from it. He scowled and put it back into the inside pocket of his jacket, laying his head back on the rock and catching his breath. His eyes rolled in his head and for a moment Tacit thought he'd fallen asleep. "Hombre Lobo," he said suddenly, laughing wickedly. Heavily, he lifted his head and thrust it in the direction of the cave. His hand was in his pocket and from it he pulled his revolver. He checked the mechanism and ensured the cylinder was full of silver coloured bullets. "Werewolves," he said, looking up and seeing that Tacit appeared puzzled.

"'Children of our faith'?" Tacit asked. "What do you mean?"

The Inquisitor sneered. "Of course you wouldn't have been told, it's one of the closest guarded secrets of the faith."

"At the very beginning," began Tocco, sweeping the dark of his hair from his forehead, "when the Inquisition was in its infancy, when its laws were first being drawn up, the Church's enemies being recognised and its methods planned, it was quickly realised that some of the fiercest laws should be kept aside for those who failed most grievously with their faith. The 'fallen deviants' the Church called them, the ones who were once mighty within the Church, who were respected, revered even, before they lost their way. To our *wise* fore-fathers, they were thought of as the true sinners of the Church, for they had sinned in the very presence of God.

"Excommunication, casting them from the Church, was felt not enough for those who had benefitted and taken so much from the Catholic faith and repaid it so badly. Only divine retribution was considered appropriate for these damned 'monsters', these high ranking Catholic officials, lords and ladies, people of power, all of whom had long taken succour from the Church and then turned their backs on it when they were replete. Not only were they were cast out of the Church, but they were cast out of society to live till the end of days as the monsters they had become, forced to live their pitiful lives under the shadow of night, no longer able to venture out beneath the glare of daylight and God's warmth, forever tormented by the desire for flesh, just as they had tormented the Lord with their greed for riches and power."

"This is terrible," muttered Tacit, his mouth wide. Tocco shrugged. "Do they still cast these people out in this way, still create these beasts?"

Tocco shook his head. "No. The mystics of the Church, those who hold the long forgotten knowledge and rarely venture from their libraries deep in the belly of the Vatican, they were the ones who devised the method. And, as far as I know, such rituals have been ripped from the pages of their tomes. None know how to perform the rite and it is unlikely that we could repeat their methods if we tried today." Tocco chuckled coldly, showing chipped teeth. "But then again, why would we want to create any more of them? We spend enough of our time trying to destroy them.

Most often they gather in clans, those cast out by the most resolute of Catholic edicts far from civilisation and the mob's persecution, together in packs plotting the downfall of those who had ensured that their own downfall had been total.

Of course, there are so many who have sinned in this way in the past and our masters of old were determined when ensuring that justice was total regarding these fallen deviants. Soon we had a problem of our own making, so many werewolves created by the Church, so many cast out by the faith, cast out by civilisation, bringing their own terror and rage to the populace near to where they settled, often in large groups, always wicked and always hungry at night. And, of course, perversely threatening the reputation and even the survival of the Catholic Church by their very existence."

Tacit understood what Inquisitor Tocco was insinuating but waited for him to continue. "If the existence of Hombre Lobo, and how they came into being, was ever revealed, then … " He looked up at the last of the sun and blinked. "We've long stopped creating their type, but whilst the last of them still exist within the world, we'll keep exterminating them."

He slapped his thigh and stood up enthusiastically. "Hence the reason we are here. To clean up our masters' dirty work. Remember," Tocco said, pulling his pack onto his back, "your generation is our future. You are one of the keepers of our faith, the protectors of our ways. We look to you to uphold the faith, Tacit, and bring damnation to our enemies." He slapped Tacit hard on the shoulder. "The world within which most people live is a falsehood. We control its secrets. We manage the direction of our faith, our Church and the way the world turns. We keep the faith strong, our prospects good and our enemies weak."

He stood and took the small bottle out of his coat pocket again. "And after everything else, we go to war." He toasted the sun before sipping from the bottle's lip. "When you think about it, after nearly two thousand years, really very little has changed," he said, before turning to face the cave with his revolver in his hand.

THIRTY THREE

22:58. Tuesday, October 13th, 1914. Arras. France.

Tacit poured himself a large measure of brandy and stared out of the window onto the square below. His face was void of any emotion, a mask; one hand on the window surround, the other snatched tightly to the glass.

He drank deeply from it and stuck a finger into an eye socket, pushing it in hard to try to unhinge a pain which had found purchase there. Headaches. They were getting worse.

Tacit coughed and drained his drink. He had been relieved when the Sister said she would not be spending any more time with him today. She'd left shortly after the Cardinal and chorister, in a flurry of waved arms and protestations. He'd ignored her, drinking, his back turned to her – his eyes on the window until the shouting had abated and the door slammed. He wanted to be alone. He always wanted to be alone but particularly this evening. He had to think in peace, to consider the murder of the Father, the confession by the chorister about the dark haired woman, the reluctance of the Cardinal to allow the boy to speak; thin threads from which he had to construct a rope with which to tie up this assignment. He'd sat on the end of his bed, turning his hands over and over, examining the deep lines within them, until a knock on the door announced the arrival of his dinner.

Over a simple mutton stew, bread and two bottles of wine, Tacit toiled with the fragments of evidence regarding the crime but nothing revealed itself, not even the freedom of thought that the second bottle of wine provided could help.

He sat in the dark, the empty plate and bottles on the table, and looked to the dark of the city outside. He felt trapped, fettered by his thoughts, the room, the assignment, his lack of understanding. Shortly before ten, no further forward in comprehending but also undissuaded from his dogged line of thinking, he had risen groggily and stumbled out. He'd headed for the East Gate and where his fuddled instincts told him to go: those people who had voiced their displeasure of the Catholic faith, the Orthodox Christians. He headed for where he knew an enclave of them lived in the city. He decided that if the answers didn't come to him, he would go to the answers.

A chill had descended on the city by the time he stepped into the streets, but Tacit never felt the cold that evening, fortified by alcohol and the theories churning in his mind. He swerved drunkenly past a couple of Arras residents taking in the last of the night air, barely able to hide his rage when he reasoned that the Father's murder *must* have been a hate crime. He couldn't see any other reason for it, the pointless savagery against a man with no apparent enemies.

At once he realised it was foolish to think of Andreas, a devout man of the Catholic Church, with no enemies. Andreas' faith and position in that persecuted oppressed religion would have assured him of enough enemies to last a lifetime, what little lifetime Andreas had had.

Tacit stumbled into a wall and held himself tight against it until his head had stopped spinning. A passing French soldier asked if he was alright, but the caustic glare he received to the question sent him sharply on his way. In that instant, Tacit felt sickened by the facile nature of the world. A soldier hadn't hesitated to help a fellow man in a street, but put a gun in his hands and he revelled in becoming a killer. Tacit muttered a passage from *Revelation* and swayed on into the night.

Now the facts were coming to him quickly. Whoever committed the crime had wanted to make a statement, make a point against the Catholic faith. Tacit knew that Orthodox Christians had long settled in the city and their ways were now growing in popularity, like a cancer. Just like weeds, the only way to deal with them would be by pulling them up by the roots. Tacit swallowed in anticipation and staggered on to where he knew their enclave to be.

They wouldn't want to talk tonight, to reveal who was responsible, to explain why. But that was their problem, it wouldn't be his.

He was fuming, bristling with fury, as he paced with exaggerated steps to the club he knew the Orthodox attended. He felt the sharp shimmer of adrenaline mix with the alcohol. It gave Tacit a potent mix of anger and invincibility.

He was relieved to find the club popular with Orthodox was still open, undamaged by bombs or failing trade. As he pushed the door open, he thought it ironic that he was pleased to find an Orthodox Christian establishment safe and well.

The barman's courtesy and welcome surprised him. He was expecting, and ready for, displeasure and possible violence, but instead received a friendly greeting from him, seemingly unperturbed at Tacit's appearance.

"Father!" he called, wiping down the bar with a towel, "a little off the beaten track aren't we?" He laughed and threw the towel to one side. There was a string band playing a perky tune and some of the patrons were doing dance turns on the available space in the cramped building. The air was heavy with smoke and incense. It made Tacit feel sick. He walked over to the bar, as the barman asked, "So, what are you doing? Recruiting or converting?" which brought a ripple of laughter from those nearby.

But Tacit was in no mood to laugh with the heretics. Spurred on with alcohol and disgusted at this jovial welcome, he shot forward and grabbed the man by the collar, dragging him over the bar to the crashing of glasses and bottles. Cries called out at once, turning to gasps and shrieks, when Tacit drew the man level with his eyes and head butted him hard across the bridge of the nose.

The barman went down like a stone, blood splattering across his face, the bar and floor. He scrabbled around, his hand to his nose, shuddering and floundering in shock and disbelief. A number of men drew forward out of the crowd towards Tacit. Before they could reach him, Tacit had dragged the bartender up off the ground and held him tight around the neck, his fingers dug deep into the man's neck, slowly strangling the life out of him.

"Take another step," Tacit growled drunkenly, "and I'll break his neck," he warned, lifting the barman clean off the ground in his fist. His feet dangled like a man on the gallows.

The men stopped in their tracks and glared at this intruder. They looked at each other, weighing up their chances of rushing the bull of a man. For the time being, they decided to stand and wait and see.

"Father Andreas, Father of Arras Cathedral," Tacit began, talking over the murmurs of the bar and the choking of the barman. "Murdered. Last night. At the Cathedral. Someone beat him up. Pretty bad. Someone who didn't much like a Catholic Father. Didn't like Catholics. He had no enemies. No reason for someone to kill him. Not that I can find. So, someone killed him who didn't like Catholics. Someone like you lot."

Tacit tightened his hand even more firmly around the neck of the barman so that his face turned crimson, and the sound that came out of him was a desperate, guttural choking.

"So," Tacit continued, peering around the club, his eyes unable to focus on anyone or anything, just peering, rolling like a blind man's eyes, "tell me who killed Father Andreas or your beer hop gets killed." Tacit gave the man's neck a squeeze. His leg seemed to jolt as if in his final death throes.

"We don't know anything!" someone cried.

"You're a crazy madman!" another voice called.

There was a movement of chairs and a slow wall of figures began to form around the bar and where Tacit stood.

Tacit looked about them. He was aware of ten, maybe twenty pairs of eyes on him. He might be able to take them. Then again, it might be tough.

But he was pissed off and fighting mad. That might even the odds a little. But the wine and the spirits. He'd had a bit too much to drink. And clearly these people didn't know anything. It was a bum steer. Bad advice. Bad idea to come here. And he reasoned that he didn't want to make a scene, not anymore. He might even have got away with not making one, as long as a brawl didn't kick off. He looked at the man in his grip and tossed him over towards one in the approaching crowd, stepping closer than the rest.

"If you hear anything," he growled, giving his hand a shake to relieve the tension within his fingers and flick the barman's blood from them, which had oozed from his pouring nose, "come and find me. I'm staying at the Hôtel Sur la Place," he said, belching loudly and stumbling backwards. He corrected the capello on his head.

"We'll come and burn it down, you bastard!" someone called, as Tacit reached the door.

"That would be murder," Tacit replied, raising a finger of warning, "one of the ten commandments. You break that, and I will come looking for you personally." He stood and stared at the crowd, before turning and stumbling into the street outside. He staggered to his knees and shook his head, fighting back the urge to vomit. *Bad mutton*, he reasoned. He wouldn't order the mutton again.

He picked himself up and stumbled on into the night. Tacit felt barren, unable to focus, to make sense of events. He found himself in a bar, several blocks from his own hotel, for a final drink of the night.

"Poldek Tacit," the figure dressed in Priest's travel gown of brown croaked, leaning alongside at the bar. "I'm surprised to find you in a place like this. You usually favour less salubrious surroundings."

Tacit slurped at his drink and set down the empty glass. Even in his drunken state he immediately recognised the short, squat figure of Father Strettavario. Strettavario was an old school Catholic. Tacit appreciated him for that. There was a rumour that once, many decades ago, Strettavario had been an Inquisitor himself. Tacit had never believed the rumour. Most Inquisitors died in their line of work before they made old bones. Strettavario was fifty, maybe sixty. Too old for an Inquisitor, too alive to have been one. But Tacit was aware that, wherever his assignments took him, Strettavario seemed always to be two steps behind him, walking, waiting, often appearing at a bar, late at night. Tacit was never sure if the Father was watching his back, or simply waiting for an opportunity to deliver the final death blow.

"I hear you're raising hell with our Orthodox friends?" the figure muttered out of the corner of his mouth. "Poldek, we can't have you going out and acting like a loose cannon," the Father said, when Tacit's attention had been drawn.

"Who's the loose cannon?" Tacit slurred, picking up his glass and finding it empty. "Just looking for answers."

"Yes, and like I said, you were looking in the wrong place. Pope Pius, God rest his soul, caused division, split opinion, caused problems, problems we need to heal."

"You don't need to give me the lecture," muttered Tacit, sagging heavily on an arm. "I know he advocated war, seeing it as a way of dealing with the Serbs, eh? Not such a bad thing."

"And that's exactly the point. What we don't need is word of an Inquisitor going around pursuing his own personal war against the Orthodox just inside the front line. Besides, they had nothing to do with the murder of Father Andreas."

"Cardinal Poré, he says it's Hombre Lobo."

"I know he does. If it is what he thinks it is, the werewolf's enjoying the hunt."

"Enjoying the hunt? What do you mean –"

"There's been a second murder. Father Aguillard. An hour ago."

"What's he doing in Arras? Father Aguillard resides in Mons?"

"Travelled here a few weeks back. Business in the area, according to his secretary. You know what he's like. Father of the people. Or was. Secretary though didn't know what the business entailed. He wasn't privy to any conversation or plans."

Tacit belched. "Obviously business didn't go well for him."

"Or it went too well," Strettavario countered.

Tacit stumbled on to his feet from the bar stool. "Need to sleep," he muttered, catching himself against the bar rail. "Long day tomorrow."

"Poldek," the Priest called, catching Tacit by the arm, as he turned to go, "They're after you, you know that, don't you? There's talk. About you. That you're off the rails, that you've lost your way." Tacit stared vacantly back at him, listing in his boots like a boat cut from its anchor. "Trust no one," the Father warned. The Inquisitor nodded dully and slumped away.

THIRTY FOUR

16:41. Tuesday, October 13th, 1914. Paris. France.

Bishop Guillaume Varsy sprinted into the northern entrance of Notre Dame from the Place de l'Evêché, his cassock pulled away from his scurrying feet by his left hand, his right snapped tight to his capello on his head. He leapt nimbly around a pair of visiting Parisians, calling an apology to them as he dived into the cool shadows of the Cathedral depths.

Ahead arrangements for the Mass for Peace were almost complete. The ambulatory for the choir had been decked with flowers and olive branches, woven with flair and skill around the shimmering marble and intricately carved wood of the raised platform before the nave where the congregated masses would sit. At the very end of the central aisle, resting bowed on his walking stick, Cardinal Bishop Monteria watched the final proceedings with a reverent look, entranced by the moving and beautiful testament to peace which had been erected before him. So captivated he was by what he saw that he only heard Varsy's cries when the young Bishop was a few strides from him.

"Good heavens!" Monteria exclaimed, staggering back at the sight of Bishop Varsy charging towards him, his hand reaching out for a pew behind where he stood in case he needed support. "What is the meaning of this?"

"Cardinal Monteria!" cheered the Bishop, beaming a broad white smile as he fought to catch his breath from his wild charge across the city. "The President! The President of France!"

"What about him?" retorted Monteria, thinking for the moment that the Bishop had been drinking, such was his level of excitement.

"President Raymond Poincaré!"

"Yes, I know who our President is!" he snapped. "What about him?"

"I have just received notice that he is to attend the Mass."

At this news, Cardinal Monteria did stumble backwards, catching himself against the pew.

"The President?" he muttered, his mouth wide. "Coming to the Mass?"

Varsy nodded inanely, like a child asked if they wished to dine on a plate of sugared bonbons for their supper.

Monteria settled himself into the pew, his hand to his chest.

"Everything," he muttered, shaking his head in disbelief. He looked up, his old eyes sparkling with renewed vigour and youth. "Everything is progressing according to plan!"

PART THREE

"The wolf has the strength of a man but the mind of nine men;
the bear has the strength of nine men but the mind of one."

Traditional Estonian Saying

THIRTY FIVE

07:23. Wednesday, October 14th, 1914. Arras. France.

The coffee hadn't worked. Sister Isabella still felt lumpen and tired. She sank her face into her hands and exhaled loudly. She groaned behind her fingers and rubbed her face in the faint hope that when she pulled her hands away she would wake up and find herself in the warm comfortable surroundings of the Vatican, a gentle assessment waiting for her on her desk, not like the one she currently faced. Maybe an assignment to tease a wandering hand from a young Bishop, already spotted admiring the younger female members of the congregation with eyes too eager for one of his station or position? How she'd welcome such an opportunity now.

Anything to avoid another moment in the company of *that* Inquisitor.

She took another glug of her coffee and rattled the cup into the saucer, rubbing an eye.

"He drew a revolver," she muttered disbelievingly, shaking her head and staring into the snaking trails of steam from the cup. "Who does that?" she asked, looking up at the Father watching her with a bored and vacant stare. "Pulls a revolver on a child? A chorister!"

Father Strettavario cleared his throat and sank his chin into his chest, so that the folds of his skin bunched like a beard of flesh. "Yes, you mentioned, last night. I thought I'd come and see you this morning. You seemed so … what's the word?"

"Disillusioned?"

"No. Revolutionary. I thought you might consider leaving the assessment?"

"I can't, can I?" she replied.

"No," Strettavario answered coldly, ending any further discussion about it.

"I'm not revealing anything more of myself to him," Isabella announced, looking over at the gown she wore yesterday. "I don't want his eyes on me." She slunk from her chair and gathered her travelling robe from the cupboard. It covered all but a circle of skin around her neck.

"He is being assessed. You must."

"He's a monster. Accept my report on him. He's a pervert. A deviant. He can't keep his eyes off me. Put that on record. Write that down, go on do it! I don't need to perform that role any more."

"But it's not true, Sister Isabella," countered her visitor, looking down his nose at her disapprovingly. "It would be a lie."

"Does it matter?" she retorted, brushing at the robe to free it of dust. "You want your report? There, I've given it to you. Tacit is a danger to women." She hung the robe on the door and looked back at him defiantly, her hands on her hips. "And about every other poor soul, as well," she muttered to herself.

"Very well," he said, writing something on the notes in front of him. "But we still need you to assess him regarding his faith."

"He has none!" she roared, as if the request was in some way ludicrous, flicking her head dismissively.

"You can't say that. Not without a thorough assessment."

"But if he had faith, he wouldn't behave in such an appalling manner. How can someone with faith be such … such a monster?"

"Actions don't always indicate faith, be it faithfulness or faithlessness. We need you to continue your assessment of Tacit," Strettavario continued, his eyes very serious. "He's engaged on the murder case. We need to see it through to fruition, however that might end."

"What about his methods? That poor chorister."

"Yes, I know. He went out last night. Beat up some people he thought might have been responsible for the Father's murder. People he thought might be useful to talk to. Orthodox Christians. Loosened their tongues a little."

She shook her head. "Are they all like him?"

"They have a hard job, Inquisitors. Sometimes it's hard for them to see the lines between right and wrong. They do the Church's dirty work. It's not always easy to stay clean. Of course, we want them to remain hard as iron; it's needed in their line of work. But it's our job to make sure they stay untarnished as well, as far as possible."

"Untarnished? Well Tacit's rusted shut," Isabella hissed, turning to look out of the window. She rested a hand against the edge of her wardrobe. She thought of her mother and her pride when her daughter entered the monastery. She wondered what she'd think if she could see her now, flirting with wayward Priests and dabbling with murderers.

"You should give him a little slack," said her hooded visitor. "Some think of him as a hero. Don't be dispirited," he said, putting the strap of his bag over his shoulder. "This is when you have the chance to shine, my dear. This is your job. Eyes are on you, important ones too. If you do well with this assessment, well, who knows where it might lead?"

THIRTY SIX

1897. Loznica. Serbia.

They stood on the outskirts of the settlement, a small collection of tents congregated around a well in the wilderness of western Serbia. As it did before every assignment, Tacit's heart beat hard within his chest. There too was the sickness in his stomach, the trepidation he always felt. But today he felt something more, something approaching repugnance, a shame at what he was about to do.

A cold breeze whipped up around them, shaking the walls of grey white tents and guy ropes of the nomadic settlers away in the distance. The Serbian town of Loznica lay just behind them. Within an hour, the settlement on the town's doorstep would be razed.

"Remember, they aren't like us," growled Tocco, checking his revolver and then feeling the weight of his studded mace in his left hand. "They're not normal people. They're heretics. They drive our faith and our God from these lands. They wish to see their Orthodox ways flourish. They trample our good Catholic name into the dirt. They call our Pope false. We need to send them a message. No mercy. No mercy for the heretics."

Tocco swung his arm and stretched his neck to loosen the tightening muscles. He looked over the young man next to him, armed similarly with a mace and revolver. "Forget what they might appear to be. Remember your past," he muttered darkly. "Don't forget what they did to you."

"I don't like you reminding me," retorted Tacit sharply, letting the weapons drop momentarily to his side. "I don't need to hear. Every time, every time we face an enemy, you remind me. I don't need to be reminded." There were tears in Tacit's eyes. He closed them and immediately he was there in the room, engulfed by the screaming, the men, the stench of their sweat, the wickedness of their laughter. The blood. The blood.

He trembled and his chest heaved.

"It's your past, Tacit," Tocco hissed, thumping his fist into Tacit's shoulder and holding it there. "You can't get away from it. It's with you. It's in you. You lived with it. Now *live* with it. Feed off its anger!"

A group of settlers from the camp had stepped out nervously to greet them. Tocco raised his pistol and without warning blew the top off the head of the tallest of the men. They squealed and instantly picked up sticks and rocks to defend themselves. A man with a dirty moustache ran up with a branch raised screaming.

Tacit thought of his mother.

The rest was easy.

THIRTY SEVEN

07:27. WEDNESDAY, OCTOBER 14TH, 1914. ARRAS. FRANCE.

Outside Tacit's hotel room, the morning was bright and clear: a stark contrast to how Tacit felt. His mouth felt like old cheroot rolling paper. Knowing it would be a mistake he opened his eyes, just a crack to peer out onto the new day. The room swirled into a blurred, churning maelstrom of light and grey shapes. The residue of last night's drinking lurched forwards and then hastily back, turning his stomach. He lay on his back with a hand across his eyes till the nausea passed. It didn't stay down for long. Tacit had known this sensation countless times, and countless times he'd felt a whole lot worse.

A long shadow was cast across the square by the Cathedral. A second night had passed without a single shell falling on Arras. Tacit would have allowed himself a moment to consider the possibility that the war was over, but neither his current mood nor general demeanour allowed for such positivity of thought. He gathered himself slowly out of his bed, onto which he had fallen last night, and watched people cross the cobbled plaza, enjoying the first of the day's sun, snatching conversations as they scurried about their business, colour in their voices and their movements. One day of peace and calm in the city and joy had begun to seep back into it. Tacit didn't like the sound of joy. It reminded him of sin.

He shivered and wrapped his arms about himself, rocking back and forth to try and get some warmth into his bones. His eyes fell on the brandy on the sideboard and he immediately stopped rocking. A dry tongue scratched across his lips. Nausea rose within him but anticipation too, anticipation of tasting the fiery liquid on his tongue. He staggered over and grabbed the bottle, stealing back to the bed and uncorking it. The first gulp made him retch. But only the first gulp. He ran the second glug from the bottle around and between the gaps in his teeth, sucking the liquor to the back of his throat. Already he felt better.

Tacit turned back to the gloom of his room and took a third, longer and more pleasurable swig on the bottle. If he had been looking out of the window, he'd have seen a darkly dressed Sister striding across the square, past the soldiers and into the building in which he was slowly reviving.

Moments later, the door to his room tore open.

"You were well out of line yesterday, Inquisitor!" Isabella cried, slamming the door so hard behind her that a trickle of dust fell from the ceiling beside her.

"And good morning to you, too," Tacit replied, turning the bottle in his fingers and lifting it so that the first of the day's sun caught in the amber depths of the liquid inside. He sat down on the end of the bed.

"There are guidelines you work within, you know?" the Sister continued, storming to the table and looking hard at the Inquisitor. The veins in her neck were straining against her skin, her face flushed. "Rules you follow! They're there for a reason, Tacit!" She pointed an accusatory finger at him. "We're a Christian family. Not a bunch of ... of monsters. You broke several of them in that interview, several rules, too many rules, enough to have you removed from this case, from your position with immediate effect."

Tacit shrugged. "Didn't hear you complaining too much at the time," he hissed. He was too tired for this, too ill to argue over the nuances of his interrogation techniques. "You needed to get the boy to talk. I got the boy to talk." He slammed the bottle down on the table and staggered wearily to his feet. He exhaled loudly, rubbing a hand across his face.

"He would have talked."

Tacit yawned and looked disinterested. "He talked," he said, in a tone which suggested the conversation was over.

Isabella shrieked, her hands and fingers wide, and threw herself down on the end of the bed, her fingers in her hair. "You're intolerable, Tacit! Do you know that?" she screamed at him, but naggingly knew he'd extracted the information from the child, no matter how dubious his technique. Not that his results were any excuse for the level of violence and intimidation used. She seethed and speared him with her glare.

The Inquisitor was staring out of the window again, his eyes on a pair of soldiers marching side by side, double time. He watched them pass up the full length of the square and then turn off into one of the side streets.

The Sister raised her head from a hand and was about to speak. Tacit spoke before her.

"This is the way it is with all Inquisitors," he said softly, and Isabella detected what she thought was sorrow in his voice.

Tacit looked across at her and noticed she was more appropriately dressed for a Sister today, more so than when she first stormed into his life. He would have been lying if he said he was pleased to see her conform. The full length brown robe covered her entirely from head to toe, save for a few inches of ankle and a thin semi-circle of flesh beneath her neck. He looked her up and down and scowled.

"What is it? Prefer me when I'm parlously dressed?" From where she sat Isabella could smell the sweetness of alcohol engulfing Tacit, the dark stubble on his chin. He smelt and looked as rough as dirt. She stood up quickly, giving the impression she wanted to fight.

He scowled and turned away from her. "In the twelfth century, not far from here, the Roman Catholic Church founded the Inquisition. Its sole purpose was to root out heresy, strengthen the Catholic Church, destroy our enemies, correct the misguided."

"Is this lesson intended to enlighten me, Inquisitor?"

Tacit ignored the question. "Heresy was so deeply rooted at the time that the Inquisitors of old had to work hard and it was not deemed enough simply to isolate the heretic and impart justice upon him or her. 'No husband should be spared because of his wife, nor wife because of her husband, and no parent spared by a helpless child.' A rhetoric we have upheld to this day. Root and branch justice, Sister. Root and branch. Within our torture chambers we Inquisitors spread out across the known world in our quest to drive heresy from the world. Within those chambers we bound and gagged, we stripped and we broke the heretics." He lowered his eyes onto Isabella and said, with relish, "And all this before we even set them upon our contraptions of torture.

"Once they had been strapped in to whatever contraption we felt appropriate, we used every skill we had learned, passed down from Inquisitor to Inquisitor, generation to generation, to extract information and a plea for forgiveness ahead of the stake's fiery release. Dismemberment. Dislocation. Flogging. Breaking of limbs. Burning. Beating. Suffocation. Rape. Gouging of eyes. Disembowelment. Drowning, with boiling water," he added, as an addendum. "Tearing of flesh. Butchery of bodies. Jellification of limbs by beating."

Isabella turned away at Tacit's recital. He caught hold of her and forced her to look at him again.

"Seven hundred and fifty thousand heretics *processed.* As a rough estimate." She turned again but Tacit caught her by the jawbone, drawing her back to look, holding her in his vice-like grip. "Seven hundred and fifty thousand over nine hundred years. And still counting," he murmured. He let go of her and turned back to the window. He filled his glass from the bottle on the table and necked two thirds of it in a vicious swig. "And you reprimand me for pointing a revolver at a boy of twelve?"

Isabella folded her arms and drew them tight in to herself.

He looked back out of the window, guzzling the rest of the liquor. "It's alright," he muttered, a resignation in his voice, something approaching regret. "You get used to it. You find a way."

Isabella watched him watch the square. He stood stock still, almost statuesque. She wanted to say something but she felt any words would be too clumsy for the moment. So they stood there in silence, Isabella's eyes on the Inquisitor, Tacit's eyes elsewhere.

"There was another murder," he said finally, looking over at her. "Last night. Father Aguillard. Same way. Murder, made to look like a werewolf attack. We should go there first."

He turned, slamming the tumbler down on the sideboard, striding past Isabella to the door. She caught him by the arm of his coat as he passed. He was solid. There was a weight about him, like stone. Intrigued, she drew her hand tighter around his biceps, forcing her long delicate fingers around it, like an iron anvil, thick and hard. She felt suddenly even more dwarfed by the man, vulnerable.

"I understand," she said, looking up into his face, feeling as if a veil had been partially lifted from her eyes. "I understand."

Tacit stared straight ahead, but his head nodded a fraction in approval. "Good," he said. And then he was away, stomping out into the corridor and down the stairs, his heavy boots thumping hard across the wooden floorboards. She watched him go. She thought back to when she stood in the Inquisitor's Hall of the Vatican, staring up at the young, proud, handsome portrait of an Inquisitor, Tacit when he was a younger man. She remembered the fire in his eye, the vague arrogance about his features, the tight cleanly shaven jaw, the strong nose, the jet black hair. What had happened to him? How had he become the man he now was?

She recalled the Cardinals' warning about Tacit before she was given the assignment, about the Inquisitor's power, both in body and mind. She shivered and hurried after him, tying her cape about her shoulders with quick nimble fingers as she went. She thrust it back across her shoulders, skipping to the stairs to catch him.

Isabella stood over the body and asked, "How do they know it's him? Father Aguillani? He's got no face."

Tacit's grunt could be heard from another room. "He has distinguishing marks. Birth mark on his right outside thigh." The Sister laid the cloth back over the torn face of the Priest and stepped in the direction of the Inquisitor's voice. She'd expected herself to blanch at the sight of the body, ripped and defiled as it was, but after seeing the body of Father Andreas laid in the crypt and having endured the gruff, dismissive attitude of Tacit for only a day, something had begun to harden within her, a new resolve, a determination not to bow or break. She heard Tacit shout, "It's also his apartment." She joined him in the bedroom, examining the open window of the room. "Door was locked from the inside. So he came home from Mass, locked the door behind him and was attacked as he stood in this room."

"Wonder why he locked the door?"

"I was thinking the same thing," Tacit replied, his eyes still firm on the window. "If you're a Father, you don't expect visitors, or unsavoury ones like the one he got. I wonder if he suspected he was being followed?"

"What's the connection then?" Isabella asked, ploughing the fingers of her hands through her hair to tie it into an unobtrusive plait. "Between Aguillard and Andreas?"

Tacit cleared something in his throat and scratched at his chin. "Doesn't seem to be one, at least not one I can see. Aguillard had visited Arras in the past, but that wouldn't have meant he'd met Father Andreas."

Isabella looked confused. Tacit explained.

"He was a travelling Priest, liked to take his sermons into the fields rather than deliver them in the constraints of the cities and towns. But he still had to return to civilisation every now and then to restock and gather new teachings. Whether he and Andreas met or knew of each other, I don't know."

The Sister had been watching Tacit hard. Something about the way he stood, staring eyes fixed on the window, intrigued her. "What is it?" she asked, sitting back on the edge of a chair and folding her arms.

"The assailant came through the window. No other way of entry into the residence."

"Unless he came through the front door."

"He'd need a key for that. And there's only one. Aguillard has that. No signs of forced entry that way."

"Is there with the window?"

"No, and that's my point. The assailant came through the window. There's no other way into the apartment other than through the window or the front door. We can discount the door, so he or she must have come in via the window. It's on street level. He opened it from outside, quite casually, drew it open and waited in here for Aguillani to come home. Quite calm. Quite prepared."

"And your point is?"

"Where's the devastation, the clawed walls, the upturned and shattered furniture, the smashed window? Where's the chaos which follows in the wake of one possessed with lycanthropy overwhelmed with rage and terror as sure as night follows day? This confirms what I thought earlier. We have someone who's got hold of a werewolf pelt."

"Werewolf pelt?"

Tacit had only encountered one werewolf pelt before, on the shores of the Black Sea, when investigating rumours of a cannibal living in the grounds of one of the churches there. The story went that thirteen members of the same family had been devoured in a single night, all that remained being their shoes and feet. Werewolf pelts were rare and malevolent things, cut from the bodies of living werewolves whilst in wolf form.

"Pelt, taken from a true wolf. Imbues the user with the wolf's powers but with a difference. The wearer is in control over their actions, their rage, at least to a degree, not like true wolves, not like Hombre Lobo."

"Well, looks like our killer's getting a taste for it. The power."

"Yes, and for Catholics."

Outside the door to the residence, they could hear the change in the rota of Catholic guards watching the door. It never failed to amaze Tacit how quickly the Vatican was able to get to crime scenes when they needed to and close them down.

"So what's the thread?" Tacit continued, blinking the last vestiges of the previous night's drinking out of his eyes. He bit hard into his lip. "Two Fathers murdered by someone masquerading as a wolf."

"And you're sure this isn't a true wolf?"

"The presence of bodies after the attack proves it's not a true wolf, as does the careful entry. When a true wolf attacks, there's nothing left. This is a planned attack, not a wanton one."

"So, where to now, Inquisitor?" asked Isabella, scratching the end of her nose.

"Seeing as we don't know the identity of this individual our opinions are limited. I think there's one place we should investigate. I just hope it gives us the information we need to catch this killer."

"And where's that?"

"Father Andreas' private residence."

THIRTY EIGHT

09:15. WEDNESDAY, OCTOBER 14TH, 1914. ARRAS. FRANCE.

It wasn't a grand building, nondescript would be the politest way of describing the residence. It was a cold stone construction tucked away at the very edge of the square where the Cathedral tower's shadow touched at sundown. There were no ornate doors welcoming returning Fathers from their communion or Mass or their work within the community, no greeting of gold scripture or holy mosaic to inspire visitors of the Priests. A single, solid plain dark wood door standing slightly ajar, set back in the sandy brickwork and up a low step, was the lowly entrance to the residence.

Tacit pushed his way in, almost filling the passageway with his size. He stomped his way to the wooden railed stairway and peered around it to the corridor beyond. Something drew his eye upwards and he climbed, taking the steps two at a time.

"Do you know where you're going?" Isabella called after him.

If he did, he didn't tell her. The stairs reached a landing thirty steps up and turned back on themselves, climbing again. Isabella was sure she could hear Tacit breathing hard, as he took the second set of steps without pause. At the top, the corridor plunged left into darkness. Along the right hand wall were a number of doors. One stood slightly ajar and there was a shuffling coming from within.

Tacit powered into the room, ready for anything.

Inside the room stood a fat man, dressed in work clothes, grimy and sweat soaked. He had a double chin, which wobbled whenever he turned his head , and a belly upon which he could comfortably rest a plate. From his face it was clear that Tacit's entrance had nearly shocked the life out of him.

"Where's all his stuff?" Tacit growled.

"Whose stuff? The Father's?" The man, dressed in trousers and a shirt, cuffs rolled roughly to his elbows, indicated the boxes. "All packed away."

"Who told you to pack up his stuff?"

"Who wants to know? You can't just storm into rooms scaring people."

Tacit took a step forward. Isabella caught him by the arm and drew him back. He surprised her by doing as she guided.

"We're investigating the Father's sudden demise," the Sister announced, stepping forward so that she could direct the conversation.

The man sized her up for a moment, and then stepped over to another box, which he manhandled to sit alongside the others had moved, huffing and straining with every ounce of his strength. "Yes," he said, his manner warming. "A bit of a shock. Particularly for Father Andreas."

"Who told you to pack up his stuff?"

"The powers that be?"

"The Vatican?"

"Cardinal Poré."

Isabella heard Tacit's breath harden. She didn't peer around.

"Any idea why?"

"Why?" the man replied. "Why am I packing up his stuff?" He laughed thinly. "Because he's dead!" The caretaker didn't look like a man much used to exercise. His neck and armpits were ringed with sweat. He mopped his brow with his handkerchief and exhaled loudly. "They need the space," he added, with a wave of it. "More Priests coming. One thing the Catholic Church has no shortage of is Priests."

"Where are these going?" Tacit asked.

"These boxes? Storage. Strange though," he said, picking up the penultimate box and struggling across the room with it.

"Strange? Why?" asked Isabella, as the man dropped it with a moan.

"Well, I've cleared out Priest stuff before. Usually it goes off to the family. You know, heirlooms, personal documents, keepsakes, all that stuff. But this stuff, it's all for storage, every last box."

"Perhaps he has no family?" Isabella suggested.

"No family?" the man laughed. "Father Andreas has family alright."

Isabella looked back at Tacit. The Inquisitor's eyes were fixed on the caretaker.

"Alessandro. Alessandro Dequois." He said it in a way as if he expected both visitors to know the name. He saw their reaction and shook his head with a sigh. "Alessandro Dequois, one of the finest butchers in Arras."

Tacit raised an eyebrow. "And can you tell us where this Alessandro lives?"
"I can do better than that. You help me shift this stuff downstairs and I'll take you directly to him. He's my neighbour."

THIRTY NINE

09:32. WEDNESDAY, OCTOBER 14TH, 1914.
THE VATICAN. VATICAN CITY.

Six ravens, squawking oily black shards in the blue heavens, circled three times around the figure crossing St. Peter's Square before coming to land in his wake. Cardinal Adansoni was walking as fast as his tired legs would carry him away from the Chair of Saint Peter and the Colonnades, his head down, his face as black as the birds pecking at his trail. He'd received word during a meeting with his younger acolytes that persons unknown were in his private quarters. Without delay he'd excused himself and left for his apartment.

"What is the meaning of this?" he called, stepping into the corridor which ran to the open doors of his residence, catching sight of a figure inside. The double doors had been flung wide and, as he neared, he saw more figures inside, black cassocked and keen featured, picking through open drawers of his desk, peering into cabinets standing against walls. At once he knew to which organisation the men belonged. He rested momentarily, a hand to the frame, catching his breath before he asked his question again, this time even more firmly. "What is the meaning of this? What business have the Sodalitium Pianum in my quarters?"

The bear that was Monsignor Benigni appeared from Adansoni's bedroom, clad all in black save for the collar of white at his neck. Behind his fine rimmed oval glasses, sitting snug against his well fed heavy features, his black darting eyes narrowed on Adansoni. A collection of newspapers was clutched in his pudgy right hand. He strode directly at him, the Cardinal retreating back out of the room, as if fearing he was to be physically assaulted by the large rotund man. As Benigni neared he clapped twice and, like obedient dogs, his team of men of the Sodalitium Pianum stopped in their searches and fell quickly into line behind him outside Adansoni's apartment.

"I asked what the meaning of this ... this intrusion is?" Adansoni demanded, regathering some of his nerve now that it seemed the Sodalitium Pianum were leaving. "Monsignor Benigni!" he roared, a sudden pique of anger thrusting out of him. "Answer me!"

At once the dark haired man at the front of the line, sweating faintly from his exertions, stopped and held up his hand, bent firm at the elbow. Behind him, the line of agents paused without word.

"Cardinal Adansoni," Monsignor Benigni began, his place at the head of the line unchanged, his eyes still firm to the corridor ahead, "you understand the work of the Sodalitium Pianum, the Fellowship of Pius?"

"I understand what it is you claim to do, to seek out those believed to be indulging in forbidden texts and doctrine. So why visit me? What have I, a loyal servant, done to attract your attentions?"

"It is not what you have necessarily done," replied Benigni mysteriously. "It is who you know," he added, before striding out of the corridor and into the depths of Vatican City.

FORTY

1898. Ural Mountains. Russia.

Inquisitor Tocco was acting strangely. He had been, for much of the journey to the Ural Mountains, irritable and prone to bouts of madness as they'd slogged across Eastern Europe, delirious and remote ever since they'd left the town in Kazakhstan Tocco had insisted on visiting, ahead of their climb into the southern foot of the mountain range.

"One night to replenish stores," he'd called to Tacit excitedly, as they'd approached the outskirts of the village. But the young Inquisitor understood what Tocco was really looking to replenish.

Tacit knew what was in the bottle Tocco fed himself. The Inquisitor never mentioned its contents but Tacit recognised the signs of laudanum, the lethargy in Tocco's movements, the remoteness of his presence after he imbibed. His stocks had run dry halfway across Europe and his mood had soured. But the Kazakhstan dealer's wares were well known to Tocco. He had frequented this place many times before when assignments had taken him north, the opium being deliciously bitter and strong. He knew he had only to hang on until they reached the herbalist's home and his redemption would be granted.

Tacit wasn't surprised or alarmed by his master's addiction. There wasn't an Inquisitor Tacit knew who didn't have a crutch of some sort to support him through the rigours of his work. To soften the blow. To mask the pain. He'd soon grown blind to Tocco's obsession. He rarely noticed how his master's tincture was forever glued to his lips.

"Remember," Tocco muttered dreamily, as he stumbled over a stone in the pathway behind the striding young disciple, climbing high into the mountains, "this is reconnaissance, not battle. We go to look and report back. We're not going to cause trouble, or go looking for it."

But in the closing dark, those words seemed to have turned foul. Standing on a rocky precipice, halfway up the ascent, Tacit's bright cold eyes fixed on the approaching figures, disfigured by the swirling mists and the ravaging wasteland in which they dwelt.

"We must go back," he heard Rocco call behind him, suddenly animated by the figures' appearance, "back to the cave we passed a short time ago. We're not fixed for battle. I'm not ready!"

They hadn't expected to find so many of the heretics gathered together, the apostates who'd been burning churches and stealing what they could. Tacit knew the Inquisitor was in no state to fight, poorly equipped for battle and ruined by his opium. But he knew they couldn't flee. There were too many of them and they were blocking the only possible route to escape.

Tacit knew they needed a magazined rifle if they were to have any hope of fighting them off, like the one the leader held in his hands.

Tacit felt the biting wind and heard Tocco cry, "What are you doing, boy?" as he raised his hands to show the approaching scrum of heretics that he was unarmed. There was laughter, and the pack gathered about him like dogs, a sharp kick to his knee and he was shackled as he fell.

He looked back and watched the clan swarm over the stoned Inquisitor; two shots rang out and then a cheer. He felt the shackles cut into his wrists. He'd bring a good bargaining price for the mob, a young one like him. The shackles were tight, but they'd been tied at the front. That was their first mistake.

The leader crouched close by, laughing as his men beat Tocco to a bloody pulp with stones and the handles of the pistols they carried. Foolish. They should have watched the captured young boy. A second mistake. It would be their last.

The first the leader knew about Tacit's escape was a foot striking him firmly in the chest. As he fell, Tacit snatched the rifle from him and had blown the leader's face clean off before he had even hit the ground. Heads turned away from the now mutilated body of Inquisitor Tocco.

Tacit targeted the bandits with pistols first, working the trigger and bolt of the Krag-Jørgensen rifle as if it were automatic. It had been adapted in its lifetime to house ten rounds. Tacit used every one of them. Nine bodies hit the hard stone. Now the rifle was a club.

He dashed the brains from the quickest of his attackers, the second man was sent tumbling over the edge of the cliff, his cry lasting several seconds before it was snuffed out by an abrupt landing on jagged rocks below. A third nonbeliever swung a fist holding a rock. He removed the thug's teeth with the butt of the rifle and crushed his windpipe with a second jab.

The two remaining figures hesitated and slunk back, their eyes on the boy and then each other. Tacit picked up a rock and hurled it at the figure on the left. It caved in the front of his forehead, crumpling him with a grunt to the ground. The other man yelped like the dog he was and turned. The young Inquisitor let him go, a warning to others that retribution for heretics was coming.

The footsteps of the fleeing bandit were swallowed up within the enveloping mists. Nothing but the sound of the wind could be heard on that rocky path where Tacit now stood. He looked over towards the pile of bodies lying motionless on the floor, spotting the thick forearm of his master amongst the misshapen torsos and limbs of the heretics. Tacit swallowed. He knew Tocco was dead. His master of the last five years was gone.

Once more he was alone.

The young Inquisitor took a step forward and at once the air around him erupted into brilliant light, bright balls of fire in front of his eyes, about his body. He shrieked and held out his hands in horror, turning them over and over, dashing left and right, waving away the flames in an attempt to extinguish them, expecting any moment to feel the searing pain of fire's angry touch.

But no pain came. There was nothing. No pain, no more fear. Instead Tacit was wrapped in nothing other than a feeling of complete protective warmth and peace, a feeling he could scarcely remember from any time previous in his life.

He looked about himself slowly, shining like a beacon on the side of the mountainside, and stretched out his arms wide. He shuddered, realising the light had lifted him from the ground and he was hanging in the air, inches from the path, bound by the might of some higher power.

And then a voice, just like his mother's, whispered in his ear.

FORTY ONE

11:00. Wednesday, October 14th, 1914.
Arras. France.

A deep, resonant bell had sounded the eleventh hour of the day by the time the landlord had moved all of Father Andreas' boxes from his residence, across the square and over to the Cathedral buildings. He wandered over to Tacit and Isabella, who had sat for the majority of the toil in the heat of approaching midday sunning themselves, dabbing his forehead and mumbling angrily under his breath.

"Well, thank you for all your help," he said sarcastically, wiping the back of his neck and forehead dry of sweat. "Did I mention that I had a heart condition and my doctor has recommended that I rest?"

"Then get another job," Tacit retorted, swinging his legs over the edge of the wall of the water fountain along which he had lain, recuperating. He was in no mood to help move boxes. If anything, he would have spent the time peering through their contents, but seeing as there were so many boxes and he didn't wish to arouse suspicion, he decided that an hour under the restorative sun would do him more good. Also the lead of Father Andreas' brother was an unexpected turn up. "Come on, let's go," Tacit clapped, helping Isabella from the wall with a politely offered hand.

"Go where?" the caretaker retorted. "I'm going for a drink first. You didn't play fair. If you'd offered to help, maybe I would have taken you there first. But seeing as you decided to lounge around waiting for me to finish my lugging, then you can damn well wait around while I do a bit of glugging."

Tacit stepped up to the man and, towering over him, shook his head. "I don't think so," he grunted. "You've kept us waiting long enough. Let's hop to it," Tacit barked, tugging at the man's coat sleeve.

The caretaker grumbled the whole way back to his house and that of Alessandro Dequois next door. When they arrived, at first they said that there must be some mistake. The house was a butcher's shop.

"He lives above the shop," the landlord gestured with his thumb. "And thank you again for your help," he said, gruffly, shuffling off to his own door. "If I die of cardiac arrest, I'll make sure you're not asked to give last rites."

"We should have helped him," Isabella suggested, watching the man slam the door of his home shut behind him. "If only to get here sooner."

"He clearly needs the exercise," Tacit growled back. "And I needed that rest. Come on, let's see what this brother knows."

Isabella grabbed the pull handled bell to the side of the wide shop fronted window. Only silence returned the greeting. Tacit pulled the handle again, more forcefully this time.

"It doesn't matter how hard you pull it," Isabella chided. "It's all on the same mechanism."

Tacit muttered something dark under his breath. He shoved his hands into his pockets and peered into the window of the shop.

"Looks closed," he mumbled, sniffing at something in his nose.

"Maybe he's in mourning?" Isabella answered, looking up the street. "Gone away. Wouldn't be surprised. If you'd lost your brother."

The Sister stood back from the building and peered up its front towards the large bay window facing down onto the street. The curtains were drawn, the room beyond dark, deserted. She turned away, looking up the street. At that moment, a dark haired woman appeared at the far end of it. She took a few steps in and then, on seeing Isabella and Tacit outside Alessandro's house, checked her step.

"Tacit!" hissed Isabella, the urgency of her tone spinning the Inquisitor to look.

Immediately, Sandrine took a couple of short steps back to the corner from which she had appeared, turned and vanished around it.

"After her!" cried Tacit, bounding up the street with his long thunderous strides. Isabella was moving with him but was lighter and swifter, running like a gazelle despite her heavy travelling robes. She flew down the street in front of him, skipping into the road down which Sandrine had slunk. At the far end of it, a hundred yards away, Isabella could see Sandrine dart right into a side street. She was quick.

Without pausing to think, pausing to look back for Tacit, Isabella shot after her, her arms pumping like pistons, her Sister's habit gathered up and drawn tight to her body as she ran. She reached the side street just as Sandrine turned off it, far off in the distance. It was a narrow and cobbled lane. There was a collapsed building halfway along it; rubble spewed out across it. She set off down it, leaping the rubble in a single bound.

She could hear Tacit huffing hard behind her, his heavy footsteps clacking echoes between the houses. Isabella thrust her head down and found another gear in her legs, tearing into the street down which Sandrine had flown. Her heart beat. The wind whistled in her hair and past her ears. She felt alive and charged.

Then, unceremoniously, she thudded head first into a baker coming the other way, loaves and baskets scattering in all directions. They went down in a cursing, tumbling tangle, dashing knees and elbows, as they fell and rolled. Tacit appeared around the corner and recovered the Sister from the man with whom she had collided. He was shouting and cursing, but his words were swallowed up when the immense figure of the Inquisitor loomed over the top of him and swiped the Sister away.

"She turned right at the top," Isabella cried, trying to find her rhythm again above the ache in her knee. Her lungs burnt, her arms and legs stung from the fall.

"She's quick," puffed Tacit, soaked with sweat.

They reached the turning and instantly stopped, hugging the wall for breath, trying to get oxygen into their tightening lungs. Ahead was a dead end. A row of terraced houses on the left and right led to a solid wall, as high as the houses either side of it.

They had her.

Breathing a little more gently, the pair wandered slowly into the cul-de-sac, their eyes wide, darting about them, their senses sharpened, looking to see any movements which might be the woman attempting to climb out of the dead end to freedom.

"You hear a door open?" Tacit demanded to know, looking along the row of terraced houses and their front doors.

Isabella shook her head.

"Me neither."

He stood in the middle of the dark cobbled street, halfway between the junction and the dead end, and turned slowly around on the spot, peering about himself in every angle. Some trickery was at play. Either that, or Isabella had been wrong and the woman had not turned right at all. For Sandrine had vanished.

Suddenly Isabella called, "Tacit! Here!"

She was looking down at a flagstone near to the far wall. The large grey coloured stone had been moved to one side, revealing a dark hole descending down into the darkness beyond.

Their eyes touched for the briefest of moments and then Tacit was heaving the large flagstone to the side to allow better access inside. They peered down into the gloom.

"Ladder," said Isabella, indicating the rusted bars sinking down into the blackness.

There was a damp vague smell of mould which rose up from the depths.

"Must be the medieval tunnels Cardinal Poré spoke about," said Tacit, his breath slowly gathering itself. He looked back up the street to the junction from which they had come. He passed the flat of his hand across his eyes, wiping sweat from them, and looked back into the blackness below.

"After me?" he asked, looking at the Sister and then back to the hole. She nodded and at once he clambered forward, dropping himself down onto the first rungs of the ladder, sinking slowly into the gloom.

Isabella watched him vanish into the yawning mouth. She hesitated for a moment and then lent forward to follow.

"It's alright," Tacit called wryly. "I won't look up."

It was almost pitch black in the tunnel. The ladder sank twenty feet down onto a hard chalk floor. The air was damp, cool, heavy with a musty smell of lichen and stale vegetables. From the light above they could make out the walls of the cavern, ten feet wide, roughly hewn from the chalk beneath the city. In front of them ran a narrow low tunnel, only darkness within it, only darkness beyond.

Tacit stepped forward and forced his way into it, his body almost too big for the opening to the tunnel. Isabella went after him, her more delicate frame more suited to the confines of the passageway.

Within a few steps, neither of them could see a thing.

"Completely black," Tacit called back, his hand on the wall beside him, feeling his way. He stopped and hung his head, gathering his breath.

"We can't go on, Tacit. It's too dark. She must have left herself a lantern down here."

Tacit peered on into the gloom. "Damn it!" he roared, and whacked a clenched fist into the smooth chalk of the right hand wall.

FORTY TWO

11:24. Wednesday, October 14th, 1914. Arras. France.

Isabella was still brushing the chalk dust from her clothes when Tacit wrenched on the door pull outside Alessandro's house in a second and now even more heated attempt to try and raise some response from inside. The hand pull reminded Tacit of the bell used to announce guests at the residence of an old Father in Prague. Tacit had broken the Father's front four teeth and his left arm the time the Father had laid a hand on his thigh when Tacit was fifteen. The Father later claimed he'd fallen down the stairs.

Isabella found herself smiling as she looked at him.

"You look like you've climbed out of the crypt," she said, raising an eyebrow and a smirk.

Tacit scowled. "You shouldn't say such things."

"For the Lord's sake. Does everything need to be so dark?" The tone of her voice caught Tacit by surprise.

"What's there to lighten up about?" he replied, grumbling and dragging on the door pull again.

"Life! Look around you,Tacit."

The Inquisitor peered about himself absently and then shook his head. His hand was back on the bell pull. "We lost our main suspect," he moaned, dragging on the pull again. "That is nothing to cheer about."

"Don't you ever realise the beauty that's around you?" asked Isabella, her face breaking with joy. Tacit caught sight of it, and didn't like it. "Don't you ever want to embrace what life is giving you?"

Tacit gave her a lean stare. "No," he spat, shaking down the sleeve of his coat.

"What is it with you?" Isabella cried, surprising herself at her reaction to the Inquisitor's dismissive attitude.

"We've chosen a path," he answered, his hand still on the pull. "You'd be wise to remember that, Sister."

"And why must the path be so dark, eh?" she hissed back, stepping towards him.

"You're not an Inquisitor," Tacit barked back, "you wouldn't understand."

"I understand people. I understand a little about life. Tell me, Tacit, when did it get so dark for you?"

The Sister was surprised to see Tacit turn his head away, as if he didn't want her to see his face. "What is it?" she asked, looking to see what Tacit was hiding from her. She peered around his bulk and was sure she saw a pain in his eyes, a real human pain. "Tacit?" she muttered, coming forward with her hands raised to place on him. "I'm sorry if I've said anything ..."

At once the Inquisitor's face hardened. A blackness forged itself within it.

"Enough talk," he snarled, heaving hard at the bell pull. "Like I said, you wouldn't understand."

A light from a lantern wavered at the far end of the butcher's shop and a figure stepped slowly up to the front of the glass, drawing both Isabella and Tacit towards it. Alessandro stood behind the plate glass, dishevelled and unkempt, straining to see who was bothering him.

"Who is it?" he asked.

"Alessandro?" Isabella called through the window.

"Who is it? What do you want?" The appearance of unexpected and unknown visitors when he felt at his most exhausted unnerved him.

"We're here about your brother. We'd like to ask you a few questions."

"I've already spoken to the Church," he answered.

"We're not with them."

"Then who are you?" he asked, looking them up and down and finding himself wondering if there was some carnival taking place in the city. "I've got nothing to say. And I've got none of his stuff, if that's what you're after."

"Alessandro Dequois!" roared Tacit, his face tight against the glass. "Get this door open and save yourself having to buy a new one!"

The kitchen was heavy with the faint smell of rot and nicotine, the residue of animal blood staining every surface. A small rickety table, one leg damaged, stood in the centre of the room with two equally wonky, and seemingly broken, chairs. Alessandro pulled at his shirt and explained that he lived alone.

"Ever get visitors?" asked Tacit, noticing the large bottle of cognac, partially drunk, and two glasses beside it.

Alessandro said nothing about Sandrine.

"No," he said.

"I heard you were quite the socialite," replied Isabella, walking over to the far side of the kitchen and resting her weight against the side of the sink. The caretaker had heard of Alessandro's political views, of his well attended gatherings, and had passed this information on to the Inquisitor and Sister. "Quite the radical, I was told."

Alessandro put his heavy eyes onto Isabella and then onto Tacit. "What is this?" he asked. "What's this all about? My brother dies of a heart attack and you come round, whoever you are, and start insulting and intimidating me?"

Isabella and Tacit's eyes met. Alessandro caught the sign between them.

"What?" he asked. "What is it?" he demanded, his hands suddenly clenched tight together.

"Is that what they told you?" asked Isabella, resting back on her elbows. "The Cathedral?"

"About the heart attack? Yes. Why?"

"Mister Dequois," grunted Tacit, "I suggest you sit down."

FORTY THREE

AUGUST 24TH, 1914. PARIS. FRANCE.

They talked long into the night, Cardinal Bishop Monteria barely pausing for breath as he unveiled his plans, Cardinal Poré listening to his every word, his eyes growing wider as the night grew darker and the Cardinal Bishop's vision became more daring and clearer. For most of the time Poré sat in silence, his hand fixed to his chin, his mouth dry, his wine standing untouched to the side in his goblet. How could he think about drinking at this time when such revelations were being unveiled. Only occasionally did he interrupt Monteria's flow, interjecting with suggestions of his own, raising occasional doubts, posing questions, both of faith and logistics.

But mostly he found himself congratulating the Cardinal Bishop on his audacious vision. "It is brilliant!" he muttered, when at last Monteria finished talking, tears coming to his eyes at the wonder of such a plan. "A Mass for Peace to bring all the peoples of the world together!" he exclaimed, candlelight flashing in his glistening eyes.

"To leave a lasting legacy for all to remember," replied Monteria gently.

"We have no time to waste." Cardinal Poré could feel the urgency rise like an energy inside him.

"Leave all the arrangements at Notre Dame to me," said the old man, reaching for his wine to clear his parched throat. He paused and looked hard at Poré. "Are you sure I can rely on you to carry out your side of the bargain?"

"Don't worry," Poré replied, lowering his head so that shadows gathered in his eye sockets, "leave everything else to me."

FORTY FOUR

11:31. Wednesday, October 14th, 1914. Arras. France.

Alessandro was truthful when he said he rarely received guests, but he was fond of visits from *one* of his friends, Paul Govain, a political sparring partner from the market with whom he shared a common interest – if rarely a similar view – in anything to do with the politics of the day. Debates between them would take place long into the night over a meal or just drinks, about politics, the market, the war. The two rickety chairs in the kitchen served a purpose – too uncomfortable to constrain thinking or encourage sleep. He explained this to the Inquisitor and Sister, as he went off to find a third chair and one sturdy enough to hold the bulk of Tacit. He returned a few minutes later brandishing a large oak chair with ornately sculpted arm rests.

"My thinking chair," Alessandro said, setting it down next to Tacit. The Inquisitor sat in it and looked like a pious judge. He took off his black capello hat and placed it on the table in front of him.

The coffee pot began to sing, filling the kitchen with its sweet rich aroma, masking the rancid stench of week-old meat from the kitchen tops and shop below. Alessandro removed the pot from the hob with a cloth and set it on a stone mat on the table.

"Would you like me to do that?" asked Isabella, watching the young man gather white chipped cups and a sugar bowl, rattling them with his trembling, tired hands. Tacit peered out of the window onto the Arras skyline. The bright hot weather was beginning to change. Bad weather was starting to move in. He could hear the sound of distant gunfire, the dull thud of exploding shells somewhere along the front. The Germans had found their voice again. He wondered if Arras would shortly be in their sights once more.

Alessandro shook his head at the Sister's offer of help and put the cups down on the table. "Can you hear them?" Alessandro asked, collecting some small spoons from a drawer. "The shells? At the front? Boom, boom. I thought I'd heard the last of them." He set himself down at the table and poured the coffee into the three cups. It looked as strong as death. "Hope you like it black? I've no milk or cream."

"No, black is fine,' Isabella replied.

"Been no milk for the last week. All this boom boom. Stopping supplies, I suppose. Not much of anything anymore. And I've not been out. Not for the last, I don't know, how many days or so." He shook his head and set the coffee pot down on the stone. He rubbed his eyes and then closed them for a while, lost in private thought.

"So," he said, drawing the word out as if expelling the weight of misery from inside him by doing so. "Tell me then, what's going on? What has happened? Don't treat me like a fool," he added, firmly.

"What do you know?" asked Isabella, "so far?"

Alessandro shook his head slowly. "First of all," he said, looking from one to the other, "who are you?"

"We're –" started Isabella but Tacit spoke over her.

"We're from the Vatican. We're here to investigate your brother's murder."

"Murder?" replied Alessandro, his head and features dropping. Isabella shut her eyes and shook her head incredulously.

"Your brother was brutally murdered two nights ago, as he closed up the Cathedral for the night. We don't know who was responsible but we have our suspicions."

"Murder?" Alessandro repeated, looking across at the Sister and then back at Tacit. Isabella's eyes were away in the corner of the room. If she could have throttled Tacit for his indelicate impatience, she would have, there and then. The Church had done much to assure that the crime had been recorded and conveyed as an expected and tragic death. They wouldn't take kindly to an Inquisitor going around revealing the truth.

Tacit looked at Alessandro. "Mr Dequois, do you know any dark haired women?"

Alessandro's looked back at Tacit.

"Dark haired women?" he stuttered, his hand working its way up his chest towards his neck. "What sort of a question is that? I know lots of dark haired women!" He said it firmly, too firmly, and Tacit's eyes narrowed.

"There was a dark haired woman. Seen at the Cathedral shortly before your brother was murdered. Who she was, we don't know. What she was doing there, we don't know. She might have nothing to do with the murder but we need to talk to her to find out."

Alessandro could feel the muscles in his chest tighten. He could feel his heart thump inside him, sweat prickle his forehead. He took up his cup and clutched it in both his hands to hide the tremble in his fingers from the sorrow and exhaustion in his heart. The light from the lantern and the candles still burning from last night drew shadows across his face and gave him an even more grievous look. He stared into the middle distance, his coffee sitting untouched in his hands.

"There was a woman we saw," Tacit continued, "outside your house. Just now."

Alessandro quickly stared at Tacit. "Who are you?" he demanded, putting down his cup.

"We're from the Church," replied Isabella, calmly.

"The woman?" Tacit pressed, his voice growing firmer.

"Why'd you want to know?"

"She was here, outside your house. She was there, before the death of your brother. We need to find her. And it seems to me you know who she is." Tacit leaned forward so that his entire weight was on his knuckles. They pressed into the creaking table beneath him and he thrust his face within inches of Alessandro's. "And seems to me that if you know who she is and you ain't saying then you've got something to hide. And hiding something in a murder enquiry, particularly the murder of your brother, is a serious offence."

"I need a drink," mumbled Alessandro, a tremor in his voice. Alessandro stared at Tacit. Tacit stared back.

Alessandro stepped away, over to the cupboard, and drew out a bottle of liquor. Tacit noticed he left the good quality cognac on the side.

"Present from someone?" he asked, indicating the voluminous bottle.

Alessandro ignored him. He gathered three glasses from a cupboard.

"I won't have any," Isabella said.

Alessandro ignored her.

"Drink," Tacit ordered Isabella, as the butcher set the glasses down on the table and uncorked the bottle. He poured three large measures into each of the glasses and pushed two of them towards the Sister and Inquisitor. He took a large swig and pulled a face against the burn. Tacit necked his in a single pull and poured himself a second.

"Please, help yourself," Alessandro called sarcastically.

"I will," he replied, filling his glass again. He proffered the bottle to Alessandro who necked the rest of his drink and set his empty glass in front of Tacit to be filled again.

"Your brother was murdered," Tacit began. "I'm sorry about –"

"How did he die?" Alessandro interrupted. He finished his second glass and shook his head as the liquid scorched his insides. Tacit refilled his own.

"Someone set upon him, beat him up. Badly. No man could have lived through what they did to him. Your brother, did he have any enemies?"

Alessandro laughed cruelly. "Enemies? He was a fucking Priest!" He held up a hand to Isabella in apology, who shrugged it off.

"Priests have enemies like anyone," Tacit suggested.

"Not my brother. He cared. Cared too much, if anything."

"This woman. She gave him a package, that day, before he was killed."

"Oh yes? Was that all she gave him?" Alessandro replied, with a smirk.

"Your brother know a lot of women then?"

"Lots. A lot of women attend church, you know?"

"This woman who came to visit your brother, she was outside your house an hour ago. Who is she? She knows you, or knows where you live." Alessandro stared into the bottom of his glass. Tacit continued. "Dark haired. Tall. Beautiful, from what I could tell. Ring any bells?"

Alessandro necked his drink and pushed it forward for Tacit to fill.

"Oh, I know her alright," he said, taking back the replenished glass. "Sandrine. Sandrine Prideux." He shook his head, almost a little sadly.

"And how did your brother come to know Miss Prideux?" Alessandro laughed again, but their was no warmth within it. "How do *you* know her?" Tacit asked, changing tack.

Alessandro shrugged. "I thought perhaps we were lovers. Perhaps my brother thought the same of her." He sat back, his eyes lolling with the alcohol and emotion. "Sandrine, she knew a lot of men."

"But your brother was a Priest."

Alessandro laughed coldly. "That meant nothing to him, not when Sandrine was involved. She had something, you know, that power, almost a power – "

"Over men?"

"Over people. Something irresistible. Something … you'd do anything for Sandrine. Whoever you were."

"Was she his girlfriend?"

Alessandro looked sadly down into his glass. He almost appeared to shrivel in size before the pair of them. A sadness drew across his face.

"Maybe?" he said with a shrug. "I wouldn't be surprised. Who wouldn't want to be her girlfriend? She was … magnificent. Beautiful and spirited and vulnerable. Everything, rolled into one. But if he was her boyfriend, he never told me."

"And she lives in Arras, this Sandrine?"

"Arras?" replied Alessandro. "She doesn't live in Arras!" He said it like a scoff, as if he thought everyone knew of Sandrine, of where she originated from.

"She doesn't?" asked Isabella, stealing forward. "Then where?"

"Fampoux," replied Alessandro, draining his glass. He turned and looked at the Sister and the Inquisitor. "She lives in Fampoux."

FORTY FIVE

11:32. Wednesday, October 14th, 1914.
Fampoux. Nr. Arras. France.

Lieutenant Henry Frost had found a table which, remarkably, still had its legs after being buried in much of the wreckage of the house. He also found a chair, plain light coloured, possessing all of its legs as well. It was a start.

He set the two by the broken window, looking out onto a rubbled side street to the ruined houses opposite. It wasn't much of a view, but it gave him some natural light on the unit diary as he wrote. After all, there was much to document. The artillery strike. The German trench. Fampoux. The patrol which never returned from last night's sortie. He stopped and thought about each man who'd gone forward and never came back. He wondered what had happened to them, what the Germans were doing to them now; for surely they'd run into a German patrol themselves, or stumbled into the German front line and been taken prisoner. He hoped they were being treated well, according to the Geneva Convention, according to the morals of man. It might be war, but they were all still gentlemen.

One thing it proved to Henry was that the Germans weren't beaten, that they were still entrenched in the nearby land. Almost on cue, the whining shriek of a barrage sounded from the east, thundering down on the far outskirts of the village. The rolling, shrieking roar sent men tumbling and careering for cover, men who twenty hours earlier had proudly stood in the ruins of Fampoux and boasted of their invincibility, of the might of the British Expeditionary Force and the cowardice of Fritz. Now they ran, charging and plunging for their holes, like foxes from a hunt.

The barrage was brutal and purposefully mean, an inhuman rampage of shells and explosive rounds full of venom and spite at the Germans' loss of Fampoux. Henry sat and listened with trepidation to the falling bombs, the cries of the injured. The French boy with the perfect teeth suddenly appeared at the window, making Henry jump and curse.

"Les Allemands viennent!" he cried and then laughed before skipping away – "*The Germans are coming!*"

A cold trepidation swept over Henry. Urgently, he stood and crossed to the far window, one which gave him a better view of the land to the east of the village. There was nothing to suggest the Germans were on the charge, no grey silhouette or slow gathering of men, bayonets glinting, eyes fixed firm to the western horizon. He chuckled and gently cursed, shaking his head at the image of the boy giggling and running away. It alarmed him that he could turn from cold panic to wry humour in the split of a second. He wondered how much more this war would reveal about himself. A fly buzzed about his face and he chased it away with a hand. Unlike the birds, which took flight at the first sound of falling bombs, the flies seemed defiantly resilient under the barrages. But they'd be foolish to leave such choice delicacies of the dead upon which to feed.

The thought of the dead drew the question of the boy's parents into Henry's mind. He wondered what had become of them. It was a pointless thing to consider and Henry quickly gave up on the idea. Henry was slowly accepting that in this war, people simply vanished, never to be seen again.

His mind turned to his own parents and his younger brother. He checked his watch and considered what they might be doing at this very moment, over the channel, back in Britain. He supposed his father Thomas would be at work at Flitchards, studiously studying lines of accounts, estimating dividends, calculating profit margins and expenditure for the company's clients. Later he would leave for home, a short walk through the Cathedral grounds of Salisbury into Harnham and the small family home on the river.

Thomas would spot his teenage son Ralph hanging by an arm from his favourite tree, or doing something equally ridiculous in their garden, as he reached the apex of the bridge across the River Avon, and he'd be considering whether he had time to slip into the Rose and Crown for a quick half before supper was on the table. His mother Ethel's meals were legendary. It was said she could make a feast out of a famine. Henry licked his lips unconsciously and heard his stomach groan.

A bitter longing for home came over him. He'd been away from home with the army many times before. After all, he was a professional soldier. It was his life now. But he'd never been out of the country for so long in such conditions. Whenever he returned home, he secretly cursed the cramped living conditions, the sterility of the life presented, its regimented sameness, and couldn't wait to leave. Now, it was all he wished to know.

To the backdrop of the falling bombs, he sat down at his desk and began to write: detailing the capture of Fampoux, the digging of trenches beyond the village's reach, the lack of resistance from the German forces, the fact that you could now turn around and see the joint British and French line behind you whilst Pewter's unit was moving ahead. The thought both charged and concerned Henry. Great gains had been achieved but, having moved forward, he was painfully aware they had pushed ahead of the accompanying lines either side of them. They were exposed on three sides, as if they had forced themselves forward into the jaws of the enemy, and at any time Fritz could take a bite.

He wrote with conviction, his tongue always firmly wedged between his teeth, his studious eyes fixed to the paper. He recalled the endless hours of handwriting practice, the sharp bite of the cane from the master when a character ran over a line, when a word was misspelled. How he had hated handwriting lessons at Winchester. But, as he looked proudly at his manuscript in the pale light of the Fampoux sun, he had a new found appreciation for them and the tyrannical master who corrected mistakes with corporal punishment.

This was how Sandrine found him, bent over the diary recording the developments in the unit, when she walked into her home. Henry nearly jumped out of his skin at the sight of her and reached for his revolver.

At first he thought her grey with age, courtesy of chalk dust, until she began to beat the dust out of her hair. He was instantly smitten by her loveliness, despite her bedraggled appearance. There was a flair and easy style about how she stood and held herself, about how she moved.

"Who are you?" she demanded curtly in French, one hand still on the edge of the door in case a sudden escape was required. Despite many hours in the tunnels between Arras and Fampoux, her senses were still honed, her mind full of distrust, her heart still beating hard within her chest. She'd cursed herself for her stupidity at returning to Alessandro's house. Returning for what?

For a loving reunion with him? As soon as she'd been told of Andreas' death she knew, somewhere and somehow, things had gone badly. To have gone back to his house had been too foolish a thing to have done. She'd found the body in the crypt, she'd seen the wounds with her own eyes. What was to be gained by returning to Alessandro? To tell him the truth, that no heart attack had killed his brother? She'd chastised herself for her good heart. She knew she had a responsibility, which stood above any such reckless care.

For all she knew, Alessandro was now probably dead too. Had she been a moment slower in recognising the danger in that street, she too might have been dead. The Priest and the Sister, they looked like killers, particularly the Priest. The net had closed. There was no question in her mind that they'd come to that place in the hope of finding her, perhaps to kill her, to silence her and the plans she'd helped to put in place. She'd experienced the ruthlessness of the Catholic Church first hand. She knew when it acted, it acted without emotion or hesitation.

When she'd pulled herself out of the tunnel hole into the light of Fampoux, her mind was still a rage of doubt and worry. How much had the Church uncovered? How much did they know of the plot? But she knew there was nothing that could be done. She just prayed that the plan still did remain undiscovered, unchanged.

Henry put down his pencil and brushed at his clothes. The fly returned and Henry rather impressed himself by catching it in the snatch of a hand.

"Lieutenant Henry Frost," he said, proffering his other hand and a smile.

Sandrine ignored it.

"What are you doing in my house?"

"Your house? Oh sorry. Uh, writing," he replied, hesitantly in French. He stepped to one side and indicated the open tome on the table.

"Writing? Writing what?"

"Our achievements." Henry shrugged and felt foolish and arrogant to have used such a word. "Events, in our unit's life."

"British?" Sandrine enquired. It was a silly question. She could tell from his accent he was as British as bowler hats and pipe smoke.

"Yes." Something about the woman transfixed him. He watched her shake herself down. "Have you ..." He stopped. "I am sorry, my French is not that good."

"Then you should have tried harder at school," Sandrine retorted in English for the first time, tying her hair back in a plait, once she was sure as much of the chalk dust as possible had been removed.

Henry laughed.

"Yes," he said. "I suppose I should. I apologise. I was just going to ask, have you climbed out of the ruins? You look, well, dusty?"

Sandrine ignored him. She was stepping her way slowly through the house, her hand to her mouth in horror.

"I'm sorry," called Henry, stepping after her. "I haven't had a chance to tidy up."

The Germans had made a mess of Sandrine's home. It seemed that everything they could ransack or damage they had. The windows had been smashed in, doors splintered. Every piece of furniture had been pushed over and emptied, all Sandrine's belongings ripped out, torn and hurled around the place. A dreadful stench hung in every room so stubbornly, it was as if the awful odour had actually seeped into the very fabric of the building.

The Germans seemed to have taken delight in wanton destruction, every plate in the house used and then thrown into a wall, every glass smashed. She stepped through into the pantry, her shoes crunching on the broken crockery as she went, and, as expected, she found the shelves stripped bare, all her jars and pots of carefully stored produce, her curing meats and vegetables gone.

She had stayed longer than most of the residents in the village when the Germans had first appeared on the horizon, a reluctant hurrying stream of refugees pouring out from Fampoux to the west. She hadn't wanted to go. She was needed in Fampoux. She had errands. She'd watched the slow progression of people tread past her house, residents driving their carts and livestock in ragtag clumps of a fleeing nation: the cranking turn of a wagon wheel, a low moan from their livestock, the shrill cry of a terrified infant. There was rumour of dark happenings within villages further east when the Germans arrived; tales of rape and torture as the invaders looked to gather information as to what lay ahead of them and take possession of what they could.

"Come away, Sandrine!" villagers had called to her, as she stood at the doorstep of her home. "Come with us before they arrive."

She'd watched the Germans' appearance on the horizon, the vague outline of a vast black army, trundling forward with their huge machines and their innumerable grey and black clad soldiers, rifles slung across shoulders, Pickelhaubes shimmering in the late summer sun. At first, barely audible above the cacophony of panicked cries and screams from those residents who had stayed, the sound of music came. As it grew louder, people stopped in their dashing about to gather their belongings and escape and, instead, turned and looked in the direction from where it was coming, out along the main road east towards Fampoux. Now the music was ringing out clearly in the air of summer morning, music from a marching band, the voluptuous thump of the bass drum, the shrill heights of the piccolo. A man shouted out 'The Faithful Hussar' and all heads turned in wonder towards this army who were playing songs as they conquered.

Row upon row of soldiers, dressed in sharp uniforms, short boots of black untanned leather, huge knapsacks straining at the seams, picks, spades and other utensils clanking from straps of the backpacks, rifles slung over shoulders, marched up the road in precise and efficient lines. At their front marched a military band, boots gleaming, instruments glinting in the early morning sun. As they neared the village, a great crowd of residents waiting for them caught hold of the tune and joined them.

So it was that the Germans took Fampoux, amid cheering and singing from the residents who stayed.

But quickly the Germans had rounded up those who had stayed behind and interrogated each of them to find out what they knew of the defences ahead, who they were and what they could offer in the village. Four men were taken out into the main square and shot without hesitation when they refused to part with information deemed pertinent to the war effort. Only a few women had stayed with their husbands or out of loyalty to their village. That evening, as the officers billeted themselves within residences, they took turns raping those women who had stayed behind, as means of recovering and recuperating from their long and arduous push across France. The husbands, if not shot for resisting the crimes beforehand, had been forced to watch and then taken to the main square and shot afterwards.

After all, why did the Germans need villagers who no longer respected their new masters?

Three officers had been billeted at Sandrine's home that first night. They'd wolf whistled and grabbed at Sandrine several times as she'd made her way around them in the small house, pulling at her clothes and cupping her breasts. They'd forced her to cook for them and watched her avidly as she'd served them a stew, made with what little she had, complimenting her with caustic German jibes or muttering dark promises of what was coming for her later.

By morning, there was no trace of them. It was suggested that a British or French patrol had taken them during a sweep of the village. Sandrine too had left the village before first light.

"I'm terribly sorry about all the mess," said Henry, "I really am. I'll help you tidy up. I just needed to update the unit's diary. I was so far behind and there was so much to document. But when I am done, I am relieved and then I can help –"

"Where are the Germans?" Sandrine asked without acknowledging him or his offer, stepping through the rooms with slow and deliberate care.

"Well, uh … we think they're probably four hundred yards east of here. We sent out a patrol last night. It …"

"Did they put up much of a fight? The Germans?"

"Well …" Henry let himself trail off from answering. "Look, would you like to sit down?" He could see Sandrine's shock at what remained of her home. "I mean, there's a lot to take in. To be honest, I'm surprised you were allowed through. I thought they weren't letting anyone back up the road."

"The Germans, did they put up much of fight?" she asked again.

"Oh, well, no, they didn't."

She was now retracing her steps through the ground floor and beginning to climb the broken stairs to the first. Henry waited at the foot of them until the woman had reached the top for fear of catching sight of her thighs beneath her dress. Sandrine stopped and looked down at him. "Are you coming up, Lieutenant Frost?"

"Please, call me Henry," said Henry, nodding and trotting up after her.

"What happened here, Henry?"

"Nothing," the Lieutenant replied. "That's the thing. There was nothing left. No Germans at all. They'd left the village. No trace of them. They'd left their forward trenches and had gone back. There were only a few we found."

"What did they say?" Sandrine asked.

He looked down at his boots and then slowly he raised his eyes up to Sandrine. She was standing three paces away from him, amid the clutter and waste of her home.

"Well, it sounds ridiculous but …"

"Tell me."

"Wolf."

There was no change in Sandrine's face. She stared hard at Henry and then looked back across the ruin of her home.

Henry shrugged and forced a chortle. "Have no idea what they meant but, well … that was what they said. I don't suppose it makes any sense to you, does it?"

She turned and stepped with deliberate slowness along the corridor, vanishing into a room at the far end.

Henry called after her but Sandrine didn't answer back. He called again and then said, "I'm coming in," before pacing along with his heavy boots. "I'm sorry," he said. "I'm in your house and I don't even know your name! It's terribly rude of me. After all, you've asked me mine."

"Sandrine," she replied, looking around at what was left of her bedroom.

"Ah," said Henry, spotting the cruel mess. "I am so sorry."

Sandrine looked at him and her features softened. Henry could feel the inside of him tingle on noticing the thawing of her frosted look.

"Why do you keep apologising, Henry?" she asked. "I don't think you started the war. I don't think you have wrecked my home. And it is only that, a home. It is not a living thing. It is not as bad as death."

Henry shrugged again. Sandrine peered out of the window which, surprisingly, had been left undamaged.

"How long have the British been in Fampoux?"

"Uh, one night," replied Henry, counting the days and nights out on his fingers. "Tonight is our second night."

"You sent out a patrol?" she asked, still peering down onto the street below.

"We did, yes. It didn't come back. We suspect the Germans got it."

"They didn't," Sandrine retorted, looking up at Henry. "You must listen to me very carefully," she said, stepping forward and taking Henry by the shoulders so that there was no question where his attention would be focused. "Send out no more patrols at night. Only during the day are you safe."

"What?"

"Make sure that all your men are secured inside at night."

"My men? They're not my –"

"Then tell whoever is in charge that every man must be locked inside a building at night. There must be no one outside when night falls."

"But that's … well, that's impossible as well as ridiculous!" Henry replied, laughing. "We need to protect –"

"The only thing you need to protect yourself against in Fampoux is the night."

"But –"

"Henry! Listen to me! You are not safe here. Why do you think there were no Germans here when you arrived?" Henry went to speak but Sandrine continued. "They were forced to retreat. There are many unspeakable things which appear here in the night."

Henry laughed nervously. Sandrine shook him.

"Listen to me, stupid British soldier!" she hissed.

"Now steady on!"

"Tell your men, they must barricade themselves in at night. Do not walk the streets at night. Do not go out into the night on patrol. Do not go into the trenches."

"But –"

"Beware the moon, Henry! Beware the wolf!"

She slipped past him and ran down the stairs.

"But … where are you going?" he called after her, rushing down the stairs and into the street to follow her.

"This door," Sandrine said, looking at the front door to the house. "Can you fix it?"

Henry looked at the smashed frame and lock where a German boot had broken it open. A few lengths of wood and nails should secure it. He was sure he could.

"And this window," Sandrine continued, "board it up. We cannot stay here tonight as it is."

"We?" replied Henry, taken aback at the suggestion of sharing the house with a female resident, especially one quite so beguiling as Sandrine. "Well, I'm not sure we could spend the night in this house together."

Sandrine looked at him, her head tilted sympathetically to one side, her hands on her hips.

"I mean," he continued, "it'll go against all contingencies that are recommended during war time service."

Sandrine allowed herself a giggle and wandered away down the street in the direction of the falling shells. "Then you better find yourself other lodgings, Mr Henry."

FORTY SIX

1898. South of the Ural Mountains. Russia.

Tacit sat in the cold dark, his back to the stone, watching the last of the embers die in the fire. The rabbit he'd caught in the trap remained skinned and uncooked on a rock next to him. He wasn't hungry. He couldn't eat. Four days ago he had been under the guidance of a master. Now he was alone. Once more alone.

He listened the sounds of the forest, the rustle of the wind through the trees, the screech of an owl. Everything seemed alive, distinct, precise. It felt as if Tacit could hear even a pin drop in that wilderness.

The lights which had come upon him were gone. If they had been fire, they were unlike any flames Tacit knew. They'd left no mark, his clothes remained whole, his body unhurt. But as Tacit sat in the dark and listened to the night and his thoughts, he realised that the flames had left a mark of sorts on him. They had purged him of doubt, invigorated his body and for the first time in many years his mind was clear.

Far off a lone wolf howled. He knew exactly how the wolf felt.

FORTY SEVEN

12:19. Wednesday, October 14th, 1914. Arras. France.

Cardinal Poré had torn the envelope open the moment he was alone in the quiet of the antechamber of the cathedral. He recognised at once the delicate spidery writing of Monteria, a man as graceful with the nib as he could be with his congregation. There were now only three days to go until the Mass for Peace. How the days had flown since they had first gathered in August to consider the event. Time was of the essence and any word from the Cardinal Bishop could not wait. Should anything require Cardinal Poré's attention, better it be done immediately than let it wait.

Poré's eyes darted indiscriminately over the words, urgently trying to discover the essence of the letter, whether there were problems or if things were progressing as planned. Patience had never been a virtue of the Cardinal's. He barely made sense of the words, just snippets of what Monteria was intending to say, and reluctantly he forced himself back to the start of the letter to read it in the order it had been written. After a moment or two, he felt as if he'd been struck a mortal blow and dropped his hands, a long breath of relief issuing from between his slowly parting lips.

Monteria indeed had news, and the news was good.

According to Monteria, all the hotels in Paris were now full, brimming with journalists and exalted guests arrived for the Mass. But there was more.

The outgoing American Ambassador to France, Myron T. Herrick, had arrived in Paris just yesterday and would also be attending the ceremony to show his support for its aims.

Monteria had made a special point to underline the line which read, 'We have America's ear!'

Poré lifted the letter back to his eyes, excitement building in the ball of his stomach, a sensation causing his fingers to tremble.

'Take care,' the letter continued, the conclusion to it taking a darker turn. 'I have heard rumour that some in the Vatican have not taken kindly to our little escapade, as they are calling it. Be doubly vigilant. Take no risks. I suggest you travel to Paris at the next available opportunity. Once here there will be nothing to derail our Mass but, whilst you are out in Arras, I fear terribly for you and your safety. Our Church is capable of many things, when it feels impelled to act.'

A sudden noise from the Cathedral drew Poré's ear. Without thinking, he put down the letter and crept slowly out into the ambulatory to see who had come visiting so early in the day.

FORTY EIGHT

18:17. WEDNESDAY, OCTOBER 14TH, 1914. ARRAS. FRANCE.

Isabella looked up at the darkening skies over the city.

"It's too late to go to Fampoux now," she said, pulling her arms around her as if to illustrate the creeping gloom and cold. "It's a good two hours' walk from Arras. We'd never get there before dark."

"I agree," replied Tacit, sticking his hands in his pockets, as he trudged through the streets of the city back towards the centre and his lodgings. The hollow echo of explosions further east forced their way between the buildings. The Germans were renewing their onslaught on the British lines with gusto.

"You're agreeing with me?" replied Isabella, with a brightening tone. "Don't tell me you're lightening up?"

Tacit ignored her comment. "We can't go there tonight. Not unless we can find transport to take us out there more quickly." A thunderous clatter sounded on the outskirts of the city, sending the last of the birds still to find shelter flocking to the skies. "And I suspect that'll be difficult." He scratched his chin and put his hand back into the depths of his pocket. "We shouldn't go to Fampoux in the dark."

"We shouldn't be out in the open either," commented the Sister, as another shell landed close to the first. The noise of it crumpling into the earth was followed, a short time later, by a cacophony of tumbling bricks and stones. Somewhere in the city a building had collapsed. "The Germans are making up for lost time. We should get inside."

"I've been thinking," said Isabella, pulling her cape tight around her.

"Really?" Tacit replied, doubtfully.

"We should go see the Cardinal."

The comment surprised him. He was impressed with the Sister's dedication to the case. After all, if he was tired, she must have been exhausted.

"Poré?" Tacit growled. "I don't see why?"

"We should tell him about Sandrine. He might know her. Be able to explain the connection."

"We know the connection," retorted Tacit, his mind turning to the drink waiting for him back in the hotel. "The Father's brother's girlfriend. Maybe even the Father's girlfriend for all we know?" The uttering of such a thought seemed to unsettle Tacit. He scowled and wiped his lips, as if the words had dirtied them. "Anyway, I don't trust him."

"Who? Poré? Why?"

"His unwillingness to allow us to interrogate the chorister."

"Who you were threatening with a gun!"

"His lack of openness about just who was with Father Andreas at the end of Mass."

"An oversight. Come on, Tacit. What have we got? Not much, and if you have your suspicions, a meeting with the Cardinal might help shed more light on just what is going on?"

Tacit scowled and sunk his thick neck into the folds of his cassock collar. "We know who the girl is and where she lives."

"Yes we do, but Poré might be able to give us something more ahead of seeking her out."

"I doubt it," grunted the Inquisitor. "He seemed to make it clear he didn't recognise her, that we'll get nothing more from him."

"Come on, Tacit. We've got nothing, other than a name and a description. We have no motive. Nothing. All we have is a body." Isabella realised then how much she was enjoying the thrill of the assignment.

"Bodies," the Inquisitor corrected.

A third shell thundered into the city, somewhere closer to where they were walking. The main square and the Cathedral were now just a few blocks away. Isabella fancied her chances more – if the barrage was intensifying – within the solid stone construct of a Cathedral, compared to the exposure of the street.

"Come on," she insisted, "the Cathedral is just up here. Let's see what Poré knows."

"He'll be starting Mass," warned Tacit.

"Perfect. We can catch him afterwards. And we can both reacquaint ourselves with the Lord during the service."

"I'd rather go around and talk to some of the locals."

"Yes, I know what you mean by talk. I think my suggestion is safer. We've got to try and find out more before we head to Fampoux."

"If she even got there," Tacit warned, looking skywards. "The Germans are regrouping and attacking. Not easy getting there by road. She might never have made it."

"*If* she went by road," Isabella countered. "Seems to me she knew the tunnels under the city pretty well. Wouldn't be surprised if she travelled underground the entire way."

The side door to the Cathedral grated across the tiles as Tacit and Isabella entered, several parishioners nearby turning to look. Cardinal Poré stood at the pulpit performing the Communion Rite.

"Behold the Lamb of God, behold him who takes away the sin of the world," Poré announced across the congregation gathered beneath the yawning heights of the Cathedral ceiling. "Blessed are those called to the supper of the Lamb." It wasn't a disappointing congregation, considering the war, considering the latest barrage upon the city. Some saw it as their absolute duty to attend the church, even more so now, to seek favour before their Lord at Mass. "Lord, I am not worthy that you should enter under my roof, but only say the word and my soul shall be healed."

Tacit and Isabella found seats at the rear of the congregation and sat waiting for the service to finish. Tacit felt around in a pocket and drew out a battered silver hip flask. He pursed his lips for a drink and felt the Sister's cold stare on him. He offered her a drink in a gentlemanly fashion, which as quickly surprised the Sister as it was rejected. The Inquisitor guzzled thirstily at the mouth of the flask, his face gathering itself into a scowl as he swallowed. He enjoyed the warmth seeping its way through his body. He wondered how he'd allowed himself to agree to visit the Cathedral tonight, why he had not stuck to his original plan in his mind and headed for the hotel and the bar. He didn't just desire another drink, he needed a drink. The nauseous vestiges of last night's wine still clung to fragments of his soul, still needing to be supplanted.

They watched the Cardinal draw the Concluding Rite to a close and with it the service. The congregation rose and slowly gathered themselves and their belongings together, shuffling out of the Cathedral. There were mutters of dismay as people drew open the doors and became aware of the falling artillery barrage spattering the far edges of the town, the Cathedral having masked much of the sound with its broad and high walls. Hats and capes were hurriedly donned and worshippers bustled out to their homes beneath a fiery sky.

Tacit and Isabella waited until the final member of the congregation had left before they wandered slowly towards the ambulatory and antechamber into which the Cardinal had disappeared. Tacit's heavy boots on the tiled floor drew Poré out to investigate.

"Inquisitor Tacit," he called, with as much warmth as a stream in December. "Sister Isabella. I trust you are both well?"

"Better than some," spat Tacit, rubbing a hand under his nose.

"Yes, I have heard about Father Aguillard."

"Did you know him?" asked Isabella, looking for somewhere to rest herself against and realising that her tired limbs would have to hold her up a little longer.

"I did," Poré replied, sounding more dismayed than when he revealed the final moments of Father Andreas' death. "Whilst he travelled much, he was a frequent visitor to Arras. I knew him well."

"Any enemies?" Tacit enquired.

"And here we are again, Inquisitor!" hissed Poré in reply, any sign of dismay dropping from his manner in an instant. "Asking the vagrant question of enemies!"

"You have any better suggestions, Poré?" Tacit growled, squaring up to the Cardinal. "You got any light to shed on what's happening here?"

"You're the Inquisitor," the inscrutable Cardinal replied, looking down his nose with a disdain which secretly delighted him. "However, it seems that I alone have my Lord's blessing." The Cardinal waited for either of them to enquire further as to what he meant by such an perplexing comment. But when they said nothing he continued. "It seems that Father Andreas or Father Aguillard were not the sole names on our *murderer's* list."

He said the word 'murderer' with scorn.

"What do you mean?" Sister Isabella asked.

"I mean, Sister, that I was attacked by the *beast*, this very lunchtime. And, yes, I say beast, for that is what I saw with my own eyes. Hombre Lobo, Tacit! Werewolf!"

If, with that address, the Cardinal had intended to draw some reaction from the Inquisitor, then he was sorely disappointed. Tacit scratched the side of his head and looked to the shadows of the Cathedral.

"So, I can see you're still not convinced?" Tacit didn't even give the question the honour of a reply. "So, you doubt the words of a Cardinal do you, Inquisitor, standing here, before you? You accuse him of lies when you doubt his words."

"I doubt my eyes."

"What's that supposed to mean?"

"I mean, you must be an apparition then, Poré. If you'd met a true wolf, there'd have been no escape."

"How did you escape?" Isabella asked, more to defuse the mounting argument between them.

Poré turned his eyes to the antechamber. "See for yourself. I locked myself in the chapel. The beast savaged the door but was unable to penetrate the rock."

"Quite an escape then?" Tacit said, in a tone heavily laden with sarcasm as he lurched in the direction of the side room.

"You mock me, Inquisitor! At least I've been able to see who our murderer is with my own eyes, which is more than you've been able to do! An Inquisitor?" the Cardinal spat, wandering a few steps behind Tacit and Isabella as they examined the gnarled and scarred stone. "Pah!"

Great claw marks ran the length of the doorway, the stone gouged and disfigured as if it was soft clay. But the stone had proved sufficiently deep and hard to deter the beast from getting to the Cardinal on the other side.

"Perhaps we've not seen the murderer, this is true," said Tacit, turning away from the door after the briefest of looks. "Or perhaps we have? I'm not sure. But we do have a name."

The Cardinal raised an eyebrow and looked at him from behind his hooded eyes. "A name, you say?"

"Sandrine Prideux."

"Who?" he asked, with an exhausted tone.

"Do you know her?" Isabella replied.

"Sandrine Prideux? Of course I don't know a Sandrine Prideux!"

"Are you sure?" Isabella pressed.

"Never heard of her. Who is she?"

"The woman who visited Father Andreas the day he was killed," growled Tacit, his eyes throughout on the Cardinal. "She lives in Fampoux. Anything you can tell us about her?"

"Like I said, I don't know her."

"She seemed to know the Father's brother," Tacit continued.

"Fascinating."

"Knew him well."

"Well? Well, what?" retorted the Cardinal, his manner now one of disdain and boredom. He stifled a yawn. "Inquisitor Tacit, I heard you were good. I now wonder if you are responsible for your own publicity?" He played with the threads on his cassock. "You come to me with the name of a woman I have never heard of and tell me she was a friend of the Father's brother?"

"I never said friend," hissed Tacit.

"What is this? Some sort of joke? And you expect me to be appreciative of your work here? Inquisitor! We have two Fathers who have been killed by a werewolf and a Cardinal who, by good fortune and sense, is lucky to be alive. The case is clear and simple. If you choose not to look at the basic facts that is fine, but don't come to me claiming you're in the middle of a detailed murder investigation when you have no details, no evidence and with nothing more than a name of some unknown woman!"

Tacit could feel the blood pump behind his ears. He recalled a similar feeling when his work eradicating a coven of witches in the Ukrainian town of Lutsk had brought derision from the local Priest, who claimed the Inquisitor was performing witchcraft himself. Tacit took the blasphemous Priest to a dry well and dropped him down it. To his knowledge, the Priest's body was never found. Tacit shot forward and took the Cardinal by the scruff of the neck, the collar of his cassock cutting into Poré's neck, bulging veins. The Cardinal's eyes burned in his head. Isabella cried out, her hands on Tacit's wrist, pulling him away.

"Oh yes, Inquisitor," hissed Poré when released from Tacit's clutches, pulling his cassock straight against his body. "You've quite shown yourself to be the man you are. No wonder they're saying things about you."

"If you didn't want an Inquisitor in your midst, why did you invite one?" Tacit seethed.

"What do you mean? Invite an Inquisitor to an already troubled city, especially one like you? Are you quite mad?" Poré almost spat the words. "Do you honestly think I would give myself the trouble of inviting one of *your* kind into my midst?"

Tacit stared across at Isabella and then at the Cardinal from the corner of his eye.

"No, I don't understand either?" Poré lamented back, spotting Tacit's perplexity. He shook his head and rubbed his shorn scalp with the flat of a hand, regaining a little of his poise and finesse. "Your coming here was not of my doing."

"So, if you didn't want an Inquisitor sniffing around, why so vocal?"

"Vocal?"

"About a werewolf attack, Cardinal? You seem awfully keen to press for their involvement here in this case."

"Because unlike you, Inquisitor, I look at the facts before me and make a judgement instead of creating a fantasy to allow me to play the big man."

Tacit looked ready to spring towards the Cardinal, but Isabella was prepared this time and set herself between the pair of them.

"Well, if that's so, Cardinal," Tacit hissed, fighting against Isabella, as she forced him from the Cathedral, "then I hope you're ready for your own day of judgement."

The Sister manhandled him onto the central aisle. As soon as his boots touched the hard stone, he instantly turned and strode from the ambulatory, as if the aisle was a river sweeping him away. Poré called after them as Tacit vanished into the gloom of the building and out into the city. "My day of judgement, Inquisitor? It seems someone already planned it, but it would appear it is not yet time for me to be judged. Perhaps, Tacit, it should be of your own judgement that you take greatest care?"

FORTY NINE

1899. The Vatican. Vatican City.

"Poldek!" Georgi cried, the moment he saw Tacit enter the main hall. He leapt from his table and bounded over to him, engulfing him in a bear hug. "Poldek! It's good to see you again! Satan's curse, I thought you were dead!" He laughed and slapped him hard across the shoulder.

"Georgi!" Tacit replied, holding onto his friend's arms. He shook his head, as if reacquainting himself with the sight of his old friend. "You think

I'm that easy to get rid of, eh?" He made to slap Georgi in the face. Georgi glanced the gentle blow aside and they wrestled each other lightly, pulling and tugging like children. "Where's everyone else?" Tacit asked eventually, holding his friend at arm's length to look at him. "Claus? Leon?"

At once Georgi shook his head and sat back down at the table. "We've lost many good friends, Poldek."

"What do you mean? Where have they gone?"

Georgi pulled the cup of coffee towards him.

"Ivan?" asked Tacit cautiously. Georgi looked into the black depths of his drink.

"We've not heard from him. For months." And then he turned and looked at Tacit fiercely, tears in his eyes. "We thought we'd lost you! Damn you, Poldek! Where've you been?"

"I lost my master. It's taken me all this time to get back," Tacit replied, grimly. He sat down on the bench next to Georgi, both revolvers at his side thumping against the wood of the table. He removed them and placed them in front of him, Georgi's eyes flashing at their terrible beauty. Tacit ran the dirt from his hair.

"I never expected it to be like this," Georgi said, lifting his eyes from the weapons to stare across the hall. "Never thought it would be so hard. Never thought as to what they would want us to do, what they would want us to become." He looked back at Tacit. There was something different about his friend, a reluctance to talk, to confide, as if a line had been crossed with him, an emotion forever excised. "Are you okay, my friend?"

Tacit nodded and picked up his master's revolver, feeling its weight.

"What are you going to do now, then?" Georgi asked, sweeping up his coffee and putting the scalding liquid to his lips.

"Now?"

"Now that you've lost your master?"

"Nothing," Tacit answered, teasing the chamber of the revolver free and spinning the cylinder with his fingers. He snapped it home. "Nothing changes, Georgi." He put his dark eyes onto his friend. "The battle still goes on."

FIFTY

18:20. Wednesday, October 14th, 1914.
Fampoux. Nr. Arras. France.

They huddled together in the cave for warmth, filthy and wretched in the foul dank gloom. September had brought a chill to the day's end and a dampness in the air. They'd allowed themselves a meagre fire, but didn't risk stoking it too high for fear that the smoke might reveal their location to a passing soldier. Of a night they need not fear but during the tormentingly long hours of daylight, they knew they were vulnerable.

Throughout the years they had sought refuge in the darkness, these pale and sallow figures, deep below where their prey walked, cast out by civilisation, terrorised by flames, fearful mobs and ignorance. For years, too numerous to count, they had eked out a meagre existence, entombed within a prison born of a curse and their enemies' fear. They were the damned, the once great now fallen, the ones cursed to walk the pitiable line between darkness and light, always longing, yearning for life, longing for salvation, craving for a final meal to satiate their hunger and thirst for a last time.

A longing always conducted at the mercy of the moon.

"Can you hear them?" asked Angulsac, referring to the sound of the soldiers digging nearby.

It was not his birth name, the name his mother had given him when he was pink and small and perfect. Too long ago it was that that name had been used, too long ago for its recollection, those days now beyond reach, like an itch unable to be scratched. It had slipped from time and mind just as the moon each morning countless times behind the horizon. Now he'd taken the name decreed by the clan, Angulsac, 'Waning of the Moon' in the tongue of the true wolves.

"I hear them," replied Baldrac wearily, shivering in the gloom despite the layers of cloth bound about him.

During daylight, Baldrac preferred to sleep but at this time his hunger gnawed at him like the incessant cold, a cruel and constant reminder of what he was, what hateful thing he had become and also what he desired beyond anything else in order to help find respite from the pain. Only by being the monster he so despised could the monster rest, embrace the troubled and hateful portion of death that was sleep.

"From the west," Baldrac croaked, trying to clear his parched throat.

"The British."

"They are coming," Angulsac said.

"The Germans, they have abandoned the village," Baldrac spoke quietly into his rags, as if to himself. Beneath his layers of cloth and threadbare fabric, he was naked, stinking and scarred by an endless lifetime of dirt and filth. Once he wore clothes of finery. Now rags were his clothes, the same as many of the clan chose to use. There was little point in fitting oneself in the attire of those who walked above in the sun. With the coming of the moon, their transformation would be sudden, their clothing ripped asunder when the curse was unleashed in flesh and fur and rage.

"I wonder if *they* will listen to the villagers?" a white haired woman, who went by the clan name of Calath, asked, shuffling a little closer to the fire to urge some warmth into her gnarled fingers. She was drawn and emaciated, half starved. Once, many years ago, she was beautiful, with the ear of kings and a host of lovers. But she was too beautiful for the liking of some and was cast down with a curse upon all of her house. Now no lover would be drawn to her fetidness, not even those she shared the underground hovel with.

"They are men," Baldrac spat, drawing the rags a little higher around him. "Foolish men. It is not in their nature to listen, to understand. Once they learn of us ..." He let his words trail off with a shake of his head.

"We were men once," a shivering figure called from the back of the cave, shrouded in shadows.

"I wish them no ill," Calath continued.

Angulsac laughed bitterly. "I wish them no ill either, but neither did I the Germans, or the French, or any who have trodden upon our paths. The moon is a cruel master."

Baldrac coughed hard in his tight, rasping chest. "Men are foolish," he said, spitting the ball of phlegm he'd brought up from his leathery lungs. "They will scoff when they are told of us. Nothing will change, not even when the moon climbs and we venture out amongst them."

"Perhaps our princess will convince them?" Calath asked, summoning a little hope within her voice.

"She was unable to convince the Germans. What makes you think she will be able to convince the British?" Baldrac drew his feet inside the folds of cloth and nestled himself into a ball inside the mass of rags.

"She will have completed her task by now," said Angulsac, staring into the measly flames of the fire.

"Perhaps she will come to us?" Calath replied, urgently. "With news?"

"News?!" Baldrac barked back, suddenly enraged. "It is not news I wish for! It is food! Food to sustain me through the night so I need not hunt for it!" He trembled and shook as he spoke, caught in his anger. "Ah! The torment! When will it end?!" he cried out, his voice echoing throughout the cavern network.

"Easy, Baldrac," urged Angulsac, his eyes heavy on the fire. "If she comes, then it will be with news *and* perhaps a little food."

"A little food is not enough though!" the wretched man spat back. "There is never enough food! For a whole month, since the war has come to these lands, we have been without our sustenance brought to us and have had to search it out like the vermin that we are!" He spat in the dirt and threw himself into a ball by the side of the cavern.

Out of the reach of torchlight, more figures could be seen stirring, a lamentable band of creatures, pallid and filthy. The raised voices had awoken them. They retched and cursed, coughing up their misery and the stinking foul residue of last night's hunger frenzy, knowing soon that the madness would return again, once the moon climbed in the sky.

Angulsac drew his rags about him. "I know we need food, but also with news then perhaps our journey's end will be a little closer. Until then, let us try and rest."

"Rest!" cackled a voice from a dark corner of the cavern. "How can we rest when we know the moon is climbing? What good is rest when soon we know we will be beyond all hope of rest?"

"If she doesn't come, I trust the Germans have given the British good warning," Baldrac growled, laying himself down against the hard rock floor for sleep that he knew would not come. "Because my hunger is terrible and already I feel my rage match it."

The soft crumbling cascade of soil and the noise of slipping shoes on damp mud drew their attention from the smouldering fire and their infected, troubled dreams. Angulsac was the first to face the intruder, low on his haunches in an instant, taut like a coiled spring in the middle of the dark and stinking cavern.

A pair of shoes and then long legs appeared at the hole of the extended passageway leading down to the cavern. Moments later, Sandrine dropped gently down the wall to the passageway floor.

"Sandrine!" Calath called, summoning up a residue of joy from the depths of her forsaken spirit.

Baldrac and another male levered themselves weakly onto their elbows, whilst Angulsac rose and strode forward naked to embrace Sandrine, his rags flung aside in readiness to spring unhampered at the appearance of the unknown intruder.

She was a joy to behold, an accepted and welcomed face from the outside, an injection of life and colour into their barren and desperate world.

They scampered forward from the fire and the dark corners of the cavern to peer on her and see what she had brought for them. She threw a sack onto the floor before her.

"I am sorry," she called, as the pack gathered around the sack and its contents. "I have not had time to gather much for you."

"Is this all there is?" cried a hairy flat faced man, looking up from the scant contents spilled out across the floor. It was being ripped apart urgently into bloody sticky pieces by the rampant crowd. "A few cats and a long dead dog?"

"I am sorry, Galath," Sandrine called back, almost overwhelmed with sorrow. "I had not the time to –"

"Is this what we are reduced to now? Scrapping for cats and dead creatures. Are we truly dogs?"

But Angulsac came forward and embraced her earnestly.

"Silence, Galath," he cried and then put his deep dark eyes onto Sandrine. "Sandrine," he said, taking her hand and kissing it. "Thank you."

"I would have brought more but …"

Angulsac raised his hand to silence her.

"I know. And your offering is kind. It will sustain some and hopefully reduce others' hunger – and their savagery a little."

Sandrine was always touched by how they tried to distance themselves and their vulgar feasting from her as they ate. She'd seen them eat a thousand times, had watched the animalistic passion with which they gorged themselves on the flesh of whatever Sandrine was able to bring. It had never revolted her in terms of a spectacle. What did repulse her was that they were forced to live like this, like animals, underground, feeding on the detritus and filth cast away from the butcher's block, unable to step beneath the sun and fend for themselves.

They gorged themselves the best they could on the bloodied offerings within the basket, stuffing food into their mouths quicker than they could swallow it; flesh, blood and fur guzzled as if it were the finest of French cuisine. Calath looked up, feasting greedily, her eyes now burning brightly.

"Calath," Sandrine called to her in greeting, her eyes moist, her hands locked in prayer to her lips. How it pained Sandrine to see her reduced to such carnality.

What had been brought by Sandrine in the bag lasted mere moments before it had been consumed, bones, skin, fur and flesh of the few dead creatures gathered from the streets of Fampoux or caught on her journey to their lair. Those who had not already done so now slunk away from the empty stained remains of the bag, like hyenas cheated from a kill.

Not a single drop of their meagre meal was wasted. They sucked fingers and wiped mouths with backs of hands, which they then licked like starving cats.

"The British," someone called from the mass of bodies, "they have come then?"

"Yes. They are in Fampoux."

"And they let you through to the village?" Baldrac asked, his face a vivid crimson from the food he had taken. Bloodied strands hung from the sides of his mouth and fingers which he began to clean meticulously.

Sandrine sat on a rock and rested her head on a hand. "I came via the tunnels. They were making preparations for defence when I left the village to come to you. They were looking elsewhere. I was able to gather up what I could and step out to you without any bother. We will see how they treat me and these errands once they have settled for a little while in the town."

"You weren't followed, were you?" Baldrac asked. He always asked that question, once his hunger had abated a little.

"I was not," replied Sandrine. "I do hope that the British will be kinder visitors in our town than the Germans." She sank her head into her hands and rubbed her eyes, exhausted. "I have hope," she said, looking over at them.

"They are men," spat Angulac grimly. "We do not hold out much hope."

"You were a man once, Angulsac," Sandrine replied.

"I was," he replied, chewing the end off a length of bone and sucking at the marrow within. "And look at me now," he said sadly. "It was too long ago now. I forget."

"I don't," Sandrine replied swiftly. "You may yet be a man again."

Angulsac laughed thinly. "I admire your optimism, my dear. But I know our curse is as firmly laid as the chalk rock about us." He crunched at the end of the bone, crushing the fragments within his mouth. He turned them about his tongue before swallowing. "We are beyond saving. All I hope is that we might be granted the final word in this most bitter of tales."

"I would not turn back," Baldrac called, shaking his head and scratching at his skull with his gnarled withered fingers.

"You would not?"

"Not if the turning back equalled the pain of the original turning. Such torment. My bones still recoil from the pain," he said, and to illustrate the bitterness of his memory he massaged his shoulder.

Calath sneered. "I too remember when they cast me down, so much so that I can remember nothing before that moment, only their wretched words, the bile and hatred uttered by them, the red heat of their curse, a brand for all of eternity." She shuddered and wept pathetically.

"At least they have stopped cursing," said Sandrine, attempting to bring a little light to the conversation.

"Yes, recognised their folly finally," spat Baldrac. "Now, instead they hunt us, like vermin. Exterminating us like rats, to ensure our silence."

Angulsac smiled darkly. "Too late for that."

"Come, tell us, how was Arras?"

"Fine."

"Did you ..."

"I did. It has been done."

"All according to plan?"

Sandrine hesitated.

"Come, what is it Sandrine?"

"It's nothing. I am just a little tired. The deed has been done. We must now wait, and pray."

"Pray?" spat Angulsac. "Ha! You forget. We all stopped praying many years ago!"

"You are so good to us, princess," Calath said, shuffling forward to the feet of Sandrine, nourished a little by the taste of blood. "Your father would be proud."

The mention of her father brought a wrench to Sandrine's heart. She never knew her father, not properly, not as other families. For so much of her life, Sandrine had been alone, cared for by distant cousins and strangers in her childhood, finding her own way in Fampoux during her adolescence. Her pain was made all the greater knowing that he had been there, just half a mile from the outskirts of the village, inaccessible but for the most restrictive of visits. And those hateful visits, which could only be short during daylight hours, brought their own demons and resentment. Sandrine always felt she was growing up in the shadow of neglect and a father she could see but could never reach. As her mother had proved, there could be no chance of a normal relationship between the father and his offspring.

The isolation had brought a self-sufficiency and a spirit to Sandrine, but it had also tormented her so much so that she wondered whether she would ever be able to love, or be loved, with truth and sincerity. At times she'd felt the almost unbearable weight of neglect and loneliness, so great she wondered how she could go on. But now, buried within that rancid cave, surrounded by those desperate souls, she felt more wretched and alone than ever.

"You look sad, little one," Calath called, a concern clenched about her words.

Sandrine forced a smile and buried her misery deep inside of her, as she always did eventually. With everything she had in her world above – compared to these lamentable creatures, doomed to remain in the filth and darkness – she refused to reveal her hidden sorrow to them. But inside her emotions churned. She felt stunted, like a seedling starved of light. She knew her heart was like that of a flower waiting to reveal itself and its true beauty, but having had so little love with which to cultivate it, the bud was firmly closed.

"I mourn for you, Calath," Sandrine replied, reaching out and drawing her to sit beside her on the rock she had found.

"You are kind, Sandrine."

"Kindness does not come into it, Calath. You are family. I just hope what my father and I have done is enough."

FIFTY ONE

22:14. Wednesday, October 14th, 1914. Paris. France.

Cardinal Monteria gently snatched the letter from Silas' hand without a word and stepped to the window to read it, a lamp standing nearby. He recognised Poré's firm pronounced letters on the envelope, a man confident in both himself and his thoughts.

It was only a short letter, written in haste, judging by some of the raggedly penned characters, a scruffiness which rarely blighted Poré's usually immaculate hand. With minimal fuss he thanked Monteria for his last letter and his excellent news regarding the American Ambassador, of which Poré announced that he had been almost overwhelmed to hear. He also acknowledged the dangers which faced them, writing that he 'would be taking steps to ensure that their plans go unimpeded by those who wish to thwart them.'

A wave of cold panic swept over Monteria and he swallowed on his dry throat, his eyes rising to the dark Paris skyline beyond his window as he wondered just what steps Poré might be inferring. He was aware of Silas's eyes on him and he scolded the servant for remaining in his presence unrequested, ushering him away with a flap of his hand.

He stared back at the letter, grasping at the final words in the hope that they might give him something to allay his fears.

'Cardinal Bishop Monteria. I will be joining you in Paris at the next available opportunity. I look forward to our meeting then.'

FIFTY TWO

19:24. Wednesday, October 14th, 1914.
Fampoux. Nr. Arras. France.

The shadows were long and a chill wind had grown from out of the north, by the time Sandrine returned back to her ruined home. She looked at the tumbledown terrace from the street and shivered, not through cold but through apprehension for the night to come. The small amount of food she had taken to the clan would do little to appease their hunger. It was like crumbs to birds. Their appreciation of the gift had been great, but, once the moon rose above the skyline, the hunger and the rage would still be terrible.

Confusion and fear racked her. She was caught in a maddening place, between trying to save her liberators and trying to stave off her clan's hunger. She took solace from the fact that soon, perhaps, maybe, she hoped, all would be over. She would pray, but it was prayer which had first delivered her and the clan into such peril and suffering.

Henry jumped when Sandrine pushed open the door to the house.

"You are not much of a soldier," she said, "jumping when a woman enters the house!"

"Wasn't expecting you," Henry smiled, recovering and unconsciously straightening his hair into some semblance of style.

"Have you made the house safe?" she asked, like an officer to one of his juniors. "It's soon dark." Henry couldn't help but laugh.

"What is this? I have two Majors ordering me about now, do I?"

But Sandrine ignored him and repeated the question again, even more seriously.

"Yes. Well, I've patched up the door. Boarded up the window. You look tired."

Sandrine was. Exhausted. She rubbed a hand across her face, as if trying to brush the weariness away from her.

"I can make tea," Henry said, in a tone which made him sound proud of the fact. "Here, take a seat." He wiped down the chair, from which he had been writing, with a hand and set it before Sandrine.

"Thank you, Lieutenant."

"Please do call me Henry."

"Thank you, Henry. Do you have anything stronger? Feel like I could do with a proper drink."

"Ah," replied Henry, bowing his head so that his chin was on his chest. "I don't think I –"

"I think the Germans would have taken all of my spirit. Let me look …" Sandrine began, levering herself up from the chair.

"No, no, let me," Henry insisted, raising his hands as a sign he could do whatever was asked of him.

"You are very kind. In the pantry, at the back under the little window, there's a tile in the wall." Henry wandered his way through to the room. "Is it untouched? Should be some bottles inside."

Henry reappeared moments later at the door.

"Empty, I'm afraid," he said, pulling a face. Sandrine looked crestfallen. "Sorry about that."

"There you go again," retorted Sandrine, although there was a lightness in her voice. "Apologising! You English! You are sorry for everything."

"Yes, I suppose you're right, bit of a national pastime of ours. Can I make you tea?"

"Tea! The other great British pastime. Is there no coffee?"

"I don't think so," replied Henry, rummaging through his stores. "I might be able to find you some from –"

"No, don't worry," said Sandrine, wearily. "I will take tea."

He headed off to the kitchen where he had set up a stove.

Sandrine listened to the sound of his knocking and tinkering as she leaned forward, resting her head into her hands, her eyes closed, enjoying the swirl of her tired mind slowing to a halt.

"I've tidied up a bit," Henry called into the room. "Don't know if you'd noticed."

Sandrine hadn't. She sat up and looked about herself.

"All I care about is whether the doors and windows are safe," she answered. But then she felt unkind and said, "But it looks much better. Thank you." It still looked a mess, but she could see the Tommy had made an effort, of sorts, a British and male effort at tidying up, which involved moving everything to the side of the room and hiding the worst of the mess where he thought it was out of sight.

"I still don't think this is a good idea," Henry said, appearing at the door and pulling a face of guilt.

"What, securing the house?"

"No, I mean ..." He shrugged awkwardly. "Cohabiting."

"My dear Henry, you English are so sweet. If you are that uncomfortable about it, you can leave anytime you like."

"No," replied Henry, quicker than someone would have if they thought it a bad idea. His response rather shocked him. "No," he said, slightly less passionately, "no, it's fine, it's just not army protocol to share residences with residents like this, especially a single female resident. Are you single?" he asked again, a little more pointedly than he was expecting.

"Single? Yes, I have no husband or boyfriend, if that is what you mean," Sandrine answered flatly, as if replying to a mundane question, but there was a mischievous light in her eyes. She looked up through her dark eyelashes and smirked. "Goodness me, Henry," she said, allowing the smile to take root on her face, "are you blushing?" She stole forward from the chair and grabbed him from turning to hide his embarrassment. "You are!" she cried, and she laughed and ran her hands through his hair. "You are blushing!"

"All right!" replied Henry, a little hotly at the teasing. Privately he adored the feel of her on him.

"You are blushing, Henry!" Sandrine laughed and she stood back and shook her head. "You are a quite remarkable man, Henry."

He swiped at his hair to smooth out any ruffles and coughed uneasily. "Stop teasing," he said.

"I'm not. I don't think I've ever met anyone like you before."

"Don't say that. I'm sure you have." He picked up his pencil and played with it absently in his fingers.

"All the men I've known, they had, how do you say in English? A head that is too big?"

"Arrogant?" he suggested.

"Arrogant!" Sandrine cried. "But you?" She came forward again and placed her hands on his jawbone, looking hard into his face to see if there was anything to suggest her thoughts where wrong. “You are a beautiful man. Do you know that?”

“Ah, right. Good,” Henry replied falteringly, easing himself back and thrusting a fist into a palm, as was his way. “Well, anyway, like I was saying,” he continued, and then suddenly rushed back to his stove to take the boiling water from the flame, cursing when he burnt his fingers.

“So,” Sandrine said, sitting on his chair and crossing her legs, watching him closely, this small and correct Englishman, the flicker of emotion catching inside her. She swept her hair over her shoulder and raised an eyebrow. “You are happy to stay here then? With me?”

“It’s just, I’m sure my superiors would have something to say about it, but that’s okay.” He noticed a line of dirt on the inside of one of the mugs and smudged it away with his thumb. “Do you like your tea strong?”

Sandrine ignored the question. “Talking of your superiors, what did they say when you passed on my message?”

Henry appeared at the door, playing sheepishly with its wooden surround . “I ...”

“You haven’t!” she snapped, leaping at once to her feet.

Henry stole forward, his hands out to try and pacify her. The way she could flash to scalding hot from cold terrified him. “I told them there was perhaps more behind the attacks than simply the British advance!”

Sandrine hand was on the door handle. “Bloody English!” she cried. “Who is your officer?”

“Major Pewter. But –”

“And where is this Pewter?”

“At the main hall. But –”

“Then if you won’t tell him, I will go and tell him myself!” She threw the door open and thrust herself outside.

“But your tea!” Henry called after her, hurrying back to the kitchen to collect it from the hob. But Sandrine was already down the street and away into the heart of the village.

FIFTY THREE

1900. Shores of the Black Sea. Romania.

The handle of Tacit's heavy case felt reassuring to him, as he stepped along the shore of the Black Sea. A cold wind came off the water. It was close to dark. Night time seemed to fall earlier and faster in this part of the world. Maybe it would have been better to wait before making the journey but it was too late for second thoughts now. He shivered and drew his long dark coat tighter around him. It was a little loose, but Tacit would grow into it. He'd taken it from his master, just as he had Tocco's revolver and case. His master would have approved. The old Inquisitor wouldn't have wanted his belongings to have languished in his Inquisitorial locker. It wasn't the Inquisitor's way to sit and gather dust. "Only in death let the dust have a chance to settle on you," Tocco always said. Tacit thought of his master's grave and unconsciously his hand fell to the revolver at his side.

Ahead he could see the outline of rocks, running down from the hills on the right, tumbling into the dark depths of the sea. Everything appeared just as it had been described to him when the assignment had been posted. A witch. On the shores of the Black Sea, Romania. Spreading witchcraft, fear and lies. To be terminated. An urgent assignment. His first on his own.

He followed the outline of the rocks down towards the sea with his eyes and shuddered as he recognised a dark shape amongst the silhouette of jagged rocks, a hunched figure staring back towards him. He swallowed and considered taking a shot at it from here.

He braced and caught hold of himself, measuring his breathing and his thoughts. *Stupid. Remember your training. Calm. Keep calm. Focus. Control. Always control.* He removed his hand from the handle of the revolver and stepped forward, muttering an ancient prayer to Saint Joseph under his breath. It was one which had always caught his imagination.

Oh, St. Joseph, whose protection is so great, so strong, so prompt before the throne of God. I place in you all my interests and desires. Oh, St. Joseph, do assist me by your powerful intercession, and obtain for me from your divine Son all spiritual blessings.

He looked up at the figure. He'd never hit her from here, not even with the Saint's help.

He walked until the pebbles of the shore slowly turned into rocks and began to climb, passing stones marked with the black etchings of witchcraft. The route up was damp with night mist and spray from the sea tide, seaweed and algae making the way treacherous. But Tacit's heavy soled boots bit firm into the rocks, his fingers like crampons within the crannies of the stone.

He pushed his case onto the topmost rock ahead of him and heaved himself after it, cursing that he'd brought the thing at all. A bullet to the witch's skull would suffice. No ointments, potions or symbols would be needed on this assignment.

"So, you have come to carry out justice then, Inquisitor?" the witch called from the far end of the spur. Tacit drew himself upright and stared down at her, her lank white hair running over her filthy brown robes. "I see it in your eyes, Inquisitor!"

"Through this dusk? That I doubt!"

"My eyes are keen, Inquisitor, it's yours that you should be wary of," the witch called back calmly.

"How do you know what I am?"

But the witch did not answer, instead stepping behind a stone and vanishing from view. Tacit grunted and picked up his case, at the same time pulling a revolver from his side. The next clean shot he promised himself he would finish the witch and he'd go back into the warm.

"So, are you happy upon the path designated for you, Inquisitor?" a voice called suddenly from behind him, causing him to turn, the revolver levelled to the empty darkness beyond. At once Tacit realised the trickery of the witch and looked back to the path he was following and the hole hidden behind the stone into which she had slipped. It led down into a hellish black. He put down his case and extracted a lantern from a deep pocket of his coat. Two clicks and the lantern instantly sprang into white light. Leaving the case behind him, he crept into the mouth of the cave.

"I asked you a question," the witch's voice asked again, seeming to rise up from all around him. Tacit kept his eyes to the path ahead, ignoring any urges to look either side or behind him. "What is it, Inquisitor? Lost your tongue?"

"I don't speak to witches," Tacit growled back into the blackness, "those who shroud themselves in darkness."

"No, of course you don't. But you speak to the lights, don't you?" the brittle voice asked and Tacit wavered in his step. "You talk to the lights, Poldek Tacit, don't you?"

"How do you know my name?" Tacit hissed, crouching a little lower in the darkness, feeling isolated and exposed.

"Oh, I know far more than just your name, Poldek. I know everything about you. How you were plucked from the bosom of your dead mother. How you were drilled in the ways of the Catholic Church. How you were set on this path of hell-bent destruction."

"I don't know what you mean?" Tacit cried, a fear beginning to form in his throat.

"Of course you don't know," the witch hissed. "You're foolish, blind to the world around you. Only a fool would allow himself to be manipulated like you have been to serve the needs of your superiors."

"I have no such choice," he stuttered, turning about himself and the dark. "This is my path."

"Of course you have choice," the voice came. "We all have choice. We can choose to do as we are bid, or we can choose to act as our soul implores us to act. Tell me, Inquisitor, do you have a soul that you still listen to?"

Tacit grimaced and thrust the trigger of the revolver hard into his forehead, scratching at his skin, relishing the dull sting of pain, the focus it brought to him. "Silence witch!" he cried. "I won't listen to your accursed words any more!"

"It does not surprise me, Poldek Tacit, that you're not listening. After all, when have you ever listened? When have you ever acted upon your own desires, your own wishes, your own judgement?"

"There is only one judgement!" Tacit called back. "The judgement of the Lord God himself!"

"Oh you are a pitiful one, Inquisitor!"

"Not so pitiful as to hide myself away. Come out! Show yourself!"

"All in good time."

Tacit shifted himself in the passageway, putting his back hard to the wall. The voice in the corridor continued.

"Tell me, is that fear that I sense?"

"I have nothing to fear from the likes of you!"

"Indeed! You need only fear The Church itself."

"Blasphemy!"

"If your Church was truly so loving, do you really think it would have put you through the trials it has? And what a gracious and fulfilling role it is! Bringing damnation and suffering to all who cross you."

"It has prepared me for this role."

"You admit it yourself then? That you have needed to feel pain in order to be prepared for all that your role brings? Well let me tell you this, Tacit, the pain you have known has not yet finished. It has barely started. More is to come, far more crippling than you could ever imagine."

"I have heard enough! Show yourself to me!"

"So that you can silence my tongue?" the witch spat and then laughed wickedly. "Patience, Inquisitor! Isn't that what your training teaches you? To be patient? To wait for the right moment to act, to strike, to bring retribution to your enemies? Well, be patient then! For I have not finished."

"Then say it and let us be done with our business."

"So, that is what you consider your faith? A business, like the stitching of uniforms and the finishing of artillery rounds?"

"You speak in riddles, witch!"

"Very well. A war is coming, the likes of which mankind has never before known. Upon you, Poldek Tacit, will fall the fate of millions. The question is whether, when the time comes, there will be enough of you, of your soul, left to act, or whether you have lost yourself completely to lights."

Instantly the darkness was thrown into blinding light from which Tacit had to shield his eyes. He winced through the searing brightness, making out the vague outline of a figure standing a little way in front of him.

"You stop using *that* part of you," the witch's voice boomed, "and it shrinks and dies."

"Enough!" Tacit cried. "I have heard enough. Be done with your message and let me be done with my business."

"Yes, let us come to your 'business'." The figure opened its arms wide, like a bird about to take flight. "You will choose poorly, Poldek Tacit. You are not nearly as big as you think."

As soon as the revolver recoiled, the cave was thrust into immediate dark, taking all sight and Tacit's thoughts with it.

FIFTY FOUR

20:44. WEDNESDAY, OCTOBER 14TH. 1914. ARRAS. FRANCE.

They stood in the darkness in the centre of the square, Tacit staring back hard at the front of the Cathedral. The clouds were now moving fast across the sky. The weather was changing. There was a storm gathering.

Isabella stood close by watching the Inquisitor, partially lit by the faint silvery shards of moonlight and the fires and light from the surrounding buildings. The dull thump of artillery fire pounded in the distance, occasionally joined with the sharp crack of small arms fire.

"What is it?" she asked, tracing his stare to the Cathedral.

Tacit said nothing, staring with his dark eyes until the muscles within them ached.

"Where are you staying?" he asked, finally. "I never enquired."

"The church has given me a private residence, just down from the main Priests' house. It is fine."

Tacit put his eyes back onto the Cathedral. "I don't care whether it's fine or not, just be careful."

The warning puzzled Isabella. She tried to find the meaning of it in Tacit's face. She found nothing but a stony grimace. But there was something else. She saw, between the cruel hard lines and the thick spread of stubble, there was a sadness which tinged the edges of his features, a quiet suffering, deep rooted like a contagion within him. She was immediately filled with an overwhelming urge to reach out and touch him, like a mother to an injured child, to take him into her arms and hold him, tell him that whatever sorrow ravaged him, it would pass in time.

"I'll see you tomorrow, Inquisitor!" she called, turning and stepping sharply away from him, her heels rapping hard on the stone slabs of the square. "Been a long day. My bed is calling!"

"It'll be a longer one tomorrow," he called back.

"That's what I like about you, Tacit. Ever the optimist. Get some sleep," the Sister called. "It might do wonders for your mood."

Tacit watched her all the way out of the square and then put his eyes back onto the Cathedral for one final time, before retiring to his lowly room above the bar.

The bar was busy, noisy. The crowd from the previous night had swollen in number, as if the recent barrage had driven people from their homes and beds for one last night of merriment, lest it all end tomorrow. The proprietor looked up as Tacit pushed himself through the doors of the establishment and stomped over to the bar.

"Welcome back, Father!" he said, flashing teeth and a look which suggested more than just a jovial welcome. "I trust you are well?"

"Just get me a drink," Tacit spat back. "Leave the bottle. And some olives."

The barman nodded and returned a moment later brandishing a full bottle of Armagnac.

"The woman," he asked with a glint, as he put the bottle down in front of the mountain of a man. "Your escort. She's not here tonight, is she, by any chance?"

At once, Tacit was across the bar and had the man by the collar, dragging him back over it. Glasses went spinning and crashing to the floor. The banter and noise from the bar immediately ceased.

"How dare you!" he hissed. "She's not a prostitute, you bastard!"

"Very good, Father," the proprietor whimpered, shuddering in the Inquisitor's grip.

"Keep your opinions to yourself." Tacit gave him a shake and threw him back from where he had come.

"Now, get me my olives!"

"Olives!" the proprietor repeated, staggering to his feet shakily. "Of course!" He set a glass next to the bottle and slunk away. Tacit seethed, staring into the depths of the bottle's rich brown liquid. Without a word, he took the bottle and glass up in his fingers and strode away, heading for the stairs and his room. His shame and anger were too great for him to reside any longer in the bar amongst strangers, their stares and their muttering all set in his direction. As he reached the first floor and his room, he could hear the first strains of music start up and the low rumble of conversation roll into it.

He thrust the glass down on the table and uncorked the bottle, drinking deeply from its lip without a moment's pause, instantly feeling soothed by the liquor inside him. He stood, thoughts festering over the barman and his impudent insults, before drinking again and putting those thoughts to the back of his brain. *Little ignorant people. They'd get their judgement, one way or the other.* He crossed over to the window, gulping at the bottle as he went, and crouched alongside it, his eyes back watching the Cathedral.

Why was he so drawn to the building? There was something that troubled him about it, something itching in a corner of his brain, an uncertainty, a doubt.

He sat on the side of the bed and gulped at the bottle, feeling enriched by the drink. Already he felt better. He put back his head and wallowed in the buzz as the first alcohol soothed his mind. He let out a long and satisfied exhale and stretched himself out on the bed, an arm behind his head, the bottle still clutched in his left hand. He peered up at the ceiling of the room, his racing thoughts slowed by the embracing hold of the Armagnac.

FIFTY FIVE

20:50. Wednesday, October 14th, 1914. Arras. France.

Isabella set the key in the lock and stepped inside. She shut the door behind her with a comforting crack and stood back, her hands flat against the wood, her head rested hard against it. The young Sister exhaled and blew strands of hair from her face.

She pushed her weary body forward with her hands and stepped lightly down the passageway to her apartment. The Catholic Church was generous with their hospitality for travelling dignitaries and official personnel. The apartment could have housed four people comfortably. In the lounge, she unlaced her boots and slipped them off her feet, nursing her cramped and bruised toes. The boots she wore were made for practicalities, not comfort; for delivering a hefty kick and scooting out of dangerous situations, not for ensuring toes remained pristine and dainty.

She unbuttoned her cape and laid it on the back of a chair, stepping into the kitchen and pouring herself a glass of water from the jug. It was warm, but she enjoyed the refreshment of it in her dry mouth. She stood there, glass in hand, staring down at the wash sink, her mind half in, half out of consciousness.

"This will never do," she whispered to herself, and set down the glass.

Her brown travelling gown had been discarded beside her empty glass. She was already unbuttoning her basque as she stepped into her bedroom, clean and tidy, and scented with the remnants of lavender. She liked that about the Catholic Church; little touches left by the maids like adding lavender fragrance to the room for women, a stronger musk for men. She threw her basque to the bed and rubbed her breasts and armpits through her brassiere to sooth their pained and crushed flesh.

Toes and breasts, Isabella thought to herself, as she unbuttoned her undershirt and let that fall, followed by her corset. She breathed deeply as they tumbled to the floor and she stepped out of them now, wearing only her lightly weighted undergarments. She stretched and bent herself sideways and down to her toes, enjoying the sensation of movement, the tight pull of her tired muscles. She knew why she put herself through the misery of such confining clothes. Men were weak minded.

It was amazing what secrets could be gleaned, what weaknesses could be exposed by the enticing beauty of the female form. But that didn't make the wearing of such garments any easier.

She stood up straight and looked out of the lace lined window to the darkness beyond. She was suddenly aware that, with the gaslight on in the room and the blinds drawn, people from the street would be able to see her. But who would be passing at this hour, who would be looking in? Everyone would be taking refuge in their homes, the bars, or within the city's tunnels, not walking the streets whilst bombs were falling. But there *was* someone, or something, looking, two flaming red eyes staring at her from the other side of the glass.

She had already turned to run by the time the feral beast smashed through the window, shattering glass to all corners. The odious stench of the wolf engulfed Isabella as soon as it was through the window. She slipped, scrambling to get away, the howling roar of the beast almost deafening her, chilling her to her bones. Glass scattered between her feet and toes, as she found purchase and leapt aside before the monstrous wolf crashed into a nearby table and chairs, flinging them aside, talons rending vast gashes into the wooden floor of the apartment.

Isabella landed and rolled behind an armchair, her feet torn with glass, terror bringing tears to her eyes. Her heart pounded in her chest, her breast rising and falling like a bellows. She grabbed a peek from behind the chair, shuddering as she watched the grotesque matted form of the grey black wolf, vast crimson jaws, scalding red eyes, raise itself up to its immense height and stare down at her.

It leapt and, as it did so, so did she, rolling and tumbling to the door of the apartment, her hand fumbling desperately at the lock of the door. No good. Her fingers were too clumsy, her fear too great. She could feel the wolf rise up to strike from behind.

All of a sudden, there was a tremendous thump which sent the Sister sprawling, dazed, to the side of the room. She guessed she'd been struck by the creature, expecting to look down and find herself drenched in her blood, bones broken, her side ripped open and torn, paralysed, unable to move as the creature sank down to feed upon her.

But her body was untouched, despite the dull ache of bruising. In front of her stood the Inquisitor, standing in the remains of the shattered door, which he had kicked clean off its hinges, thrusting Isabella to one side, silver revolver raised in his right hand. The cylinder turned and the gun exploded. In a blur the wolf was upon him, casting him back through the open door, the pair of them rolling like fighting cats.

Isabella tried to lever herself up. Her ribs screamed in agony, her head span. In the corridor outside her apartment, barks and roars sounded as if a frightful feeding frenzy was underway.

"Tacit!" Isabella cried, rising up onto a knee and forcing herself onto her feet. "Tac –!"

With that, the wolf came sprawling through the doorway, its nose thick with blood and gore. Tacit came after it a moment later, like a great black bull, fists raised, thumping and thrusting as the wolf tried to find its balance. A taloned claw swooshed through the air and Tacit deflected it with the barrel of his revolver, punching hard up into the ribcage of the creature. It lowered its jaws and crunched hard onto the Inquisitor's thrusting forearm, snapping and tearing like a rabid dog, the Inquisitor's weapon falling away.

Beneath his robes, Tacit's intricately woven dress of steel, forged in the hottest fires of the Vatican's smithies and hammered impenetrable and light by its most skilled of blacksmiths, hung impervious against the creature's terrible teeth. Tacit raised his left fist and thrust it once, twice, into the eye of the wolf. The beast drew back, blinking hard. An upper cut and it stumbled up groggily onto its hind legs. It tottered left and then right, floundering into furniture.

A sharp grip of claw on stone thrust the wolf forward again, striking Tacit hard in his side with a taloned hand, slashing open his cassock, rending a great gash in his inquisitorial chain mail, blood staining dark crimson against the fabric. The Inquisitor went down in a heap. Immediately the beast turned and focused its fiery glare onto the Sister. It leapt, but as quickly as it did so, it stopped, mid air, and staggered to the ground, Tacit having grasped the creature by the tail. He wrenched it back towards him and gathered it into a bear hug, tightening hard about its yawning jaws and neck.

It was then that Isabella caught sight of Tacit's silver revolver on the ground. She rushed forward and took it up. It felt cold and terrible in her hands, the weight of it unsettling. She raised the gun and fired. The shot rang about the apartment like a thunderbolt. The wolf barked out in pain, going down on one leg. Immediately it pulled itself free from Tacit and spun on the Sister. She levelled the revolver at the creature's chest. And then it was gone, launched like a spring from its good right leg, through the door and out of the building as if pursued by unseen furies.

She charged after it as far as the door, but already it had fled into the dark of the city. She looked back and watched the Inquisitor stumble onto the floor, his hand at his side, his face broken and bruised.

"Tacit!" she called, rushing to him, a hand to his ribs, another to the back of his head, supporting his body down to the flat of the floor. "Tacit, are you okay?"

The Inquisitor scowled in pain, and then chuckled coldly.

"Tacit, I fail to see what is so funny!" the Sister retorted, pushing the hair from his face and wincing as she peered down at the cruel wound in his side.

"Shame. I do. It would seem our enemy is scared."

"Scared?!" stuttered Isabella. If anyone was scared, it was her. "If you say so, Inquisitor." She pulled her hand away from his side, fingers and palm drenched in his blood. "Tsk, this is nasty. I'll get some water and a cloth."

She ran for the kitchen to gather the water jug. She was suddenly aware of how her feet smarted with glass embedded deep within them. She stopped and hobbled to a chair to examine the sole of her left foot.

Tacit tried to get up. "Yes, scared," he muttered, turning awkwardly onto an elbow. "Clearly they don't want us going to Fampoux." He growled out his words like a prophecy. "I wonder what it is we will find there that so terrifies?"

FIFTY SIX

19:28. Wednesday, October 14th, 1914.
Fampoux. Nr. Arras. France.

There was a style and a poise in the way Sandrine stepped briskly through the shattered streets of Fampoux. It brought a colour and a light to the surroundings even as a sombre shade of night fell about it. She passed lines of soldiers marching out towards low trenches being dug and constructed at the eastern outskirts of the village, standard issue folding spades strapped to their backs. She could smell the sweat and gun oil from them as they passed. Several times she was called to "Halt" by a barking sentry, but each time she ignored the order, striding past with a flippant turn of her head. A grumbling, "Bloody Froggies," or words to similar effect, were always levelled back at her, but the sentries clearly thought the woman not enough of a threat to their growing defences to follow up their shouts with bullets.

Once again the German guns had fallen quiet. No longer was there the distinct growl of artillery. A hesitant peace had come to the lands. After the hell of fighting and bombardment, to see the soldiers march past in formation or dig in their units at the harsh chalky land; it felt like watching a scene from a huge exercise, with just a darkening sky above, the smell of horse dung, sweat and hay all around.

The town hall had been badly damaged from an earlier onslaught, a direct hit decapitating the bell tower and bashing a great hole in one side of it. Pigeons now roosted in the ruins of what was once a finely carved stone rampart, taking startled flight whenever the shells fell again. Dust and stone littered the ground before the grey stone brick building. It broke Sandrine's heart to see it as it was, the cobbled square before it cast light grey by fallen masonry and dust. The hall held so many great memories for her, of dances and fetes, of her first proper kiss.

There was a bored looking soldier at the door, resting against the lintel, a cigarette balanced precariously between his lips. He watched Sandrine studiously as she strode up, stepping into her path before she could reach out to the door.

"What is the meaning of this?" Sandrine cried, throwing her hands in the air. "This is my town hall."

"Major's headquarters now," replied the sentry, dutifully. He gripped his rifle in his hands and measured himself against the woman, moving a little to the right to better block the way through.

"Piss on your Major!" hissed Sandrine, making to push him to one side.

The soldier swept Sandrine's hands to the side with the body of the rifle and tried to usher her away. She was stronger than he expected and it was in fact he who found himself pushed aside. He lost his footing and stumbled over, down onto his knee. Sandrine was through the door and inside before he could reach back to grab her.

She pranced lightly over the wooden floor of the hall, long ruined by the endless trudging of military boots. At the far end of the hall, a set of sweeping staircases ran upwards either side of double doors. The rich pile carpet which had adorned the stairs had long since been ripped up and disposed of. With the soldier fast on her heels, Sandrine gambled on the lower doors and headed towards them, casting them wide. The balding figure behind the desk looked up and roared at the unexpected interruption.

"What is the meaning of …!"

And then the words were stripped from his throat the instant he recognised the woman before him.

"You!" Sandrine hissed, stuttering to a stop on the carpeted floor of his office.

The sentry caught hold of her roughly by the arm, and began to draw her away. "I'm so sorry sir," he called apologetically, expecting any moment a torrent of abuse to be unleashed upon him by the Major. But Pewter's face was a mix of surprise and cautious delight. His mouth hung partially open, his eyes burning into Sandrine.

"No, leave us, Ponting," he ordered, gathering himself to his feet and stepping slowly around the desk. "Shut the door behind you please, as you leave."

The sentry did as he was bid, bowing dutifully. Pewter stalked towards her, like a hunter approaching a triggered trap. She watched him with uncertainty, turning so that she always faced him, as if expecting a lunge or a killing blow from behind.

"Well, well," Pewter smiled, showing teeth. He brushed back his wisps of hair and stepped close. Sandrine could smell his stale breath and took a step away but the Major's hands were around her back in an instant, snatching her to him, his mouth to hers. She pushed him away and wiped his spittle from her lips, snarling at him, her eyes like fire.

"How dare you!" she hissed.

"How dare *you* walk out on me like that?!" he retorted, his tongue gently touching across his lips to taste her saliva. He gave an eyebrow a surreptitious little raise and sat back on his desk with an arrogant ease, feeling in his pockets for cigarettes. "You know, you shouldn't have turned me down like that. Just as I was getting a little excited about the whole thing too. You really are quite a tease. And quite a delicious thing." His eyes played over her body. "I'm certainly glad to see you again. Why on earth you chose Lieutenant Colonel Wood, I just do not know. You naughty thing. I've had women flogged for less."

Sandrine spat at his feet. "I don't care what you think!"

"Oh, but clearly you do. I mean, why else have you come back to me?" he asked, drawing out his packet of woodbines and placing one into his lips. "Realised your mistake have you?" He laughed, a high haughty laugh. "I must say you must be desperate, padding all the way across the British front, but I do agree that I am a bit of a catch."

Sandrine seethed, her eyes thin and hostile.

"Oh, I see," chuckled the Major, coldly, "this is just a happy chance, you turning up like this, is it?" he asked, his hands raised in mock question. "Cigarette, my dear?" Sandrine's silent response gave him his answer.

"Look!" he said, adopting a more conciliatory tone, "let's not worry about what went on back in Arras, shall we?" He pushed himself forward, at which Sandrine immediately stepped back, expecting another assault. Pewter raised his hands in submission and stepped slowly to one side, circling about the woman, studying her as he went. She looked filthy and exhausted but he could still feel the urge grow within him at seeing her again, her natural beauty no war could ever diminish. "You played with me," he went on, "really rather well, too, I'll admit. But I survived and so did you. And here we are, once again. I say it's a jolly good omen, don't you?" He chortled manically. Sandrine glared at him.

"Be quiet you fool!" she shouted back, her body still taut, ready to spring aside if the Major tried anything. "I haven't come to see you."

"Of course not," he replied, smugness filling his features, then suddenly saying, "my God! Your body is a gift!" He stood back to admire it, shaking his head with exaggerated wonder.

Sandrine gritted her teeth and shook off his nonsense. "I have come to warn you."

"Warn me? Warn me of what, exactly?" replied Pewter, his face and manner darkening. "No one, particularly women, warns me about anything. I am my own man."

"Keep your men indoors at night when in Fampoux."

"Good heavens!" Pewter exclaimed, shaking his head and now laughing. "Are you in any way connected to Lieutenant Frost? The damned fool said exactly the same to me earlier!"

"I know Henry, yes."

"Oh, it's Henry is it? On first name terms, are we?" There was a jealous glint in the Major's eyes. "My, you do get around. Lieutenant Colonel Wood one minute, Lieutenant Frost the next?" He leaned close to her. "I have bad news for you. You are going down the ranks, not up them."

"You should listen to your Lieutenant. Keep your men indoors on a night in Fampoux!"

"And why exactly should I do that, pray tell?" he asked, sitting on the arm of an armchair and crossing his legs.

"The wolves," Sandrine replied, coldly.

"The wolves?" replied Pewter doubtfully, with a smirk.

"The wolves of Fampoux. They are what defeated the Germans. The Germans were warned and they did not listen. Listen to me now," Sandrine urged, coming forward a little into the centre of the carpet. "Do not let your men outside after dark."

The Major sat back and looked at her blankly. He then started to laugh, a high forced mocking laugh. Sandrine crossed her arms and stared back at him.

"Very good!" he chortled, putting a cigarette between his lips and clapping. "Very good! I am most impressed!" He stood up and started walking again, his time in the opposite direction to which he had first surveyed the woman.

"I don't understand what you have to be impressed about? You just have to do it. Give the order. Keep your men indoors and safe."

But the Major was still laughing. "So, what are you? A German spy?"

"No!" Sandrine shot back.

"A German sympathiser?"

"How dare you! The Germans invaded my country, enslaved my people, ruined my village!"

"Yes, and took you as their little fuck puppet, no doubt?!" the Major cried, dropping his cigarette to the carpet and crushing it beneath his boot. "What did they do? Fuck you so well that they won you over to their side? I do suggest that you must have a delightful and eager cunt. Moist. Well worked. At least that was the impression I got from what you allowed me to feel."

"You are sick!" Sandrine cried, turning and heading for the door.

"All lined up and fucked you, one by one, was that it? Worked you over to their side so that you'd be encouraged to spy for them? Eh?! Thought you'd get secrets from the Lieutenant Colonel, did you? Thought you'd try the Major next, did you?"

Sandrine threw the doors open. She turned back and stared at him in the doorway. "You are sending your men to their deaths! I have tried to warn you. I ask you one final time, keep them indoors."

"No, I won't oblige you with your request to remove my troops from my defensive trenches," Pewter shouted after her, storming through to the entrance hall into which she had now gone. "No, I won't give the Germans free passage back into the village I won from them. I am terribly sorry, German whore! Go and tell them that now. Tell them that I am waiting for them and we will give them a typically British hospitable welcome, when they come!"

Sandrine stopped before the main doors of the hall and turned around. She looked at the Major and then over his shoulder at the carpet in his office, before steering her eyes back to him. "I remember when that carpet was first laid down, laid down by my family twenty two years ago." There were tears in Sandrine's eyes, tears of rage. "I would prefer if you showed it a little more courtesy than to stamp your cigarettes out on it," she warned, before turning and striding away.

"Silly bloody woman," Pewter cursed, his eyes still trained on the open door. "Ponting!" he shouted. At once the sentry rushed through the open doors. "Go and pass orders to all the officers. Tell them they and their men are all to take sentry duty this evening. Tell them I have received intelligence of an imminent German attack. Tell them I expect all defences to be occupied and primed within twenty minutes. Do you understand?"

"Yes, sir," nodded Ponting.

"Good, now go."

At once the young soldier tore out of the hall. Pewter watched him go from a window of the building. He looked out to the horizon. The moon was just beginning to rise silver and sleek above it. Somewhere in the darkness, a wolf howled.

FIFTY SEVEN

19:34. Wednesday, October 14th, 1914. Paris. France.

Cardinal Bishop Casado was signing papers at his desk when Bishop Basquez swept in unannounced through the open door, the only sound coming from the swish of his cape as he approached the table.

"Cardinal Adansoni is guiltless then?" Casado asked not looking up, knowing his visitor to be the serpentine man who seemed to be everywhere in the Vatican. He knew of no one else who would enter his room without first declaring his arrival.

"Monsignor Benigni and the Sodalitium Pianum found newspaper cuttings in his residence," the Bishop countered, leaning forward on the desk with a gloved hand, "regarding this Mass for Peace."

"And?" replied Casado, his eyes still fixed to the papers he was signing. He waved with his left hand, like a king might do to a favoured subject, in the direction of a tall pile of paper where the cuttings now sat.

"This material is dangerous," Basquez insisted, his eyes turning from the papers to the Cardinal Bishop.

But Casado showed little in the way of agreement. He scratched angrily with his pen across several documents without reply, only eventually looking up to skewer the scowling man with a stare of his own to match. "Don't be ridiculous!" he spat. At once Basquez drew his hand away from the desk, as if burned. "This material is available in every home in Europe! Indeed, it seems that everyone within the Church is talking about this event, some even with both great hope and admiration for those with the gumption to attempt to forge peace through the power of prayer!"

"But –" Basquez tried to protest.

"This is nothing which requires further investigation!" Casado roared, picking up the sheets of newspaper and tossing them forcefully to floor of his office. With that, his anger seemed to evaporate, the heat within him cooling to something which resembled shame. "And I feel foolish for agreeing to the Sodalitium Pianum's involvement. Cardinal Adansoni is many things, but he's not a traitor or heretic."

"As you wish," replied Basquez cautiously, bowing with his head subserviently and stepping back from the desk. He put his hand to his chin, in a way which suggested he was concocting some new evidence to use, walking a tight circle in the carpet in front of Casado's desk. "May I ask a question, Cardinal Bishop?" Casado sighed. By now he had gathered his pen into his fingers with the intention of showing that Basquez's time with him was at an end. "Just as we're talking about Adansoni," Basquez continued, "knowing how much he was against the assessment of Inquisitor Tacit."

"Is it important?"

"Probably not. But may I ask it anyway?"

"Very well. As long as it's your final question." The old man behind the desk cast one eye onto the clock on the far wall. "I am busy."

"Why was Tacit sent for assessment in Arras? I mean, there are far more appropriate, one could say challenging, places to test an Inquisitor than somewhere, dare I say it, mundane like Arras. What was the Holy See's thinking?"

"It was not of their choosing," Casado replied, his pen beginning to scratch across the coarse surface of parchment in front of him. "So who'sedecision was it?"

"Pope Pius X. He requested it, in a final letter to me shortly before he died."

FIFTY EIGHT

1901. VERONA. ITALY.

The tavern smelt of vomit and mould. Neither Tacit or Georgi paid the stench any mind. They supposed it probably helped mask their own odour, four days on the road riding hard to bring news of their first assignment together back to the Vatican. They still had another four days ahead of them till they got there and the pair felt the need for a night under cover and a little more comfort than the land could offer. A hot meal cooked by another's hand and wine on tap would beat what fare they could gather on the road and drink from their wineskins.

Tacit guzzled his third goblet of wine, before filling it again and pushing back his chair into the shadows of the tavern corner. He gulped another mouthful of the weak house red and stared into middle space.

Georgi chuckled and filled his second cup of wine. He put down the empty jug and leaned on his elbows, peering hard at his friend.

"Considering the success of our first assignment together, Poldek, and our first night in a tavern after, how many days is it? ... eight? ... you really are quite dismal company this evening."

Tacit sniffed.

"So what's wrong?" Georgi continued, taking up his goblet but not drinking.

"Wrong?"

"Wrong. With you? Face like Cardinal Konstantinov," he said, referring to the irritable Cardinal from Bulgaria whose face resembled a scowling backside.

Tacit chuckled at the comment and shook his head. He necked his wine and thrust his cup down on the table. "Any more?" he asked.

"Jug's empty," Georgi replied. "You want another?"

"I do."

Tacit's partner and friend caught the attention of the barmaid and she brought another jug over to their table. Tacit filled his cup immediately and sat back in the shadows.

"Got a bit of a thirst on tonight, Poldek?" suggested Georgi.

Tacit ignored him. "How many witches have you killed?" he asked, draining his goblet and nursing it in his lap.

Georgi raised his eyebrows and wondered, wrong-footed by the question. After a moment searching he said, "I have no idea. Not many. A few. The correct answer would probably be 'not enough'. Why do you ask?" He brought his drink to his lips and sipped.

Tacit shrugged, leaned forward and reached clumsily for the jug, showing the first signs of heavy limbed drunkenness.

"Would you believe anything a witch told you?"

"Depends what it was they told me," Georgi shot back, winking. "Here, let me." He lifted the jug and poured a broad stream of wine into Tacit's goblet. "Again, why do you ask?"

Tacit shrugged again and took the drink, thanking him. He looked across the tavern.

"Best not to worry yourself, Georgi. How many of us are there left?" he asked, drinking again but this time more leisurely.

"From our original thirteen?" Tacit nodded without looking at him, as if drawn by the other scenes in the tavern or unable to look at his friend. "I don't know. Petr went north. We've not heard from him in over six months."

"Five," Tacit growled in answer, almost upending the goblet into his mouth so wine ran either side of his lips, down his black cassock. "There's five of us left, Georgi." He turned his eyes onto his friend. "More than half of us killed."

"We're Inquisitors," Georgi replied. "We know the dangers. We've always known them."

"I thought only monsters could behave in such a manner."

"What's that supposed to mean?" Georgi laughed, but it was more in an attempt to lighten his friend's mood.

"That those who command us, who send us out, can act with such little care."

Tacit's melancholy had begun to make Georgi uncomfortable. He snatched up his wine and sat back, eying him cautiously.

"And our superiors? What do they say?" Tacit continued drowsily, as if reading from a script. "Nothing. They say nothing but draw up the next assignment. They're killing us, Georgi. They're killing my family all over again." There was silence between the pair of them. "Do you ever see lights?" Tacit asked his friend – now looking as sullen as Tacit with the drift of the conversation.

"Lights? What do you mean, 'lights'?" he replied testily.

"Exactly that. Lights, all around you?"

"God, Poldek, are you drunk? Course I've not seen lights all around me! Who has?!"

"I have. Or I did. Once. No, that's a lie. I saw them when I was younger once before that, before I'd joined the Inquisition. Just before I joined. And then once afterwards, when … when my master had been killed and I was left all alone." He stared, as if hypnotised by the knots of the table, with his unwavering eyes. "They've not come to me since. Never. Not for over three years now. When they came to me it felt like I'd been touched by the Lord God himself. I felt his power and his greatness. I'd never experienced anything like it before. Such power. Such warmth and belonging." He drew a filthy nail across the grain in the wood of the table and made a mark. "I can't help but think I've been abandoned by him. That he knows my thoughts. For cursing our superiors. For questioning their judgement. For raging at them for killing us, one by one." Tacit drained his goblet. "That God knows my weaknesses."

FIFTY NINE

22:28. Wednesday, October 14th, 1914.
The front line. Fampoux. Nr. Arras. France.

"Can you hear something?" Private Dawson asked, standing from the divot he had dug into the trench wall to act as a rest. He craned his ear to the sound. He listened for several moments, those around him looking on with growing trepidation. Suddenly, his face, illuminated by the patchy moonlight, brightened and he said, "There! Can you hear that? What is it? Is that singing?"

All of them gathered in the trench and listened hard. Between the distant thump of shells and the wind rustling the grasses of No Man's Land, one by one they caught the sound that Dawson had first detected. Singing, "Deutschland, Deutschland, über alles", drifting like a fog over their lines. It was beautiful and moving and terrible, all at once bringing home the aching honesty and pointlessness of the two enemies' rivalry. The British soldiers stood in reverent silence, their heads bowed, listening to the harmonic voices sounding like a choir from beyond the grave, so very distant, the voices alien and strange, but bound up with such warmth and humanity.

A little way along the line, a couple of Tommies started singing a retort to the lush, ghostly sound, with china chipped voices and high pitched warbles. "Pack up your troubles in your old kit bag, and smile, smile, smile." They sang with faltering gusto, and all along the line, the song was picked up, bit by bit, man by man, until the entire front sang the song back at the Germans, as if a riposte of melody to match the musical foray from the enemy; sung not to spar with them, but to share the moment and the camaraderie, their troubles forgotten when a simple thing like the human voice had the power to overcome distrust and hatred of each other.

Eventually both lines of singing subsided and a cheer went up, first from the German lines and then from the British at the end of this war of melodies, this little battle of songmanship. With that, the cheers and the laughter were promptly extinguished by Sergeants on both sides storming down the trenches demanding silence and diligent focus on the hundreds of yards of No Man's Land between the rival trenches.

A tense tranquillity once more suffocated the peace of the place. But not for long. All at once, a tumultuous cacophony of explosions broke forth from vast German guns away in the east. Like the thundering birth sounds of some beast unleashing itself from the very bowels of hell, the heavy artillery tore into life, casting their rain of death upon the British hunkered down in their trenches.

Along the British lines, shells fell with wicked rapidity and deadly precision, dirt and dust; flaming iron and mangled flesh, cries and shouts, smoke and cordite cast about the wide front that they had thrown up. Wire and mud was blasted into the sky, showering and whipping those caught beneath as it fell. Everything turned to orange and red as the shells landed, blinding and disorientating with their glare.

There was no hole for Henry within which to hide. His time and dedication spent preparing Sandrine's house against an unseen and unknown, – and for all he began to suspect, non-existent foe – now seemed a futile exercise, as he clapped his hands to his ears and hunkered down tight to the trench's floor. Every inch of his body seemed to tremble and shake, every sinew was taut and sense utterly shattered. If he had been able to hear he'd have heard his men roaring near him, clamouring for the barrage to stop, praying for a higher power to help them make it through the carnage and let them live for one night more. Nearby Sergeant Holmes stuck his head between his legs and waited for the end to come, however that might be.

Sandrine had begged Henry not to go. She pleaded with him and had hung onto him like a wife bidding farewell to a husband leaving for war. But he could not abandon his men. The order had been given that all were to man the eastern trench outside the village. And whilst his heart wished not to go forward into the trench, there was never any question that he would not.

There appeared to be no end to the barrage. Even in the cool of the night, German artillerymen stripped to their vests with wiped brows and drenched clothing as they worked rounds into the vast and terrible barrels of their cannons. Such was the fury of the onslaught that the earth shook and tumbled from the walls of the trenches, partially covering Henry as he lay at the base of one of them. He pulled himself clear of the fallen dirt and crouched on his haunches, his fingers in his ears, his head cowed. So it was that he never heard the first sharp bite of rifles being fired, he never saw the enemy when they first appeared.

It was the movement in the trees which first drew the British sentries' eyes, a wave of grey, lit by the multitude of flares shot high into the darkening sky, spiralling downwards like slowly falling stars. Movement in front of the trees suggested that there was something alive within the wood, some four hundred yards in front of the British lines, away to the right of the main German line. Suddenly the grainy movement of grey condensed and became more precise, crystallising into the muddied blue of uniforms, German uniforms, a vast army of Germans materialising out from the woods and from the spell which had been their rousing song ahead of taking to the battlefield as a legion of death.

Out of the trees they came, beneath the sharp luminescence of British flares, trotting at a slow but steady pace, packed shoulder to shoulder, so tight not even a bullet could pass untouched, an immense river of them, surging with assured and steady pace over the distance of No Man's Land towards the British lines.

Once out of the shadows of the wood they moved quicker, adopting an odd unnatural gait across the undulating fields of the land, not running but not walking either, an awkward middle speed which both perplexed the British defenders in the trenches, as it did the attackers in the open fields.

All along the British lines roared orders drove men to take to their positions on their trench walls. Sergeant Holmes threw himself alongside Henry and pushed a cartridge into his rifle with trembling fingers.

"Bloody hell, Lieutenant," he cried, finally fitting the magazine into place. "This is bloody it! This is bloody it!"

SIXTY

1904. Tirana. Albania.

Tacit followed the lead of the other Inquisitors and sank to his haunches in the long grass. He drew a hand across his face and rubbed the exhaustion from his eyes. He swatted at a fly and surreptitiously sipped at his hipflask. Dawn rose behind them. Tacit felt rough and unhinged. He'd not slept for days, tracking the clan of heretics as they made their way over the border into Albania. The Inquisitor squad was biding its time, waiting for the most opportune moment to strike.

Tacit knew this was it.

He stowed the flask and grimaced as the liquid burned inside him, sparking his senses into some sort of focus. When he was younger, adrenaline would have fired him up for his task ahead. Now he felt as lumpen as the bodies which would soon be piled up on the banks of the river at which the deviants had gone to pray.

Antonio looked across at him and winked, kissing the signet ring on his right hand. It had been a gift from his father when he'd first been accepted into the Church. He wondered if his father would be proud of Antonio still, the charming boy from Padua near Venice, whose party trick was eviscerating enemies with his bowie knife.

A series of clicks sounded down the line, the signal that the attack had begun. The squad leader had given the nonconformists long enough to finish their prayers. He wasn't a complete monster.

The crack of a rifle sounded and Antonio's eye was ripped from his face, throwing him backwards into the long grass. Instantly Tacit gathered him into his arms, holding the shuddering young man, as he looked down into his one dead eye. An inane mumbling bubbled from Antonio's lips before he fell silent.

Tacit laid him gently on the earth and closed his lifeless eye with his fingers. Then he rose, like an elemental explosion rising from the bowels of the earth, and thundered into a run, screaming and roaring towards the hordes of heretics waiting for them on the river bank.

SIXTY ONE

22:34. Wednesday, October 14th, 1914.
The front line. Fampoux. Nr. Arras. France.

A volley of shots rang out across No Man's Land from the approaching German army.

"Bloody bastards are hopeful!" cried Private Dawson. "They think they can hit us from here?!"

A vast wall of German infantry had appeared in the clinging grey dusk of No Man's Land, a grey blue smudge against the horizon and fading light.

"They're not firing at us," replied Henry, peering up and over a sandbag with the periscope, directly in front of his firing position. "They're shooting into the air, as if to warn us!"

"Warn us?! Do they think we don't know they're coming?!"

And they were coming, jogging now through No Man's Land, their rifles turned towards the sky, firing off rounds in a show of bravado and strength.

"Stay your ground!" growled a Sergeant from the ranks, pacing the trench behind the line of soldiers. "And when you get the order, don't you stop shooting till every one of those bastards is dead. Do you hear me?"

"Can we start shooting then, sir?" came a dispiriting voice from somewhere in the line.

"No you cannot shoot. You do not shoot until you hear the order. Is that understood?!"

Now the Germans were gaining ground on the trench, two hundred yards away, the sheen from their badges and belts catching the glare of the fizzing flares above. They lowered their rifles and fired as they ran, their rounds buffeting the ground about the trench and whizzing through the air above it. The British soldiers crouched down into their trenches and firing holes and watched with ever growing fear and trepidation.

"Now can we shoot, sir?" someone cried imploringly.

"If I hear another request to fire, I will rip the bloody balls off that man!" roared the Sergeant. "You wait for my order, you bloody riff-raff."

Now the Germans were running, not a sprint, but a steady pace, cantering over the ground, one hundred yards away, a massed wall of bayoneted rifles and young Germans, looking to tumble into the waiting British lines and down onto the Tommies. And they were firing. Rounds peppered the ground before and beyond the British line. Every now and then, a British soldier would snap back, crumpled into the back wall of the trench.

Seventy five yards. You could make out the eyes of the enemy, dark pits in white, ashen faces, drawn into stern frowns. Their hands worked furiously over their rifle bolts, shooting from their hips towards the British lines.

Fifty yards. The German soldiers seemed so close now that the British could simply reach out and touch them. The edges of their bayonets glinted.

All of a sudden, from along the entire British front, the cry of the Sergeants took hold. The infantrymen lining the walls needed no more than the merest of nods from their superiors before their rain of death was unleashed. The British fired and the call was given to move to 'rapid fire'. The approaching Germans stumbled and fell like pins in a skittle alley, man after man, set after set, the following lines climbing over the bodies of the fallen without hesitation to continue the suicidal advance forward.

There seemed no end to their number but greater still was the stock of bullets possessed by the British. For what seemed an eternity the British lines fired, for so long and so ruthlessly that the wooden casings of the rifles grew too hot to hold and soldiers rested their stocks on the trench lips as they fired, or gathered cooling soil and grass into their hands to act as a padding against the heat. Wave after wave of them came, scrambling over the dead and the dying to continue their grim pursuit forward.

"They're bloody off their trollies!" roared Private Dawson, inserting another magazine. "What do think they can do? Walk through bullets?"

The ratta-tat of a machine gun sounded from somewhere and a vast swathe of German soldiers crumpled, the line behind them collapsing moments later. A wall of Germans now lay in front of the British lines, a hundred yards into No Man's Land, a wedge of bleeding quivering flesh, grey and black and crimson.

From the woods there suddenly came a second wave, shoulder to shoulder as their predecessors had done, moving with slow steady strides over the ground, firing a warning to the heavens as if to announce their arrival and then, as they drew closer, firing towards the trenches with more rapidity and running with fleeter feet. Once again the British rifles replied and the German lines fell. The wall of dead and dying grew taller and broader still, until it became a great surging torrent of death sweeping the entire length of this part of the front. But still the Germans were not done. Another wave came, and was broken as before, followed by another, and then another, and then yet a following wave, each time broken and despatched before the wall of dead was ever breached.

"Fritz is a bloody madman!" cried Holmes, shaking his hand and cursing, after burning it on the stock of his smoking rifle.

"Or his officers are as cruel as ours," Henry replied, setting down his rifle and rubbing the dirt and grime out of his eyes. "This is sheer bloody murder."

Eventually, finally, the attacks faltered. The Germans stumbled uncertainly backwards and then fell back altogether, broken in a blind racing panic.

"Alright, lads," Sergeant Holmes cried. "Hold your fire." He climbed up onto the observation plate and peered over the sprawling mass of trembling, moaning bodies to the line of desperate Germans in flight, far off across No Man's Land. "Good shooting lads," he called, hopping down and brushing his hands clean of mud. "Taught bloody Fritz a lesson there. No doubt about that."

"Not quite what I was expecting," said Dawson, sounding hollow.

"Be happy it wasn't you on the charge," replied Holmes. "It might be, next time."

"Sheer bloody madness!" Henry muttered to himself, sinking down the wall, his back to No Man's Land, as if unable to any longer look on the horror of the scene beyond. And yet, his mind wasn't trained solely on the dead. He was also aware of the nagging fact that if he'd pushed through with Sandrine's advice and withdrawn his troops to the houses, they would have been overrun. Fampoux would have been lost. He felt confused and sickened at the betrayal.

All that night the moans and howls of the injured haunted British trenches. They could hear sounds in the darkness of No Man's Land, the retrieval of the wounded and of dear comrades fallen in the suicidal assault. At least, that was how it seemed to those listening in the British trench. They didn't fire at the noises. How could they hit anything in the dark? And, after all, enough blood had been spilt for that day.

When dawn broke, they were surprised at how efficient the Germans had been at clearing away their dead.

PART FOUR

"Hell is empty for all the devils are here."
William Shakespeare, *The Tempest*

SIXTY TWO

06:57. Thursday, October 15th, 1914. Arras. France.

Isabella woke with the sun across her face. She shielded her eyes with the crook of her arm and swallowed, her tongue exploring the dry chapped landscape of her lips. She swallowed again and opened an eye cautiously to the light. The soles of her feet ached. Her back and ribs ached. But her one open eye felt more or less unharmed, which gave her confidence that she was not totally damaged. She opened a second eye and squinted at the window, the thin blind a paper shield against the morning glare.

As she looked around she realised that Tacit was no longer sitting in the chair, silhouetted against the window, as he had been when sleep had finally taken the Sister in the early hours of the morning, despite her most determined resolve to stay awake with him. She was surprised to find herself disappointed by his absence. Her last memory had been of the Inquisitor, sat with his chin on his hands, staring hard out of the window of the hotel room he had found them, stock still as if he was made out of stone. She thought how apt it was to think of him as stone, hard of body, hard of heart. It had been her final memory when her thoughts span and dissipated with the first embracing charms of sleep.

The chair on which Tacit had spent the night was still drawn to face the window, the paper thin blind crumpled to one side to allow Tacit a view of the street outside and the only entrance to the building.

Tacit had chosen the hotel without a moment's hesitation, as if he'd known it well, as if he'd known it would ensure safe solitude for the night. It was too dangerous to stay at the Catholic residence any longer, too dangerous to return to Tacit's old decrepit hotel.

He'd carried her from the residence, despite his far more terrible wounds, to save her feet, across the city to this hotel, without a thought for himself. Though his wounds must have roared in their resistance to his new burden, he made no noise nor gave any sign as to his discomfort. No one took any notice of them as they crossed the city, Isabella clutched in his arms, the Inquisitor bleeding profusely. German bombs had fallen across many parts of the city. The injured being carried was a common sight. In his arms, she felt like a child who had climbed into an old and ancient oak tree and sought refuge within its thick branches. She remarked to herself that, in the past, she would have rallied against being treated quite so gallantly by any man.

But after last night she felt a very different person to the one who had met Tacit just those few days before.

She caught sight of herself in the mirror on the wall and saw that she was smiling wistfully. She raised her fingers to her lips, as if to test what the vision in the mirror was telling her; whether the thought of Tacit had really brought a smile and a warmth to her. She closed her eyes and shook her head gently, both appalled and amused at her weakness in being drawn to this dreadful man, this brutish, rude, proud, protective, honourable man. She breathed deeply and told herself to get a hold of herself.

Isabella listened to the sound of the city outside, the babble of voices, the soft rumble of feet on the street. She moved a hand to her side and felt her ribs. They were sore and tender, crying out when she moved. She waggled her feet carefully. Last night, when they'd arrived at the room, Tacit had laid her gently onto the bed and, under candlelight, had delicately extracted every shard of glass he'd had been able to locate from the soles of them. His dexterity and care had touched her deeply. This brute of a man was perhaps less of a brute than she, and others, had previously taken him for.

With that thought, she now felt guilty for lounging in the bed and forced herself to sit up, almost weeping as her ribs curled over themselves. She threw her legs over the side of the bed and gently settled them onto the carpeted floor. They took her weight and there was little pain returned by them. She levered herself upright, battling through the agony of her side to finally stand straight. The pain ebbed away in waves as she did so, her breath returning to her. She stepped carefully, deliberately, towards the mirror, guarding her side against too much movement which might aggravate the ribs again. She wondered if she'd broken them. She took a deep breath and there was only a little pain which bit back at her. Bruised. Just bruised.

She peered into the bathroom, on the unlikely chance that Tacit had taken to sleeping in the bath and was still there, languishing against the porcelain. She imagined him sleeping, snoring as he slept. The thought brought a wry smile to her lips, quickly lost when she caught sight of herself in the mirror, her bruised and battered face, one blackened eye, the white of it bloodied and demonic. She played with her hair in an attempt to improve the picture and waved a hand at her reflection in defeat.

Carefully she crossed her hands around herself and lifted her undergarment slowly, very slowly, over her head, wincing as delicate white fabric slipped over her buttocks, her breasts and her head. She set it on the bed knob and turned back to the mirror to regard her bruised side. Where china white skin had once been there was now black and deep crimson- looking flesh, down her side to her hip bone and back up around the heavy hang of her breast, her raspberry coloured nipple and into her armpit. She stood looking at her reflection and shook her head to see how battered she appeared.

"You're a mess, Sister," she said to herself, but inside she could feel the tingle of excitement that this world of adventure and danger gave her.

Footsteps suddenly sounded in the corridor outside, their approach catching Isabella by surprise. Before she could cover herself, the door was thrust open and Tacit burst in. His eyes fell upon the topless Sister – Isabella's wide eyes upon Tacit, her hands shooting across herself to conceal her nakedness.

Instantly, Tacit stepped back out, pulling the door hard behind him.

Isabella grabbed back the undergarment and tumbled it over her head, forgetting the pain and discomfort the rapid act of dressing caused. Her heart beat and she could feel an arousal shimmer inside of her as she called out, "Sorry! You can come in!"

Slowly the Inquisitor opened the door and with a childlike awkwardness shuffled sheepishly into the room, his eyes fixed firmly to the floor.

"Sorry about that, Tacit," Isabella soothed, tousling her hair in an attempt to improve her respectability. "I'm sure you've seen women's breasts before?"

Tacit mumbled something indiscernible and thumped the basket of provisions he had bought down onto the sideboard. Isabella heard the sound of chinking glass and correctly guessed Tacit had bought not only food. Still without looking at her, he pulled the bottle of cognac from the bag by the neck and gathered up a glass. He dropped himself into his chair and uncorked the bottle, filling the glass to the top with the rich brown liquid.

"There's food in the bag," he grunted, necking the drink and refilling the glass. "Bread."

"Are you eating?"

"No," Tacit answered, downing the second glass and refilling it for a third time.

Isabella peered into the bag. Sure enough, there was bread, but also fruit. Isabella was touched by Tacit's consideration. She didn't realise how hungry she was until she smelt the aroma of the freshly baked bread rising from inside. She fished inside and took a roll out, sitting on the bed near to Tacit and taking a greedy bite.

"Don't you ever eat?" she asked, taking a second bite and catching the falling crumbs in a hand.

"When I need to," Tacit replied, drinking half his drink and nursing the remains of it in his lap.

Isabella nodded. It seemed a fair answer. She just wondered how a man so big had never needed to eat as long as she had been in his company.

"How's the side?" she asked.

"Fine," replied Tacit, as enthusiastic as the room's plain decor. "It was a good field dressing. Thank you."

"Pleasure," Isabella replied. "Goes to show they teach you something of use at Catechism classes.What time is it?" she asked, finishing the hard, round roll and reaching for something else to eat from the bag.

"Late," muttered Tacit, allowing himself a brief look at the Sister before returning his gaze to the window. Isabella wasn't sure if it was said with annoyance or was typical of the Inquisitor's gruff manner.

"Much happening out there?" she asked, picking an apple from the bag and brushing crumbs from her clothing. She knew it was pointless to try and engage Tacit in idle conversation but she felt the urge to try. It felt daring and wild to sit as she was, beside him, dressed in just her nightgown.

Tacit stared solemnly out of the window, one hand clenched to the glass, one hand clenched to the bottle, as if they were the two most important things to him on the planet.

"Sounds like no more bombs –"

"So why've they sent you?" Tacit interrupted, his eyes still fixed the skyline.

"Sent me? I don't know what you mean."

Tacit ignored the Sister's apparent ignorance. "Why've they sent you? Do they think I've lost my way?"

"I don't know what you mean," Isabella insisted, trying to sound surprised.

"Don't lie to me!" Tacit hissed, now putting his eyes firmly onto the Sister. They were cold and dark. There was no light in them at all. He looked exhausted, as if he'd taken no sleep all night. The rings beneath them were as black as coal. "You said to me there was an assignment," he continued, "when we first met."

"I never –"

"Hombre Lobo."

"And that was true."

"You don't need to play tricks with me, Sister. This wasn't about protecting the Catholic Church, was it? This is about investigating me. I'm the assessment. I'm being assessed for my suitability as an Inquisitor, aren't I?

What is it? File a report on me every night?"

"I don't know –"

"Don't you dare lie to me, Sister! I know. You slipped up. You knew about my interrogation of the Orthodox Christians the other night. My methods. And yet you were never with me, never knew about what I'd done. Never knew, unless you'd been told, of course. Which you were, weren't you? Briefed. Updated. Advised, as to my behaviour. Did Father Strettavario come and tell you that night? Wake you from your bed with news of my disdainful actions?"

Isabella shook her head. Her heart sank and her mind rushed in on itself like a whirlpool. She silently cursed herself for her reckless comment but still she was unable to bring herself to make an open admission.

"No, there was never any assignment *for* me. There was only yours, your assignment *about* me, to assess me, to see if I've fallen. Just so happened that when you found me, a murder had just taken place. Never part of the original assessment. The assessment was just about me. Whether you could corrupt me, see if I'd gone awry. Then the murder happened. A useful chance to test me further and to hide the true intentions of your appearance. A fluke. You've been sent by the Vatican, haven't you, to assess me?"

Now it was Isabella's turn to look away. She stared blindly through the shade into the sunlight, her eyes seeing nothing.

"They think I've lost my faith, don't they?"

"Have you?" Isabella shot back.

Tacit scowled. "Who sent you? Cardinal Delvoria? Cardinal –"

"Who cares who sent me, Tacit? Have you lost your way?" Isabella asked again.

"What do you think?"

"I can only comment on what I see."

"And what's that?"

"Oh come on, Tacit. Do I really have to answer that? The drinking? The brooding?"

"The exorcism? Was that …"

"Part of the assessment?" she hissed. She swept back her scarlet hair, her hands clenched firm. "Yes. They wanted to see if you'd lost your edge."

"Clearly I hadn't. That should have been the end of it." He went to drink and found his glass empty. "But no, they wanted to dig deeper. Wasn't enough for me to battle with the Church's greatest enemy, eh?" He refilled the glass and drained it in a single neck. "And you?" he asked, a voice like granite, his finger pointing accusatorially, "What's your role in all this, eh? To tempt me? To see if I would fail in the temptations of the flesh? Done this before have you, Sister?"

Isabella nodded wearily.

"I doubt it. I'm your first, aren't I? You don't fill me with confidence, Sister."

Isabella shook her hair in front of her face as a way of hiding from the questions and stole her way mournfully to the bathroom, taking her clothes from the end of the bed as she went.

"What do they think?" Tacit shouted from his chair. His anger terrified her. He was going to storm up out of his chair after her, but, despite his rage, he couldn't summon the energy to do so. "Do they think I've fallen from the path with more than my drinking and my faith? Thought that I would be tempted? That I would wish to fuck a whore of the Vatican?"

The words tormented and disgusted her. "How dare you!" roared Isabella, storming forward to strike him. Her hands were drawn white with rage. "How dare you call me such a thing?"

"Well, look at you. You never looked like any Sister I've ever seen!" he cried, climbing out of his chair.

"And you're not like any Inquisitor, Inquisitor! What happened to the man who's hanging on the wall of the Vatican? The Inquisitor of honour? The one with a light in his eyes and a urgency in his features?"

"He got old."

"That's rubbish, Tacit. You're not –"

"What? Old?" Tacit spat. He stopped and stepped towards her. She fell away from him, terrified by his size and anger, until she hit the wall behind her. Tacit loomed over her, so close she could smell the reek of his alcohol -soaked breath, see the deep blue of his irises. He pressed himself tight to her, his thigh against hers, one hand flat to the wall to the left of her head, the other flat against the wall to her right, locking her inside a cage of his making. She could feel her breath surge in and out, her breast rise and fall beneath her flimsy nightdress. She knew she could slip away, under his left hand, but something held her firm, some invisible power clenching her tight to the wall. She felt herself go weak, about to swoon in front of the Inquisitor's firm and fierce glare. But as she felt her legs begin to buckle, he turned and stepped away, back to his chair, his back to the wall and to Isabella.

"You might have assessed Bishops and Priests in the past but not Inquisitors. If you'd known any Inquisitors, properly known any Inquisitors, then you'd know. This is what this role does to you," he said, opening his arms, as if to reveal himself to her. "There's a weight which is applied, a burden which all Inquisitors must carry. The Catholic Church has been busy for too long with its misdemeanours. We spend our lives cleaning up what our superiors within the Church have deemed necessary to ensure the heretics are silenced and the Church continues. And the only signs the Lord gives us are the creatures and the things he sends for us to contend with."

"I don't like the rhetoric, Inquisitor," said Isabella, regaining her voice and her composure.

"You're not alone. Neither do the accused who've had their arms torn out during confession. Neither do the heretics whose bones have been powdered and flesh liquefied whilst repentances have been beaten from them. Neither does the pregnant rape victim whose unborn child has been ripped from her belly and burnt in front of her eyes. How many exorcisms have you attended?"

Isabella hesitated. "I don't see what that has to do with anything?"

"Then you will never have seen the way the demon looks at you. The way it watches you out of the corner of its evil eye."

"What has that got to do with anything?"

"Everything. You know why it looks at you like it does?" Isabella shook her head. "Because it knows it's winning!"

"I don't know what you mean?"

"Look around you, Sister. Look at how we act, the deeds we carry out. Look outside of that window. Look to the horizon. Look at what mankind is doing to itself? Can you not see the devil's hand in everything we do?"

"By that I suppose you mean this war? War has always been part of the fabric of our very being. We go to war to ensure good is preserved."

"Precisely. Perhaps there is no need any more for the devil for we have taken over his role in bringing darkness to the planet. Perhaps we have become so infected by his wickedness that we are all his vessels now. We are legion."

"Say not such things! War is, Tacit. It has always been."

Tacit spat dismissively. "War is the devil's plaything. But if you think war's an acceptable face of mankind …"

"I never said that."

"… there's more delicious examples of how far we have fallen as a race that I can share with you."

"I do not need to hear."

"Yes you do! How many more times do I have to visit the scene of a child rape, unpick the butchery of a senseless street attack? How many more times must I do my Church's bidding and interrogate suspects so long that their bones break and their organs fail? How many more men, women and children must I kill with these bare hands, in order to ensure frailty and respect for the Church? How many more times must I wash blood from my hands, innocent blood; innocent but for their alternative faiths and beliefs? Last week I came upon a family butchered because they weren't Catholic."

"Alright!" cried Isabella. "Enough!"

"The mother and daughters had been raped, the father and sons run through with bayonets. All because they weren't Catholics."

Isabella looked out of the window, avoiding Tacit's gaze.

"Of course, it's not just us who are to blame. The protestants and the jews and the muslims and the hindus and the shintos and the sikhs, they all give as good as they get. An eye for an eye. A tooth for a tooth. An endless spiral downwards." Tacit paused and drew breath, shaking his head. He tapped his foot on the floorboards. "An endless spiral down there."

"So, you don't think we're winning then, Tacit?" asked Isabella, "winning the fight against our foes? Is that what you're saying?"

"Winning? No. But that's the point, Sister. We never will. It's war without end. And that's why I'll keep squeezing the life out of our opponents, correcting our superiors' mistakes, washing the blood from my hands and breaking the unworthy, because it's the only life I know. There is no other direction to go other than onwards, spiralling ever down, down, down."

"And what about you, Tacit?"

"What about me?"

"Have you lost your way?

He shook his head. "No, you and your Vatican lackeys don't need to worry about me. Because there's only one way we're going so it's impossible to get lost."

SIXTY THREE

1904. Naples. Italy.

It was a large farm and Tacit was surprised to find the woman worked it alone.

"My husband died springtime. Typhus," she said, addressing him on the steps to her farmhouse. She admired the size of him, his broad shoulders and strong back, visible beneath his long black coat. "You don't look like any Priest I've ever seen," she continued, sweeping a black curl from her face. "Are you sure you're from the Church?"

Tacit ignored the question and turned to look out across her fields. "You work all these alone?" he asked, placing a boot on the step above where he was standing.

"Not alone. I have farm hands."

"No children?"

"We were only married a few months."

"I'm sorry," he replied, looking at her. She was dressed in black trousers, patched at the knees, a white cotton smock hanging loose over her body and hips. Her beauty came to her naturally. There was a pragmatism about how she looked, dressing for the fields and for work but not hiding the woman she still was. He'd never seen anything so lovely. He forced his eyes aside. "So, I've been told you have a poltergeist?" he asked, looking at his boots. He waited for an answer, which never came. He looked up and found she was smiling at him, her head tilted to one side.

"You have handsome eyes," she said, and Tacit could feel his face redden. He coughed nervously and played with the handle of the bag in his hand. "I'm sorry. I probably shouldn't say such a thing to a Priest."

"Probably not," Tacit replied, but a smile came to his mouth and he tilted his capello hat back on his head.

He realised he was staring at her captivated, their eyes locked together in an embrace. He shook his head and cleared this throat, stepping back to put some distance between himself and the woman.

"I'm sorry," he said, pulling at the lapel of his coat. "I … I suppose you should show me where the activity has been happening."

She pushed herself away from the post at the top of the stairs and told Tacit to follow her inside.

"It's in the main house?" he called, climbing the three steps onto the porch and dabbing his dry tongue on the roof of his mouth. "I thought it might be in one of the barns." He looked back one final time to the fields outside and then stepped inside like a man condemned.

"Yes, it's the room at the back of the house. I think it used to be the bedroom of my husband's grandfather. I never go in there. There's no need. There's never been any need."

"When were you first aware of the activity?" asked Tacit, stepping after her. His eyes fell upon the open doorway to her bedroom and a charge of excitement spun through him. He swallowed and looked straight ahead down the dark passageway he was being led. It turned right and ended promptly at a closed door.

"It's always been there," she said, standing across the corridor from him, a foot away, "noises, bangs and occasionally moans. Sometimes sounds of things being thrown."

Tacit could hear the sound of her breathing. He could feel the sweat on his brow. He surreptitiously moved back, as she fiddled in a pocket of her smock and produced a key.

"We've always kept the door locked. Here." She handed it to him. Tacit noticed how long and graceful her fingers were but that her nails were short and had dirt under them. Hard working hands. Honest hands.

He looked at the key and then at the door. He felt muddled and confused. He couldn't understand why he wanted to lean forward and kiss her. The urge terrified and shocked him but he felt charged and alive, as at no time before in his life. Not even when the lights had picked him up in their glare. He looked back at her and smiled.

"Thank you," he said.

"Are you going in now?" she asked.

"I am. I'm sorry," he asked, "I don't know your name."

"Mila," she replied.

SIXTY FOUR

07:03. THURSDAY, OCTOBER 15TH, 1914.
THE FRONT LINE. FAMPOUX. NR. ARRAS. FRANCE.

A grey dawn was rising over Fampoux and the battlefield to the east, its searching rays like tendrils of light, filling cracks and doorways with their insipid glow. There was the heavy weight of smoke in the air, the stench of gunpowder and grease. Across the vast plains of No Man's Land, a pitted and blasted landscape revealed itself. All remarked at how efficient the Germans must have been at disposing of their dead during the night. Barely a body was left in the field.

Over cigarettes and morning brews, soldiers hunkered down in the trench units and discussed the assault and the night that had followed. Most had a view and that was that the Germans cared more for the dead than the living. Who else would have stripped the battlefield so clean of their fallen?

But there were others who drew themselves away from the discussions and kept their own counsel. Strange things had been seen and heard last night, although no one was able to explain them. Such was the nature of war. One quickly learnt that it was better to not ask questions and just carry on as one always did, accepting that once in the trenches you were no longer a human being but merely an insignificant piece in the giant puzzle that was the war.

"Did I dream it?" Private Dawson asked, peering through disbelieving eyes on the empty landscape.

"Count your casings, Dawson, and then decide," answered Sergeant Holmes helpfully.

Henry staggered out of the trench feeling sick with exhaustion and doubt. The village of Fampoux looked as if a giant had recently shaken its very foundations, the buildings appearing even more tumbledown and decrepit than those Henry had left nine hours before. He wandered wearily back through the streets, aware that the air was thick with flies, fat bluebottles, buzzing and circling around his head. He stumbled on newly fallen rubble in the street, his eyes too weary to take care, his body too exhausted to balance itself. He fell against a group of soldiers lined up along the front of a house. He wasn't sure if they were about to head out to the trenches, or had just returned from them, and neither did he care.

"Bloody watch where you're going!" one of them called, pushing Henry back into the road. He stumbled to regain his composure and footing, and shrank away from them, not caring if he'd been shoved by a fellow officer or a lowly infantryman. All he cared about was returning to his bed and sleep. The desire was like a madness.

The boy with the beautiful teeth appeared, scooting around a corner, almost bundling into the Lieutenant. He spun circles around Henry, bidding him good morning and laughing, before tearing away up the broken up street, as if for him the whole war was a big game. Henry tried to remember when he had felt so carefree and alive as the boy, before he'd undergone his baptism into manhood courtesy of the war. He couldn't – and stumbled on, back to Sandrine's home.

He didn't see the relief in Sandrine's face as he collapsed in from the street and staggered over to his desk. "I didn't expect to see you back," she sniffed, looking down her nose. "I thought the night would be the death of you."

She rested her hands on the end of a broom and looked at him hard, shaking her head disapprovingly. Inside she felt a tangle of joy and thanks at his returning. In the confusion of anxiety after he had left, she had busied herself in making the house more respectable, far more efficiently than Henry's rather feeble efforts. The windows were open and there was a sense of normality returning to the home.

"Thank you for the optimism," muttered Henry, drawing out the diary and taking up his pencil. He yearned for rest but knew he'd rest more easily with his unit diary written up.

"You're welcome," replied Sandrine, brushing absently at the floor, and hiding a smile behind her hair.

Henry covered a yawn with his hand and scratched away at the open page. Sandrine brushed closer and closer towards him, eventually brushing beneath this feet.

"Do you want me to move?" asked Henry, a tension coming to his voice.

"No, no, you are fine," she replied, turning away and brushing the remaining dirt from the side of the room. From the corner of her eye she watched the arch of his back, the curve of his neck vanishing into the base of his military haircut. "So, did they come?" she asked, at length.

"Depends who you mean by 'they'," replied Henry coolly, his pencil momentarily resting on the paper. He continued scratching his recollections of the night until Sandrine interrupted him with an exhausted cry.

"The wolves, of course! Who else?"

Henry turned on her, his anger finally spitting out of him. "Sandrine!

Do you take me for a fool?! There were no wolves! Only Germans! As there's only ever been! Hundreds of them! Yes, they did come. And thank God we were there in our trenches when they did. Because if we weren't …" He turned back to his diary and brushed the dust from the page. "Thank God we were. If we'd taken your advice, stayed in our homes, locked away, we'd have been wiped out, overrun, Fampoux lost! The unit, lost!"

"You mock me!"

"For Christ's sake, Sandrine, put a sock in it, will you?! I'm not mocking you. I'm just telling you, had we done as you'd told us, like you said, well …" He let his voice trail to silence, his composure slowly returning. He turned back to his book and picked up his pencil, but didn't write. He stared at the blank yellow stained paper, the lines blurring into and out of focus. Finally he asked, "Tell me. Tell me, please," turning back to face her, his features grim, drawn. "Tell me you're not working for them are you? The Germans?"

At that accusation, it was Sandrine who now flew into a rage. "Them?!" she screamed, throwing her broom at Henry and charging after it. She battered him from his chair with the back of her hand, sending him tumbling and groaning across the room. He slid into the wall where he lay, both stunned and shocked from the force of Sandrine's outburst. He cowered as her shadow drew across him, shielding his head with his hands, waiting for the blows to rain down on him.

But nothing followed the initial onslaught. He lay there, his eyes tightly shut, waiting for the sharp rap of her fists, too exhausted to fight back and only offering the most pitiful of defences. But the next thing he knew was Sandrine's hands on his hair and then around his face, helping him gingerly to his feet, her tone mournful and apologetic. There were tears in her eyes and she enveloped Henry in an embrace.

"I'm sorry," she sobbed. "I'm so sorry, Henry," and she slowly moved her head around his to face him, her hands on his cheeks which she kissed. She then drew forward and kissed his lips twice and hugged him again. Henry felt the warmth of her pour into him like a tonic. He closed his eyes and his head swooned. "I'm sorry. Please forgive me. Sometimes … sometimes it is hard."

Henry raised his hands to her back and held her tight to him, the confusion of his mind from the blows replaced with a delirium of a quite different kind. He allowed the wonder of the embrace to wash away the weight of hurt and exhaustion he felt. He could smell her skin, feel her warmth. In that moment, he felt he could just fall into her, merge as one, as they were, and stay like that for ever.

Sandrine felt it too, a connectivity like pieces of a puzzle being dropped to the floor and all of them bouncing perfectly into place. All her life she had searched for this moment to be held like this, a simple uncomplicated embrace of kindness and honesty. She'd found herself falling into countless clasps with lovers, but each time something had felt amiss about the situation, incomplete, insincere, demanding. Now, at last, she knew she had found someone in whose arms she felt she could rest forever.

Neither of them said anything for a long time, holding onto each other like heavyweights in the final round, crippled by the moment. Finally, it was Sandrine who spoke. "So the Germans," she said, extracting herself from Henry and wearily gathering up the broom. "They came?" How he wished she hadn't pulled away.

"They did," he said, watching her for a few moments and then picking up the chair which had been knocked from him as he fell.

"And you won?"

"For now, yes."

"Good. I am pleased." She smiled and manoeuvred the pile of dirt she had gathered over towards the open door.

Henry stared at her as if he'd taken leave of his senses. In that moment he could have both throttled her and swept her up off her feet and cradled her in his arms. He was more confused than ever, about what Sandrine had said last night and why she had said it. He also knew, in that moment, he was desperately in love.

Sandrine looked down at the dirt and with two sharp sweeps she sent it as a cloud into the street. "So," she said, placing the broom against the wall and gathering up a cloth, "did you see anything unusual?" so matter-of-factly that Henry wondered if the strike, the kiss and the embrace had ever happened at all, or if he had simply dreamed it.

"Unusual?" the Lieutenant replied.

"What are you writing in your diary?"

"What happened."

"And that is my point. What happened?"

"Oh, I see!" he replied. "Yes, of course." He turned back to his book and then paused, looking back at Sandrine with a scowl. "What happened? A crime," he said, putting down his pencil and rubbing his eyes with his hands. "Another bloody crime in this bloody war." He picked up the pencil and continued to write. "The Germans, they kept on coming, over and over the horizon."

"Just the Germans?" Sandrine asked, pointedly.

Henry put his eyes onto the wall and sat back from the book. He then turned and looked around. "No, not only Germans," he said, no longer able to deny what his eyes and ears had witnessed later, when the pitch of night had come into the lands. "There *was* something. You were right, Sandrine. You could hear them, after the Germans had pulled back. Howling. Terrible howling and crying in the darkness of the night. We didn't dare send up flares. We didn't wish to draw them towards us. We could see very little, in the dark, in the wreckage of the battlefield, all those mounds of bodies, lying still or shuddering in their final ghastly moments. But the howls, you could hear the howls. And you could see … well, you could see shadows, great big shadows, the shapes of giant dogs, going amongst the bodies, grabbing and tearing away, or sitting and feeding. You could hear the sound of them, the dreadful crunching, the slap of blood and flesh, as if the soldiers were being eaten beneath our bullets and bombs."

"I did warn you."

"I know you did." He swallowed and nodded. "I know you did."

"They didn't come for you?"

"Into the British trench? No, they did not."

"I suspect they were suitably well fed by other means."

Henry swallowed. "There was nothing remaining that following morning of the battle. The word was that the Germans had cleared the battlefield that night of bodies. The official word, anyway."

"Are you writing about it, in the diary?"

Henry breathed deeply, staring into the white of paper. "I am … writing what facts I know," he said.

"So you're not."

"I am writing what is … what would be expected."

Sandrine tutted and shook her head. She swept into the kitchen. "I will make you a coffee."

"I would prefer a tea, if you're boiling up some water."

"I know you would," she replied, without turning around.

"So how come you know so much?" he asked nervously, "about the wolves?" Henry called to her through the open door of the kitchen. The sound of her preparing the tea clattered back.

"They are legendary around here. We all know of the wolves in Fampoux."

"I don't understand."

"Then that is good. There are some things not worth knowing, especially if they are not to go into your diary! I will give you a little cake with your tea."

"Cake?!" replied Henry, with a start. "But I don't have any cake!"

"No, but I do. I found some. It's a little dry. But it is still good, after you have had nothing for so long."

"Found? Where on earth did you find some cake?'

"This is my village. Some secrets will stay secret. You write up your silly book of lies. I will fix you some tea and cake."

"You sound like my wife."

"You have a wife?"

"No, but you are talking like one!"

Sandrine felt relief rush into her. She came to the door and folded her hands, looking at Henry, who had turned back to the diary.

"The Major," she said.

"Major Pewter?" Henry replied, scribbling away.

"What do you know of him? Do you like him?"

"Well, I wouldn't say I like him. But he is my commanding officer. I don't suppose you're meant to like them too much."

"Yes, he's an ignorant man."

"Yes, I think he probably is. You worked that out from your meeting with him, did you?"

"Something like that."

"I suspect he sees this whole war as a jolly old jaunt. Would probably do him good to have a little taste of the front line trench, once in a while."

Sandrine laughed and said, "Henry, it is not so bad for you. After all, you have a roof over your head!"

Henry turned, his arm across the back of the chair. "Yes, I suppose you're right," he said, smiling wearily.

"And a wife making you tea and cake!"

SIXTY FIVE

1905. Naples. Italy.

She was standing in a field with her back to the track, pulling sugar beets from the long lines of piled earth, when she heard the crank of the horse's cart. She turned and strained her eyes to see the figure in the cab, her hand across her forehead. In an instant she knew it was him.

"You're back?" she called, and at once Tacit felt awkward and foolish for having returned to the farm and to her. She saw his uncertainty and smirked. "I wasn't aware of any more hauntings."

"I was just passing through," Tacit replied, drawing the horse to a halt. He tried to keep his voice flat, matter of fact, but inside his heart yearned for Mila. She appeared more beautiful than when they had last met. "Just on my way to Salerno." A moment hadn't passed when Tacit had not thought about her. His conscience raced and spun at what he was doing, at his daring and foolishness in returning. He took hold of the guilt building in his head and throttled the life out of it with the resentment he felt at how his friends had been slain in the line of duty.

She smiled and swung the beet over her shoulder, holding onto its stalks like a hunter with a kill. "It's good to see you again, Poldek," she said. "It's been ..."

"A while," Tacit said. "I'm sorry," he said, gathering the reins, "I shouldn't have come."

"No. I'm glad you did," Mila replied, and she flashed a smile at him. "Please." She stepped back from the cart as a sign for Tacit to climb down. "Come into the house. I was just breaking for the morning. It's been a hot day. Would you like a drink?"

Tacit could feel his heart beat hard within him. His mouth was dry, his hands clammy. He felt sickened and ashamed at the recklessness of his coming. He thought of his training, his masters, the Inquisition, the witch, his soul, and he climbed from the cart and led the horse to the stable alongside the house.

The night sky above the farm was like glitter dust. They'd eaten a good earthy supper of rabbit stew and a peach tart, which had made Tacit's eyes water with pleasure. Over the meal and a bottle of red Mila had gathered from the cellar of the house, they'd talked long into the night. The air was still and hot. Crickets chirped endlessly. The peace of it all was complete. Tacit felt unburdened by their talk. Much of the time they had laughed, their conversation at times tantalising and risqué, at other times open and poignant, the talk of their dreams, of the Church, of Mila's loss, of Tacit's service. Finally she yawned and apologised.

"I'm sorry," she said, rubbing a hand across her face.

"No, don't apologise," replied Tacit, reaching across the table with his hand. He placed it within touching distance, unable to move it any closer to her. "I should be the one apologising. I'm keeping you up. You've had a long day."

"And a longer one tomorrow. But thank you for your help, Poldek," she smiled, referring to his assistance gathering beets in the afternoon, stripped to his waist save only for his vest, the hot sun on his back, the sweat drenching his broad chest and shoulders. He'd enjoyed the toil of it. "You work hard, for a Priest," she added, and reached forward to touch his hand with hers.

Tacit laughed quietly and lowered his eyes to their hands.

"Why are you sad?" she asked suddenly.

"I'm sorry?"

The question stung Tacit like a thorn, tearing him from his moment and back to the present.

"Why are you sad, Poldek?" Mila asked again. She leant forward, her hand now on his forearm. "There is a sadness, in your eyes."

"I think you're mistaken," Tacit replied, trying to laugh. "There's …"

"It is not our place to be sad within this world. I know a troubled soul when I see one." She moved her hand back down his arm onto his hand. It felt warm and soft, as she cupped his knuckles and fingers gently.

Not for the first time their gazes locked. Tacit could feel the soft rubbing of her thumb against his hand, could smell the loveliness of her skin. He was trapped by the urge to reach across and kiss her, to take her into his arms. But a shadow drew itself across him and he shivered, his eyes filling with tears.

He turned his eyes down to his lap.

"Don't live with sadness, Poldek. It is not your Lord's bidding to be sad all your life."

She squeezed his hand a final time and stepped silently from the porch into the house.

He lingered at the entrance to her bedroom, the door wide open like an invitation to enter. He could see her shape in the bed, the white cotton of the sheets caught by the silver moonlight streaming through the open window. He pushed the door open a little more, and it groaned on its hinges. Tacit hesitated, as if the noise was somehow a warning against him entering. A passion coursed within him. He could hear his own breath, could see the light sheen of Mila's skin, the dark spray of her hair across the pillow.

He placed a hand to his chest. It touched the cross hanging there and closed around the cool of the metal. He caught hold of himself and stepped backward into the passageway.

Mila turned quietly over beneath the sheets and stared up at the crescent moon climbing high into the brilliant night sky.

SIXTY SIX

09:51. Thursday, October 15th, 1914. Paris. France.

Cardinal Monteria had only recently returned from his visit to Notre Dame when he heard Silas enter his office. He hadn't bothered to look up as his servant stepped up to the desk at which he wrote, the first task of the day's administration to be done. A lifetime of recognising the different footsteps and their business told him who he needed to acknowledge and who he could answer with the opening of a palm. The letter was pressed into the Cardinal's outstretched hand and its messenger slunk away from sight. Monteria opened it absently, his eyes still on the speech in front of him, silently mouthing the words he was going to speak in two days' time.

He finished the paragraph he was reciting and turned his eyes to the open letter. At once his jaw slackened and his eyes burnt into the paper. He raced across the words several times over, back and forth, each time recounting fewer and fewer of the details. Something clutched at his throat, snatching the breath from out of him. He crushed the letter into a ball in his palm and reached out for his walking stick where it usually stood, knocking it to the floor. He hissed angrily, and reached down over the arm of the chair to gather it into his shaking hands.

"Silas!" he called, pushing back his chair and gathering himself to his feet. "Silas! Where are you?!" he asked of the young man, not caring if his irritability got the better of him.

"Is everything okay, Cardinal?" called the young acolyte, hurrying back to the Cardinal's chamber as fast as he was able.

"Have you heard news of Cardinal Poré in Arras?" Monteria asked, clacking past the young man with his cane and then realising there was nowhere else which needed his attendance more urgently than where he currently was. He stopped and stared at the young man. "Has he left for Paris yet?"

"I believe he was going to leave in the next day or so," Silas replied anxiously.

"Get news to him. At once! Tell him he's to leave immediately. Without delay."

"Yes. Of course. We will wire him. Is anything the matter?"

"No, it's like anything," the venerable Cardinal replied, regaining a little of his composure. "With every action there is a reaction," and he looked back to the window with the rain pouring down outside. "As we in the

Catholic Church always do, we simply need to ensure we act faster and with more conviction than our enemies."

SIXTY SEVEN

10:14. THURSDAY, OCTOBER 15TH, 1914. ARRAS. FRANCE.

The lateness of the hour by which they left Arras had done little to improve Tacit's mood. With his battered brown suitcase in one hand, the pockets of his black coat laden down and bulging, they filed along the road out of the city, quickly realising that it would be impossible to hail a taxi for passage to the front. There was no choice other than to walk the four miles to Fampoux. Any motorised vehicles they had seen had been commandeered for army use, carrying fat Generals up and down the Rue D'Arras and to 'important briefings'.

Hot, thirsty and hungry when they finally arrived at the outskirts of the village, they were little enthused to see an endless stream of soldiers and vehicles going into and out of the front, the line of military being the only feature visible. The entire landscape, for as far as Tacit and Isabella could see to the north and the south, had been battered into blackened charred featurelessness.

"You think Sandrine Prideux came back this way?" Isabella asked, doubtfully.

Tacit scratched his chin and sneered. "If she did, you have to ask what on earth for?"

As they'd left the city, a mournful bell had tolled somewhere in its depths, a haunting farewell for their departure. It sounded tuneless and despairing, as if the bell itself had been broken. It fell silent prematurely, midway through its peal. Every church they subsequently passed on the eastern road to Fampoux never once announced the hour. A strong, cold north-easterly swept over the sunken road, making the leaves on the few remaining trees rustle and fall like a shower upon the two lonely figures.

At many times they passed great formations of soldiers, singing and sharply dressed, going east, bloodied, blackened and shambling units coming west. An occasional lorry load of men, jolting and tilting over ruts and holes in the road, would shudder noisily past. A company of men was stretched out on a patch of grass, all of them motionless and silent. Isabella thought the area a makeshift morgue until one of the men tossed noisily in his sleep and turned over.

Always they were accompanied by traffic of one sort or another going towards or away from the front line. The road resembled a huge long traffic jam of soldiers, vehicles, refugees, supply lorries, cattle, cavalry and horse-drawn ambulances filled with the wounded. Incongruous in the churn and the industrialised hell of the scene, suddenly a well dressed woman in a fur coat appeared in the distance and passed them, her head held at a lofty angle, no shoes on her feet. And all the time, the noise of artillery hung in the background.

It took longer than four hours, once the traffic and the crowds and the sentry points had been traversed, to reach the outskirts of Fampoux. And they were still not at the village. Beyond where Tacit and Sandrine now stood, the road had been ground up by the great network of trenches, consumed back into the vast, churned earth from which it had been dug many centuries before. Back then it had been a track along which horses and carts had ridden from Arras to the east and back again. Now it was a metalled road broken up and lost in the myriad of support trenches, dug-outs, officer posts, ammunition stores, latrines, feeding stations, hospitals and the harsh front line.

Great groups of soldiers were gathered in ragtag tired bands near mud stained field tents, chatting and smoking, congregating around tea urns or spread out on the earth under the very last of the heat from the sun that year. Officers marched in tight, conspicuous groups, their sparkling belts and boots as sharp as their clipped English accents. A proud troop of horses trotted by, their coats shimmering in the late French sun, riders saddled on them like proud birds atop pristine nests.

The great trenches had been hand carved into the earth, a rambling, chaotic interconnecting mesh of corridors and pathways winding their way spasmodically, but always gradually away towards the east. Teams of diggers were at work all across the vista, thrusting their spades into the sides of the trenches to widen and enhance, others forcing the first blades into new trenches. Wherever one looked, toil and sweat was the scene. With the drudgery came a muttering too, a jumble of accents talking of home, of Wigan and Hull, a debate about the industrial might of Liverpool or Newcastle, a sparring of words regarding the beauty of the Lancashire dales versus that of Cornish moors.

In the distance, over the rise in the land, they could see the broken tops of houses and leaning chimney stacks of Fampoux.

They passed lines of soldiers, heavily dressed, too heavily dressed for the weather, marching under sharp barked orders from Sergeants, perched high up on man-made mounds along the route, so they could look down as they shouted at the passing units. Artillery sets were being heaved by teams of sweat drenched horses and men, horses pulling at tethers, men groaning and cursing beneath the weight and the cloying soil. They passed a group of men, stripped to the waist, washing themselves with water taken from open drums. They cheered and called when they caught sight of Isabella.

"Alright, Sister?" one of them called, "any chance of a blessing?" to much laughter and cheer. Tacit's cold stare quickly silenced any further hilarity.

They passed a field hospital. An officer and a number of juniors hung around outside it, puffing leisurely on cigarettes, whilst blood splattered doctors filed in and out of the tent openings, pursued by nurses carrying metal containers and trays of bloodied and defaced utensils. A constant stream of soldiers on stretchers carried by weary looking stretcher bearers came out of the trenches. Tacit looked at the wounded as they passed, their bodies pulverised by the shrapnel, flayed and torn.

Tacit looked towards the eastern horizon and watched it with heavy eyes.

The pair of them were regarded sceptically by the gathered ranks as they assembled to enter the labyrinth of the soldiers' endeavours. But no one stopped to question them as they turned into the high walled trenches, most thinking them to be a Priest and a nurse heading to the front line to bless and tend to the wounded. The smell, the musty bite of charcoal mixed with the sweet aroma of hot metal, hung like a shroud across the devastated landscape, thick and clinging, so much so that the sun could barely penetrate and light the ground before them.

All around them, field hospitals consisting of flimsy makeshift and hastily constructed tents spewed an endless stream of nurses and bloodied stretcher borne soldiers and sucked nurses and bloodied and burnt soldiers in. It was like an endless conveyor belt of grief and mutilation.

Like entering a plane of hell.

Tacit and Isabella drew their clothes tight around them and stepped inside.

SIXTY EIGHT

1906. Toulouse Inquisitional prison. Toulouse. France.

The heavy clank of an iron gate opening was followed by heavy feet descending damp stone steps. There were cries and a pleading coming up from the darkness below, the staircase leading down lit by flickering torches on the wall. The stench of defecation and decay was everywhere. Water fell from high places and splashed with a maddening persistence. The darkness had an enveloping chill about it, felt by all save those dressed in furs.

The tall lithe figure of an Inquisitor, clad in black loose fitting clothing, marked with symbols of the Catholic faith, was waiting for Tacit at the bottom of the circling stone steps, a cruel leer on his face. He said something Tacit couldn't hear and the jailer next to him laughed, showing a mouthful of rotten teeth.

"You look nervous, Tacit," the black clad Inquisitor called up. "This is your first visit to Toulouse prison, isn't it? Well you are welcome here of course." It was not said as a greeting. It was meant as a threat, a wicked tease to someone visiting an underworld few had ever witnessed and, of those, few ever wished to return to afterwards.

The Inquisitor turned and banged hard on the large wooden door behind them. A rustle of keys and turning of a heavy lock sounded moments later and the vast door was pulled open, a gaggle of filthy leering men with great rings of keys on belts, whips in hand, peered out, smiling and laughing.

"Glad you could make it, Tacit," the Inquisitor mocked, putting an arm around him. "I've heard great things about you from the field. Building quite a reputation, from the sounds of things. But you've only done part of the job." He thrust a finger into Tacit's shoulder and looked hard into his eyes. His face cracked with a smile and he smoothed the part of the coat that he had just prodded. "This is the best bit, the bit where we separate the men from the boys, where we dispense justice to those who really deserve it. You've never been down here, have you?"

Tacit shook his head and tried to mask his abhorrence. "Oh, you've been missing out," Inquisitor Salamanca continued, turning and stepping through the door. "We used to carry out sentences in the Vatican, in the main Inquisitional Chamber, but some of the Cardinals … well, they didn't have the appetite for it. So …" He looked across the passageway at Tacit. "It was decided to move to these salubrious surroundings. And do you know what? I think they were right. Down here we can work unmolested, untethered by the reticent hand of those who would see us adopt a more conciliatory approach towards our enemies."

Suddenly, Salamanca stopped and thrust an arm across Tacit's chest. "Which, of course, would be an extremely foolish thing to do. The last thing we want to do is give the initiative back to them. The only way to win this war is to keep up the pressure. No remorse. No hesitation. No weakness." He looked at the jailer, grinning fiendishly alongside. "Is the witch prepared?" he asked and the jailer nodded eagerly.

The smell of rot and putrefaction was almost overwhelming in the stinking claustrophobic corridor, lined either side with wooden doorways, filled with a persistent wailing from behind most of them.

The jailer pushed past Tacit and unlocked the door in front of them, heaving it open on creaking hinges. A squeak of alarm came from the gloom beyond, along with a stench like an animal's cage. Salamanca stepped inside and a heavy hand on Tacit's shoulder coaxed him inside a stride behind.

"Restrain her, Inquisitor," Inquisitor Salamanca demanded, as he stripped beneath the waist and fondled at his crotch. The jailer laughed wickedly as he took Salamanca's clothes from him. Tacit was aware of sweat on his brow, on the top of his lip, a fear and trepidation like that he had felt once before, long long ago.

"Who is she?" he asked, peering into the far darkness of the rank, stinking cell. The bleached white form of a naked woman scampered weeping across his vision, her greying long hair trailing behind her as she ran.

"Does it matter?" Salamanca called. There was a lightness in his voice, as if he took great pleasure from his work. He caught hold of the woman and manhandled her to the table in the centre of the room, ignoring her blows, pushing her over the length of it. "She's a witch," he hissed. "That's all that matters. Take her hands quickly!" he demanded, his eyes flashing at Tacit, his weight on top of her. Without question, Tacit did as he was told but there was doubt in his eyes and fear in his face as he held onto her hands. "She's created armies of bastard warlocks," the Inquisitor hissed. "This is the only way!"

The witch's imploring eyes were on Tacit's. He closed his own as loathing built within him. He saw his mother, and then almost at once, Mila.

"Inquisitor Salamanca!" he muttered. Nausea washed over him. His head was spinning. He could hear cruel laughter. He opened his eyes. Froth and blood, everywhere. He removed his hands from hers. "Stop!" he implored. Freed, at once the woman turned on her attacker, rending deep scars in Salamanca's face.

"Stop!" Tacit cried again, this time at the woman, at the chaotic scene, as Salamanca roared in pain and anguish at his wounds. The woman was on top of him, biting and tearing with her teeth and hands, the Inquisitor's face resembling a torn knuckle of meat.

The door to the cell was thrown open. Guards rushed in, cudgels suppressing the witch almost instantly. Tacit watched in revulsion as they crowded around her, their blows only ending when she lay lifeless on the floor.

Salamanca held his face, his wild eyes turned on the young upstart.

"She's now dead because of you, Tacit!" he hissed, reaching out to the table for support. "You put those cudgels on her body. You took her life. Instead of being cleansed, she's dead." He raised a finger, drenched in the blood from his raked face, and pointed.

Tacit stumbled backwards against the wall of the cell, lowering his head into his trembling hands, the vision slowly passing away from his eyes.

SIXTY NINE

12:43. Thursday, October 15th, 1914.
The front line. Arras. France.

The rain fell with unrelenting vigour, quickly drenching Tacit and Isabella, turning the trench floor to a clinging bog. There was a stink about the place, of defecation and decay, a putrescence which was as thick as it was fetid. It embraced you like a rag, filling every pore, every orifice, clinging like a parasitic layer, a thing neither gas nor liquid, a spectre of death become real.

If there had ever been any drainage in the trenches, it had long become blocked with the detritus of war. Puddles had become pools which, after heavy rainfall, became running rivers. The pair of them tried to walk either side of the river but always found themselves slipping back into the filthy brown water. Eventually it was easier to splash along it rather than try to avoid it and risk twisting an ankle in the mud. Any shelter provided by occasional small sections of corrugated tin roofs directed the falling rain into the trench.

It was a tortuous journey through that labyrinth of twisting and turning tunnels full of injured, often quiet, soldiers, filthy caked specimens, faces scorched by gunpowder and smoke. On several occasions, soldiers, numbed and senseless with shock, stumbled forward through the rain, blindly grasping out to the Inquisitor and Sister, pleading and praying for salvation, only to be shouted at by their Sergeants to "Get your filthy hands off them and get back into place. You're beyond salvation, you infested little worm!"

With every step there were objects to avoid, splintered pieces of wood, discharged and ripped clothing, cartridge cases, bits of equipment, a semi-buried limb, as well as deep hidden holes and the river growing ever deeper in the middle of the trench. Every now and then, a large rat would scurry across the trench in front of them, diving into a hole alongside the entrance to a dugout or an officer's bunker, two wretched creatures living together, side by side.

"You okay?" Tacit asked Isabella, as they eventually emerged from the far side of the complex of trenches, drenched to the skin and shivering. Ahead of them lay the ruined outline of Fampoux.

She nodded, her teeth chattering, and drew her sodden clothes tight around her.

"No place for a woman," Tacit grunted, dispiritingly.

Isabella shivered and gulped at the cleaner air outside the trench. One wouldn't call the air fresh, for there was the lingering malevolence of rot and feculence about it, but to breathe away from those corridors of death was as cleansing as having the rain wash the dirt and grime from their clothing.

"Come on," muttered Tacit darkly, "we need to press on."

They walked, side by side, up the rutted and blasted track, to the first rubbled house on the outskirts of the village. Green foliage climbed up a spoiled wall of the house, its feelers finding plenty of purchase within the crumbled exterior of the building. Isabella stopped and looked down the length of a street where entire buildings had been blasted to piles of stones.

Suddenly there came the sound of light feet running quickly in the rain soaked ruins of the streets. They moved with a lightness and an urgency, incongruous with the weight of war. The boy with the broad white smile charged around the corner. Immediately, Tacit drew back, his body low and coiled, his mind instantly suspicious, fearing an attack. Isabella struck him playfully on the shoulder and strode in front of him.

"Keep your gun away, Tacit!" she warned jokingly, turning to greet the boy.

"Hello young man!" she called in perfect French.

"Hello pretty Sister!" the boy called back. "Have you come to bless the troops?"

"Yes," replied Isabella. "That, and other things."

"So, you've come to get rid of the wolves as well, then?"

The question struck her dumb, like a hard glancing blow. "The wolves?" asked Isabella recovering, sensing Tacit's fierce eyes on the boy. "Yes. We have," she said.

The boy smiled more broadly than ever. He stood up straight, as if to attention. "Then follow me!" he called. "I will show you!" He dashed off up the street.

"Wait!" Isabella called after him, trundling into a short – and within three steps – aborted run. The boy took no notice and flew from view. The Sister stopped and called again, peering back to Tacit with a shrug. "Youthful enthusiasm," she said.

Tacit grunted and clutched the handle of his case tight so that his knuckles turned white. He was too wet and cold to chase children. They would have to come back and find him. If there were wolves here, they would make their presence known eventually, in their own way. Wolves weren't subtle in how they revealed themselves.

He walked with slow methodical steps up the road, realising he'd not packed nearly enough bottles of brandy to sustain him, particularly in the cold. The realisation made him scowl and he muttered irritably under his breath.

SEVENTY

1906. Perugia. Italy.

All day the back streets roasted in the Perugia heat. Goats had plodded wearily from the scorched brush, seeking shade amongst the city's outlying buildings, their bells clonking dully on their rusted neck ties. Lizards had scampered over hot stones in search of insects and little delicacies dropped between cracks in the road, whilst high above, buzzards had cut silent circles in the endlessly blue sky.

But in the orphan-house dormitory, the temperature had quickly dropped to below freezing.

Water froze glasses and shattered bottles in the sudden cold of the room. The sun which had streamed in from the many windows had been cast out with the slamming of the shutters by invisible hands, the room now thrown into almost complete darkness, but for the piercing shards of light from holes in the shutters and the vague radiant blue hue emanating from the restrained body in the bed.

Inquisitor Tacit stood at the foot of the bed, his chest tight from the cold and exhaustion, his breath billowing as great white palls in front of him. For hours he'd fought the forces within the room. He felt burdened down by weariness, but then again he could barely remember a time in the last four years when he hadn't felt exhausted. In the dark of the room he was almost invisible, clad as always in his black cassock and full length jacket, black bible clutched in his left hand. He raised up his colossal hands, bringing down God's condemnation upon the creature in his fieriest and fiercest rhetoric.

The small figure, tied tight upon the bed, hissed and twisted against its bonds. It spat and cursed venomously, the sound seeming to come from another voice, one from far away. Whilst its form and size suggested it was a little girl, the swollen mottled features, like those of a badly beaten dwarf, suggested something else, something far less innocent. It howled like a wolf, vomiting a putrid stinking stream of grey black pus across the bed.

Tacit looked back at it, his dark eyes narrowing. Many Inquisitors disliked carrying out exorcisms. "Priest work," they would call it mockingly. "Send a Father to tend a child," they would say, whilst testing the weight of their weapons in their hands.

But Tacit thought them wrong. When else was one afforded the opportunity to pit oneself against the Church's ultimate foe?

"You are finished, demon," he announced.

The figure began to writhe even more furiously, as if touched by an unseen fire. It pulled tight at the cords binding it to the bed posts, cutting hard into the scarred and scaled skin of its wrists.

"Release the vessel!" Tacit commanded, looking up into the space above the bed and thrusting the wooden crucifix towards the figure, the moonlight squeezing through the shutters catching its length and giving it an almost holy glow.

The body pulled back and cried out in an ungodly voice, the straps about its legs going taut. There was fear in the demon's eyes, fear but a wickedness as well. It hissed at Tacit like a snake and its mouth widened to a ungodly yawning sneer. The demon glowered and smiled, showing a fouled set of broken blackened teeth.

"What's the matter, Inquisitor?" it croaked. "Tired?"

Tacit put his eyes onto the wretched child. It was particularly strong, this possession. They often were stronger when they fell upon victims during puberty. He raised his forearm to pat his drenched brow and instantly the crucifix burst into flames. Tacit cursed his foolishness and threw the flaming symbol to one side. He'd been lucky. He'd seen Priests blinded by doing such a thing in the past, a momentary lapse of concentration allowing the bound wicked beast to strike. Exhaustion was a dangerous companion in an Inquisitor's line of work.

The demon sat staring at him quite calmly, mocking with an unerring smile.

"Trust me," it croaked, the smile unchanging, "it's not going to get any easier. Did you think you could just work your way through your problems? It's not that easy, Tacit. It'll never get any easier, you know? This is your burden. It's yours alone to carry."

Tacit ignored the figure and dug deep into a coat pocket, searching for his bottle of holy water. He always took great pleasure in burning demons with it, particularly when they had fought as hard as this one. It was the one weapon which would leave no discernible mark on the possessed once they had been freed from the possession. Bruises, cuts, broken bones inflicted by the exorciser had a tendency to carry through to the possessed, once the demon had been expelled. When explaining multiple injuries to a twelve year old child, excuses could sometimes run short. But holy water allowed the exorciser to unleash heaven's furies on the demon.

"Your mother, the rampant whore, she sucks Slavic cocks in hell." If the devil was looking for a reaction, he didn't get one. "She likes it when they hurt her," the demon smirked. Its voice softened and, at once, it spoke as if Tacit's mother. The sound of her voice struck Tacit like an uppercut. He rocked back on his heels, steadying himself on the bed post. "You failed me, Poldek," the voice of his mother called. "You could have saved me, but you were too slow. You were always too slow. You've always been too slow," his hardening mother's voice said.

Tacit glowered behind his eyebrows, an anger bubbling within him. The demon allowed a smile to latch itself onto its mottled face.

"Like with your master. Like with Antonio. All dead because of you." At once the voice deepened. Tacit's father spoke. "And me. You failed me. It's the story of your life, son. Never good enough."

Tacit knew they were just words, formed from memories which the demon was drawing out from Tacit's mind, out of his presence. Nevertheless, the intrusion into his family, his mother and father, raked at his very soul. He wished desperately to step forward, to lash out at the beast, batter it into bloody submission.

But then he'd be playing the devil's game.

Tacit pulled out a bottle from his pocket. The figure in the bed cackled. The Inquisitor looked down at it uncertainly.

"What are you going to do, Tacit?" it shrieked mockingly, recognising the Inquisitor's quarter bottle of Spanish brandy in his hand, its voice now ragged and bestial. "Toast me?"

Tacit uncorked the bottle and scowled at the demon.

"One thing I've never been," he growled, lifting the bottle to his lips and draining it in a long and satisfying pull, "is slow."

"Ah yes, Tacit, that's it. Drink your cares away. Redemption lies at the bottom."

He threw the empty bottle at the figure who, in return, vomited a syrupy stream of glass and iron shards towards him. Tacit wiped it from the front of his coat and retrieved the correct bottle from deep within his pockets.

The demon's face immediately dropped.

Tacit unstoppered the bottle and raised it above his head, bringing it down sharply whilst speaking incantations passed down since the Church's first battles with demonic possession. He showered the figure with spots of the water taken from the holy font at St Peter's Square. The beast howled, writhed and smoked as the droplets touched its flesh.

The guidance for exorcisms insisted that between three and five castings of holy water would usually be sufficient to unsettle the demon and sometimes be enough to force it from its host.

Inquisitor Tacit, however, rarely read guidelines.

He cast the bottle backwards and forwards at the squirming figure until the bottle was empty, the demon straining and tearing at its bonds, engulfed in snaking trails of vile stinking smoke from its burning flesh. Harder and harder it fought at the cords, scarred and enraged by holy liquid. It jarred its hands tight against the ties so that the skin tore from its wrists, drenching the bedsheets in black putrid blood. The bonds stretched to the limit of their capacity.

Tacit's eyes widened. He realised, too late, that demon was about to rip itself free of its bonds. The top right tie broke lose, followed by the left. It sprang forwards at the Inquisitor, screaming and hissing like a wild animal, both leg straps snapping at the ferocity of the leap.

It fell upon Tacit, its hands and nails scratching dementedly at his face.

Tacit caught hold of the beast by its neck and held it at arm's length, the possessed child's arms flailing wildly to grab hold of flesh into which to gouge its filthy nails. It spat and cursed and cried every obscenity it was able to dredge from the very depths of hell's vocabulary. Tacit's hand slowly tightened about the child's neck, until the curses were squeezed into silence.

A long purple black tongue, like the proboscis of a butterfly, flashed forward from the child's mouth and lassoed itself tight around Tacit's neck. Tacit grunted and felt at his belt for his revolver. He drew it from his holster and set the barrel of the gun snugly to the forehead of the demon. His finger whitened against the curve of the trigger. He closed his eye out of habit. He always did when he aimed.

The demon's eyes flashed and a grin spread across its face. At once Tacit caught hold of his senses. He loosened his grip on the trigger and threw the revolver onto the bed. The beast's tongue drew itself tighter still around the Inquisitor's neck. Tacit felt within the folds of his coat and drew out his silver crucifix, his most treasured possession. It had never failed him. He thrust it hard against the face of the child. Steam and hissing flesh drew up into the air as the demon rocked and convulsed within Tacit's grip. Tacit cried out above the screams of the beast and the hiss of its burning flesh, repeating holy words and invocations to cast the beast from the poor unfortunate host, once and for all. Over and over he spoke them, each time his voice growing louder, his commands growing firmer. The writhing of the body weakened, the appearance of the creature's skin softened until, moments later, in his grip hung the body of a young girl, pure and perfect. The only evidence that some evil had taken place was the child's wretchedly soiled sleeping gown and a slowly rising trail of smoke, snaking out of the top of her head.

He turned and dropped the body onto the bed before looking up into the ceiling of the room to where the shadowy smoke hung like a death mist, dissipating amongst the shards of sunlight striking through the shutter holes. He took out a small glass jar from the folds of his coat and trapped some of the last of the smoke within it. Tacit had always been a hoarder of curiosities from vanquished foes. In his experience, curiosities would often have a value when least expected.

He sat down on the edge of the bed and exhaled loudly. He rubbed his eyes with a thick thumb and forefinger. He looked down at his hands and turned them over, examining the cuts and calluses about them. Busy hands, too busy to be of use for the devil.

SEVENTY ONE

11:44. THURSDAY, OCTOBER 15TH, 1914.

FAMPOUX. NR. ARRAS. FRANCE.

A shadow moved across Henry's eyes, shielding the light and warmth from his face. It drew him awake and instinctively he smiled, his eyes still closed against the sun, listening to and smelling the world around him. He smelt roses and damp earth. He could hear the idle chatter of men, the uniform pounding of spades in the dirt, as another trench was being dug. He felt a weight on the mattress beside him and stretched himself out, enjoying the tightness in his limbs, the groaning of his muscles that only a long and nourishing sleep could bring.

"Hello," he said, opening his eyes to Sandrine sitting next to him.

"You snore," she said, smiling.

"I do when I'm *that* tired," Henry replied, masking a yawn with a hand. "What time is it?"

"I brought you a cup of tea." She handed the cracked cup over to him with the handle facing.

"You are a very kind woman," he said, taking it from her. He shuffled himself up into a sitting position against the wall at the head of the bed, careful not to spill any of the tea onto the sheets, this despite them looking grey with filth. He sipped cautiously at the hot brown liquid, aware of Sandrine's eyes on him. "What?" he asked finally, looking over the brim of the cup and smiling, his spirit teased by her attention. "What is it?"

"You," she replied, stretching forward with her hands just short of Henry's leg beneath the covers.

"Me?"

"Yes, you," she said, coyly, scrunching up her nose and looking to the window. She looked back and saw that Henry's deep blue eyes were focused on her intently. For so long she had chased love, longing for the feeling of being desired, being adored, being cherished as something of value and worth. For so long she had wanted someone, anyone, to show her love beyond lust, beyond a base carnal desire. Since she'd left Fampoux she'd sought out love, as if it was a prize to be hunted. For too long she'd felt starved, using the brief relationships she took in Arras to snatch brief glimpses beyond love's ajar door. But always, when she looked through it, she'd found that nothing lay beyond.

She'd lain in the arms of so many men since leaving her village, soldiers and businessmen, traders and Priests. Alessandro had lavished her with gifts and praise but his attention had always been too cloying, too anxious. His brother had loved her with a passion and desire which almost overwhelmed her, but his remorse after every climax cast a shadow across their afternoon dalliances, an abrupt curtain drawn across the confessional box.

She remembered the politician she'd seduced at the Central Hotel in Arras, with the large belly and small manhood, who liked to be beaten, and how he'd promised her wealth and the power of his connections if she came away with him. But none of them had fired her soul like this quiet and gentle man, drinking tea in bed in front of her. She thought it funny how, after all her chasing, she felt peace and the first pangs of love within the ruins of her village, from where she had set out to find love she'd never known as a child.

She reached forward and pushed the short curl from his eye. He blushed and she sat back, saying with a shake of her head, "You really are not my type, Henry."

"And what is your type, may I ask?"

She hesitated because she didn't know. And then she realised that he was sitting in front of her; someone who loved her for who she was, not what she was. In short, the opposite of her father.

Henry grew uncomfortable at the silence and coughed quietly. "What time is it?" he asked.

"It is lunchtime. Maybe two o'clock?"

"Two o'clock!" he cried desperately, setting down the cup on the floor and springing from the bed in a single leap. "I didn't expect to sleep so long! Why didn't you wake me?" he asked, hopping about the room with a leg in his trousers.

"Because you looked so at peace."

"I won't be when I'm in front of Major Pewter for sleeping in. Bloody hell, I'll be for the chop! I should be securing defences, not lounging in my bed."

He drew up his trousers and secured them with his braces. Urgently he pulled his shirt over his arms, hiding the vest and his keenly muscled chest beneath.

"You have good arms," said Sandrine, pretending to test her own biceps.

"They'll do me no good when I'm on report!"

He sprang from the room and tumbled down the first few steps. He then stopped and stuck his head back through the open door.

"Thank you," he added, "for the tea." He vanished again and Sandrine listened to the thump of his heavy feet down the steps, the sudden stop and curse as he manhandled his boots on, and further heavy footsteps out of the house. She looked down at the bed and lowered her hand onto the tangled warmth of the sheet where he had lain.

SEVENTY TWO

14:00. Thursday, October 15th, 1914. Arras. France

Cardinal Poré knew there was something different about the communiqué due to the fact it had been typed. He tore the delicate bond which kept the message secret and stared at it hard. Unlike Monteria's letters which could be long winded and detailed, touched with the use of beautiful language, this letter was abrupt, cold, precise. The Inquisitor, unnamed (but Poré knew who was meant) was heading east to Fampoux. Arras was no longer safe. The plan was in jeopardy. The Cardinal was to leave immediately.

Poré roared, tearing the letter into shreds, which he let fall like confetti into the waste bin beneath. Was he to be forever cursed by their kind? Would he never be free of them? Everything he had worked for, everything he had envisaged, had dreamed of achieving: was it to be snatched from him at the eleventh hour?

He looked up at the clock and thought of what he needed to take with him. He wouldn't need much, and much was already packed and ready to be loaded into his own private carriage. Once in Paris, as Monteria had previously said, he would be safe, the plan too. Tacit was too far behind, with no time to catch them now. Indeed, there was all probability that he would never even leave Fampoux.

Pain shot up his leg as he turned without thinking, having forgotten momentarily about his wound. His hand clutched around the seeping hole. He'd noticed how it had started to smell. He needed to find medical help. But not yet. Not till he was finished. Once his part had been played, he would seek help then. Until that moment, he would carry his wound as Christ had on his final journey to Calvary.

Grimacing, he limped from his office and into his waiting carriage.

SEVENTY THREE

14:02. THURSDAY, OCTOBER 15TH, 1914.
FAMPOUX. NR. ARRAS. FRANCE.

There was no sun. Just mist and a haze, hanging in the air like a shroud. The rain had come to a halt. The ground was damp and mud clung to the soles of boots like glue. Henry tore out of the house, still tugging his coat over his shirt. He careered down the street, leaping sideways to avoid a patrol of soldiers coming the other way. One of them shouted something and the group laughed. Henry put his head down and ran.

He had never been on report. It was rare that officers were on report, more something reserved for the infantry, the engine of the British Expeditionary Force. As he ran he wondered what it would take for an officer to be put on report. Abandoning his post? Sleeping when he should have been at his post? He cursed as he ran and considered his fate all the way down to the front. But, within that tangle of uncertainty and fear of what Major Pewter might say, he could feel the indiscernible prick of excitement, the gush of adrenaline within him as he recalled the voice and vision that woke him from his sleep, the sight of Sandrine beside the bed as he lurched back into consciousness. And as he ran for his life, he smiled remembering the warm glow created within his chest.

He turned into the sunken road which had once been the main street through the village, pitted and scarred by so much shell fire that no wagon or carriage could pass down it any longer. He spotted Major Pewter, standing stiffly in the road, his hands clenched sharp behind his back, deep in conversation with two figures dressed in the garb of a Priest and a Sister, but quite unlike any religious persons Henry had seen before. The Priest appeared to be a bear of a man, more suited – if appearances were anything to go by – to patrolling the more insalubrious clubs Henry had visited with his unit in Nantes. The woman, whilst clearly dressed as a Sister, had a style and a flair at odds with her profession. If anything, she looked more like some of the female workers at those same clubs in Nantes, her flaming red hair giving her a seductive, slightly dangerous appearance.

Henry slowed to a canter and then to a walk as he neared, to give the pretence that he was not rushing, that he was in no urgent hurry to reach his position in his trench to direct his men.

Pewter looked over at him and called. "Ah, Lieutenant Frost!" he said, his head turned sideways, a supercilious look upon his face.

"Major Pewter. I am sincerely sorry I am late. I –"

"Don't you worry, Frost. I am sure you had more pressing matters to deal with," he said, his eyes narrowing above his cold, thin smile. "This here is Father Tacit and Sister Isabella," he continued, removing a hand from behind his back and raising it as a host might to direct a plate of hors d'oeuvres.

Henry nodded in greeting. He began a smile but noticed that their faces were stern and chose not to proffer a hand.

"They have come to Fampoux in search of someone."

"Oh, I see," replied Henry, turning from the Major back to the darkly clad pair. "I do hope it's not someone who's been reported missing. I mean, that is, most of the villagers have now moved west, back to Arras or beyond." Henry looked back over his shoulder, as if to indicate the direction of Arras, and immediately felt foolish for having done so. "I think all have been accounted for, either safe or deceased."

Pewter chuckled and rocked himself on his feet between his heels and toes. "No, Lieutenant, they're not looking for someone who's been reported missing. They're looking for someone who's very much alive."

"Oh?"

"Sandrine Prideux." There was a relish in Pewter's eye as he said the name. He couldn't resist watching Henry's reaction and was impressed when the Lieutenant feigned ignorance.

There was something in the way in Major said it, combined with the Father and Sister's grim appearance, that suggested all was not well with Sandrine or the reasons the pair were keen to locate her.

"Sir?" he replied, adopting his most perplexed of faces, so much so he was sure the bear of a Father watched him with even greater suspicion.

"Sandrine Prideux. Come come, Lieutenant. You know her, don't you? Lives in Fampoux."

"I'm afraid the name isn't ringing any bells, sir," Henry insisted, looking between his commanding officer and the visitors from the church.

"Let me remind you, Lieutenant. She's quite memorable, from the sounds of things. Tall. Dark. Quite beautiful."

Henry rose his eyes to the haze of the horizon and beyond in a bluff of thought. He narrowed his eyes, feigning deep consideration. "No, sir," he said, now rocking himself on his toes, his arms too tight behind his back for comfort.

"You surprise me, Frost. I thought you and this woman were quite well acquainted."

Henry could feel the heat rise within his collar. "Forgive me, sir, I'm afraid I'm at a total loss."

Tacit grunted and began to move away. Isabella stayed and stared at Henry. He could feel the colour in his cheeks. He shrugged ignorantly, as a way of deflecting the gaze. He looked across to the Major and was a unsettled to find Pewter staring at him, smirking. Pewter turned his eyes back onto the woman. The Father had distanced himself from them and was now peering up into the heavens, as if checking for rain. Henry thought him then to be a most peculiar fellow, silent and suspect.

"Well, there we go, Sister," said the Major, turning to face her with the hint of a smirk still on his face. "I'm afraid it appears that you've drawn a blank. Disappointing. She sounds a lovely filly. Would have quite liked to have met the girl myself, judging by the description, not that you would appreciate that, I am sure!" he said, feigning a laugh. "Now, I am sorry to move you along but we have defences to secure."

They watched the pair of visitors from the Church step into the depths of the village. Eventually Pewter said, his eyes still in the direction the pair had gone, "You're as bad a liar as you are a soldier, Frost. She'll do you no good, you know?"

"Sir?"

"Oh, come on now, Frost! Play the game!" Pewter spat, ending his words with cold laughter. "Why's she so important to you, eh? Why lie to them about her? To a Priest and Sister as well! Goodness me, she must mean the world to you."

"I don't know what you mean ..."

"I should point out that I touched her, Frost," he announced, turning to Henry, his eyes wild with an insidious pleasure. "You do know that, don't you? In case you're getting any ideas. I touched her on leave in Arras. Between the legs. Just the other day, as it turns out. She parted them for me and urged me inside her."

"Again, I don't know what you mean, Major," replied Henry, but Pewter could sense the tension in the Lieutenant's voice and how he held himself.

"Of course you don't," Pewter sneered.

Henry could feel the heat rising within him again. "So why didn't you say something?" he snapped back angrily.

"I'm rather enjoying your pathetic little dalliance with the strumpet," he hissed, leaning close, savouring the anger rippling Henry's face. "And I do like a nice hunt." Pewter looked in the direction the Father and Sister had gone and then back at Henry. He cracked a smile and stood up, smirking and shaking his head. He felt in a breast pocket for his cigarettes. "I'll enjoy it even more when those two from the Church find her and drag her away screaming." He removed a cigarette from the packet and set it between his moist lips, the edges of which curled in quiet delight. "Do they still burn witches? If not, they should."

Rage shook every fibre of Henry's being. With hands drawn tight to his sides in balls of fury, the veins in his neck and face standing proud, he wrenched his face away and turned to leave, but Pewter called after him, drawing him to a halt. "She came back to me, Lieutenant. Followed me to Fampoux. Came back to find me. Yesterday, was it? Well, who could blame her, after what I could have done to her? What I could have given her?"

Despite his wrath, Henry stood staring towards the network of trenches to the east of the village. He watched the slow labour of the men, heard the strike of match and crackle of lit tobacco from the Major's cigarette. "She realised her mistake, you see. Regretted not taking me home that night in Arras. She came to me begging. Pleading. Thought she might have a chance to win me back. But I showed her the door. Not my way, to go back when I've moved on. Not my way, at all. But, each to their own, Frost. Afraid to break it to you old boy like this, it would seem you are her second choice."

At that Henry walked on, his hands still clenched by his side as he marched, his teeth gritted in his skull.

"I just hope you fuck her as well as old Lieutenant Colonel Wood did, from what I heard. She's a good lay, they say. You don't want to lose her because of any lack of skill on your part. And I hope you fight better than you lie. Rumour is the Hun is on the move again. Don't let anything cloud your judgement, now. Oh, and Lieutenant," Pewter called, louder still, "I took the liberty of giving some of your men an order. They'll be engaging in their assault just about now, hoping to catch old Fritz unawares."

Henry twisted in the dirt, as if skewered to the spot. "What?" he cried. "But there's not enough of them to carry out a forward assault, even if you used the entire unit!" Henry cried, looking with startled horror to the front line and, at that moment, hearing the shrill peep of a whistle blown in the distance. "They'll be annihilated!" He threw himself forward into a sprint.

"Not my problem, Frost. Sadly, you weren't around to take charge, so I did." But Henry never heard him. He was away, down the road, charging towards the front trench. "If you choose to sleep ahead of commanding your men," Pewter continued to bellow after him, "on your head be it."

In the street into which Tacit and Isabella had turned, the Sister leant close to the Inquisitor and asked, "Is he lying about Prideux?"

"Of course he's lying," muttered Tacit, his hand instinctively dropping his side and onto the handle of the revolver strapped to his thigh. "It's not a big village. Let's track her down."

SEVENTY FOUR

1906. The Vatican. Vatican City.

The mood in the Inquisitional Chamber was bleak. Talk had been of the ending of the Russo-Japanese war, a massacre of twenty four Catholics in the Middle East and the rape of a young acolyte by a senior Cardinal, the acolyte apparently turning out to be the son of a prominent Italian politician. It was little improved when the agenda moved onto Poldek Tacit.

"They say he's weak," a Cardinal announced, his tongue too big for his mouth, the sound he made making Tacit appear even more pathetic and loathsome.

"He has deficiencies, certainly," replied another Cardinal, dressed in red. His eyes flickered about the council. "But he is still one of our finest. He struggles with the act of torture, but in the field …"

"Something to do with his past," said a greying Cardinal, dressed in a cassock of green. "Apparently, he can't cleanse the whores."

"Not all can," replied the red dressed Cardinal. "Some are best used for field work."

"I heard he collapsed?" spat a Cardinal from the far side of the room. "Inquisitor Salamanca's face is torn to shreds, according to the report I've read." He looked at his notes and appeared to check his facts, before peering down the line of Cardinals and adding, "Courtesy of a witch," knowingly.

"He's been heard to question our methods," the green clad Cardinal said, shaking his head. "The very nerve!"

The red cassocked Cardinal shrugged and sat back in his chair. "He's the last of two left from his original class. We knew the risks when he was first brought into the Inquisition. The loss of his family …" the Cardinal said, pulling a face.

"He now talks about having lost his family twice," the green dressed Cardinal spat, wrinkling up his nose.

"He should be thankful," a corpulent officious looking Cardinal sitting at the head of the circle replied, shaking his head so that his fat neck wobbled. "If Adansoni hadn't saved him when he did, he would have perished on that hillside."

"Adansoni raised his doubts about Tacit becoming an Inquisitor the very first time he was brought to this chamber," the most elderly looking Cardinal murmured. "I should know. I was there."

"Don't forget, Adansoni was the one who finally brought him before the Inquisitional panel to push for his acceptance within the Inquisition," the large tongued Cardinal mumbled, shaking his head crossly.

There was nodding in agreement.

"He'll find a way," the fat Cardinal concluded. "They always go through these funny patches. Have doubts. Inquisitors always find a way through, eventually. Either that, or they die in the field." He turned and addressed the whole of the council. "Personally I think we ignore the issue and move on with the next point on the agenda. After all, there's nothing we can do about him and, really, where can he go?"

SEVENTY FIVE

14:03. Thursday, October 15th, 1914.
The front line. Fampoux. Nr. Arras. France.

Fifty or sixty soldiers gathered in the foot of the front trench, swarming about their Sergeants, attaching bayonets whilst receiving final orders. A few military chaplains wandered between the crowded masses, offering words of encouragement and support, passing blessings to any who wanted them.

From deep within the confines of the British trench network, a whole volley of metallic claps clattered from gun barrels. A wave of lyddite shells flew forward with the sound and force of a fleet of express trains. They arched into the sky and dropped along the German front, casting vast mounds of yellowed earth high into the air from where they fell.

An order was given and the soldiers wordlessly slipped to the base of the trench. Ladders were produced and placed up against the facing wall of the trench. Sergeants, revolvers in hands, eyes on wrist watches, whistles firmly embedded between tightly clenched jaws, stood crouched on the first or second rungs of the ladders, counting down the final few seconds. The tension of the soldiers grew like a storm, until the pressures were unleashed in a single shrill moment.

A whistle blew, then another and a third. Up the ladders and out of the trenches the soldiers poured, faces set with determination, rifles firmly held, terrified wide eyes on the horizon and the German trenches many hundred yards away. Sergeants stepped purposefully on, their loyal men following behind, a creeping, resolute wall of British khaki and brown heading off away into the haze of No Man's Land.

There came a sudden tumultuous roar of gunfire from the distance, followed by the strained cries of men, the blowing of many whistles, the steel ring of shells and the thump and bang as they landed. The noise sounded very far off from the bottom of the trench.

"Sergeant!" Henry cried, leaping down into the trench and scrambling along it. The relentless angry clatter of gunfire confirmed that he had missed the party. "What the hell's going on? Why've the men gone over?"

"Received an order to make a forward assault, sir, from Major Pewter. The Major thought it would be prudent to keep Jerry on his toes, make him think we're weren't slacking, weren't bedding in for the long stay."

Henry stared beseechingly to the east. "Madness!" he screamed, his hands to his temples. "Sheer fucking madness! Why would the Major do such a thing?"

"Respectfully, ours isn't the place to ask, sir. We just do as told."

"Tell me then," snarled the Lieutenant, "how many did we send over the top?"

Holmes blanched and then seemed to take hold of himself. "Too many, sir."

Henry scampered up the front of the trench and peered out cautiously. The sounds of the whistles and the cries of men seemed to grow louder and, through the grime of smoke floating across No Man's Land, he began to make out shapes, running and stumbling shapes coming back towards the British lines.

"Jesus Christ," he swore under his breath, straining to see into the blackened swirling mists. "Someone's coming back!" he called, his voice breaking. "I think it's the Hun. It's the bloody Hun! Get me my rifle!" he snapped, clicking his fingers and then pointing down the trench towards it.

"Can't be!" Sergeant Holmes cried, scrambling alongside side. He strained his eyes towards the approaching figures. "No. It's the bloody platoon!" Holmes cried, lamentably, "or what's left of them," he added, watching as they got closer, a scrabbling dribble of men, blackened by fire and ash, many bloodied and torn inside their uniforms and panic stricken.

Amongst the infantry the occasional Sergeant could be seen, urging the men back, but the entourage of young officers, who had set out moments before, had been cruelly decimated.

"Over 'ere!" Henry called towards a floundering soldier, who had lost his rifle and cap somewhere in the melee. The top right of his forehead had been blown off and blood gushed – a rivulet down the right side of his head. He moved towards the sound and collapsed to his knees, metres from the trench parapet. Henry and Sergeant Holmes reached forward and took him by the shoulders, pulling him headlong into the trench. He slithered down the side of it and was manhandled onto his backside at the bottom. He threw his head back against the trench wall and closed his eyes, exhaling loudly.

"You want a bandage on that, mate," said Sergeant Holmes, indicating the wound on his forehead. Either a bullet or shrapnel had carved a neat furrow across the soldier's head. He was lucky its path had been shallow enough to take only bone and skin.

"I'll get some bandages," said Henry, slipping away and appearing a short time later, rolls of them sweeping from his fingers like ticker tape.

"Lucky bugger, you," Holmes laughed, tapping the shoulder of the soldier and offering him a swig of a water bottle. "Nice little trophy that," he said, pointing to his head. "Be able to show that off when you're home. A little trophy from the war." Holmes laughed again and winked at the soldier.

The soldier took the bottle and had a swig from it, enough to moisten his lips. "It's not war, chum," he mumbled breathlessly, taking another, this time longer, swig. Henry could hear the rattle of the soldier's throat. "It's bloody murder."

SEVENTY SIX

14:24. Thursday, October 15th, 1914.
Fampoux. Nr. Arras. France.

"You bastard!" Henry cried, having cast open the doors to the Major's office without warning and stormed into the room. He was filthy from the trench and the tending of the wounded. "What the bloody hell did you think you were doing? Don't you know you've just sent thirty four good men to their deaths?"

Major Pewter looked up nonchalantly from his desk and set down his pen, as if the question had as much importance to him as a query regarding the weather. "Alright Lieutenant," he said, placing both hands onto the desk, palms down, "pipe down. I could have you shot, Lieutenant, for surrendering your post when you should have been commanding it! You should consider yourself most fortunate."

"You did that on purpose!"

"Did what exactly?" he asked, the root of a smile on his face.

"Sent my men across to the German front line."

"Ah, that." Pewter sat back and swept at the strands of hair. He chuckled. "Did they not achieve their goal?"

"No they did not bloody achieve their goal! There was never any hope of that! There was never enough of them!" Henry stalked to the front of the desk, as Ponting came running to investigate the outburst. "Where was the artillery support? Where was the smoke screen to conceal them? It was the middle of the bloody day, for Christ's sake!"

Alerted by Henry's cursing, the sentry stuck his head around the corner of the Major's door.

"It's okay, Ponting", Pewter said to the sentry, "the Lieutenant and I are just having a little chinwag. You can go."

The sentry nodded, eyeing the Lieutenant suspiciously before returning to his post.

"I suggest," Pewter began, his cold eyes boring into Henry, "that you calm down a little and remember just who you are talking to." The Major crossed his legs and picked at a spot on his trousers. "I'm afraid you gave me no choice," he said, a supercilious smirk coming to his face.

"No choice? They were my men!" Henry cried, tears welling in his eyes.

"Exactly. They were *your* men. So where exactly were you, Lieutenant?"

"I ..."

"You'd vanished. Quite abandoned your men."

"I was exhausted. I'd not slept for two days."

"Neither had your men, but they weren't sleeping. No, they were dying, just like you should have been."

Rage surged inside Henry. He tore over the desk and wrestled Pewter from his chair, picking him up and dashing him hard against the wall of the room. Henry heard the air gush out of the Major and he raised his fists to batter the winded officer.

"Strike me, Frost," he hissed, snatching at tight breaths, "and I will see to it that you are strung up as an example to all who cannot control their emotions. This is war, Lieutenant. Death is part of it." Pewter tore himself from Henry's grip. Panting, he retreated and crossed his arms, eyebrows raised. "So," he said, clearing his throat and correcting his tie and jacket, "you were sleeping, were you, Lieutenant?"

"Resting. I needed to rest, once the unit's diary had been written. Just for an hour, or two."

"Yes, of course, write the diary and then take to your bed. You didn't, by any chance, take anyone else to your bed at the same time did you, Lieutenant?"

"I beg your pardon?"

The Major's face had begun to grow a little crimson in colour, a rouging of the cheeks and across the temples. "Oh come on, Frost! Don't play dumb with me! I know what you were up to! Sleeping in your bed? That I doubt very much. What do you take me for? A fool? Sleeping?" he said, spitting the words, as if they insulted his mouth. "Fucking more like! Fucking that whore whilst your men were dying!"

Henry threw himself forward again, making another grab for the Major.

"Go on, Lieutenant. Strike me. I'll have you in front of the firing squad before you have time to let your dick go dry. Don't you dare question me, you have no authority. You weren't here. Simple as that. I took command."

Henry drew back, his chest heaving, his shoulders sagging, his head down but his eyes still fixed fiercely upon the Major, staring at him from under his eyebrows. As Henry did so, Pewter stepped out towards him.

"It's a disgraceful state of affairs, Frost, you indulging yourself in the middle of battle. I've never quite known anything like it. It would be all the more tragic if your men got word. It's the sort of thing that a junior officer never recovers from. She's a woman, Frost," he said, brushing a speck from his sleeve. "Only a woman. She's not worth any more thought, any more debate on the matter. The Hun, they should be first in our mind. We've battled hard to take Fampoux, in no small part due to my own leadership and verve. Already we are the model unit in the eye of the British Expeditionary Force. No one else has achieved our gains since Fritz was held in their big push. I do not intend to lose our gains because of the charms of a woman or her lovestruck beau."

But Henry had heard enough. Whilst Pewter was finishing, he'd been striding towards the closed doors. He thrust them open and strode out, without another word.

"Where are you going?" Pewter demanded, annoyed his speech had been interrupted by the officer's insolence.

"Going to my men," Henry called back over his shoulder. "I might have missed the last party but I don't intend to miss any more."

"Very wise, Lieutenant," the Major called back, sitting on the edge of the desk. "Very wise. Try not to get yourself killed, mind. A well-rested soldier like you is a valuable asset."

The doors to the hall swung back behind the Lieutenant, slicing a brief snippet of noise from the village outside into the hall, before silence returned again when the door swung back shut.

Henry strode from the hall, tears in his eyes. He stopped, his hands on his hips, and stared down at his feet, shaking his head in confusion and disgust. In that moment he felt anger and revulsion at both himself and the Major. How could he have slept as his men had toiled? How could his commanding officer have sent them to their death in so fickle a manner? He thought of the men, recalling their faces and their names, and drew his hands to the sides of his head, slipping his fingers under his cap and tearing at the strands of hair beneath.

"You alright sir?"

Henry recognised the voice at once as Sergeant Holmes.

"Bill," replied Henry. "No, not really."

"I do understand sir. It's a bastard, isn't it?"

He stepped over and leant against the wall alongside Henry, looking back to the fields and the front line, the churned brown fields of No Man's Land and the outline of trees which marked the German front. He coughed and removed his cap, wiping his hair flat.

"It's like I tell the men sir, if you excuse me, that they're all bastards in a bastard war and if I ever find the scoundrel responsible for all these bastards, I'll tie a knot in it for him personally."

"Bill, please, call me Henry."

"Very well, Henry." He coughed again. "Uh, is there anything I can do?"

The young officer turned his head away to face the wall of the building, dragging his cap from his head and leaning himself towards it. He rested his forehead against the rough stonework. "No thanks, Bill. It's just, just hard to take."

"Yes, I suppose it is sir, isn't it sir?" said Holmes, aware of how awkward he felt standing next to him, witnessing his grieving senior officer break down. "Don't envy you, sir, if I may say so," he said kindly. "That's why I'm happy being who I am sir, Henry, I mean. Just me, with no responsibility, just following orders, making sure those bastards in the trenches behave themselves, do as they are told, like, get up when they should, keep down when they should at other times. That's the thing sir, try not to get too attached. Think of them as poor bastards, and everything seems less … difficult. But they was good lads, those that went forward and didn't come back. Try not to let it get to you sir.

"After all, that's the nature of our business, sir, if you don't mind me saying. We are all tools, sir, is how I look at it, tools of war. Sometimes we're picked up and used, sometimes we get blunt and need to be fixed. Other times, we get broken and the only good thing for us is to be chucked away. No point in thinking anything more deeply about it than that. We ain't the craftsman who wields 'em. We're just the tools. Tools of war, sir. That's how I look at it, anyway. When you think of it like that, well, it gives a sort of comfort, sir, if you know what I mean?"

Henry nodded, his head still pressed tight to the wall.

"Can you …" Henry began slowly, clearing his throat, "can you give the order to dig in please, Bill?"

"Yes sir."

"No one is to go forward. There will be no more assaults today."

"Yes sir, very good sir."

"Bill," said Henry, wearily, "please call me Henry."

"Yes, sir, Henry," replied Holmes, with a tight smile. "Force of habit, Henry. Are you coming back to the trenches, sir?" he asked, peering over his shoulder to where the trenches lay defended and then back to the Lieutenant, who had now turned his back to the wall and was resting against it, his hands on his knees, as if he was about to vomit.

"Yes, in a bit. I just need to run an errand."

SEVENTY SEVEN

14:28. Thursday, October 15th, 1914. Paris. France.

Bishop Guillaume Varsy appeared at Cardinal Bishop Monteria's door with a strained and serious look upon his face.

"I know what you're up to," – he spoke seriously, tears gathering in his eyes, staring firmly at the man reclining on his chaise longue.

Monteria's eyes darkened and he sat up, his hand reaching for his cane, wondering whether or not he possessed the strength to wield it and subdue the young Bishop.

"I don't know what you mean," he replied, swallowing slowly and feeling the weight of the wooden shaft in his hand. He'd never killed a man before and trusted that God would guide his arm with both precision and forgiveness should he need to. He made to push himself up, to be ready to face the Bishop standing so that he might be able to strike him with more force than he could sitting, but Varsy threw himself forward, too quick for the old man.

At once Monteria feared the worst, but rather than grapple him to the floor, Varsy fell upon it instead in front of him, gathering the end of his cassock into his hands and kissing it, weeping openly as he did so.

"What is the meaning of this?" cried the Cardinal Bishop, both bemused and relieved in equal measure, his hand loosening its hold on the cane.

Varsy looked up, his wide beseeching eyes on the one man he admired above all others, even more now for discovering what he had just heard.

"Such piety!" he wept, burying his face into the folds of Monteria's cloak, as if it was a treasured relic.

"For God's sake man!" replied Monteria, pulling himself clear of the Bishop and his tears. "Stop talking in riddles! What do you mean?"

"The banning of all guards, of all soldiers, of all security at the Mass!"

"What of it?"

"I have just heard it is what you have stipulated for the Mass. It is inspired! How can there be a Mass for Peace, a true Mass for Peace, if we fill Notre Dame, every doorway, every aisle, every entrance and exit with men armed and prepared for violence? Only peace, and those with peace in their hearts and their minds can possibly bring the vision to fruition."

Monteria's mind slowed and he smiled cautiously, dropping his hand to the young Bishop's head.

"Let us cast away all our weapons," Varsy continued, his eyes very wide.

"Let us embrace this opportunity, show the world we can live as one!"

"Good," Monteria muttered, his breath slowly recovering, "I am glad you have recognised the significance of such a demand. Yes, there will be no one armed as we sit down to pray in the Cathedral." He smiled, cautiously at first. "We come together sharing the same hope that by casting our weapons aside, we can find a new and compassionate future for us all."

SEVENTY EIGHT

14:59. THURSDAY, OCTOBER 15TH, 1914.
FAMPOUX. NR. ARRAS. FRANCE.

"I have no idea who they are or what they want with you," Henry cried, the moment he reached Sandrine's house, "but there's a Priest and a Sister looking for you!"

As he'd wound his way through the dusty, blasted streets of the village back to Sandrine's house, he'd caught sight of the Priest and the Sister, emerging from a building, immediately turning and passing into another. They were searching from house to house. It was then that he'd started to run.

"Who? What?" Sandrine gasped, leaving the table at which she was reading and hurrying over to him.

"There's a Priest and a Sister, here, in the village," Henry faltered, trying to catch his breath. "At least that's what they said they were, but they look like no clergy I've ever seen."

"What did they want?" asked Sandrine, immediately drawn to think of the two figures outside of Alessandro's house and knowing in her heart that they were the same.

"You. They want to find you."

"How do you know?"

"I was there, when they asked Pewter."

"Did he tell them where I was?"

"No," said Henry, turning away.

When Henry turned back to face her, Sandrine could see the pain and guilt in his eyes.

"Don't worry for me, Henry," she soothed. "All my life I have lived as one hunted, always on the run. They will not find me."

But Henry twisted his head to the side as if the words somehow pained him. "What is it, Henry?" Sandrine asked. "What is wrong?"

"Nothing."

"Don't lie to me." Sandrine's tone suggested he would be wise not to.

"It's not just you that I fear. This war. This wanton merciless war!" He sank his head into his hands, his fingers white against his eye sockets. "My men. Whilst I was sleeping my men, they were instructed to attack the Germans. They were all but wiped out."

"Oh Henry, I am so sorry. Who gave the order?"

Henry didn't say. He couldn't. He looked to the window and stared.

But Sandrine knew. "It was him, wasn't it?" she spat, walking around him so she could look into his face. "The Major?"

Henry moved away, trying to avoid her gaze. He raised a hand to the wall to steady himself and hung his head.

"Henry! What is it?" Sandrine called.

"The Major. He said that you were …" He twisted his head, as if ashamed, ashamed to question the woman he loved, ashamed to say such things about her. "He said that you might have been lovers."

Sandrine laughed cruelly.

"Lovers?! What's this?"

"Exactly that!" he retorted, allowing the anger out of him.

"Lovers?" she spat back. "Maybe he wished for such a thing, but I did not! I would never let him touch me!" She threw her hands into the air. "Pah!" she exclaimed.

"You weren't lovers?"

"Of course we were never lovers, no!" she replied, crossing her arms and staring down him. "Ah! Henry! What is this? You tell me one moment that you are sad that you lost your men, then you tell me next that you are sad because of idle rumour about the Major and me?"

Henry hung his head, ashamed. "I am sorry, Sandrine," he muttered, fighting against his confusion and pain. "I am sorry."

She could feel his torment. Sandrine reached forward and drew herself around him. "My dear Henry," she soothed gently into his ear, her arms sweeping the full length of his broad back. They held onto each other in silence, closing their eyes, shutting out the numbing horror all about them.

Eventually Henry looked up at her. "You must hide," he urged.

"And you must go to your war," she said, easing herself out from the embrace.

"Sandrine," he said urgently, grappling her into his arms. "I love you, damn it! I love you!" And then he kissed her, quite unexpectedly and passionately, holding her to him with no resistance, until she pulled away from him, a look of shock on her face. She stared at him aghast, and instantly he wilted under her fierce glare. Then, without warning she threw herself forward and her mouth was on his, their hands in each other's hair, across their backs, fingers clawing at their clothes. Their mouths locked together in an embrace not even the strongest of forces could tear apart. They devoured each other and, when they finally separated, both were exhausted and all was forgiven.

"Go!" wept Sandrine, pushing Henry gently towards the door.

"Please, Sandrine!" Henry begged, "whatever you do, don't let them find you."

She kissed him again, this time sensually, enjoying every moment of his lips on hers. "I will not let them find me, Henry," she said, kissing him one final time. "I will come back to you, now go."

SEVENTY NINE

18:43. Thursday, October 15th, 1914.
The front line. Fampoux. Nr. Arras. France.

Private Doughty thrust the spade into the dirt of the trench and dug, just as he'd been told to by his superiors. The thin pale sun was finally giving up the struggle to bring light to the world and night was swiftly approaching. A chill had settled on the land and the full moon was already visible, casting a cold light of its own. Not that Private Doughty or Private Wrigley felt the cold, nor did any of the soldiers toiling along the entire length of the front line. The order had been passed down to dig, and as the chill of evening settled, that is what every man did, working with rough, calloused hands, cigarettes balanced from corners of mouths, sleeves rolled up to elbows, cursing and chatting and singing through their work.

For two days, since they'd arrived at Fampoux, all it seemed that one did was dig, defend or die in lunatic assaults on the enemy line, which achieved nought but kept the blood stations busy.

Doughty's back was stiff. He thought back to 'Badger' Thomas, his mate from childhood, who had died attacking the German front line earlier in the day. "Join the army, and be stiff," Badger used to say, "Bored stiff, frozen stiff, scared stiff."

For three hours they'd been at this same portion of earth, Private Doughty and Private Wrigley, digging at a part of the trench at the very far end of the front line. "Just our bloody luck," Doughty had said, "to get the part of the front with all the stones."

He threw the blade of his spade with all his anger and annoyance and was confused when it vanished halfway up the neck of the handle in the earth. He stopped, perplexed, and withdrew the spade, which came out easily, too easily for a spade buried blade and handle deep in trench soil. He kicked forward with a boot into the small hole he'd left and fell forward, his boot vanishing up to his shin in the earth.

"'Ere, Mick! There's a hole here!" he called to Private Wrigley behind him, extracting his foot and kicking forward with it again to enlarge it further. Soil tumbled away into darkness below.

"What's that, Doug?" Private Wrigley asked, wiping a sleeve across his forehead. "Found a hole? Should bloody think so! You've dug it, you daft bastard."

"No, there's a hole," replied Doughty, peering closer to the blackness and trying to look inside. He reached forward with his spade and shovelled a blade-full of earth to one side, and then another and another, his digging growing quicker and more urgent, as if he'd discovered buried treasure. "Tell you what," he stammered, getting down on his knees and heaving the dirt aside with his hands, "it's a bloody tunnel!"

He sat to one side to allow his mate to have a look.

"Blimey," exclaimed Wrigley, stepping nearer, "wonder if it's one of ours."

"Course it's not one of ours," Doughty shot back, "we'd have the plan of it on one of our maps if it was one of ours, you daft bugger!" He stuck his head down into the hole and peered into the gloom of it. "It must be one of theirs," he said, pulling himself out.

"Who? The Germans?!" Private Wrigley took a step back and crouched behind his spade.

"Dunno." Doughty put his head back into the hole. He then retracted it. "Bloody dark in there. Can't see a flaming thing. 'Ere," he said, looking up the trench, "pass us that there lantern."

"You should go back and tell the Lieutenant," Wrigley advised, handing him the lantern at arm's length.

Doughty lit it, corrected the height of the flame and lowered it into the hole, following with his head and shoulders. "Coo-eee," he called, his voice muffled by the depths of earth into which he had plunged. He pulled himself out and looked up at his chum, who was now inching forward, hooked by the intrigue of it. "It goes back a long way."

"Must be a German tunnel," Wrigley continued, turning the handle of the spade in his hands. "Do you think it's a tunnel?"

"Course it's a bloody tunnel!"

"Let's go back and tell Lieutenant Frost."

But Doughty was lowering himself in feet first and vanishing into the darkness, taking up the lantern after him.

"Where you going, Doug?" Wrigley hissed quietly, as if fearful of being overheard. Private Doughty's head appeared up out of the hole. "Come on. Let's go and have a little explore!" he urged, before vanishing back into the darkness.

"Doug!" Wrigley called under his breath, glancing back down the trench to see if anyone was looking and then back at the hole. "Dougie?" he muttered at the dark yawning mouth in the middle of the trench. Just silence and dark. He called again, inching his way forward, his hands around the shaft of the spade, as if strangling the life out of it. "Doug!" he cried, kneeling down at the dark edge and peering into it. A head suddenly reared up from inside, tumbling the Private backwards, swearing and cursing quietly.

"It's ever so murky in here," Doughty warned, chuckling at his friend scrambling in the dirt of the trench. "Don't look like no German trench, neither. Can't see any supports. And it's wide. Very wide. And tall. Come on in and have a look." His head vanished again and Wrigley, still cursing and muttering, scrambled after him into the blackness.

It was only a short drop down to the tunnel floor, maybe four feet. The floor was smooth and felt dry underfoot, although there was a chill and a dampness in the air. There was also a peculiar smell, not dissimilar to rotting vegetables.

"Cor, that pongs a bit!" said Wrigley, holding his nose, more to illustrate his dislike rather than an attempt to block out the smell.

"Must be old stores," suggested Doughty, holding up the lantern and stepping forward with wonder. "See what I mean?" he said, when he'd gone a few steps, the light giving his face a shadowed and demonic appearance in the black of the tunnel. "Don't look like no Boche tunnel I've ever been told about. Nor no Tommy tunnel, neither. No supports. No tool marks."

The tunnel ran on for ten or so feet, before turning left into pitch black.

They walked to the corner and peered down into the dark.

"See what I mean?" said Doughty again, reaching up and placing his hand on the roof. "No beams. How's it stay up?"

"Maybe we should go back," suggested Wrigley, looking back to the grey hole down which they had come. "The whole thing might come down on us at any minute."

But Doughty ignored him, walking on. "It's big," he said, "a big tunnel. Some serious work has gone on here." He stopped and looked back to Wrigley who was loitering at the corner, peering between the lantern light and the light of the trench behind. "You coming or what?"

"I think we should go back."

Doughty laughed and looked to the tunnel's depths.

"What if the whole lot falls down on us?"

"It's not going to fall on us!"

"How'd you know? You an engineer?"

"No, but it's stayed up this long, it'll stay up a bit longer. Come on!" Doughty walked on, his light slowly being swallowed by the utter blackness of the passage.

Wrigley wavered between going forward and going back, eventually cursing and trotting after his mate.

"Have you got enough fuel in that lantern?" he asked, placing his hand on the wall and feeling its rough edge as he walked. "Don't fancy being stuck down here in the dark."

"No idea. Mind your head," warned Doughty, pointing out a dip in the roof of the tunnel. "Cor!" he said, chuckling, "stinks worse than the medical tent back at Fampoux!"

"Hang on," replied Wrigley, craning his neck to the right, "the path's turning around to the side here."

"Cor," whispered Doughty, pushing back his cap and scratching his head. He moved the lantern into his left hand and held it up to shine a little more light into the passageway beyond. "This is a big tunnel. I mean, look. We're standing up. Most of the tunnels our boys make, you have to crawl down 'em."

"Bloody Boche engineering," replied Wrigley solemnly. "Look," he said, taking hold of his friend's arm and looking at him seriously, "I think we should go back."

"Let's just go on a little further, see if this passage goes anywhere. Then we'll go back and tell the Lieutenant."

Reluctantly, Wrigley agreed and side by side they stepped into the gloom, aware of the delicate crunch their boots made on the ground.

"Should have brought a rifle," Wrigley whispered into Doughty's ear, as loudly as he dared. Doughty nodded. "Have you got your knife?"

"No!"

"You're bloody useless! Come on!"

Ahead of them the passage seemed to be widening and dropping down into a larger tunnel, perhaps a room along the tunnel path. Both of the soldiers stopped, instinctively, when they saw how the corridor widened out, and they now moved forward with a dead creeping pace, one foot slowly in front of the other. Each of them was aware of the other's breathing, unsettling wavering breaths, tight and concealed in the cold silent darkness of the tunnel. They inched forward like snails, stopping every now and then to listen to any sounds from the cavern ahead, turning their heads to catch any noise. But none came.

Private Doughty giggled and Wrigley stabbed him with a glare.

"What you playing at?" he hissed, hitting him with the back of his hand and then crouching and looking into the inky blackness ahead.

"Look at us?" muttered Doughty, in a hushed voice. "Right pair of turkeys. There's nothing here?" he said, standing taller and holding up the lantern.

A dark shape moved across the room at the very edge of the lantern light. "What the bugger was that?" hissed Wrigley, his eyes wide.

Another dark shape loped across the lantern light, followed by a low, animalistic growl.

Wrigley was stepping backwards, tugging hard at this mate's arm. "What the fuck was that?" he asked, urging Doughty away. A dark shadow lunged towards them. There was a splattering sound, like that of a heavy object being thrown down into water. Wrigley was aware of the light of the lantern moving, moving up the wall, now across the ceiling, now over in an arch towards the floor. As it flew past, it caught the soldier in its full glare, Doughty's headless corpse, blood pumping down his uniform from a neatly severed neck, turning and falling, following the lantern down onto the floor of the tunnel.

Wrigley tried to scream, but nothing escaped from his mouth. He turned and ran, thundering back up the tunnel into the pitch black, charging headlong into the end of the passageway, his hand flapping wildly to find the corridor on the left in the utter dark. His head crunched hard into the dip in the ceiling of the tunnel, stars swarming, a sharp stinging pain on his forehead. The young private crumpled backwards onto the floor, stunned, the black entombing him like a casket. He felt warmth and wetness on his forehead, in his eye socket, on his face. He turned himself onto his hands and knees and scrambled forwards, wherever that was, lost in the pitch black, weeping, finding the wall and scurrying along it like a lost child. From behind him came the crunching of bones and of flesh, the tearing of uniform, a blood curdling howl. And then feet, many many feet, scrambling after him.

At the end of the tunnel, Private Wrigley could see a grey tinge, the grey tinge of light from the hole down which they had first slid. The light of the few torches they'd left in the trenches and the glow of the full moon, just ahead, just around the corner. He rose to his feet and leapt forwards. A sharp pain jammed hard into his left leg. He felt something rip into his left thigh and then the pain came, too great for him to think of anything else. He fell forward, mud encasing his torn limb. He cried pitifully but it was almost a mercy when jaws settled and with a crunch bit the top of his head clean off, flecking the dark mud with white.

Out of the hole they tore, feral wolves, terrible and crazed, their grey and brown hides caked with dirt and a lifetime's filth from their world below. They tore out into the trench, the moonlight stinging their burning red eyes, glinting on their flashing talons and blood red jaws. They charged down the trench, gashing and gnashing at soldiers as they went, decapitating, amputating, disembowelling, mortally wounding with single blows from their vile claws.

The sound was terrible, like a host of berserk dogs high on the scent of blood and half-starved by their wicked owners, unleashed and sent after a desperate fleeing prey. And no prey could run from such a terrible enemy.

Amid the cries of the butchered and the howls of the wolves, blood gushed, organs flew, bodies fell and were dashed into the earth or crunched and consumed in seconds by the following feeding pack. A cry went up, a gun fired, its bullet buffeting harmlessly into the wave of insatiable blood lusting beasts. Further up the trench a bell was rung desperately.

Alarm! Alarm! Enemy in the trench! Enemy in the trench!

Soldiers scampered out of dugouts and scrambled from the outskirts of Fampoux, tumbling down into the trenches, rifles and bayonets at the ready, expecting to find the Hun, only to be dashed apart like seeds beneath a threshing machine, their bodies torn open, their blood and body parts showering the trench walls. Those who tried to flee were caught after their first few steps.

Henry saw a soldier stumble out of his trench and watched wide eyed as the wolves he was hopelessly trying to flee engulfed him. The first bite took the soldier's head and part of his shoulder clean off, the second swallowed his lungs, ribs and most of his organs. Not a single morsel was left.

Henry turned the machine gun down the length of the trench and pulled the trigger. He watched as the stream of bullets thudded into the head of the wave of wolves leaping and howling along it. But it did little to halt their merciless drive up the trench's length under the hail of bullets, snapping and devouring all in their path. The lead wolf leapt up at where Henry was positioned, his jaws snapping hard down on the muzzle of the gun. The beast was huge, the size of a lion, long limbed, stinking and emanating evil from every strand of its fetid coat, every inch of its terrible, taut body.

Henry pulled the trigger. The gun exploded, blasting him backwards into the gunner's hole, showering him with shrapnel, as tumbling rocks and debris fell on top of him, throwing the wolf back down into the trench, dazed and burnt, wilder and more wrathful than ever. Henry fell, seemingly for an age. The back of his head hit something hard and sharp. Everything went black and the world faded to nothingness.

EIGHTY

19:07. Thursday, October 15th, 1914.
The front line. Fampoux. Nr. Arras. France.

Tacit stopped dead in his tracks as he strode through the village and turned his head urgently to the cacophony of horror coming from the front. His eyes were wide and full of alarm.

"What is it?" Isabella cried, her hands to her mouth.

"Someone has opened a door to hell," roared Tacit, trundling into a run. He charged to the end of the road, where the ground rose and gave them a better view of the front line, two hundred yards away. He stared and without a word ran on through the village, Isabella racing after him, using the buildings for cover. The howling of the wolves and the cries of the soldiers were dreadful to hear, as if countless wild packs of dogs were snarling as they closed on helpless prey.

"Where are you going?" Isabella cried. "The wolves aren't this way."

"I am well aware."

Tacit thundered up the battered side street and turned into the main square, charging across its broken stones to the crumpled remains of the hall. He reached the main doors and dug into a coat pocket.

"Here," he said, handing a silver coloured revolver to the Sister. "Six rounds. Use them if you need to, but use them wisely."

She took it and held it in trembling hands, as if it were a thing of terrible mystery. These weapons were part of the sacred arsenal, passed down from Inquisitor to Inquisitor for generations. Tacit put his hand up on the door of the village hall and thrust his way inside. There was no sentry to be seen. He stormed across the room and pushed at the doors on the far side of it. They were locked. He raised a boot and kicked it hard, busting the doors open. Behind the desk, the figure of the Major jumped and he flinched backwards into his chair.

"You've got a problem," Tacit growled, striding to the desk. He put his immense fists down on the table in front of him. "You can't solve it. Only we can."

"This is the British Army. Of course we can solve it!" Pewter spat back, but his eyes didn't look at Tacit. Instead, they were fixed to the window and the trenches far off in the distance, to the howling and the chaos unfolding outside. He shuddered and it looked as if tears were forming in his eyes.

"You can't beat them," replied the Inquisitor grimly. "Trust me."

There was a sudden noise from the door of the hall and Ponting ran inside, his eyes half-crazed, his face drawn and very white. He had lost his cap and his hair was wild with haste.

"Sir, it's your horse, sir!" he announced, hopping anxiously from foot to foot, as if the ground was on fire. "It's been killed!"

"My what?"

"Your horse, sir."

"Good God, she was a beauty!"

Isabella scowled. "You're more worried about your horse?" she cried. "Major, you're losing entire units out there."

"Help us," Pewter stuttered, swallowing hard on his dry throat. "Help, God damn it. Help us."

"It might be too late," Tacit replied, staring at the window. "Seems you have tunnelled into hell." He looked back at the Major, who cowered under the Inquisitor's gaze. "Give the order to pull back. There is nothing you can do out there tonight."

"Pull back? Are you mad? If we pull back, we'll give the Boche our trench! I won't allow it. If they take the trench, they'll be able to take the village! No, I'm sorry, I won't allow it."

"You're going to lose the village whether you stay in your trenches or not. Tell your men to retreat back to the village. They need shelter. They need to get indoors. Lock themselves in. If you want to stay and fight, you'll die. You asked for my advice. You have it. Pull them out of there."

Tacit levered himself back and strode swiftly from the room, Isabella in his wake.

"What are you going to do?" asked Pewter desperately, tears running down his cheeks. All his dreams lay in tatters.

"Me?" replied Tacit, stopping at the door and looking back to the window. "Sleep. There's nothing that can be done, not during night time. Not with this many of them." He stepped past the sentry and pulled out another silver revolver, opening the chamber and checking the silver bullets were in place. "Just pray they're not still hungry by morning."

PART FIVE

"And praise be to God Most High, who delivered your enemies into your hand."

Genesis, 14, Verse 20

EIGHTY ONE

05:23. Friday, October 16th, 1914. Fampoux. Nr. Arras. France.

Safe within the tunnels beneath Fampoux, all night Sandrine had listened to the wolves stalking through the ruined village, searching for any prey who had managed to escape the trenches and attempted to find refuge amongst the ruins. The sounds had been dreadful. Only with the very first rays of light did the creatures and their savage and terrible howls recede and then vanish.

Sandrine pushed the flagstone of the tunnel mouth aside and peered out into the fresh light of a new day. She'd heard a wolf sniffing and scraping at the tunnel's entrance last night but by morning there was no trace that they had come, save for the multitude of immense pad prints deep in the dewy dust of the road.

She pulled herself out into the thin light of the morning and tumbled from the tunnel like a rag doll, her limbs heavy, her footsteps clumsy and slow, as if she couldn't walk through the village for fear of what she would see, what she might find. But she was unable to turn away from the task. She *had* to find Henry.

There was no debris left from the night time's hunting in the street in which her ruined house stood but, turning into the main street which ran from it, Sandrine began to encounter the evidence of the dreadful feeding frenzy which had taken place in the village and the outlying lands last night. Trails of blood were everywhere, splashed across roads and up walls, splurged from bodies as they fell or from jaws as they shook the flesh from their victims' bones. Bits of bodies, torn uniforms, broken weapons, detritus and mess lay across every street down which Sandrine walked. She expected to see a few numbed souls, soldiers staggering and faltering in the cool dawn, but the village was deserted, like a ghost town.

She wept, clawing at her chest and tearing at her clothes to witness such scenes, for she knew the ones she loved, her people, had been the architects of such devastation.

Sandrine reached the main square. She looked across the village hall, long ruined and broken from its once fine appearance. She looked across the square in the opposite direction to where the trenches lay and the worst of the onslaught had taken place. Sandrine forced herself in that direction, wandering slowly towards the butchery which awaited her. She didn't even know what she'd discover, if she'd find the remains of Henry. All she knew was that she had to try. She owed him that.

"Is there anyone alive?" called a small voice from behind her. She immediately knew its owner without even turning to see. Tears of rage welled in her eyes. *Why him? Why did he have to live when Henry and all the others had been taken?*

"No."

It was all she could bring herself to say to him.

Realising he had survived, Pewter's eyes flashed evilly. His plans lay in tatters, his promotion gone. But he had survived. And there was still hope. He could go back to the support trenches, commandeer another unit, bring them to the village. It could call be done by lunchtime.

But what would HQ say when he returned alone, with none of his men? He'd be ridiculed, ruined, probably put on trial for desertion, cowardice. He knew his career was over. But not all was lost.

He leered at Sandrine and swallowed slowly.

"You and me then, again?" he said, licking his lips. "That's good." He said it with a light now coming to his voice, which made Sandrine feel wretched to the core.

"What's that meant to mean?"

"My horse," he mused sadly. "They killed my bloody horse!" The Major dragged a hand across his scalp and held it there, clutching tight to his skull.

"They killed your men," Sandrine hissed. "Fuck your horse!"

She turned her back on him and stepped away. She could feel the Major's eyes on her as she walked. She felt violated by his staring but she refused to turn back and look, to give him the satisfaction of turning around. At the lip of the trench, she stopped and peered into it, her hands on her mouth and across her stomach. She wandered along its upper bank, looking down, looking for anything which might identify Henry, but there was nothing to distinguish the remains of one body from the next. Everything was bloodied and spoiled. Not one single identifying element remained. A cold wind blew fluttering paper and waste across the barren landscape. The silence seemed almost utter. Even the crows had fallen silent.

A wretchedness grew in the pit of her stomach. The desolation was total, all life having been choked out of this stretch of earth. She imagined even the worms were dead.

She turned and walked back to the village, aware of a strangled choking sound, like weeping which failed to come. She realised the sound was coming from herself. She was relieved to see that the Major had vanished. She wished never to show him any sign of weakness. She hoped she'd never see him again. However, as she stepped up into the square, he appeared from the doors of the hall grinning. A cold shiver drew across her. Pewter had a small pack upon his back and a cigarette was smoking between his lips. He removed it and blew out a big cloud of smoke.

"Failed to find anything?" he asked, smirking.

Sandrine ignored him, and walked on by.

"It's a mess down there," Pewter called. "A bloody mess, quite literally. They did more than rip the bloody heart out of this unit. They ripped the bloody unit apart." He sounded almost remorseful.

He watched Sandrine stride out of the square and turned to follow her, throwing his cigarette away. He was suddenly aware of being watched himself and looked up to see the boy with the china white teeth staring at him from the edge of the square. The boy was grinning, but there was no joy in the smile. It was a smile of immorality and licentiousness, like the leer of a gargoyle on a castle wall.

"What do you want?" the Major called to him, unsettled by the stare. "Thought you'd have died last night. More's the pity. Thought I was the only one left. Is there anyone left?"

The boy stared at him.

"Come on, speak up! What's the matter? Lost your tongue?"

"Les loups ont pris tous vos hommes!" the boy called

"No, that's no good," Pewter replied, stepping over to him. "You'll have to speak English. Can't be dealing with all this froggie nonsense."

"Vous auriez du écouter ce que vous avez dit."

"What is it?" asked the Major hotly. He rested the palm of his hand on the grip of his revolver. "Do you speak no English at all?"

"Maintenant vous devez vivre avec leur sang sur les mains." The boy crossed his arms and for the first time the grin was replaced with a scowl.

"No need for that," hissed Pewter. He looked to where Sandrine had walked and went to step after her. The child caught hold of his arm as he turned to go. Immediately the revolver was in the Major's hand and a deafening bang bounced amongst the walls of the square. The child's head rocked backwards and he slumped to the floor, a gaping hole in his temple. Slowly blood began to draw down his face, into his mouth and seep across his perfect white teeth.

Pewter felt sickened. He knew he was too important to have to do the dirty work of killing children in this war. He turned his mind and eyes back to the woman. He recalled the smoothness of her thighs and hurried in the direction she had gone.

No wind had reached the depths of the village, but the air was still cool, the sun only just beginning to rise above the horizon, casting long shadows. Sandrine's brown skin prickled as she thought of those huddled in the cold and the damp of their underground lair the day before. She shivered. How cruel a fate that those she loved had taken someone who …

She shook her head and tried to chase any thoughts of Henry away.

Through the pale morning light, she stared at the imprint of a bloodied figure, dashed against a wall of the village, his final violent ending captured in crimson on the white stone of the building. Fampoux was a very different place to the one she had left a month ago. It was a very different place to the one she had returned to just a day or so ago. The silence was dreadful. Then a single sudden gunshot shattered the bubble of calm. Sandrine stopped dead in her tracks and looked behind her to where the noise came from. The square. She hoped the Major had done the decent thing and his brain had been the bullet's final destination.

"Not leaving without saying goodbye I hope?" Major Pewter called to her from the end of the ruined street. Her heart sank.

He stepped over beams and mortar, which had fallen from the house on the corner, and made his way towards her.

She turned her back and ignored the officer, walking to the other end of the street before turning to face him. She was too tired for the attention, too sick for any confrontation. It was at these times she wished she had been short and ordinary.

"Leave me alone!" she hissed, squaring up to him. His cap was pushed back high up on his hair line, giving him a cowboyish appearance. "Don't follow me. Go back to your men."

"My men are all dead."

"Then go back to your commanders," she said, thrusting her arm towards Arras.

"Come on my darling, the war's over for us. At least afford me the opportunity of a little taste of your company? You did once. You might be the last woman I ever get to feast my eyes on." He made a move to put his hands upon her, but Sandrine pushed him away.

"Get away from me, you pig. You disgust me!"

"I didn't disgust you once. You wanted me that time, didn't you. I could feel it, the heat from your underwear. Come on, for old time's sake? What do you say?"

"Keep away from me!"

"But like me, you have no one left. Lieutenant Frost is dead. They're all dead."

Sandrine shook her head, revolted. She turned on her heel and crossed over the road, her cheeks sodden with tears, her mind racked with pain and grief. She heard him following her and cursed. This had now gone too far.

She walked a little faster. She could hear him murmuring to himself, keeping step with her some ten or so paces behind. She quickened her pace again and noticed Major did the same. Sandrine's heart beat a little faster. Her throat tightened and her mouth felt even more dry.

She slipped from the main street and turned into a narrow side alley. It was a different route to the one she usually would have taken to get home, a detour, a longer way around to tire out her pursuer. She was aware she might lose him in the depths of the village. At her home she knew there would be no hope of escape.

Ten paces later Pewter turned too. She could hear him say something wicked and obscene. The alley was deserted, high walled and windowless. Blackness hugged every inch of it. No more than six feet across, it was almost perfect for an unwitnessed and silent assault. Rats fled ahead of Sandrine over rubbish sacks. The ground was thick with their waste. The stale stench of rotted vegetables clung to her nostrils like a thick paste.

Pewter chuckled and felt a shimmer of excitement and anticipation ripple through him. "Did I ever tell you I like a nice hunt?" he called after her, pursing his sweaty lips.

He watched Sandrine turn right and hurried after her, a desire building in his heart and loins. He imagined the sweat on her chest, the tantalising taste of salt on her skin. He imagined her struggling in his grasp, at least until he finally squeezed her into submission. He swallowed and hardened his eyes on the route ahead.

Sandrine rushed forward, turning right again and then left almost immediately into a very narrow alleyway which ran behind the street in which she lived. She rested against the wall of the alley and listened, looking back to where she had come.

There was no longer any sign of him. She wondered if she'd lost him. For several moments she waited, listening for the slightest sound, the crunch of boot on gravel, the hurried snatch of breath. She was aware of her own – slow, measured, cautious. She was aware of a sudden tension gripping her. A tingling anticipation in her mouth.

A wretched voice croaked from behind her. "Not hiding from me, I hope?" asked Pewter, leaning against the wall and absently flicking at a trail of dust on his tattered lapel.

"What do you want?" cried Sandrine.

"What I should have had back in Arras." He thrust himself forward, grabbing out with his hands. Sandrine battered him to the side and sent him down onto his knees, kicking him over and away with a foot. She ran out of the alleyway, Pewter laughing and watching her as she went. He liked the passionate ones, the ones who fought. He found they were always the most satisfying of buds to pluck.

He climbed to his feet and shot after her, crouched low like an ape as he ran, his arms and fingers spread wide. Up the street Sandrine was fumbling with the lock of her door. She spun around at the sound of Pewter's invidious giggling as he drew near.

"Why have you followed me?" Sandrine asked quietly.

She swept back her hair and glared. The Major watched her out of the corner of his wicked eyes, a devilish look on his face. He swayed uneasily lightheadedly overtaken by a cocktail of fatigue and desire. And suddenly Pewter's face hardened. "Boring!" he shouted. "Oh, don't play games with me, woman! You might be the last chance I have to feel a woman. Lord knows what my fate will be back at HQ? Whole unit wiped out? Only one to survive? Don't fancy my chances much in front of the panel."

In the darkness of the street, the whites of the officer's eyeballs made his pupils look like coals. "It's entirely your choice my lovely. You can either indulge me here, or you can allow me inside. I'm not choosy but I'm sure we'll be more comfortable inside. Either way," the sandy haired officer said, forcing Sandrine to look at him again, "you're going to indulge me."

At this, the officer made a grab for her, taking her by the neck and pulling her face closer to his. "You can start by giving me a kiss."

Sandrine pulled a little away from him. The officer felt the strength in her and placed a second hand around her head to stop her escaping from his grasp. She looked into his black coal eyes. Dead eyes. There was no warmth in them. They'd seen little joy but had witnessed much cruelty. She wondered how much their owner had inflicted himself.

"Not here," Sandrine whispered, easing her fight within his grip.

"There's a good girl," Pewter soothed.

She reached back and turned the handle of the door. In his passionate state, Pewter never saw the light which had now appeared in Sandrine's eye. Instead, as if the opening of the front door was taken as an invitation, Pewter bundled Sandrine inside, pushing her into the first room he could find, closing the door fast behind him with a trailing boot.

He looked at Sandrine hard. "Take off your dress," he demanded, swallowing back his desire, his hand unconsciously falling to the stiffness at his crotch.

Sandrine reached to the buttons at the top of her dress and unfastened them. It fell away from her and she stepped out of it, placing it gently to one side. She knew one thing and that was she wouldn't let her dress become ruined in what was about to unfurl.

She stood confidently before him in her white brassiere and panties. Pewter cooed. "Bloody hell," he muttered, his breath short and hesitant with lust. Sandrine could hear the dry swallow in his neck. The sound revolted her.

"Let me draw the shutters," she called, stepping across the room. Her hands shook as she did so.

"Of course, we want a little privacy," the officer replied, barely able to suppress his excitement with a snigger. "Don't know from whom, but I want to make sure you're comfortably relaxed my love."

The shutter clunked shut and, as darkness devoured the room, Sandrine began to change. She hung her head down between her shoulders, heaving heavily like a woman in labour, as the transformation began to take place. She'd endured this a hundred times in her lifetime and the pain of its demands on her body had never eased. She could feel the bones burn within her as they elongated, the skin shriek as it stretched about her body.

She heard Pewter saying something from behind her but the sound was muffled and faint, as if she were under water. Rage ripped through her. Her face contorted and she wrenched her head upwards, forcing herself forwards onto her hands and knees. She was aware of her head banging into the wall of her room as her muscles hardened and enlarged. She suddenly felt hot and drenched in sweat, as hair sprouted from every inch of her body. Her panties and brassiere split and fell away from her body as a raging and insatiable hunger coursed within her.

She leapt to her feet with only one urge, to feed and satisfy her desire for blood.

In front of her, Pewter stumbled backwards, moaning pathetically. He whimpered, holding his hands up in front of his face. She took a step forward and he screamed. She hated it when prey screamed, even though they always screamed when she came upon them.

Pewter bolted for the door. One swing decapitated him. She grabbed his body and drank greedily at the blood pumping out of the neck. She bit down into the chest with vast cruel jaws, snapping at the tender lungs and heart, and feeding greedily on organs and his warm cruor. The officer's fluid flowed down into Sandrine's belly, the smouldering fire in her eyes seeming to burn lower with every gulp she took.

"Sandrine?" came a shaky, unsteady voice from the door of the house.

The red of her eyes flared again and she turned, blood drenched and snarling. She cast the remains of Pewter's body to one side and stalked towards the open door of the room, just as Henry appeared through it, bruised, bloodied but alive. She crouched low and leapt, talons raised, her jaws wide, ready to snap and feed once again.

EIGHTY TWO

1908. Naples. Italy.

He was still holding the letter in his grasp as he drove his cart up the track to the farm, eight hours since it had been pressed into his hand by the messenger, a young Catholic boy who wouldn't look him in the eye. Tacit knew the seriousness of the letter by the mark on the envelope. He'd torn it open and read it immediately in the hope that it wasn't what he knew it to be.

She came out to meet him on the track, as she always did when he visited, whether heading out or back from an assignment, cleaning her hands on her apron after preparing meals for the farm hands in the kitchen. But this time she knew that something was wrong. He hadn't waved from the track and he was driving the cart hard.

Mila stepped aside as he thundered the cart to a halt and tumbled from the cab into her arms, tears in his eyes.

He howled like child as she held him, right there on the track, like a child who had lost his favourite toy, knowing it would never return to him. Eventually, she spotted the paper clutched tight in his fingers.

"I am the last one left," he wept, as Mila read the letter. "Georgi. Georgi has been killed."

Mila felt she knew the young man Georgi like her own. Tacit had littered the stories he told her with mention of him, tales of daring and kindness and a love only brothers could appreciate. As she read the note from the church, her own eyes filled with tears.

"Poldek ..." she muttered, but she could find no other words.

"I've had enough," he replied and he reached out to her. She resisted, at first afraid, but his hold was firm and she allowed her herself to be drawn towards him. He leant forward and kissed her for the very first time and she swooned in his arms, wrapping her arms around his neck and kissing him passionately back – the two lost completely in each other. "I'm leaving the Church," he murmured finally, pulling away from her just a little. "They've lost me. I want no more of them. They are dead to me."

Mila wept and kissed him again, and Tacit bound her up into his arms, carrying her back to the homestead.

EIGHTY THREE

06:17. Friday, October 16th, 1914. Fampoux. Nr. Arras. France.

It had been the first time she'd watched him sleep. Pale golden rays of morning sun were striking through the holes of a broken shutter and falling upon the Inquisitor's face in pools of light, giving him a more youthful and softer appearance than she'd seen. It was as if a good night's sleep and the morning sun had erased all the evidence of the exhaustion which had spoiled Tacit's handsome features for so long.

His breathing was very slight, despite the size of him, his chest rising and falling almost silently beneath his cassock. Isabella pulled her knees up beneath her chin and sat watching him, trying to imagine the life he'd lived, the things which had touched him, the people who had meant anything to him. She wondered if anyone had, if he'd ever let anyone close to him, anyone in. She realised at that moment she was imagining her and Tacit together.

"Silly girl," she hissed at herself, under her breath. *You don't fall in love with assignments.*

But she had fallen in love; she'd felt something change when he'd rescued her from the wolf. And whilst she teased herself, claiming she didn't know how, she knew why she'd fallen for the man. He was so complete, Tacit, and yet he was damaged. Broken. If only she was able to mend him. If only she could get close enough to hold the pieces together and let them heal.

He'd slept where he had thrown himself, directly onto the floor of the derelict house, once he'd checked the windows and doors were secure. There'd been no idle chatter, no discussion as to the plan for the following day, no 'goodnight'. He'd gone about his business securing the building and then had stretched himself out and fallen into a deep and immediate sleep.

Outside she could hear the unfolding horror, the stalking of the terrible beasts, their howls and their cries echoing throughout the ruined village, the grotesque slash and splutter of gutted bodies, freshly slaughtered prey. But in here, she felt assured and safe, knowing he would have left nothing to chance. Nevertheless, she looked at him and wondered how the pair of them could hope to defeat so many, armed as they were with just two silver revolvers between them.

Tacit stirred under the beams of sunlight. He swallowed, his lips moving in slow pursed circles. He scowled and exhaled loudly, blowing the air through his lips, making them tremble. His eyes flickered and drew themselves open. He stared up, hard at the ceiling of the place into which they had barricaded themselves, as if taking a moment to reacquaint himself with his surroundings, their predicament. He took in the cracks and the undulations of the room and listened to the sounds of the morning. Then, without hesitation, he levered himself up and onto his feet, striding with purpose and vigour to the table and his case, where it had been set the previous night.

"Morning," Isabella called lightly, sitting up on an elbow and stifling a yawn. She had found herself a mattress upon which to lie, which had given her a little more comfort than the Inquisitor appeared to need.

"Morning," he grunted and thrust the case open. "Did you sleep well?"

"I did, thank you. Took me a little while to drop off. You?"

He nodded. "Like the dead."

Isabella climbed gingerly from the mattress and stretched, leaning back to coax her spine into place, her ribs yelping dully from their bruising. She tousled her hair and began opening shutters to the room, the light almost too bright to bear.

The Inquisitor had begun methodically to unload the case – contraptions of all shapes, sizes and types being removed and carefully placed to one side on the table. Every now and then he would inspect an item closely, work its mechanism, if it had one, and place it into the folds of his long coat. Sometimes these items would go from the case into his coat without a moment's hesitation; bags, a clutch of bullets, a holy symbol.

All the while Isabella had been surveying the house for evidence of food. She reappeared as Tacit closed the lid of the case with a thump.

"Are you hungry? We should eat," she said. "I've not got much. Some nuts. Dried fruit."

Tacit dropped his hand to his outer pocket and drew out a bottle, swirling the remains of the amber liquid inside. He turned and sat on the edge of the table, uncorking the bottle.

"You hungry?" Isabella asked again, leaning against the door frame.

"I'll take some nuts and fruit," Tacit replied, putting the bottle to his lips and drinking deeply. He frowned and offered the bottle to her. She raised an eyebrow and crinkled her nose, before giving him a knowing shake of her head and turning back to the kitchen. "I'll bring what I can with us," she called.

"You're not coming." Tacit took another long swig on the bottle, almost draining it. Isabella stepped back to the doorway.

"What do you mean?" she demanded.

"It's too dangerous. I'm going alone."

"No, I won't have that," Isabella replied adamantly, crossing her arms. She could feel a hammering pain in her chest. "We've come this far."

"This is far enough. From now on it gets serious."

"And it's not been so far?" she cried.

"You stay here." He necked the remainder of the bottle and put it down on the table. A good night's sleep and a quarter of the bottle of spirits in him. Now he felt ready. "There's no more booze in the kitchen, is there?" he asked, scratching the side of his heavily whiskered face. The heat of the drink coursed through him, bolstering his limbs, enriching his senses.

"I'm not staying here. You can't leave me behind, Tacit! I am coming with you!"

"You're not. You're staying here. I need you to stay safe."

"Need, Tacit? You *need* me to stay safe? What does that mean?"

"I need someone to tell the Vatican, if I don't come back. If I don't, they will need to send a squad of Inquisitors to enter the lair and wipe the clan out."

"A squad?" Isabella moaned desperately. "A squad?!" She came forward and caught Tacit by the elbows, turning him to her. He resisted, briefly, but her touch was firm and determined. "Tacit, you don't have to do this! You've already proved yourself. Proved yourself to me. With the assessment. You have nothing more to prove. On that you have my word. Tacit –" She drew him closer to her. She no longer cared what he thought of her, of how she behaved with him. To hell with opinions and religious etiquette. "Tacit, I don't … I don't want to lose you."

The hope and expectation had tumbled out of her. She couldn't see how he would survive, going into the lair alone, one against so many. The mission seemed hopeless. She felt crestfallen and forlorn. If he was to die, she wanted to die alongside him. She wanted so dearly to tell him just what … just how she felt.

Tacit pulled himself away and stood back facing her, a stride apart. If he wished, he could have reached out with his long arms and touched her face. How Isabella longed for him to do so. Her heart burned to feel his fingers on her skin. And from an ember buried deep in his heart, Tacit too felt the heat of emotion urge his hand forward towards her, a desire he'd long fought to contain. How she reminded him of her, of Mila, of her spirit and her independence. But she wasn't Mila. She couldn't be. And after all that had happened …

He resisted, burying the stupidity of his thoughts and, instead, the Inquisitor stood and watched her with his sad, distant eyes.

"What I'm about to do," he said, eventually, "it isn't about the assessment. This isn't even about the Church. This is about putting right what was done wrong long ago. I'm an Inquisitor, Isabella. I'm not a man. I don't feel, I don't think and I don't brood. I act and I do. Anything else is dead to me."

"Is that what I am to you, Tacit? Dead to you?" He looked away to the windows. "So what am I to do then?" she muttered, her eyes filling with tears. She raised a trembling hand to her mouth. "Sit and wait for you to come back or not to come back?"

"No," Tacit growled, checking the cylinder of his gun, "I need you to find Sandrine Prideux."

EIGHTY FOUR

05:53. FRIDAY, OCTOBER 16TH, 1914.
FAMPOUX, NR. ARRAS. FRANCE.

The beast leapt forward, dripping talons raised, foul jaws wide, any moment about to snap down upon Henry. He cried out and stumbled backwards, his head striking the wall of the house, his mind spinning. An acute pain shot down into the base of his skull and surged across his shoulders. For the second time in twelve hours darkness poured into his vision but this time he fought it off, his consciousness burning, desperate just to stay alive. He raised his arms to his face in a feeble attempt to defend himself from the monstrous wolf.

He could smell the stench from it, its hot breath on his face and neck. He cried out Sandrine's name in a pathetic attempt to warn her away from returning home and stumbling into the same fate that was clearly going to be his.

And then, suddenly, with a high pitched shriek like the sound of a dog triggering a trap, the creature threw itself back. At first Henry thought he was dead, the shriek his point of entry into heaven, or hell. But he was aware of sounds around him, light on his face, the smell of the house. He drew his arms away from his eyes and looked on the wolf, shuddering and trembling against the far wall. Before him, the creature began to change, slowly and indefinable in its transformation, but certainly changing. Its talons shrivelled away on its fingers, the glowering of its eyes cooled, the fetid coarse hair covering the beast's body receding and sinking back into beautiful cream skin. As the quivering grotesque of twisted stretched limbs shrank down to the elegant perfection that was Sandrine, the trembling slowed and then stopped. Within an instant, the transformation was over. The feral wolf had shrunk and slipped back and in its place Sandrine lay naked and exhausted on the floor of the house, her white skin shimmering with a fine coating of sweat.

Henry gazed on in bewilderment. The palms of his hands were flat to floor, his back pressed tight against the wall. He was aware of a throbbing in his skull and a fogginess in his vision. But there was no doubt what he was looking at now, and what he had seen. Sandrine lay prickled with sweat across the floor, unmoving, save for her sharp breaths, as if she was wounded. He stared and he stared, unable to take in just what he had witnessed. The wolves. The murder and carnage. The decimation of his men.

Sandrine? Surely not her?

He was aware of a searing heat on the skin of his throat. His hand shot to his neck and tightened about the pendant of Francis of Assisi about it, the circle of metal feeling hot in his sweaty palm. At once it cooled, Henry feeling its indentations and marks against his palm. He was aware of his breathing, loud and urgent, the cool of the metal seeming to pass like a shiver through his body. He trembled and stared.

Sandrine slowly raised her head. Her face was crimson and dashed with the blood of the Major. Her eyes were dark and deep, like coals awaiting fire's touch. She was breathing hard. They stayed as they were, Sandrine prostrate on the ground, her eyes turned to Henry; he with his back hard to the wall, hand on the pendant, eyes fixed to hers for what seemed an age before finally they spoke.

"What are you?" he cried, fear in his eyes and in his voice as he pressed himself as far into the wall as possible. "What …" Henry started again, trying desperately to find the right words. But they didn't come.

"I'm not like them, Henry," she said, still prone on the floor. "You must believe me."

Henry tried to reply, but his head span and his tongue was still. His eyes fell on the bloodied remains of a body, the lower torso, legs still attached, a bloody mincemeat mess to the side of the room, its arms cast nearby in the frenzy of feeding. He turned his head away, his eyes closed, repulsed by the vision. There was blood up the walls, dashed like paint thrown wantonly from a paint pot. He thought he was going to be sick, but the sensation soon passed when he closed his eyes. He breathed in deeply and asked, "Was that – was that your handywork?"

"It was," Sandrine replied without hesitation. "It was Major Pewter, he came looking for me, came to try and take what I wouldn't give him before."

The fear began to leave Henry's eyes. "Remind me never to get on the wrong side of you," Henry retorted, exhaling and inhaling deeply.

"Don't joke," Sandrine hissed.

"I'm not," Henry replied, putting his head slowly back against the wall. The back of his skull pounded with pain. He used the feeling to focus himself back on the room, back to his discovery and the revelations about Sandrine, to stop himself from collapsing into unconsciousness. He let go of his pendant and put his hand gingerly behind his head, nursing the wound.

"Francis of Assisi," Sandrine muttered on seeing the pendant fall free. Slowly she moved, easing herself up. She sat, resting on an arm for balance, her left leg crossed under her. She gave no consideration to the fact she was naked in front of Henry. She raised a hand and smeared the drying blood from her face. Henry couldn't stop his eyes from falling onto her dark nipples, tracing the line of them down to her belly button and the dark forest of hair further below. "Your pendant."

"Oh, that? Yes. A gift. From my grandmother. To keep me safe."

"She is a wise woman."

"Maybe," he said. He winced and pulled his hand in front of his face to inspect his crimsoned fingers. "What makes her so wise?"

"Assisi. The tamer of wolves."

"Is that what you are, Sandrine? A wolf?"

He asked it like the question was a dart to be thrown, dead straight, with no deviation or doubt.

Sandrine looked at Henry hard. "I'm not one of them."

"Then what are you?!" he cried passionately, looking back to the remains of Pewter and then away, wrenching his eyes to the side.

"I am a 'half wolf'."

The answer more confused than helped him. He looked back at her, his attention caught, for the moment.

Sandrine sat up, pushing her hair from her face. "I was born of human and werewolf. My father was a werewolf, a 'true wolf', as they are called by some. My mother, she was his sweetheart, when they were both … human."

The word appeared to stick hard within Sandrine's throat. She rose onto her feet and padded slowly to the kitchen, Henry turning to look away out of decency to her. She returned wearing an apron.

"It's all I could find," she said, recognising how ridiculous she looked with her front partially covered, her buttocks and back entirely exposed, save for a tie around the spine of her back.

Henry felt his face crack a little in mirth, but his features tightened when he remembered the scene into which he had walked, the blood lust and violence by the woman in front of him, if indeed she even was a woman.

"Your mother," Henry began, still trying to find the words, "she loved a werewolf?!"

"You do not understand, Henry."

"No, I don't."

"You stare at me with such cold eyes, Henry. All our lives we have felt this look. It is not fair."

"Try telling that to Pewter. Try telling that to my men!" His voice cracked as he cried the words.

"Are they all dead?" asked Sandrine, quietly.

Henry nodded. "We're the only ones left."

"How did you …? Oh, my dear Henry!" Sandrine sobbed, beginning to weep. "I thought you were dead?"

At first Henry resisted the urge to come forward and console her. But as she broke down and wept uncontrollably, he saw, for the first time, the fragility within her. Without hesitation any longer, he scrambled forward from the wall and took Sandrine into his arms. His mind swam, his skull cried, his heart felt fit to burst. If she changed before him now into the beast; if this was merely some ruse to fool him into her arms so that she could devour him, to hell with it! Let it be so! Everything Henry had known, or thought he knew, had crumbled and fallen like sand through his fingers. In that moment he knew he was as ignorant and as helpless as a newborn baby. All he knew, the only thing he felt, was that the woman whom he held crying and whimpering in his arms he loved; he loved her with all his heart and his passion and every part of his being. So if this was a trick, let him be ripped asunder and devoured, bones and skin and all. For if she did not love him or she would not let him love her, then he would rather be dead than live never knowing. He thrust his arms around her and held her tight. He felt her body shudder beneath him and he refused to pull away for a long time.

When he did, he cupped her face in his hands and looked deep into her eyes. He wiped the tears from them with the tips of his fingers and kissed her gently on the lips, holding her tightly into his chest.

"I was on a machine-gun post. The wolves, they came up the trench. One of them leapt for me. Caught the gun in its mouth. I pulled the trigger, the gun exploded. I was thrown backwards. I went down into a hole. I hit my head. I remembered no more. I awoke covered in debris. Clearly the fall saved me. I am sorry. I speak of the werewolf as *it*. *It* might have been your father."

"No, it can't have been my father," replied Sandrine, drawing herself into a tight ball within Henry's arms. "For my father is dead."

"I am sorry to hear that."

The dark haired woman shook her head, as if his death was not of importance or had passed too long ago to affect her now.

Sandrine reached forward and took the pendant into the tips of her fingers.

"Your grandmother," she asked, "did she know of the wolves?"

"If she did, she never said anything."

"Rescue me, O Lord," Sandrine began, "from evil men. Preserve me from violent men, who despise evil things in their hearts, they continually stir up wars. They sharpen their tongues as a serpent. Poison of a viper is under their lips."

"You know your bible better than me."

"Francis of Assisi," replied Sandrine, reaching forward and tracing the contours of Henry's face with her fingers. "He asked for it to be read as he died. Henry," she said, a serious and august look on her face, "let me tell you about my people."

EIGHTY FIVE

06:32. Friday, October 16th, 1914.
The front line. Fampoux. Nr. Arras. France.

Tacit's heavy coat, packed with ammunition, holy relics, lanterns and oil, weaponry, gauntlets, iron provisions and stakes, hung taut from his immense frame, tight across his shoulders, pockets bulging, the fabric of the coat so stretched that it seemed it would never return to its former shape. Every imaginable tool, apparatus, symbol and weapon had been stowed somewhere within, buried in a pocket or slipped inside a fold of the coat. The Inquisitor clinked as he walked, every footstep seeming a little bit heavier than the last.

Sister Isabella watched from the outskirts of Fampoux, her arms wrapped tight around her waist. Tacit stopped and peered into the grey skies of morning, taking in the light, as if it might be the last time he saw it. He looked back over his shoulder, to the frail dark figure in the distance. He raised a hand and held it aloft until the figure returned the farewell. He felt something he hadn't felt before. Whatever it was, he didn't like it. It made him feel mortal, and where he was going, feeling mortal was not a good feeling to have.

He bowed his head and vanished into the yawning black of the lair.

Tacit was surprised that the stench from the passage wasn't greater. It smelt cleaner than most werewolf caves he had visited, sweetish, with only the vague scent of rot in the air. He removed a small lantern from a deep pocket and, with a click, it sprang into life.

Bowing as he went due to his height, Tacit stepped forward, his senses alert to the smallest movement, the lightest of noises. His right hand he held out to the side of him, his fingers wide, almost like a counterbalance to the rest of his bulk, ready to spring forward, to move sharply to the side. He felt his revolver knock against his thigh and the silver bolted crossbow against his rib cage. There was no need to draw these weapons yet. The wolves would be sleeping, slumbering in human form. Daytime was the only time one could attempt an extermination. Night assaults on werewolf lairs weren't called 'Hombre Lunatic Assaults' for nothing. They were carried out in only the most urgent of cases.

Tacit stopped and bent down. The ground here was churned, not the pathway cut by a multitude of wolf paws but by a body that had fallen and had struggled back to its feet. The sides of the pathway showed where it had floundered. Tacit reached up and felt the lip in the ceiling of the cave. There was a residue of blood on it. So the British had come this way and unleashed the creatures. Tacit shook his head and cursed. *Mankind's inquisitiveness. It would be the death of us.*

The passage turned to the right and then widened to a cavern, deep and widely cut. The stench from this cavern was greater than in the corridor and quickly Tacit saw why, a multitude of bones, piled high and cast about the floor, gnawed and snapped open for the nutritious marrow inside. But there was an even greater stench coming from the way beyond, like an animal's cage uncleaned for a thousand years. Its smell stuck in his throat. It came from the dark yawning archway beyond. Without hesitation, Tacit raised the lantern and stepped towards it.

It was a wide and well trodden tunnel. The cavern through which he had just passed was an outpost, he guessed, a place to gather to listen to the village, or perhaps somewhere where the villagers would bring offerings and sustenance to the clan. It was well known that people living close to wolf clans would bring them offerings as a way to appease them, to encourage them to look elsewhere, an ineffective ruse to try and deflect their hunger. Tacit shook his head disdainfully and strode on. Little did people know that when their rage came, wolves would look for food wherever their senses told them food was to be found. No offerings would, or could, appease them, not in Tacit's opinion. Leaving offerings was as effective as telling a circling shark that you couldn't swim.

The passageway ran downwards, curving down, down into the chalky earth. There were ruts in the ground, up and down where wolves had passed for countless decades, maybe longer. Tacit went slowly, knowing that a slip might be fatal, his hand on the wall, his feet feeling his way forward. The passage began to level out, turning slowly around to the right. Now there were corridors, running off from the main passageway, giving the underground network a labyrinthine feel. Tacit stuck his head down each he passed and sniffed, but each time he turned back to the main corridor and continued along it. There was a strong smell of excretion and evisceration down these side passageways, in part oddly familiar. Whilst the wolves were monsters, they were still part human. Tacit was heading where the air was less rancid, the stench less foul. To the heart of their clan.

There was a cry from the tunnels ahead, a lonesome mournful cry, full of pity and sorrow. Tacit stopped and listened. He wondered if they knew he was coming. When he fought werewolves during daylight hours before, often they would lie down before him as he executed them one by one, as if relieved that the end had come. It gave Tacit no joy at giving them their final relief. In many ways he felt he was betraying his Church by ending their curse ahead of God's allotted time. But increasingly, the worry that the truth behind the existence of wolves, that they'd been created by the Catholic Church's meddling, might somehow find its way out into the wider population, had caused the Church to make executions a necessity to keep the wolves' secret remaining just that. Secret and unspoken. The problem was the Church had been so busy throughout the many centuries it had cursed and condemned that the werewolves were so many.

The Inquisitor walked on, but now his hand was on the handle of his holstered gun. Just in case.

Ahead the passageway stopped and opened wide into a vast cavern. The heart of the clan. Tacit could see a multitude of shadows moving within it, wretchedly thin and foul looking figures, slinking away from the lantern light, broken and desperate souls weeping and creeping away as the Inquisitor entered. Had Tacit had a heart for the putrid creatures, he would have wept at their pathetic existence. As it was, they filled him with loathing and revulsion as he stood at the doorway of the passageway and cried, in a voice darker than pitch, "Hombre Lobo! My name is Inquisitor Tacit! For your crimes against the church you have lived out your pitiful wretched existence down here in the bowels of the earth. I am here to end your suffering. This sickness is not to end in death, but for the glory of God, so that the Son of God may be glorified by it. Consider this your redemption!"

A few of the figures howled and cried out, slapping themselves about the face and body, whether in joy or torment Tacit did not know. But the Inquisitor was surprised. He had expected more of a reaction from the clan, knowing that their end was nigh. Instead, most stared at him in silence, with their hollow, grey eyes, staring, unmoving. Suddenly one of the figures drew itself out of the crowd, more wretched and broken than any of the others. He looked as old as the hills and rotten within his very soul. He limped forward and kneeled in the very centre of the hall, his head bowed, as if awaiting his execution.

Tacit's eyes flittered around the cavern. He sensed a trap. The silence was too great, the wolves' subservience too apparent. He took out his silver revolver and held it up, the cylinder facing the wolves, to show he was armed and armed appropriately. Silver was the only weapon of use against the wolf, silver like that of the moonbeams which so confounded them in the dead of night. One or two of them again wept at the weapon's appearance, but the rest sat and eyed the Inquisitor with a melancholy quiet.

For several moments Tacit held the gun in the air, waiting for anything which confirmed a trap, a reaction, a muttering, a sudden movement. But all the massed wolves, thirty or forty of them, sat staring at him, unmoving.

"Hmm," muttered Tacit, and for once he was at a loss. But there was nothing else for it. He stepped forward towards the human wolf kneeling before him. He lowered the revolver at the rank head of the creature and cocked the hammer.

And it was then that all hell broke loose. From every angle, the wolves leapt. Tacit turned and fired twice, two wolves cartwheeling backwards, dead in the air, then ground under foot by the hordes of others bearing down on him. Within the maelstrom of bodies, Tacit's lantern was lost, darkness enveloping him. He struck a figure square in the face, breaking his jaw and sending him sprawling. He got a thumb into an eye socket of another and dug deep, pressing through the eye ball and into the brain beyond. But there were too many hands on him, hard fingers groping and striking, pinning him down. He butted another figure in the nose and sent it reeling backwards but, unable to fight against the tide of wretchedness, his limbs were spread and his face was pushed firm into the rancid dirt of the cavern. And then a hard sharp object struck the back of his head and everything went black.

EIGHTY SIX

06:12. Friday, October 16th, 1914. Fampoux. Nr. Arras. France.

Sandrine crouched in the corner of the room, her head bowed and buried in her hands. She drew back her hair with them, pulling the cascading dark river over one shoulder. Then she looked up and stared hard at Henry.

"We're not as we appear, to *normal* people. I know how that is, how we are viewed by the *civilised* world." She feigned a laugh and said, "Civilised" again sarcastically. "We're not monsters, Henry," Sandrine insisted, standing in the middle of the room, "not unless falling from your faith makes you a monster?"

"But ..." Henry started. Sandrine shook her head.

"Let me speak. Throughout the ages, since the founding of the Catholic Church, the damned have walked the land."

"The damned?"

"Whom we call wolves. Outcasts, Catholics excommunicated from the Church in a most terrible way. Not satisfied with simply turning them out of the Church, those with the power and the authority cast some of the most senior and important of those excommunicated into the abyss of lycanthropy, condemning them to a tormented and terrible existence on the very fringes of society, cast out by their faith, spurned by their people, cast out by their families, their friends, their villages and towns, to be monsters, desperate and pitiful souls during the day, half starved and tormented by their shame and their eternal insatiable hunger, vengeful and driven mad by their rage at night under the moon. The true werewolves. Hombre Lobo.

"Across all lands where the Catholic Church has taken root they can be found, hiding in their lairs, cast out, on the edge of civilisation, surviving as best they can, every day agony, every waking hour tortuous for knowing who they were, what they have become and what they are compelled to do. Their rage drives them and it is their rage which disgusts them so. Every painful hour of daylight is beyond measure, every moment of night time horror agony to themselves, cursed to perform such barbarous acts in order to satiate the insatiable. Their endless hunger."

"But you," began Henry, finding a chair and sitting in it, intrigued and enthralled by her utterly, "why do you say you're not like those wolves at the front, those wolves you mention, driven insane by hunger when night comes?"

"As I said, I am a half wolf. My rage and the wolf lies within, but I have control over it. I am not at the mercy of the moon's cycle, I am not corrupted by the agony of daylight's rays."

"And yet you are still a werewolf?"

"A half wolf," Sandrine corrected.

"But must you … do you feel compelled to fly into a rage and become a werewolf? Must you feed as a werewolf to survive?"

"No. I can control my rages. I am not forced to feed like the wolves to satisfy my hunger. But there are times when controlling my rages is a severe trial. Like the fault lines of the earth, sometimes they give and the resulting anger is terrible."

"As Pewter found," muttered Henry coldly.

"Indeed."

"So these wolves of Fampoux, they are not alone. There are others?"

Sandrine nodded, pulling out a chair from the table and sitting herself upon it opposite Henry. "As far as the Catholic Church has reached there are werewolves. Some of us within Fampoux, we knew of the wolves. Of course, my father was one of them. We would feed them, do what we could to lessen their agony during the night time with offerings and food that we could spare. But when the Germans came, our errands to their lair were stopped. And then the wolves, half starved, came for them."

"Are all werewolves, true wolves, cursed?"

"True wolves have been cursed by the Church, true Catholics who have lost their faith and been excommunicated. However, there are some people who are foolish and admire the might of the wolves and the strength and cunning it gives to the individual. These people have sought to choose the path of wolf themselves, thinking it will give them power that they desire, that they believe they can control. Power, yes, it does give them, but they are unable to control it in any way."

"How would they become one of these werewolves?"

"By drinking water from the footprint of a true wolf. But by doing this you are only brought misery and pain, held forever under the control of the wolf from whose footprint you drank. Some within the clan here at Fampoux have chosen such a route, and they are the most wretched and broken of them all. There are others who can adopt the appearance of a wolf by donning the skin of a werewolf. These are rare items, for they must be taken from a werewolf whilst the wolf is still in werewolf form. Great is the pain and great must be the determination of the wolf to withstand the rage and the pain as the skin is cut from them. For when in werewolf form, the wolf's only desires are food and survival. To stand as a wolf and allow yourself to be skinned alive, few are able to endure such a task."

Sandrine reached forward and took Henry's hands into hers.

"What of your mother?" he asked.

"My mother?" Sandrine shook her head. "My mother is dead. My father, he killed her. They loved each other very much but such is the curse of the wolf. She would not leave him; she could not bear to be parted from him. Even on a night. Despite his most fervent protestations. She would rather die than be parted from him. One night, she left me safe within the village and stole into his lair, hoping that her love could cast the curse from him. He devoured her, an act which haunted him to his final days.

"So you see Henry, monsters we are, yet we were made so by those who consider themselves most holy. It is the belief of all of us who carry the curse that perhaps the true monsters are those who wield the power in the Church to condemn and cast down, not those who have been cursed themselves."

"How did this all come to be?" asked Henry as he struggled to comprehend the enormity of what she was telling him.

"No doubt the Catholic Church, who first created the mechanism and blended the secret rites to bring the curse upon the victim, would be able to say. But they have banned any mention of the tradition for nearly fifty years, burying it and its secrets deep within their libraries and vaults. They make no reference of it in public, deny all knowledge of the practice or even that they hunt and persecute those they have created. All historical documents have been destroyed. All but one. A story is told of a man, a werewolf, Peter Stumpp. Three hundred years ago, Stumpp, a Catholic, was cursed and thrown from the Catholic Faith for lying with a married woman who was not his wife. Afterwards, possessed as a wolf, his atrocities, if you wish to call them that, were terrible. He devoured many including his wife. Men, women and children, eighteen in total, until he was caught and brought before the Cardinal of Cologne.

"After his short trial, he was taken and put on a wheel, where his flesh was stripped from his body with red-hot pincers. As a bloody, weeping thing, his limbs were broken with the blunt side of an axehead, so that when he was tossed into his grave his broken form could get no purchase in the earth to heave himself out towards the moon. This broken, torn thing was then beheaded and his remains burned on a pyre. As this punishment was being meted out, before Stumpp's eyes his daughter and mistress were flayed, raped and strangled, and their bodies tossed alongside Stumpp's in the fire."

Henry swallowed and gritted his teeth. But Sandrine had not finished. "As a warning to others, the Church hung the torture wheel from a mast for all to see, the body of a wolf set in the centre of the wheel and, at the very top, they placed Peter Stumpp's severed head."

"Good God."

"Or not."

"How d'you know all this?"

"We wolves have talked and passed on memories and stories. The hours are long for werewolves to sit in the silence of their lairs, waiting for the passing of the days and coming of the infernal moon."

"Is there nothing that can be done? Is there no way to reverse what has happened? To end the curse?"

"There is a plan."

"What plan? For the salvation of werewolves?"

Sandrine laughed thinly. "The wolves are beyond salvation. But there is a greater threat coming to the church. Revenge. Revenge for all the years they have forced my people to live in the wilderness. And when it arrives, all the foundations of the Church will be washed away for eternity."

EIGHTY SEVEN

1908. Naples. Italy.

"There's a pony and trap coming up the track," Mila called from the field, but Tacit had already spotted it. He lent his shovel against the front of the trailer and collected the shotgun from the cab. He'd told Mila everything. He told her trouble would eventually come looking for him. It appeared that it had.

"You're not welcome here," he called to the figures aboard the cart, as it drew to a halt on the track.

"Inquisitor Tacit," the passenger in the trap replied in greeting, looking down at him and feigning a smile. Tacit recognised him from the Vatican, one of the Bishops who used to clean up around the Cardinals. It was clear he was still doing the Cardinals' bidding. The Bishop looked up and surveyed the farm. He spotted Mila and his eyes narrowed on her.

"You're on my land," Tacit warned.

"Your land?" the Bishop retorted, pulling a face in mock admiration. "My, you have come a long way since falling from grace, haven't you, Inquisitor?"

"Who said anything about falling?"

"You don't turn your back on the holy faith, Tacit!" he spat venomously, his eyes burning with an unholy rage. "You don't simply walk away from the Inquisition."

Mila had moved a little closer in order to hear what the visitors were saying. The Bishop looked at her and scowled.

"Who's she?"

"Turn this cart around and leave," Tacit growled, ignoring the question. The Bishop looked down at him and shook his head.

"Good heavens," he swore. "Are there really no limits to your degradation?"

One handed, Tacit broke open the shotgun and checked the rounds in the barrels. He flicked the gun shut and leaned it over his shoulder.

"Murder's not beyond me, if that's what you mean?" he growled.

"Cut the nonsense, Tacit! We need you back," the driver called, his eyes shifting between the black of the gun barrel and Tacit.

"I'm not coming back. I've had enough. My days with the Church are over."

The Bishop laughed. "You don't just leave the Inquisition," he said, looking over to Mila and back again. He wiped his brow, sweaty under the Italian sun and from the confrontation. "This is not a role you turn away from and leave. You gave your life to it."

"You took my friends' lives," Tacit spat back, his nose flaring. "All of them." He fought hard against his rising anger. "You took my best friend, my only true friend Georgi. You won't take anything else from me."

"Inquisitor Tacit, we *gave* you your life," countered the Bishop, shaking his head dismissively. "Before us you were nothing."

"Enough talk," Tacit grunted, taking a step towards them. "Get off my land."

"You'll be back, Tacit. You're nothing without the Inquisition. It's all you know."

"I know how to count to ten," he growled. "And when I get there, I start shooting. One," he began, but the Bishop had already given the order to turn the cart around.

"You've stumbled from the path, Tacit," he shouted, as the cart pulled away. "Damnation is all that awaits you!"

Tacit watched them all the way up the track until they vanished in the cloud of dust kicked up by the pony's hooves and the wheels of the trap.

EIGHTY EIGHT

07:07. Friday, October 16th, 1914.
The front line. Fampoux. Nr. Arras. France.

Tacit was aware of a stinging pain in his head and the smell of wet coals in his nostrils. He could feel the damp of earth on his cheek and forehead. His mouth was dry, fouled with the metallic taste of blood. He grunted and tried to move. Hard fingers and hands held him down. He opened an eye. There was a fire in the middle of the cavern around which the filthy pallid clan of human wolves had congregated, watching the Inquisitor from a distance. When he stirred there was a hooting and crying from the assembled.

Bony fingers caught hold of his hair and pulled his head up from the ground, almost breaking his neck by the severity of the tug.

"So, the Inquisitor awakes," Angulsac muttered, stepping forward from the throng of gruesome white bodies, more like maggots with limbs than the men they must once have been. Angulsac's matted black hair hung in lank clumps down his neck, across his shoulders, his wretchedly thin face drawn tight over his skull. "So good of the Church to have sent us one of its Inquisitors to bid us greeting. Tell me, Inquisitor, does the Church send you in regret and shame or anger and rage?"

Tacit spat dirt from the corner of his mouth and stared on, silently.

"Speak when you're spoken to," called the wolf holding Tacit's head back.

"Seems to me," Tacit hissed, "the only ones with anger and rage are you. You should consider my presence a blessing. A gift. I offer you redemption and escape from your captivity, from your pain."

Angulsac laughed and a few wolves laughed with him, but there were others who hid their faces or turned away. "We have no need of your redemption, Inquisitor!" Angulsac hissed.

"Then would you prefer to be left as you are, wolves, never at peace within these cold caverns of earth beneath the accursed moon?"

"What sort of a question is that, Inquisitor? Of course peace from our madness is desired. For countless years we have lain here in the darkness or stalked beneath the moon, half mad with our anger and our shame. For too long we have been forced to live an existence more wretched than any sentence for a crime in the land of man. And for what, Inquisitor? And for what, tell me? For turning away from the Church, for turning our back on the Lord?"

"The most wretched of sins!" Tacit roared back in defiance.

"So wretched that our very being was accursed from that day forward, unable to live, unable to die, unable to love for fear of what it might bring – only filled with hate."

"If you turn from the good Lord then you can expect nothing more than hate to be brought unto you!"

"Turning from the good Lord? The good Lord, eh? So good that he would curse his flock in such a way, so good that he would enforce damnation upon all who turned from his path."

"There is only his path," Tacit muttered.

"Only his path, you say? Yet, you sound none too sure yourself." Angulsac stole forward, crouching down on his knee so he was but a spit away from Tacit. The Inquisitor could smell the stench of him, excreta and blood. "Tell me, Tacit, now that you see us as we are, as poor unfortunates, now that you yourself are forsaken by your Lord and left amongst us, the fallen, tell me, do you still believe there is only one true path?"

Tacit didn't reply. Instead he tested the weight which held him down. Someone was on his legs, another on his back, as well as the creature holding his head. Difficult odds to free himself, but not impossible with the right manoeuvre.

"I …" Tacit began, but Angulsac spoke across him.

"It is there in your eyes, Inquisitor. I can see it. Doubt. Doubt as to your own Lord's path, his salvation, his love. Look about you," said the wolf, standing and holding his hands wide. "Look about you, Inquisitor. Look about you and ask yourself if you feel the shame of the damnation that he has brought down upon us, upon you, upon your Church. For every action in the name of your Church, there is a reaction of pain, of hate and of heartbreak. When you curse to uphold your Church's laws, you tear open another hole into the world of lawlessness that you and your Church are creating." Angulsac turned and stared hard at the Inquisitor. "For too long we have suffered whilst you and your fellow Inquisitors and Cardinals have tried to wash your hands of the horror you have created. No more. The time has come for the truth to come out. You ask why we wish no redemption from you? Because we wish to stand witness to the downfall of your faith. The end is nigh for you Inquisitor, and all of your kind! But before that it is high time that the Inquisition tasted the pain and revulsion that we feel every day of our waking lives."

Angulsac dug at the ground with his foot, churning the earth aside to form a large footprint in the dirt. He turned to another within the clan and nodded. The figure, a woman, bent double with age and disease, came forward with a bowl clutched in her claw-like grip. She handed the bowl carefully over to Angulsac, who, after looking briefly at Tacit, sank to the ground and poured the water into the print.

"Bring him!" Angulsac commanded.

Unease gripped the Inquisitor, as hard as the firm hands which held him. He knew the ceremony. He knew what it was they were planning to do, to turn the hunter into one of the cursed and hunted. Tacit fought against the hands which held him but their grip was unyielding. They half carried, half dragged him to the lip of the puddle. Tacit well knew what drinking from the puddle would mean, a curse set upon him, forever casting him under the power and control of the wolf whose footprint it was he drank from. Under Angulsac's control he would be a whipped and pathetic dog at the foot of his master, thrown the carrion of his master's night time hunts, forever tormented. He wrestled and thrust like a fish on a line, freeing a hand momentarily. Just enough.

"Hold him!" Angulsac cried, and more bloodless bodies piled on top of him, his hand wedged tight beneath him.

Angulsac lowered himself down so that he was mere inches from the Inquisitor's face.

"So, Inquisitor," he hissed, "this is when *you* stumble from the path of your Lord and find yourself on another very different one. Let us see how walking in the shadow of the moon fares with you after having stalked the shadow for so long?"

Angulsac looked up and nodded. The hand which held Tacit's hair now ushered his head downwards, pushing his face towards the surface of the water. Tacit fought with all his might, but the hand, whilst wretched and shrunken, possessed all the strength and force of a werewolf's, full of sinew and wrath. Tacit grimaced, fighting with every ounce of his might to keep his lips from touching the surface of the puddle. But, bit by bit, the strength in his neck weakened and his face lowered ever closer towards the surface of that insipid pool.

And then the memory flashed across Tacit's skull. With his hand still wedged tight beneath him, he felt with searching fingers inside a pocket, his hand closing around a small container. Quickly, and as carefully as he was able, he drew out the glass container of the demon's breath he'd taken from the exorcism in Perugia years ago. With the last of his failing strength, he levered his arm up beneath his chin and crushed the glass in his hand, shattering its fragments over the surface of the water. At once, the possessed contents hissed and squealed free, running over and around the puddle. As soon as the evil gaseous spirit touched the water, it froze it in an instant. Tacit groaned and fought the forcing hands no more. His face thumped hard against the solid ice of the frozen puddle.

Shrieks of disbelief and anger exploded in the cavern.

"Witchcraft!" one cried, leaping from thin yellowed foot to thin yellowed foot.

"Accursed Catholic magic!" another called.

"It is the mercy of the Lord!" one wept on seeing the puddle turn to ice in front of him. A cacophony of shouting, howling and crying shook the foundations of the cave. Figures sprang for doorways, whilst others threw themselves down on the ground, their faces buried in the grime of the lair.

Tacit took his chance. He threw himself backwards, now easily casting the distracted and desperate creatures from on top of him. He roared like a wild thing at the astonished and bewildered clan, appearing to grow like a bear before the wailing and weeping creatures, circling desperately in pain and anguish. Their scheme to curse the Inquisitor for the rest of eternity had failed. Some lay down and refused to move, accepting now the Lord's judgement upon them. Some still had some fight in them, filled with a rage and torment unlike any they had known before. They circled and snarled at the Inquisitor, waiting for their moment to attack. If they could not bind him within their clan, then they would now have to satisfy their rage by ripping him limb from limb.

As they closed in around him, Tacit ripped a bag from his coat pocket and threw it onto the smouldering fire, shrinking down as small as he could go on the ground, his back turned. Seconds later, an almighty explosion shook the cavern, blasting shrapnel to all corners of the room. A million fragments of scorching hot silver ripped through the cavern.

Pain tore into Tacit's back and buttocks as the silver bomb exploded. He ignored the need to cry out and stay crouched to protect his wounds, instead leaping to his feet, the revolver and crossbow drawn. Around him was a scene of bloodied smoking devastation, the vile bodies of the human wolves ripped and pulverised by the deadly explosive. Bodies and body parts scattered the floor, headless, limbless, dead eyed and despoiled. There was a whimpering and a gurgling from shattered throats. Pallid chunks of flesh lay quivering against walls, blackened and burnt from the explosion, like bully beef turned out from soldiers' meat tins. Several figures still shook and stumbled about the cavern, stunned and deafened by the blast, staggering blindly, eyes blown from faces, feet feeling their way in the darkness.

The detonated silver, deadly to these creatures, would eventually kill all those caught within the bomb's blast, but Tacit was never one to leave any job half finished, to leave anything to chance.

He aimed the revolver and blew the head off one of the wolves. He turned and killed another. A female wolf whimpered before him. The silver round blew a hole through her ribcage and she slumped lifeless to the ground. He turned, just in time to avoid the full impact of a tottering blow from Baldrac, the left side of his face utterly blown from his head. Tacit inserted the barrel of the revolver into the wound and blasted out what was left of his brains.

Two wolves turned and bolted for the archway, their natural instinct for survival overcoming their desire for release from the misery of the curse. Tacit shot one in the back of the head, tumbling him down in the dirt. The other was caught behind the heart and slumped into the wall alongside him, dead.

Tacit loaded six more sliver bullets into the barrel of the revolver and cocked it. A tall gangly figure leapt at him. Tacit caught sight of him out of the corner of his eye through the grimy light of the cavern. The crossbow pinged and the bolt thundered with a sickening thunk through his eye socket and lodged firmly in his brain. A wolf on the ground reached up at the Inquisitor as if to ask for release. Tacit struck the poor creature to the side and blasted a red hole in its temple. Another crawled away from a huddle of bodies and the Inquisitor stopped its movement with a bullet in the rear of its skull. He stepped with rapid feet, wading between the bodies, his keen eye watching for movement, for any signs of life that remained in their carnal murdering hole. He put four remaining wolves out of their misery. It was ironic how after he had been warned by Angulsac of his Church's lack of mercy he showed the repugnant creatures exactly that in their final moments.

Tacit turned, two rounds left in his revolver's cylinder, and surveyed the cavern. Death hung like a thick fog over the place, silent and complete. Movement caught his eye from the far edge of the cave where there lay a mass of bodies, dashed and bleeding from the full force of the explosion. Tacit stepped over, reloading the revolver from the bullets in his belt. He looked down. It was Angulsac, the wolf who had tried to bring him under his own curse.

Tacit stared down at him, a vague smudge of satisfaction across the Inquisitor's face.

"You asked if I would stumble from the path," said Tacit, pushing the cylinder back into place. "Who says I already haven't?" he asked, raising the barrel of the gun to the forehead of the matted grim faced being. "You're a doomed and finished race from another time, wolf," Tacit hissed. "Don't worry, your time is nigh. Your suffering will one day end."

"Do you really think so, Inquisitor?" Angulsac croaked, blood pouring from the wound in his throat. "What do you see, Inquisitor? Do you see a wolf or do you see a man, a man cursed by your Church's evilness."

"I've heard enough of your sermons, wolf," replied Tacit, cocking the weapon.

Angulsac laughed. "You're too late. The truth will out, Inquisitor. All around you, your kind are turning. The downfall of your Church and a new age for mankind is nigh. Watch for the signs, Inquisitor. Watch for –."

The revolver exploded in Tacit's hand. Angulsac's brain exploded across the mound of churned and torn bodies behind him. Tacit opened his aiming eye.

EIGHTY NINE

08:34. FRIDAY, OCTOBER 16TH. 1914, FAMPOUX. NR. ARRAS. FRANCE.

Henry took Sandrine's hand and led her from the doorway of the house. She had dressed, finding herself a pair of blue grey pantaloons and shirt, over which she wore a shawl. Henry had changed into clean fatigues. A new shirt and trousers. They smelt of lanolin and polish. He left his old clothes in a heap on the floor. His abandonment of order thrilled him.

They looked set for a journey back to civilisation. Henry watched Sandrine gather together the few things she wanted to take back with her, including the dress she had carefully folded and put to one side when Pewter had come upon her. He adored her, even though he still understood so little. The fact that she was willing to share her secrets with him was not lost on Henry. She had opened her heart to him. There was no question he would give his heart to her.

As he sat in the silence of the house whilst she was changing, so much more began to make sense to him, her strength of mind and body, her determination, her passion and her drive. He could never imagine meeting another like her. She was bewitchingly unique. They said nothing as they walked from the house down the street, their heads bowed, as if in silent procession to church. Sandrine didn't even turn to bid her home goodbye. She had long ago left her childhood home, in every way.

Henry's mind was still a mass of questions and fears, but there was no time to consider them now. Fampoux was lost. Soon the Germans would learn the news of the British defeat, or their disappearance from the village, and they would come upon it with their strengthened units. Henry and Sandrine had to be away – better to travel lightly and quickly and be assured of their escape rather than weighed down with unnecessary items from the past. For all that history and violence and terror was behind them now. He would mourn his men for the rest of his life but only the future lay before them. Its unpredictability was enticing.

All Henry had brought with him from the house was the unit's diary, tucked under his right arm as he walked. Whilst Sandrine had been changing he had written up his final entry. He'd left nothing out. He'd not been sparse with his details. The wolves, the method of their creation by the Church, the devastation, the fall of Fampoux. He breathed deeply and contentedly as he closed the cover of the book, his last act as an officer in the British Expeditionary Force. His gun, his packs, his iron rations, all his standard issue, he left behind at the house, the only trace of his ever having been in the village.

"There is nothing for me here now," Sandrine announced, as they stepped away with urgent strides.

They reached the junction where the street turned onto the main road. Away to their left they could see the desolation of the trench, quiet as the grave. Beyond No Man's Land, along the line of trees and built up earth, which marked the line of the German trench, figures like ants in the distance could be seen gathering and preparing for an assault with urgency.

To their right, climbing the slight incline to the apex of the sweeping hill, was the vast network of the British support trenches, ominous, silent and grey black.

"We'll never get through them," Henry warned, shaking his head. "Not that way."

All his optimism now drained out of him, all his hope had come to nought in that moment, in the realisation that there was nowhere they could go. To the east, they would come upon the Germans. Henry would be taken as a prisoner of war, perhaps even shot and discarded in an unmarked grave. Sandrine, he wished not to think what might happen to her in German hands, whether she allowed the rage to come upon her or not.

To the west, they would arrive in the support trenches, be processed and interrogated. Henry would be posted to another unit, if lucky, more likely shot for desertion, for leaving his post, suspicions being raised as to how he could have survived, to have been the last one out of there alive. To the north and south they would be caught up within the warring fronts of both sides, their fates no different, no better than going east or west. "It's desperate, my darling," he said, shaking his head.

She turned and stroked her fingers through his hair and kissed him gently. "Nothing's truly desperate. Not after you've lived as long as my kind have," she replied. "Come on!"

They hurried back into the tangled depths of the ruined village.

"Where are we going?"

"You'll see!" Sandrine called, tugging him by the hand.

But at the next turning, they shuddered to a dead halt.

Up ahead stood Sister Isabella, her legs astride the middle of the grey white road, her hands extended around a silver coloured revolver pointed directly at the pair of them.

"It's you!" Sandrine hissed, letting go of Henry's hand and dropping back onto her haunches like an animal about to spring.

"It's me," replied Isabella hollowly. The revolver trembled in her hands.

"How did you find me?"

"Does it matter?" Isabella asked, gently unclamping and clamping her fingers on the grip.

Henry raised a weary hand. "Please!" he said, stepping forward with both his hands raised. "Please! Let us go!"

"Be quiet, Henry!" Sandrine hissed, her eyes firm on the Sister. "Are you going to try and take me?"

The revolver wavered in Isabella's hand. Her finger whitened against the trigger. She closed an eye, focusing on Sandrine's heart. She felt the pressure of the trigger. One more little pull.

"No," Isabella then said, and let the gun drop to her side.

"Why?" Sandrine asked, standing again and facing down her opponent.

"Just tell me," Isabella asked, raising her hands and the gun lifelessly in front of her and then dropping them to her side. "Did you kill them?

"Them?"

"The Fathers?"

Sandrine hesitated, as if confused by the question. "No."

"Then who did?"

"I don't know."

"You lie!"

"It's true. I don't know who killed Father Andreas or the others."

"Then tell me, Sandrine, tell me why?"

"I only know why I did what I did, no matter how small my role."

"That will suffice."

Sandrine chuckled. "Peace," she said, and then her tone darkened. "And revenge."

"Peace and revenge?" the Sister scoffed. "By the killing of two Priests?"

"Like I said, I do not know who killed them, or expected them to be murdered," replied Sandrine, turning to Henry who watched her closely.

"But you still think the killing of two Fathers, two peaceful and kindly Fathers, will grant you the revenge you so sought and in doing so bring you peace?! I should shoot you now and put you out of your ignorant misery."

"You think this is about the killing of two Catholic Fathers?"

"But you said –"

"I said peace and revenge. I did not tell you the means or indeed when such a thing shall be achieved."

"So, the deaths of the Fathers –"

"Enough of the Fathers!" cried Sandrine. "Sister, if you were provided with the opportunity to both achieve peace on earth and salvation for your people, would you not grasp such an opportunity, no matter what the cost?"

"Every life is sacred."

"Yes, but what is the deaths of two when set against the salvation of millions? An everlasting peace? What better goal can there be for mankind?" Isabella shook her head, but there was the hint of admiration in her eyes at Sandrine's vision. "You really believe you can achieve what you say?"

But Sandrine was no longer looking at her. Instead she was staring at Henry, whose manner had changed to surprise at what he had heard. "Yes," she said finally, "I want to end these terrible wars, both of mankind and against *my* people." And finally she turned to look at Isabella. "Don't you think there's been enough killing?" Something caught Isabella's attention. Sandrine and Henry followed her gaze to the horizon. Germans, a vast band of grey and black massing in the distance, coming towards Fampoux.

"The war," said Isabella. "What's this got to do with it? With you? With the Fathers? I have to know."

"You will see, Sister. You will see."

"I must know."

"Be prepared for disappointment. Your Church will need to learn to cope with disappointment from now on."

"Meaning?"

Sandrine raised an eyebrow indicating that the Sister would have to wait. That only time would tell.

And now Isabella suddenly chuckled and looked away. She shook her head, peering about the ruins and rubble. "I wish you luck," she said, striding forward and past the pair of them.

"Luck?"

"If it is peace you seek, then may all luck go with you. And you should go yourselves," she warned, "the Germans will be here any minute."

"Tell me," Sandrine called after the Sister. "Why didn't you kill me? Just now?"

Isabella stopped and looked back. "Like you say, it seems to me there's been enough killing."

NINETY

1909. Naples. Italy.

Tacit filled a jug from the pump and drank long and deeply from it. He felt spent and burnt from the merciless sun but he had also never felt so empowered and alive, such utter contentment in his life. Beneath the relentless heat, the harvest had grown fine and strong, the finest Mila had ever known on the farm, or so she had said two nights before, whilst they lay naked in each other's arms. A surge of joy struck him quite unexpectedly as he drank, and he smiled and shook his head, draining the remains of the jug in a final long draw.

"What are you looking so pleased with yourself about?" demanded Mila playfully, stepping into the kitchen. He lunged forward and took hold of her in his arms, lifting her off the ground as if she were a child, enveloped in his vast strong arms.

"What are you doing, you fool?" she laughed, giggling and batting at him with her hands.

He kissed her behind the ear and shook her gently.

"Careful!" she warned, eventually wriggling free of him and reaching for the safety of the kitchen side.

"What is it?" asked Tacit, wrapping himself around her and kissing her neck again. "What's wrong?"

"Wrong?" she replied, turning in his grasp to face him and kissing him gently. "Nothing's wrong, Poldek." She put her hands to his face and kissed him again. "I'm pregnant."

NINETY ONE

08:44. Friday, October 16th, 1914.
Fampoux, Nr. Arras. France.

"Come on," cried Sandrine, dragging Henry into a narrow side street, so ruined that they had to climb over piles of collapsed walls and roofs to get through it. "Let's go!"

"Where are we going?" asked Henry.

"The tunnels."

They slithered and staggered over the mounds of broken masonry and stones, all the time listening for the approach of the Germans, for the whine of their shells, the sharp bark of their rifles. But they heard nothing, cocooned within the tumbled ruins through which Sandrine led them.

She pushed him left into a short cul-de-sac and suddenly stopped, dropping to the floor of the road. "In here," she called, lifting a stone to the side with ease. A dark square tunnel was revealed, leading downwards into the black, a ladder running down one wall. "Down here," she said, pointing to the tunnel.

"What's down here?" Henry asked, ominously.

Sandrine smiled and Henry longed to kiss her. "Escape," she said. "These tunnels lead all the way to Arras."

Henry beamed. "Sandrine, I think I love you!" he announced.

She blew a raspberry and tutted. "Only think?" she replied, hiding a smirk. "We will have to do something about that!" She swung her legs over the edge of the hole.

"Do you have a lantern or a light? It looks awfully dark in there?"

She gave her lover an odd look. "Henry, do you even need to ask? You know I think of everything! There's a lantern at the bottom of the ladder." She was soon swallowed up in the darkness below. Henry looked back one final time to the devastation of the village. Everywhere he looked he saw only signs of death and destruction. He looked back to the yawning hole. He knew it was time to leave.

NINETY TWO

08:42. FRIDAY, OCTOBER 16TH, 1914.
THE FRONT LINE. FAMPOUX, NR. ARRAS. FRANCE.

Forward they came, the massed ranks of the German forces, striding across the ravaged shell holes and undulations of No Man's Land with caution and uncertainty as to what lay ahead. There had been jubilation within the German ranks at the news that they were to go forward *into* Fampoux, jubilation mixed with hysteria because of how the scouts had insisted that Fampoux had been deserted. Some said that it was a trap, others said there was a curse on the place, recounting how the Germans had been driven from the village less than a week ago. Expectancy was mixed with terror; fear became aggression.

They attached bayonets and shouted their loyalty and allegiance to the Kaiser. They lined up in their trenches, mumbling final prayers and kissing rings and necklaces. There was not one who did not reflect upon – in those final few moments before the whistle was blown and they filed up the ladder and out into No Man's Land – the catastrophic assault made the other night. Their Sergeants screamed for loyalty and belief in their commanding officers and told them to go forward and do their duty.

Isabella staggered towards the hole in the trench into which Tacit had vanished. The pale rays of sunlight scorched across the landscape, reflecting on the wave of bayonets moving slowly closer towards the trench and Fampoux. She sank to her knees, her eyes welling with tears. She shuddered and roared a long and terrible cry of loss and pain, which scattered birds from the trees and rang about the land like a wail from beyond the grave.

He was gone.

Once night fell, she knew the wolves would tear out from the hole, the Germans would be torn and decimated: the British would steal forward and recapture the village; and the pitiless cycle of horror would begin again – capture, destruction, capture, destruction. An aimless, endless machine of death and devastation, all the soldiers and wolves small cogs in the great device. She knew she should leave, return to Arras, take a train to Rome and the Vatican, tell them the news, give her report on the assessment. Clear Tacit of all charges. Tell them he was the bravest and the most honourable man she'd ever met. But not yet. She owed Tacit a few more minutes of her time, reflecting on his grim resolve and their bond.

She hung her head and clapped her face within her hands, sobbing uncontrollably with grief as the emotion engulfed her utterly. She wailed, wretched tears streaming down her face.

She was crying so hard that she almost missed the crunch of earth from the trench. She lifted her head, blinking with pain, rubbing a sleeve across her nose, rubbing the tears from her eyes. She wept and looked again.

It was him!

She threw herself forward, sliding down the edge of the trench and diving into his vast frame, wrapping her arms around him.

"You're alive!" she moaned. "You're alive," hugging him tight to her body.

Tacit stood stock still, his arms drawn out away from his body as if crucified on an invisible cross, the Sister weeping and tugging at him, her hands on his back, her head on his chest. Momentarily, something inside him softened and gave way, and he drew an arm forward and rested a comforting hand on the top of her back as she wept into him.

"You're alive, you're alive," she kept whispering over and over until her voice finally shrank to silence.

Tacit loosened his grip on the Sister and pulled her a little away from him, wincing as the adrenaline ebbed out of him and the pain from his wounds returned.

"Are you hurt?" she asked, seeing the tattered remains of his coat hanging from his side. "You are!" she exclaimed with horror, looking closer and seeing his clothes sodden with his blood, chainmail hanging in blasted, matted rags.

"It is nothing," Tacit hissed back.

"But your side!" Isabella fussed.

Tacit took her hands and drew them from their inquisitive search of his bloodied flesh. "There's something back in Arras," he said urgently, holding her fast at arm's length in front of him.

"What?" muttered Isabella, wiping the last of the tears from her eyes.

"I'm not sure. Within the lair, a wolf, perhaps he was their leader, he was certainly the last one alive before I was finished, he said something about 'you and your kind turning'."

"Turning?"

"We need to go back and see the Cardinal."

"Cardinal?"

"Poré. What about the Prideux woman? Did you find her?"

Isabella turned her eyes from Tacit's face. Her faced flushed with shame but then, almost at once, a resolve grew within her. "Yes, I found her." She looked hard into Tacit's eyes. "But I let her go," she said, staring into Tacit's impassive face. "I let her live."

Their eyes bored into each other. Isabella shuddered, imagining all the hateful things Tacit was summoning within his vocabulary to castigate her for this act of foolish kindness. But he wasn't thinking anything of the sort. He was recalling the face of his mother in the contours of Isabella's and his life when she was alive.

"Then our only move is to Arras," he growled, as if coming out of a dream.

"If we want to catch Poré we should hurry," suggested Isabella. "He'll be leaving for the Mass for Peace shortly." And then Isabella stopped. "Peace," she muttered to herself, recollecting Sandrine's words.

"What is it?"

"Nothing. Nothing," said the Sister, shaking her head.

Tacit found a steep pathway out of the trench and scrambled his way up it, proffering his hand to Isabella once he was out. His grip was like a vice around her wrist.

They half ran, half walked along the top of the trench and up the sunken road beside the retaken village.

"The Germans will find nothing left," Isabella mused, looking over her shoulder towards where the Germans were scrambling across No Man's Land. "Nothing except shadows of the past."

PART SIX

"And I have filled him with the spirit of God, in wisdom, and in understanding, and in knowledge, and in all manner of workmanship."

Exodus, 31, Verse 3

NINETY THREE

13:02. Friday, October 16th, 1914. Arras. France.

The newly elected, and rapidly promoted, Father of the Cathedral of Arras, Father Xabier couldn't have been more unfriendly if he had tried. He scowled when Isabella asked where Poré was to be found.

"He's not at his residence," Tacit added, unconsciously thumping a fist into a palm.

"He won't be."

"And why's that?"

"Because he's gone," the Father replied briskly, striding across the ambulatory in a manner which showed his impatience and irritation.

The ambulatory, where it had first begun.

He was young and squat and well fed, Father Xabier. He had a complexion which suggested he preferred the outdoors to the cool confines of Cathedral interiors. He'd been brought in from the Basque region of France, where war was only rumour. Tacit secretly gave him six months before he reckoned the Father would apply for a secondment to a position more suited to his preference for the outdoors and warmer climes.

"All the other Fathers have gone off to war," he revealed. "More fool them." He said it with a scowl and an unconscious smoothing of his short, greasy hair. "So, for now, Arras has got me, whether the congregation like it or not. And, at the moment, I am late, my sermon is barely written, the books have yet to be set out and the new chorister is yet to learn his parts after the last one quit."

Isabella cast a fierce glare at the Inquisitor at this particular piece of news.

"Where's he gone?" asked Isabella. "Poré?"

"Paris. Left yesterday. Abruptly, by his personal carriage. For the Mass for Peace." At this moment, the guns along the front started up their distant rumble and the ground began to shake, such was the massed barrage's combined devastation. "Mass for Peace," grumbled Father Xabier doubtfully, in reply to the rumble, ambling over to the pulpit and thrusting down his sermon notes. "Mass for Peace indeed. If the power of prayer hasn't worked already, then I have no reason to believe that a Mass for Peace will work now. It would require something extraordinary to happen in order for the warring nations to sit up and take note, to listen to our combined Catholic voices." He waved his hands as he spoke, conducting an invisible orchestra.

"And more to the point, act in all our combined interests. In other words, not act solely for the Catholic Church, but for every religion, every person in the world to bring everyone together and act as one single combined force for good. And that, frankly, is a step too far, as far as I am concerned, seeing as we don't even talk to half of them and they certainly don't talk to us. It'll take a miracle. And, if I am honest, the miracle that I currently need is for someone to ensure that this Cathedral is ready for its own Mass in just twenty minutes."

He stopped and looked up, aware that the visitors had fallen silent during his rant. It was then that the Father found that he was alone.

The Cardinal's door to his private quarters broke with a single kick of Tacit's boot, the wood splintering around the lock and sending it tumbling noisily across the wood panelled floor.

"Church spends a fortune on quality locks and buys the cheapest wooden doors," muttered Tacit, thrusting the doors wide.

"What are we looking for?" Isabella asked, stepping over the splinters into his study and peering around the small tome-lined room. Every available inch of wall, every surface appeared covered. The early afternoon Arras sun smudged the spines of books with its thin light.

"I don't know," Tacit replied, working his way along a shelf of books, tugging tomes from their place, letting some fall straight to the floor, whilst with others taking more time to peer through their pages before throwing them to the ornate carpet beneath his booted feet.

Across Pore's desk were personal letters and oddments, letters from his congregation asking for assistance or prayers during the difficulties of war. All were innocuous, nothing which suggested anything untoward. Isabella shrieked in frustration and shook her hair into her face.

"Maybe it's nothing after all," she suggested, holding two handfuls of paper up. "Maybe this is just a dead end. Maybe the wolf was playing with you, a final parting gift, a trick to plant suspicion? A red herring?"

"No," Tacit replied, gruffly. "There's something. The wolf said it, like a taunt, like I knew those personally who were turning. We've gone full circle. The only place left now is with Poré. He must know something, something that can help."

"What on earth do you think you are doing?" called an officious voice suddenly from the shattered open door to Poré's apartment. "If you don't leave at once, then I will call the Sodalitium Pianum!"

"If you don't leave at once," Tacit roared in reply, "I'll break your nose!"

The Priest, dark haired with greying flecks, cassock bound, blanched and shook his head in disdain. He turned on his heel and marched away, his shoes clipping on the polished marble.

"Hey, hold yourself!" the Inquisitor called, thundering after the man and dragging him back to the busted doorway. "Where does Cardinal Poré keep his correspondence?!" he demanded to know, shaking him.

"If you think I am going to tell a common stranger like you, you, you, whoever you are, you have another think coming!"

But the Inquisitor and Sister traced where his eyes fell onto a wooden box in the corner of the room, hidden beneath piles of books and lengths of cloth.

"Thanks!" growled Tacit, connecting his ham-like fist with the bridge of the Priest's nose. He went down with a cry, a dead weight, flat out unconscious, his nose split, blood pouring from his nostrils.

"You're an excellent negotiator, Tacit," Isabella mocked, as the Inquisitor heaved the partially hidden box from the shelf and manhandled it onto the table. She tried the catch.

Locked.

"We need a key," said Isabella, looking around the walls, searching across the mantlepiece. She heard Tacit mumble something and the next thing she heard was the cracking of wood, as he inserted his fingernails into the space between the lid and the main body of the box and wrenched it open, shattering the lock and its casement. A number of papers shone like white gold inside.

"And an excellent lock picker, too," she added, pulling the first few papers from the top of the pile. Tacit did the same, his eyes flittering across the pages. With each valueless sheet, disdainfully he let it drop to the floor or the desk. A sudden intake of breath from the Sister drew him away from his studies.

"Oh my God," said Isabella, her hand to her mouth, "I think it's Poré!"

Tacit stole forward, his face grim, and snatched the paper from her fingers.

"It can't be!" hissed Tacit, his eyes keen on the paper. "Poré was attacked by the wolf!"

It was a letter, written on an old vellum parchment in a wild and chaotic scrawl, the words almost impossible to decipher, such was their savage and desperate style. The letters and words all ran into each other, as if the writer was possessed or incoherent with madness. But there could be no question that it was undoubtedly a letter written for and to Cardinal Poré. Within it, the sender had assured the Cardinal of his ultimate gift, his very own wolf pelt, in exchange for *the task* to be done, '... to accomplish our differing but combined ends.' 'An eye for an eye,' the letter read in a bold and menacing font. 'A tooth for a tooth,' it finished.

It was signed 'Frederick Prideux'.

"Prideux," muttered Tacit.

"Sandrine Prideux's father?" Isabella stuttered. "What do you think he means when he writes, 'to accomplish our differing but combined ends'?"

Tacit shook his head. "I don't know, but I've been so blind." He turned on the Sister. "We should never have believed Poré when he said he was attacked! Stupid! Stupid!" he cried, casting the box of papers from the table with a crash, letters and documents tumbling out and over the floor. "Took his word for it. Took the word of a liar as gospel. So stupid." He slammed a palm hard into his forehead, the sound like the crack of a circus master's whip.

"So what do we do now?"

"Now? We catch a train. To Paris."

"I just don't believe it. Poré, he attacked the Fathers?" Isabella stuttered, sitting back on the desk and shaking her head incredulously. "He used the pelt! He attacked me! But why? What's to be gained by killing the Fathers?"

"And why is he attending the Mass for Peace with it in his possession?"

Isabella rose her hand to her mouth and appeared to sob. "I can't believe it. Everything you thought was sacred, everything you believed in and then suddenly, it's gone."

Tacit put his heavy eyes onto her. "Finally," he growled darkly, "you're beginning to understand."

NINETY FOUR

1910. NAPLES. ITALY.

It was a hard winter, the hardest Tacit had known since he'd settled at the farm. Deep snow and driving winds buried most of the fields and the north face of the farmhouse. They'd warned him at the market, the old hands who gently mocked the Priest who had turned his back on the fruits of

God to worship the fruits of the land. But the 'foolish' Priest had not been lazy or unprepared. The house was well shuttered and warm, the stores well stocked and the fires roared beneath well swept chimneys.

Nevertheless, Tacit couldn't control the elements and word reached his ears that a tree had come down across a fence in the southern field and some livestock had escaped. Mila, heavily pregnant, had asked him not to go, but he knew he couldn't leave the cattle to wander the night unhoused. Tacit, as well as anyone, knew what dangers lurked in the dark. It wasn't far, just down to the bottom field. Three miles there and back. He assured her he wouldn't be long, and he'd take the cart and a lantern, to speed his way.

As ever, he stowed the shotgun under the rug in the back of the cart, just in case, and waved back to her as he took the reins. The Church hadn't returned since that short visit two years ago, but his memory was long and he knew their memory would be longer.

"Get back in the house!" he cried. "Keep our baby you're growing, warm!"

She laughed and blew him a kiss before shutting the door hard against the elements.

He'd lost a bull and two cows in the blackness of the night and the storm, but the fence hadn't taken long to fix. A good enough job with the tools and materials he had with him. Perhaps in the morning he'd set out and find the animals. For now, he'd take his cold whipped body home and warm it beside his love and the fire.

It was the light on the hill which first caught his attention, a blaze on the horizon, ahead of him, in line with the path up which he was driving. It took just a moment for the cold horror to creep into his soul. The farm! The farm was on fire!

He threw the horse forward into a gallop and roared up the hill towards the flames, weeping and crying out in anger and disbelief, as he leapt from the cart towards the raging building alight, staggering to a halt and dropping to his knees a few paces from the front porch when he saw her there. His hands tore at his face and hair, screaming against the wind in anguish and horror at the naked, bloodied figure prostrate on the stairs. They'd cut her from chest to pelvis, her entrails and unborn foetus spread about her in the blood stained snow, as if a specimen in some monstrous ritual.

He lunged forward and bound the frozen remains of his unborn child and Mila into his arms, his head turned skyward, a roar screamed to the heavens above.

NINETY FIVE

16:12. Friday, October 16th. 1914, Paris. France.

Cardinal Poré turned the gilded handle of the door to his personal quarters in Paris and pushed it open. He hobbled inside and shut the door firmly behind him, dropping his hand to the key and turning it in the lock with a reassuring clack. Finally, he allowed his face to crack with the pain and discomfort he felt so cruelly in his leg, his head lolling back against the door, his mouth wide, eyes tight shut, swimming in the agony coming from his thigh.

He pulled roughly at the buttons of his cassock and ripped the garment from his body, allowing it fall. The cool of the Parisian October air wrapped itself around the Cardinal's thigh and unconsciously his hand dropped to his wound, snatching at the gash, as if in vain hope of being able to claw the bullet wound closed. The trauma to his leg, inflicted by Sister Isabella when she'd shot him with Tacit's revolver, shrieked in anger and Poré moaned hopelessly and desperately in pain. He pictured the bullet, lodged deep within his leg, scraping hard against his thigh bone with every movement. It made Poré feel sick and hot. He gulped at the air in an attempt to calm himself and the pain. He had to be strong. He was too close now to fail.

Cardinal Bishop Monteria had looked more grave than Poré had ever seen him when the younger Cardinal first hobbled in. Monteria recognised at once that Poré had been wounded, not believing the excuse the ailing Cardinal had given to Bishop Varsy that the autumn air had disagreed with his joints. He immediately suspected that Poré's earlier promise to 'take steps' must have, as he feared it might do at the time, backfired. Those within his flock commented that they had never seen the usually cordial Cardinal Bishop look so private and subdued.

"It must be nerves," Varsy had said, but Poré knew it was his injury, and the manner by which it had been received, which so concerned the architect of the Mass.

"Don't worry," hissed Poré through his pain, when the pair had a moment of quiet together. "Tacit's in Arras. He knows nothing of Paris, of our plan."

That seemed to calm Monteria and he brightened as the final rehearsal ran its course.

In the safety of his apartment, Poré hobbled to the chair in front of his desk and lowered himself gingerly onto it, trying to straighten his leg with a cry. He forced his hand hard into the bullet hole, a pathetic attempt to stem the blood which had begun to stream from the wound after hours on his feet. He shook his head and wiped his sweating forehead with his unbloodied hand. Just one more night. *Just one more night*, he thought to himself. Just one more night and his work would be done. It would all be over then.

The sallow looking Cardinal looked about himself for something to help stem the blood trickling down his thigh and onto the chair on which he sat. His eyes fell on the sleeve of his shirt and moments later he was tearing strips from it, inserting a ball of wadding into the crimson hole. It made him howl and he collapsed into unconsciousness from his labours.

He came to, he knew not how long later, to the sound of a knock at the door. *Thank Heavens I locked it*, he thought to himself, as he clawed his way back to consciousness.

"Cardinal Poré?" came a voice the Cardinal recognised as Father Gugan's outside his door.

"Yes? Who is it?" Poré replied, more alarmed than he wished to sound.

"It is Father Gugan. I just wanted to check you were alright, Cardinal Poré?" he asked, into the frame of the door. "You looked and seemed a little out of sorts at the Mass rehearsal. A little white, if I may say so. I just wished to make sure you were okay?"

"Yes, yes, I am fine, Father Gugan," Poré replied, looking down at his shattered leg and blood-soaked wrapping bound loosely around the wound.

"I do hope you're not ailing with something, Cardinal?"

"No. No, I am just a little tired from my travels, that is all. I will rest tonight and am I sure I will be fine in the morning."

"Very good, Cardinal Poré. Is there anything I can bring you, Cardinal?"

"No, I am fine thank you, Father Gugan. Please be at rest."

Poré waited until he heard no more footsteps outside his door. He wept and bit hard into his fist, shoved tight into his mouth to mask his cries. Slowly, with all the energy and nerve he could muster, he levered himself up out of his chair and hobbled like a broken thing to the cupboard. He inserted a key, which he had gathered from the desk, and unlocked the door of the tall dark wooden cupboard. He could no longer resist looking at it, to check it was still there. He had to look on the foul thing inside one more time before he retired to his bed, the source of his agony, his turmoil.

It hung alone on the inside rail, limp and grey, stinking, tufted with dirt and dried black blood where it had been roughly hacked from Frederick Prideux. There was a vulgar smell of rot about the pelt, an animalistic musk which seemed to seep through and outside the wooden cupboard which housed it. It looked vile, more belonging in the window of a demonic curiosity shop or a coven's lair of sorcery. Its very essence seemed to emanate a dark power.

Poré stared at it, like a King surveying a great and terrible weapon, locked in a deep chamber beneath his castle walls, with which he would destroy his foes. Tomorrow everything would be completed. After tomorrow nothing would ever be the same again.

NINETY SIX

16:56. FRIDAY, OCTOBER 16TH, 1914. ARRAS. FRANCE.

Tacit and Isabella stumbled from the Cathedral's residences in the hope of finding some swift method of transport. They were greeted with a rare prize, a taxi, a Renault Freres motor car, stood empty in the square, rattling and cranking on its robust frame and hard wheels, engine still hot from its previous journey. Amiens was the closest city to Arras with a station on a direct line to the capital. Speed was not of the essence, it was a necessity.

"Amiens," called Isabella, climbing under the canopy and into the back of the vehicle.

"Amiens?!" the driver called, sounding relieved. "Just came from there. Will be a pleasure to get back there too," he added, indicating the screams and the thundering of shells encroaching on the city's outlying lands.

"Fortune favours the brave, Tacit," the Sister chirped from the back, as the Inquisitor stepped on the footplate and into the front seat of the car, the vehicle buckling under his weight.

"And I favour a passenger a little more on the smaller size, begging your pardon, Father," mumbled the driver, cranking his gears and inching the vehicle forward.

"How long to Amiens?" asked Tacit, leaning forward in his compact seat to relieve the pressure on his wounds.

"An hour," replied the driver of the car. "But with you on board, more likely two," he grumbled, looking over at his vast size and shaking his head. "My springs," he mumbled to himself. "My poor springs."

Isabella leant forward to the ear of the driver. "Do you know when the last train to Paris is tonight?"

"From Amiens? Six o'clock."

"What time is it now?"

"Nearly five," replied the driver, checking his wrist watch

"We're not going to make it," Tacit grunted, clenching his fists into balls.

"Can this car not go any quicker?" she asked.

"Yes. You can lose your oversized passenger and you can get out and push." He pushed his foot firmer down on the accelerator pedal and the tone of the engine yelled a little higher.

"Keep your foot there, driver," Tacit advised, feeling in his pockets for something to sooth his aching body. "If your car goes up in smoke, the Church will buy you a new one."

"If the car goes up in smoke and me with it, at least I'm in good company," the driver added, with a shrug. "Don't forget to give me my last rites, Sister."

"Why the Sister?" asked Tacit, uncorking the bottle and preparing to take a sip. "Why not me?"

"Because if the engine goes, we're both sitting on top of it."

Tacit drank long from the bottle. It was nearly half empty by the time he took it from his lips. He shut his eyes and felt the whistle of the wind on his face, felt the surge of alcohol fire his body and prickle within his mind. He raised the bottle to his lips and then paused, turning and proffering it to the Sister.

"I thought you'd never ask," she replied, snatching it from him and setting the lip of the bottle to her mouth. She drank deeply. She grimaced and set the bottle in her lap, staring out at the other traffic on the road, some going out of Arras, most going into the ravaged city; lorries laden with men, soldiers marching weary beneath packs, long lines of horses, panic-stricken civilians, a vortex of humanity, running, walking, riding, but all caught up and confused in the machinations of the war. Some lucky ones, like Tacit and Isabella, had found escape courtesy of other motor cars. They drove slowly through crowds, hooting their way through the slow moving throng of exhausted people, until they were out into the open lands of Picardian France and could take the metalled roads at a pace.

Isabella raised the bottle to her lips again and drank, toasting the city farewell.

As the driver turned the car at the front of the station, Tacit and Isabella were already leaping from it, long before it had shuddered to a halt.-"If there's a train leaving for Paris at six o'clock … " cried Tacit, charging behind Isabella sprinting ahead of him.

"That gives us three minutes to board it!" Isabella called back, checking the clock tower in the square at front of the station. "What platform?"

Tacit grunted back.

"I said, what platform?"

"Who do you think I am?" he growled in reply, "a station hand?"

They raced over the forecourt and into the brisk cool shadows of the station entrance hall, skidding to a halt before the black departures board.

"Paris … Paris … Paris …" Isabella called to herself, scouring the lists as quickly as her eyes and brain could work. She cursed her stupidity at sharing Tacit's bottle. "Paris!" she exclaimed, grabbing his arm. "Platform thirteen!"They both looked to the clock tower.

"Gonna be close!" Tacit warned, as they thundered down the station towards the platform at the far end of the building.

"Typical!" roared the Inquisitor, weaving in and out of the meandering crowd. "It's always the platform at the far end of the station when you're in a rush!"

There was a goods train standing at platform two, steam pouring from every facet of its vast black engine. The air about it and the platform hung heavy with the caustic bite of coal fire and oil, the engine's sooty belch engulfing the assembled throng; nervous soldiers, cheering and singing civilians, flustered station hands hurrying this way and that with baggage carts creaking under luggage.

The doors of the train wagons were open. From them had leapt reservists, still dressed in their civilian clothes, waving and laughing, smacking each other on the back and ambling out from the platform in the direction all the other newly arrived men appeared to be heading. The atmosphere had been charged and urgent. Long after they had gone, and with them their songs and the laughter and the spirit of belief, lines of silent bleeding men were carried or assisted onto the train in their place.

By the time Tacit and Isabella jumped over the closing barrier and heaved themselves up the black pigiron steps into the train, it had changed from being a transport of hope and proud defiance to being a train carrying the decimated reality of those dreams. The vast black train cranked and heaved itself forward, and slowly, like a beast battling against chains, it slipped from the station and into the closing light of early evening.

They found a compartment to themselves. Much of the train consisted of wagons into which the injured had been laid. Few healthy soldiers or officers who could sit in compartments were going west.

"How long to Paris?" growled Tacit, dropping cautiously into the seat.

"Four hours," replied Isabella. "Back still paining you?" she asked, watching him wince as he sat.

"Some." He felt deep in the left hand side of his coat and then in the right.

"You want me to look?" she asked.

"No," he replied, sitting back and uncorking the new bottle he had retrieved from somewhere in the folds of his long jacket.

Isabella shook her head but she was smiling. "How many of those do you have in there?"

"Usually enough," he replied, as he glugged three times and wiped his mouth, exhaling gratefully. "But never enough when you really need them." He offered the bottle but Isaballa shook her still spinning head.

The train trundled west through the creeping darkness with an extraordinary lack of urgency.

"You've not brought your case," noted Isabella.

Tacit shook his head and closed his eyes, the bottle gripped firmly in his crotch. He teased the folds of his jacket apart to reveal the silver revolver strapped to his thigh. "It's all I need now," he replied, blowing with exhaustion and relief silently out through his lips.

"Are you going to kill him? Poré, I mean?"

"Depends," replied Tacit, his eyes closed.

"On what?"

"If he tries to kill me. And …" He ran a hand across his head, placing his capello on the seat next to him.

"And?" Isabella asked, but the silence told her she'd never know the answer. "Well," she said, sitting back. "It's been an interesting few days, Tacit." She reflected on events as her reflection stared back at her from the train window.

But the Inquisitor was already fast asleep.

NINETY SEVEN

13:34. Friday, October 16th, 1914. Arras. France.

Sandrine climbed the final few rungs and pulled herself clear, setting down the lantern and killing the flame within it. She reached down and held out her hand to Henry, coming up out of the darkness after her.

"I do hope you didn't look up?" she said, sniggering like a love struck teenager.

"Perish the thought," replied Henry, adopting a look of mock surprise at the accusation. He laughed and then caught the rumble of the latest artillery barrage upon the city. "So they're at it again," he mused sadly, as Sandrine knelt and pushed the cover back over the hole to conceal it.

"It won't be for long, Henry, trust me."

She took his hand and stepped quickly away.

"I do like your optimism, my darling, but I fail to share in it. It seems to me that everything has, well, stalled. I can't see us ever getting over it, or out of France."

She stopped and drew him into her arms, kissing him briefly but passionately.

"But for you, Henry Frost, it *is* over. These clothes," she said, tugging at his shirt, "say good bye to them, for after today, you will not wear a uniform again." She took the diary from under his arm. "What are you going to do with this?"

Henry looked at it and pursed his lips.

"I don't know. I should probably have left it behind, like everything else but I felt, well, I just thought I owed it to them, to Sergeant Holmes and Dawson and, well, all the men, that they shouldn't be forgotten."

"We will post it," Sandrine announced, nodding with satisfaction at her suggestion. "We will post it, in the morning, and then you will be free of it."

Henry smiled and drew her to him, showering kisses on her mouth and her cheeks.

"Now, where the hell are we going to stay until then? I'm afraid I have no money and I really don't fancy a day or night on the streets!" he said, on hearing a loud bang not far from where they stood.

"It is okay, Henry, I know someone who will help us and I owe him one final visit, if only to say goodbye."

Sandrine led Henry by the hand along side streets and back alleyways, her pace light and swift. She didn't want to risk anything now, not to meet other British soldiers, not with Henry still dressed in his soldier's fatigues, the shirt, trousers and boots of his unit, not when they were so close to their escape. The grime of the weak afternoon light and the barren streets gave the impression that they were the only people left within the city. Henry hated it. It reminded him of Fampoux but on a far larger scale. He longed for somewhere where there was life and noise and colour, not infernal greys and browns and the endless whining sounds of falling shells.

"We're nearly there," Sandrine announced, turning down into an alley where buildings loomed over the route.

"Will Alessandro be okay with this, with us just turning up?"

"He will be fine," Sandrine insisted, although there was now doubt beginning to grow in her mind the closer they drew to his home. She remembered his tears and his pain at their last meeting. But she also thought of Alessandro's lightness of character and the joy in his manner. "No, he will be fine," she insisted, almost to herself. But on turning the corner to his street, the words were torn from her mouth.

In front of her stood Alessandro's house, boarded up.

She gasped and ran towards it, standing in the middle of the street looking up into the windows of the building.

"What has happened?!" she cried, storming forward and ripping the boarding from the front door effortlessly.

"Maybe it was hit by shell fire?" suggested Henry, but he could see that the building and its roof appeared intact.

"The door!" Sandrine cried, burrowing her way between the boards. "The door has been smashed in! There are marks, Henry! Claw marks!"

He heard her cry and the sound of her feet vanishing into the building. At once, Henry thrust his way inside after her, terrified by what he might find. He thought he'd seen the last of gruesome scenes the moment he'd sunk into the depths of the tunnel of Fampoux to leave. He reached the steps of the house and raced up, taking them three at a time. Above him he could hear nothing, no screams, no sobbing, just silence. He reached the top of the flight of stairs, looking left and then right.

Sandrine was standing in the middle of a small wrecked bedroom, furniture dashed and shattered around the room, the walls and floor covered with darkened dried blood. Every surface, every wall was splashed with the gore. Henry swallowed and stepped slowly up behind Sandrine, wrapping his arms about her. She turned and buried herself into him.

"Poor Alessandro," she wept. "Poor, poor Alessandro."

He kissed the top of her head and held her tight through her sobbing.
"Henry, is everything I touch cursed?"
He soothed her gently and rocked her in his arms. "No, of course not!"
"This horror, will it never end? Will we ever be free of it?"
"Yes, it will end. Tomorrow we leave Arras and everything behind us."

NINETY EIGHT

1910. ROME. ITALY.

Cardinal Adansoni had frequented some inauspicious places in his time; brothels, bars, places of ill virtue. But the tavern in which he found himself was by far the worst establishment he had ever known. There was a man laid across the main path through the inn, face down in the thick dirt of the tavern floor, unmoving. For all Adansoni knew, he was dead.

Vomit, excrement and blood seemed everywhere within the place, the landlord too traumatised, lazy or drunk himself to attempt to clean up. The smell was obscene, rank and fetid, like a seeping cloud of rancid flesh.

Adansoni put his handkerchief to his nose and shuffled gingerly forward.

He stepped over the prostrate body and continued to work his way through the place, ducking under oddments, heavy with dust and grime hanging from the beams above, peering around corners in the hope of finding him. How he prayed he wouldn't find him. Not here, not in this place.

And then he saw him, and it broke his heart, as it had twenty one years ago when he laid his eyes on him for the very first time.

Alone and weeping, drunk out of his mind in the darkest, most remote corner of the tavern, the man Adansoni used to call 'gallant' sat broken and ruined.

"It's me, old friend," he called, stepping closer. Tacit barely acknowledged him, fumbling blindly for his glass. "May I sit with you?" Adansoni asked. He waited for an answer which never came.

Tacit stared unseeingly towards the figure and guzzled the drink in his glass clumsily. Finally, Adansoni gave up waiting for his request to be answered and sat down opposite him. The stench off his old acolyte, despite the smell of the tavern, was atrocious.

"It's me, Poldek," the Cardinal said, leaning forward and touching his arm. The touch on his arm seemed to spark activity within Tacit and, at once, he sat up and tried to focus on his visitor.

"It's me, Poldek," he continued. "I am so sorry, Poldek." Adansoni removed his hat and placed it on the table next to him, ignoring the vomit and other detritus into which it was set.

Tacit peered at him inanely, but slowly a semblance of recognition seemed to register with him. His eyes narrowed and then widened in his head, as if trying to comprehend, to remember.

"Ad …," he muttered quietly. "Ada … Adan …," he persisted, trying to form the words on his tongue. "Adansoni?"

"Yes," replied the Cardinal, tears in his eyes. Tacit shuddered and a bubbling of air escaped from his lungs. "It is me, Poldek. I have come for you."

Adansoni was aware of crying but he refused to look, turning his eyes firmly to the table. Only when Tacit spoke did he raise them and put them on the pathetic figure.

"They … they killed her," he wept. "They killed my love," he roared. "They killed my love and my child!"

"It was the Orthodox," replied the Cardinal, his eyes firm, making sure Tacit heard and understood. "They'd been moving north, burning farms, looting wherever they went. Taking everything they could find."

Tacit leaned his head back and wept, strains of spittle lining his lips like a mask.

"We caught them, Poldek. We caught them. They've admitted to everything and have been charged. The punishment was carried out over the last few weeks. They've all been hung." Adansoni noticed how dry his throat had become, how his mouth trembled. He swallowed painfully. "They suffered," he said quietly, bowing his head.

Tacit sobbed, closing his eyes, his head still turned to the ceiling. "She was everything to me," he said, his sobs becoming howls of pain. "Now I am nothing!" he roared, so loud that all heads turned in his direction. "Nothing without her!"

"The war goes on, Poldek," replied Adansoni, his cold words charged with passion and belief. "The war goes on. People come. Lovers go. But nothing really changes. Our loved ones? Our friends? They touch our lives briefly, like stones skimming across a pond. We will see them in the next life, of that there is no doubt. All that really matters is the war, the war against our enemies, those who wish to wrong us. Those who have wronged us, like those who have wronged you."

Tacit had stopped howling now. His head had sunk onto his chest, his body shaking, his dark eyes locked on the Cardinal.

"Take up the banner again, Poldek. Make your war on those who have dared to take away everything that you thought you held safe. Make them suffer. Make them suffer double what you have suffered, every single one of them. It is your fate, Inquisitor. It is your fate."

And slowly, like a gathering storm, the figure seemed to grow large in the chair in which he sat. "You want a war on our enemies?" Tacit growled, suddenly fierce, his eyes wild. "I'll give them a war."

NINETY NINE

Midnight. Saturday, October 17th, 1914. Paris. France.

They stood in the cold dark of midnight on the streets of Paris, the Inquisitor and the Sister, their eyes set on Notre Dame. The train had made its slow and painful journey south to the capital without incident or delay. An hour and a half after leaving the train, they stood before the immense gothic Cathedral.

"Do we go in now?" asked Isabella.

"No, we'll never gain access at this hour, at least not quietly. It'll all be locked. We wait until morning. First thing. Mass is at eleven. We have plenty of time to take Poré before he causes any more trouble."

Isabella nodded and surreptitiously moved a little closer to the Inquisitor.

"So, any ideas where are we staying tonight? You usually have something up your sleeve."

"I know somewhere, but you might not like it."

Isabella laughed and pulled her shawl tight around her shoulders. "Tacit, it's fine," turning her large brown eyes onto him. "After a week with you, I'm learning to lower my expectations."

PART SEVEN

"If my house were not right with God, surely he would not have made with me an everlasting covenant, arranged and secured in every part; surely he would not bring to fruition my salvation and grant me my every desire."

Samuel, 23, Verse 3

ONE HUNDRED

09:00. Saturday, October 17th, 1914. Paris. France.

The Sister and Inquisitor entered the Parisian Catholic residency building as the clock struck nine in the morning. There were no guards, no security, no measures to impede their entry.

"I thought we might be stopped," said Isabella, scurrying alongside the black clad Tacit, as he paced across the white marble entry hall.

"That's good. He clearly thinks he's clear. And no one else is involved. Just him. You," Tacit asked abruptly a passing Priest, who appeared to have an air of superiority and importance about him. "Do you know who is staying in the apartments at the moment, and where?"

The red gowned Priest looked his questioner up and down in surprise and shock, correcting the skull cap on his head. "I do," he retorted, "but you'll get no such information from me, I can assure you!"

They bundled him silently, secretly, into a side room and Tacit effortlessly broke his wrist.

"Next time it's your neck. Where's Cardinal Poré?"

"You sure you didn't hit him too hard?" asked Isabella, as they reached the third floor and skipped through the door to the long corridor at the end of which, they'd been told, was Poré's apartment.

Tacit scowled and unholstered his revolver from his belt, checking he had all six silver rounds in place, just in case. "One thing I know, Sister, is how hard and where to hit people if you want them to stay quiet for a while, or permanently."

They reached the door to Poré's suite. Tacit knocked, Isabella thought surprisingly lightly for the Inquisitor, and a voice called from within.

"Father Gugan, you may come in. It is open."

Cardinal Poré was bent over his table with his back to the door. He didn't look up but finished signing his letters as the Inquisitor and Sister stepped inside. Only when he heard the lock of the door click shut did he turn.

"Tacit!" he hissed. "How did you …?"

"It doesn't matter, Cardinal," Tacit growled, powering forward towards him. "Your little game, it's over."

Poré staggered to his feet, his chair falling as he pushed away from it and the desk to put some distance between himself and the hulking Inquisitor.

"How could you …?" he stammered. "Where …?"

"We know everything, Cardinal," Isabella warned, reaching down and picking up the chair, inserting it neatly and precisely at the desk. "Your *allies* are slain."

Poré eyes boiled in his skull. "The girl! She talked!"

Isabella sat on the edge of the desk, her arms crossed. "It doesn't matter how we know. All that matters is we know."

"What in God's name are you up to, Poré?" demanded Tacit. The Cardinal stumbled away from him, his eyes looking furtively about the room for an escape. He staggered over to the window, but it was locked and the fall from it too dreadful to consider. "For centuries we've fought to conceal the truth of Hombre Lobo, of their existence. Why now? Why reveal it at all? What's to be gained?"

"What's to be gained?" cried Poré, working his way around the room, his back pressed tight to the wall. And then a semblance of control gripped his face. "Instead of asking that, Inquisitor, why not ask yourself what could be lost?" He reached the door and tore at the lock. Isabella waved the key at him and his shoulders slumped in defeat. "We stand on the precipice of humanity any moment," he began, limping forward into the room towards the pair of them, "falling headlong into a war which will engulf the whole of the world. Do I need to remind you that this war has been sanctioned, one could even use the word encouraged, by our very own Pope, Pope Pius X?"

"Pope Pius X is dead, God rest his soul," muttered Tacit.

"What does that matter? For he was one of the architects who helped set in motion the wheels of war which have since swept across Russia, Austro-Hungary, Serbia and France. Such was his hatred of the Orthodox Christians that there was rarely a moment when he did not contrive to plot their destruction."

"You watch your tongue, Poré," seethed the Inquisitor, drawing himself into a shape to spring at the Cardinal.

"Come come, Inquisitor, I know you share our Pope's dislike of that misguided group as much as many within the Catholic Church. Indeed, I do not doubt that, if you were Pope, you too would be inciting the Emperor Francis Joseph of Austria-Hungary to 'chastise the Serbians' for their heresy against your rule and our faith. Didn't you know, after the assassination in Sarajevo, Baron Ritter, the Bavarian representative at the Holy See, wrote to his government saying that, I quote, 'The Pope approves of Austria's harsh treatment of Serbia. He has no great opinion of the armies of Russia and France in the event of a war with Germany. The Cardinal

Secretary of State does not see when Austria could make war if she does not decide to do so now.'"

Cardinal Poré's eyes flashed and he gritted his teeth, hissing, "There, there in the Pope's very own hand was the sign given for Austro-Hungary to act and so draw the whole of Europe into a bloody war the likes of which the world has never before seen!" He thrust a finger accusatorially at Tacit, before wiping his hands on his gown and dragging the chair away from the desk, sitting himself down in it. "You don't mind if I sit, do you? I am rather incapacitated," he said, indicating his leg. "Of course," he continued, from the comfort of the chair, "to speak out at such actions, at such wickedness would have brought me condemnations and undoubtedly a visit from from the Sodalitium Pianum or one of your fellow Inquisitors. It was only when he died and Benedict XI succeeded him, a Pope of kinder tones with a more determined desire for peace within Europe, that I felt I could dare to talk and share my thoughts, and so begin to put my plans into action, to attempt to undo the horror that the Catholic Church had sanctioned.

"And I found that I was not alone in such thinking. Many came forward when they heard me speak in secret council and dialogue, and together we agreed to create a plan which would not only stop the conflict but turn back the tide of evil which we have fed too often and for too long.

"For nearly a millennium, the Catholic Church has fought against the tide of heresy and depravation in its own chosen way. With some there is corrective therapy, namely torture, to draw confession from the accused. With others, more intensive and longer serving methods need to be applied, such as full excommunication. I do not need to labour the point, Inquisitor. After all, you are famed for your work in upholding the integrity and the honour of the banner of Catholicism.

"In our time, in order to ensure the prosperity of our faith, the imposition of our values and our beliefs upon the wider populace we have done – I am sure even you will agree, Tacit – some terrible things. We have also created monsters, the sorts which are spoken of only in hushed voices or with vile repugnance, told to children to keep them silent in their beds at night. Of course, these monsters we have made, we encourage that they be ridiculed in public to keep them as nothing more than a fancy, make believe for those outside the Catholic circle of knowledge.

"Those rooted deep within the Church have achieved, with the help of authorities and governments, an excellent job in keeping our dark past and creations a secret and our current clandestine activities exactly that. Secret. You for one, Inquisitor, are an excellent example of how we have manipulated the truth to suggest you and your kind no longer exist and yet, here you are, carrying out your own Inquisition, in flesh and blood, unless you are an apparition. Are you an apparition, Tacit?" the Cardinal asked, with a cold smirk.

"My patience is running thin, Poré. Get on with it."

"Should the truth of these creations ever become public, should the activities and knowledge of the Church's meddling, both past and present, carried out by Inquisitors, Priests, Cardinals and the Holy See, ever be made public, then, well, it would be the end of the Catholic Church as we know it, perhaps even of the faith itself."

"So that's it! You wish to destroy the Church!"

"My dear Inquisitor, have you listened to nothing? The Church is not what concerns me. But its potential destruction certainly did appeal to those poor beasts you discovered outside Fampoux. It is a shame they will not see their wishes be made real. No, I have a greater target in my sights. A way to end this and all future wars, for mankind to focus in on itself and set itself to the task of defeating far darker and more insidious creatures, darker than men's old black hearts, if that is at all possible."

"The wolf pelt."

"And at last the penny drops. Or does it? You have a vagueness about your eyes. I think I should explain further, so you are fully in the picture. The destruction of the Catholic Church is only the first step to achieving an even greater goal."

"The wolves! They gave the wolf pelt in exchange for their prize, the end of the Catholic Church."

"Peace and revenge!" cried Isabella.

"A very neat way of putting it, Sister."

"The woman, Sandrine Prideux, she took the pelt from her father."

"Indeed, and she in turn gave it to Father Andreas."

"Who you murdered."

At this, Cardinal Poré's head slipped forwards onto his chest. He drew a trembling hand to his face to hide tears which had come suddenly to his eyes.

"I did," he said, at length. He turned away, but almost immediately turned back to face them. "I am not a monster!" he cried, clubbing his fist against his chest. "I am not a monster," he said again, softer this time, almost like a plea. "I did what I had to do."

"Yes! Murder another of the cloth," hissed Tacit.

The Cardinal raised an eyebrow. "And you would never do such a thing would you, Inquisitor?"

Poré stepped slowly over to the window and looked out on the bustle of Paris below. "Yes, I killed Father Andreas. He worried so much about what he had done, what it would mean for him. He couldn't tell me of his concerns, of course. He'd tried to, the day he died, but I knew anyway. I knew his fears without him telling me them. Eternal damnation he feared, eternal damnation for what he had done, what he was planning to do. Whilst he could appreciate the larger picture, he couldn't tear his mind from the consequences of his actions. I knew he was a liability. He had to be silenced."

"You've no right to sit in the house of our Lord," Tacit growled.

"There is only one God, Inquisitor. As long as we have a faith, I am sure he does not mind at whose door we pray."

"You're worse than the heretics that I have processed in the Russian mountains of Sayan!"

"And your temper needs watching, Inquisitor. It will get you into trouble one day. Just like Father Aguillard."

"What was his –"

"Role? The contact, with the wolves. He travelled far, saw many things, dealt with many of the fallen. He negotiated the dialogue between us and the wolves. But, as with all these things, you can't leave a trail. You, more than anyone, should know about that, Inquisitor. After all, you don't just kill the heretic do you? You kill his family too. And when Aguillard found out what had happened to Father Andreas, well, he rather lost his head. Quite literally."

"I still don't get it. So what if you have the wolf's pelt? So what if you can transform? It doesn't make you an army. One bullet and ..."

"See, you need to think big, Tacit."

"Think for me."

"I will. Imagine, at the Mass for Peace, of all places in the world at any one time where you have dignitaries from all over the world, not only Catholics but persons from all faiths and denominations, politicians, royal families, celebrities, soldiers, the world's media, joined in unison to show solidarity, to pray together for peace. And imagine, if you will, that as the Cardinal is giving his sermon, perhaps about the recklessness of mankind and how we create things too terrible and dreadful to comprehend, he suddenly, there and then, transforms into the single most hideous, vile and wretched of killing machines of all upon the pulpit of Notre Dame? The resulting death count within the Cathedral would be terrible. The injuries monstrous."

"So that's it. Cold blooded murder?! You're as bad as war itself, Poré!"

"Hold yourself, Inquisitor. I asked you to see the bigger picture. I have not finished painting it. Imagine the news, the horror, the resulting aftershock, that in front of an audience of one thousand aristocrats, royals, politicians, religious figureheads, a senior Cardinal denounced the Catholic Church and asked people to rise up for the common good, cast down this war and fight the real evils of the world, after which he promptly turned into one of the very creatures he reviled, one of those things spoken of only in hushed voices with vile repugnance, only told to children to keep them silent in their beds. It would be the only news worthy of reporting for, well, who knows? Oh, and have no doubt, we have all papers from all countries waiting to write their terrible front page news. 'Wolves from hell walk our earth!' 'Put aside our petty differences and rise up to fight his new dreadful enemy!' People would talk about it for weeks, months, perhaps even years, that a dark and terrible breed of creature prowled within our midst. That they were one of many. That they were growing in number and that they were coming for all of civilisation. That they came from one Church. That they were legion. The shock alone would be enough to silence howitzers. Mankind could have no choice other than to bring itself to the table to talk, friend and foe aligned, to reconsider their differences, to recognise their similarities and to work together to fight this single foe."

"You're mad! It would never work."

"It will work because of the setting, because of the media circus sitting with their pads and their cameras in Notre Dame at the moment, because of the carnage to be unleashed and, not least, because of who it is who will transform."

"Don't think that you're that important, Poré," hissed Tacit. "And, anyway, you aren't getting out of here alive. This is where the plan ends."

"Ends? I think not. Indeed, I think it's just about to begin. Good heavens, it's not me giving the Mass service? No, no, you're quite right. I am not nearly important enough. I am just the messenger. Cardinal Bishop Monteria is holding the Mass."

Tacit heard Isabella stifle a gasp.

"We still have time," hissed Tacit, his knuckles white.

"Wrong again, Inquisitor. I am not so stupid as to tell you my entire plan simply so you can foil it. Too many of have died for it to not come to fruition. Too much time and effort has been put into its planning. No, I am dreadfully sorry to tell you that Mass was moved to the earlier time of ten o'clock. And so," he said, looking at the grandfather clock on the far wall, "the transformation should be happening right about now."

ONE HUNDRED AND ONE

1912. MARSEILLE. FRANCE.

The synagogue collapsed with a groan, like that of a falling giant. Flames licked up from the broken foundations, as the central tower fell in on itself and fire sprang across to nearby buildings. All about the city, the air was rent with the sound of people screaming and shouting, masonry falling, the tolling of bells in alarm. Teams of people scuttled desperately about the wreckage, pulling bodies from the rubble, directing ambulances and water to quell the flames. Carnage and panic was everywhere, everyone doing what they could to help in the maelstrom of terror.

All except one.

Inquisitor Tacit strode out of the flames of the building into the shadows of the opposite street, his face lean and dark, his eyes like opals. He never looked back. A team of firemen rushed past him, yelping like dogs, arms waving and gesticulating towards the ruined building ablaze.

"Father!" one of them pleaded, reaching out to him and then recoiling instantly when Tacit's eyes turned to him. The cold glare burnt him like the flaming joists at the foundations of church. He stumbled on with his colleagues, his face racked with horror, as if he had seen the devil with his own eyes whilst Tacit turned into the quiet of the side street.

There was a tavern there, now empty, the patrons having run to aid those Jews still caught inside or injured beneath the falling rubble. Tacit pushed the door open and strode up to the bar, his hard hob nailed boots clacking on the wooden floor boards of the building.

"Father," stuttered the barman, perplexed by the nearby fire and the size of the man now leaning over him. "What can I do for you?"

"Brandy," Tacit replied, resting his tired body against the bar. "Brandy. And leave the bottle."

ONE HUNDRED AND TWO

10:17. SATURDAY, OCTOBER 17TH, 1914. PARIS. FRANCE.

They charged from Poré's apartment but, four strides down the corridor, Isabella stopped and turned back to the door, locking it quickly.

"What are you doing?!" roared the Inquisitor, as she tested the handle and hurried back after him, disposing of the key in a helpfully positioned plant pot near the top of the stairs. "We don't have time to waste!"

Tacit lunged for the stairs, but Isabella slipped a hand beneath his armpit and led him from them to a narrow landing, running alongside.

"You want to save time?" she retorted. "Then follow me."

She swept into the corridor, Tacit on her heels, the thundering of their footsteps on the floorboards echoing around the enclosed wooden aisle. She had been told of a secret passageway at the end of the ornate wooden walkway by a Sister friend of hers who'd spent time at Notre Dame, linking the residence building to the Cathedral. "Perfect for Cardinals who sleep a little too late for Mass," she called back, thundering around the bend in the passageway and sending a passing Priest skidding to the wall to avoid being crushed. "Being a Sister," she gasped, her lungs burning with the race, "means you get to learn all the gossip."

The corridor ended at an inauspicious wooden panelled dead end.

"Wrong turn?" asked Tacit urgently.

But Isabella ignored him, searching for the little sculpted nose protruding from the dark wood engraving. *And who said the Catholics had no sense of humour?* She spotted the merry looking Father, depicted sitting under a tree. His nose disappeared easily into the wood when Isabella pressed it and a door in the panelling swung gently open with a reassuring crack.

The dark tunnel beyond wound downwards, the walls carved smooth and white. Every twenty or thirty strides, a single dimly flickering lantern burnt, providing enough light to see one's steps and ensure the way was clear of obstacles.

"You sure this is right, Sister?"

"For once, Tacit, have some faith. And call me Isabella!"

They could smell the air of the Paris morning and beyond could see the vague dull outline of a door set firm at the dead end of the sloping tunnel down which they tore. There was a pull handle on the vast stone door, connected to a chain and mechanism set somehow within it. The handle turned on a well-oiled apparatus and the door creaked open a few inches. Tacit inserted his fingers into the crack and heaved the door wide, just enough for Isabella and himself to be able to squeeze through.

Ahead lay the Rue de Cloître Notre Dame and Notre Dame itself, just across the road, the northern transept of the Cathedral almost opposite the secret tunnel down which they had run.

"We might already be too late," said Isabella, pushing herself forward through the crack in the door. "Come on!" Her heart raged, her spirit charged. But Tacit took hold of her and pulled her back into the dark confines of the tunnel corridor.

"What are you doing?!" she asked. "There's no time to waste."

"You're staying here," said Tacit.

"No, I am not, Tacit!" she spat, whipping her arm free and turning to crawl back into the sunlight.

She felt Tacit's firm hands on her and battled hopelessly against them, kicking and punching out with her limbs. "Don't you try and leave me behind again, Inquisitor! You did that once before. Never again!" she cried and threw wild punches at him in a fruitless attempt to get him to loosen his grip on her.

Tacit pushed her hard into the wall, and set himself against her, closer to her than he had ever done before, even closer than in the hotel room that time. She could feel his hot breath on her face and neck.

"Let me go, Tacit!" she wailed, kicking out at him. "I can't have you going in there alone."

"I must!"

"And I must too!"

"No! Do you know what we're about to do? We're about to kill a senior Cardinal Bishop in front of a thousand high ranking country officials and politicians, Catholics and non-Catholics alike. Cold blooded murder in front of a thousand witnesses. If you're caught with me then you'll be guilty too. They'll string you up. I cannot have that. I go alone! This is not your battle."

He let go of her and set himself into the crack of the door, but Isabella caught hold of him.

"This is because of the assessment isn't it, Tacit? You're still trying to prove yourself! Still trying to prove, not just to the Church, but to yourself that you've not lost your way."

"It's got nothing to do with that!"

"Don't lie to me Tacit! Why, Tacit? Why do you have to prove it to yourself?"

"It's nothing to do with that!" he cried, and Isabella saw tenderness in the Inquisitor's eyes for the first time. "It's because …" he muttered, "it's because I care, Isabella." He raised a hand to her cheek and cradled it in his hands, holding her gaze with his. In that instant, that fraction of a moment, a thousand images swept within their minds, the teasing ripple of romance, the warm touch of human flesh, the burning passion of an embrace, the laughter of shared love. And Tacit felt Mila and his mother's presence there with him, and was filled with a spirit of love almost overwhelming. And his eyes filled with tears and the weight of sorrow fell away from him, like plate armour unbuckled from his body.

Then, without a word, he slipped his hand to her neck and squeezed. His grip was like a tight iron collar. In seconds darkness swept in around her and Isabella was falling. Tacit caught her body and brushed the hair from her face. He looked into her features as he laid her down unconscious on the floor of the tunnel. Without another moment wasted, he then stood and faced the door, his teeth gritted in grim defiance and determination.

He tore the door open and ran, charging like a maddened bear across the street, past wandering groups of tourists and Parisians. He bolted into the closed door of the transept. It burst with a terrific crash, sending soldiers, Priests and gathered clergy behind it tumbling and flying into the congregation. At the pulpit in the middle of the nave where the north and south transepts met, Cardinal Bishop Monteria shuddered and looked over to the noise like the gates of hell had been broken open.

Tacit ran and as he ran his hand dropped to his holster, his fingers wrapping tight around the grip of the revolver. Uproar and chaos broke across the congregation, shouts and cries of shock and disdain rippling like a tidal wave of astonishment throughout the building. Tacit couldn't see it, but hidden beneath the pulpit, the Cardinal Bishop was fingering the vile pelt he'd just removed from a box in his hands. It stank, stank like a thousand fox earths, a guttural clinging stench which ravaged the back of the throat. Monteria stuttered over his words, hurrying to the devastating climax of his speech, trying to make himself heard above the clamour of the crowd. He needed to be heard. He had to be heard, before he put on the pelt.

Tacit's gun was now out and raised. He was aware of a mob of people charging towards him, like an enveloping crowd of hounds about to leap on a cornered fox. He could see something grey and black and matted appear from behind the pulpit and rise closer, closer to the Cardinal Bishop's head. Tacit shut one eye and pulled the trigger.

He felt nothing and heard nothing, not even the recoil of his revolver, the explosion as the silver bullet flashed from the barrel of the gun, nor the impact as the bodies flew onto him, soldiers and brave or foolish men from the congregation grappling and forcing his vast bulk to the ground. But as he felt hands on his back, felt the sharp pain of his wrists being drawn tight behind him, he heard the horrified cries of the congregation and the staggered collapse and fall of the Cardinal from the pulpit. And then silence.

Silence.

Tacit closed his eyes, and smiled.

EPILOGUE

ONE HUNDRED AND THREE

06:43. Sunday, October 18th, 1914. Arras. France.

The rain fell on Arras with the power of a biblical flood. The downpour woke Henry from his sleep. He rolled over on the kitchen floor of the house and drew Alessandro's coat tight to his chin in an effort to fight off the morning chill. They'd chosen to sleep on the kitchen floor. There was no question of them sleeping in *that* room where Alessandro's final moments had taken place. There was too much squalor within it, terror and violence captured on the walls and floor, too many bad spirits.

Henry watched the rain teem down the window pane in swollen rivulets, combining with other rivulets to make rivers, which washed down off the window to the sill and finally to the street below. A clash of thunder rippled around the city. He peered over to Sandrine sleeping beside him, her breathing barely audible over the rain. She looked at peace, still dressed in the clothes she had worn when she'd left her home.

Her home. *Where was their home now?*, Henry wondered.

The thought stirred him into action. Silently, he rose from the makeshift bed and slipped into the bedroom where the attack had taken place. He felt wicked, violating Alessandro's peace by searching through his cupboards for clothes, but Sandrine had insisted he must before they left in the morning. Luckily, Henry was nearly the same size as Alessandro, maybe a little longer in the leg and larger in the foot, giving Henry a rather puzzled, imbecilic look with his toe pinched shoes and raised trousers, but he guessed it would suffice for now, at least until they were out of the city.

He stole slowly back to the kitchen. Sandrine still slept in peaceful abandon, beautiful and alluring, amongst the ragtag sheets of the hastily assembled bed. Picking up the coat and the unit diary, he crept downstairs and out into the thundering downpour.

Already it had begun to flood outside the boarded up house, the street turned to a river of murky water. He snuck the diary under his coat and hurried on. A platoon of soldiers, drenched and dismal in their sodden clothes, tramped past under the watchful glare of their platoon Sergeant. Panic gripped Henry's throat, but the soldiers moved away with neither a look nor a word to him. Henry could feel the tension shimmer up his throat and gather in the base of his skull. He breathed deeply and moved on. He didn't know how far it was he had to go. Sandrine had explained it to him and made him memorise the route, there and back, so there would be no chance of him becoming lost in the depths of the city. Anything to avoid unnecessary risks. Anything to avoid the chance of capture and arrest.

At the end of the street was a square, badly buffeted by shell fire. Lined by trees, three had been uprooted and lay snapped and gouged from their cobble lined beds. By now the rain had intensified and was blown on strengthening winds, whipping across the square almost horizontal to the ground. Henry bent himself against it and staggered on. At the edge of the square was the street he remembered from Sandrine's description he was to take. It offered some respite from the wind and Henry drew a little breath as he trotted down it, hugging the diary tight. It was then that he cursed himself and his loyalty to his unit, for taking such a risk for the sake of a record of a lost unit. He doubted anyone would ever read it anyway. He was minded to throw it away, cast it into a bin or the gutter and be done with it. But he thought of his colleagues who had fallen and knew he could never do such a thing. He owed them that much. He owed them the truth being revealed.

Halfway down the street he found the lane Sandrine had gone on to mention. The wind blew even stronger down this, casting rain and hail and broken vegetation down the channel the buildings either side created. Signs swung wildly on chains or lay snapped and broken across the floor. Henry peered through the downpour and there, in the distance he could make out the custard yellow of the post office. He half staggered, half ran to the door and cast it open, throwing himself inside.

The postmaster looked up from behind his desk and chuckled, asking him something in French.

"I'm sorry," Henry replied in his basic grasp of French, suddenly aware of the flaw in his plan. "I don't speak very good French."

The postmaster shrugged and shook his head.

"Paper?" Henry asked, removing the book from his coat, but hiding its cover from the postmaster's eyes.

"Paper?"

"Yes, paper."

"Ah, papier?" the postmaster nodded, gathering him a roll. "Ficelle?" he then asked. Henry hesitated. "Ficelle?" the smart looking elderly gentleman asked again. "String?"

"Oh, string, yes, please," said Henry, taking both and stealing over to the side of the shop to wrap the diary in the privacy of a corner. No sooner had he crept away than the door to the post office flew open and two British officers staggered in, laughing and cursing at the buffeting they'd received from the elements. They stood in the middle of the office, brushing themselves down and chortling, tall, slick haired moustached men, a Major and Lieutenant Colonel.

"Blasted weather!" one called, flapping his cap into his hand.

"One feels that summer is well and truly over now, Nicholas," the Major called, approaching the desk. Henry's eyes were on the pair of them and then the postmaster. His gaze was drawn by Henry's and he looked at him hard before looking back at the Major.

"Now then my good man, do you speak English?"

"Oui," said the man, looking across at Henry and then back at the officer. "A little."

"Good stuff. Look here, I'm expecting a package from home. Not coming in via usual circles. Don't want it go by army post. I was wondering if I could have the parcel sent here and then I come and pick it up from you?"

"Parcel? Sent here?" replied the man, torn between looking at the officer and glancing with suspicion at the British man in civilian dress in the corner of the room.

"Yes, that's right. Get it sent here. That way I might get a chance of getting it before Christmas, what?" The officer chortled and the distracted postmaster feigned the same. His distraction caught the officer's eye and he peered over at Henry, clasping the bound and addressed book in his hands. "Everything alright, chum?" he asked him.

Henry could feel the blood drain from him, his head go light. It felt like his entire world was turning in on itself. His heart felt like a battered anvil in his chest. He nodded and avoided any eye contact, retreating a little into the corner in the pretence of finishing addressing the parcel.

"What have we got here then?" the Major asked, stepping forward and tugging the package around so he could read to whom it was addressed.

"No, non," muttered Henry, but he knew the game was up and didn't resist further. They'd take him to the red caps. From there he'd be sent for court martial. He thought of Sandrine, awaking to find him gone. How long would she wait till she realised he would not be coming back?

"For the British HQ, Arras, eh?" muttered the Major.

Henry nodded and swallowed hard.

"Well why don't you let me take that?" he said, raising an eyebrow. "We're heading back there now. Save you the price of a stamp."

Dumbfounded, Henry let the parcel be plucked from his grasp, the across the office counter, producing a pad from an inside pocket.

"So, what's the address here?" he asked.

The postmaster told him, and the officer wrote it down, telling the man his name.

"So, when the package arrives, you will hold it for me? Here?"

The postmaster nodded and looked back at Henry, his eyes like slits.

"Good-oh!" the Major announced, wrenching the door open. "Ready?" he called to the Lieutenant Colonel, and together the officers fought their way back out into the street and the torrential wind and rain.

A smile lightened the face of the postmaster.

"Go on then," he muttered, nodding to the door. "On y va."

He was drenched to the bone and shivering when he reached the stairs of Alessandro's house. He could hear the rain fall on the roof and the street just outside the terraced row of buildings, swelling the puddle at the front into a flood. Henry stopped and closed his eyes, his hand on the banister of the stairs, his ears alert to the sounds of the city. And it seemed to him that he could hear each individual raindrop of the torrential downpour, and the splash of a resident running through the puddles, and the cry from an officer turning his soldiers in the storm. If he listened very hard he could make out the booms and the rumble from the front, the rusted tight deadlock of the units and the battalions and the divisions facing each other, starting up their hate-filled offensives once again.

And then it struck him – in the middle of that tempest from God and the warring forces – the majesty, the beauty and the miracle that was life. The realisation hit him like a thunderbolt, so strong and so dramatically that it drenched his eyes with tears and took away his breath. How everything in life was finite and balanced so precariously.

He climbed the stairs slowly, reverently, and gathered Sandrine into his arms on their makeshift bed. He kissed her back to consciousness.

"Come on," he said, "let's go and live."

ONE HUNDRED AND FOUR

November, 1914. Toulouse Inquisitional prison.
Toulouse. France.

They'd dragged Tacit to the cell and chained him where he'd been thrown. There'd been no need to drag him. He would have gone with them willingly. Where else was he to go? Where else had he to go? He knew what was to befall him. It didn't scare him. Nothing scared him any more. Not now.

He felt blessed, truly blessed, even in that loathsome place, amongst the rot and the stench, in between the beatings.

But nothing could touch him now. He felt complete. After all, there were those who went their entire lives never having known love, true love, never having felt its touch upon them or their lives. And yet Tacit had felt it, and he had felt it three times.

A Holy presence.

Tacit closed his eyes and remembered the lightly scented smell of his mother, the haven he always found within her embrace. Suddenly he heard the laugh of Mila in his ears, the spirit of her voice, filling him and enriching him. And then he felt the touch of Isabella's fingers on his face, the delicate warmth of her fingertips, spreading across his skin like ripples on a pond.

He felt the emotion of love swell around him, like an energy manifested within the prison cell. He then opened his eyes and he laughed, and then he roared with unrestrained joy. There were lights again! Lights all around him! Warming him with their wonder and whispering softly in his ear.

ACKNOWLEDGEMENTS

My thanks must go to my father, John, and my brother-in-law, Maurice East, who accompanied me on an inspirational and moving visit to France and Belgium in 2012 on the trail of my great uncles who fought and died in the Great War. That trip acted as the catalyst for this novel. Estelle, of the Terres de Memoire, and Jacques, of the Flanders Battlefield Tour Belgium, were compelling and eloquent guides.

Thanks to my parents, John and Janet Richardson, who I think secretly knew those comics I read as a kid would be put to good use one day, and my grandfather Fred Clarkson and his wife Denise. Thanks to my sister, Vicky, and niece, Georgia, my parents-in-law, Tony and Brigid Maddocks and sister-in-law, Katie, for all their support.

Huge thanks goes to Ben Clark at LAW for believing in me and my writing. Knowing you have someone of his wisdom and vision on your side gives you the confidence to write with freedom and purpose.

Thanks also goes to Andrew Lockett and everyone at Duckworth for letting Poldek Tacit into their beautiful home, despite the state of his boots.

I must also thank my proof readers who gave me the belief and determination to keep going; Joanna Pitkin-Parsons, Rob Swan, Paul Malone and Maurice East.

In a world away from novels, trenches and werewolves, there are people who help keep me sane on a daily basis. Thank you Jamie Gilman and James Fry for doing exactly that, and thank you Jon Phillips for providing the soundtrack to my writing sessions. And, finally, Mrs Jones, who read me The Hobbit when I was eight and opened my eyes and imagination. Long gone, but not forgotten.

NOTES

A huge number of books, articles and websites have provided me with the information required to write a compelling and factual account of the early months of the Great War. Too numerous to list all of them, I would like to give particular credit to the following books: The Great War, by Peter Hart; Valour in the Trenches, by N S Nash; Raiding on the Western Front, by Anthony Saunders; Trench Talk, by Peter Doyle and Julian Walker; The Beauty and the Sorrow, by Peter Englund; The Soldier's War, by Richard Van Emden; 1914-1918, by David Stevenson; Last Post, by Max Arthur.

The National Archives at Kew and their beautifully kept war diaries have proved invaluable to better understanding movements and morale of troops at the start of the war.

The two battles featured within the book are based on real events. The German attack was taken from the accounts of Corporal Charlie Parke, 2nd Gordon Highlanders, regarding the first German assault he faced. The British attack was taken from the accounts of Major George Walker, 59th Field Coy, RE.

NOW AVAILABLE AS A FREE EBOOK

ALSO BY TARN RICHARDSON

The Hunted is the free prequel to the full length novel *The Damned,* the first book in Tarn Richardson's gritty and compelling *Darkest Hand Trilogy* featuring flawed inquisitor Tacit Poldek

In the bustling streets of Sarajevo in June 1914, the dead body of a priest lies, head shattered by the impact of a fall from a building high above. As the city prepares for the arrival Archduke Franz Ferdinand, grim-faced inquisitor Tacit Poldek is faced not only with the challenge of discovering why the priest has been killed but also confronting other menaces: the demon rumoured to be at large in the city and the conspirators of the Black Hand organisation who plan to assassinate the Archduke.

With terrible danger only ever one step away and his private demons silenced only by strong drink, *The Hunted* introduces us to the damaged soul that is the unorthodox Catholic inquisitor Tacit Poldek. It is a world both like and unlike our own but in which the Inquisition, is alive and well yet existing in the shadows; in which history is poised to take dangerous and unpredictable paths; where evil assumes many horrific forms, from werewolves to the institutional slaughter of the trenches; and the threat to humanity (in all senses of the word) - and to love - is ever constant.

NOW AVAILABLE

Dave Zeltserman is the author of several horror and crime novels – two of which, *Outsourced* and *A Killer's Essence,* have been optioned for film. His novel *Pariah* was selected by *The Washington Post* as one of the best books of 2009. He currently lives with his wife in Boston.

THE BOY WHO KILLED DEMONS

A very scary thriller written with verve and flashes of great humour, *The Boy Who Killed Demons is* Dave Zeltserman's most accomplished and entertaining horror novel yet.

"Like Stephen King, Dave Zeltserman makes the incredible come alive."
Bookreporter.com

"Will stir the hearts of adult and YA action fantasy fans"
Library Journal

'My name's Henry Dudlow.
I'm fifteen and a half. And I'm cursed. Or damned. Take your pick. The reason?
I see demons.'

So begins the latest thriller by horror master Dave Zeltserman. The setting is quiet Newton, MA, where nothing ever happens. Nothing, that is, until two months after Henry Dudlow's 13th birthday, when his neighbour, Mr. Hanley, suddenly starts to look . . . different. While everyone else sees a balding man with a beer belly, Henry suddenly sees a nasty, bilious, rage-filled demon.

Once Henry catches onto the real Mr. Hanley, he starts to see demons all around him, and his boring, adolescent life is transformed. There's no more time for friends or sports or the lovely Sally Freeman-Henry must work his way through ancient texts and hunt down the demons before they kill any more innocent children. And if hunting demons is hard at any age, it's borderline impossible when your parents are on your case, and your grades are getting worse, and you can't tell anyone about your mission.